Far Side of the Sea

California Rising
Book 2

PAULA SCOTT

FAR SIDE OF THE SEA by Paula Scott
www.psbicknell.com

This is a work of fiction. Names, characters, places, and incidents are products of the author's imagination or are used fictitiously. Any similarity to actual people, organizations, and/or events is purely coincidental.

Cover Designer: Jenny Quinlan
Editor: Jenny Quinlan, Historical Editor, historicaleditorial.com
Cover Image Credit: © ILINA SIMEONOVA / Trevillion Images
Typesetter: Jeff Gerke, www.jeffgerke.com

International Standard Book Number (13): 978-0-692-82178-7

Printed in the United States of America

Part One

Where can I go from your Spirit?
Where can I flee from your presence?

Psalm 139:7

Chapter One

Monterey, California, 1846

Maria rode into the village alongside Joshua Tyler with an army of vaqueros in their wake. The moon shone so brightly she could see every ship silhouetted in the harbor. Joshua led them directly to the church. By now, American soldiers had noted their arrival. With guns drawn, the soldiers surrounded them in the churchyard.

"Why are you here?" demanded the leader of the US Army detachment, a large man with long, bushy sideburns.

Joshua stepped down from his horse with an easy smile. "I've come to marry my fiancée." He motioned to Maria, perched in a sidesaddle on her palomino. "We've ridden a long way today."

"The padre's asleep. You'll have to wait till morning."

Joshua reached into his saddlebags and pulled out a sack of coins.

The soldiers looked at one another speculatively. "The padre isn't going to like this. He's a pious old priest," said the soldier in charge.

Joshua retrieved a handful of silver coins from the pouch, showing them to the soldiers. "My bride is a gently bred Californiana. Certainly, the good padre will understand the need for vows before we take a room for the night."

The soldiers stared unabashedly at Maria. She glared back. Her fiery auburn hair tumbled down her back, tangled with dirt and leaves from a fall from her horse while trying to escape after leaving the hacienda.

"Does she understand English?" asked the soldier, thoughtfully stroking his sideburns. "Do you speak English, señorita?" He walked toward Maria, tucking the silver Joshua handed him into the pocket of his uniform.

"She speaks only Spanish." Joshua gave Maria a warning look. She reined her horse away from the approaching soldier about the same time one of Joshua's vaqueros cut him off. The other vaqueros circled Maria with their horses.

"Gavilan, go rouse the good padre," Joshua told one of his horsemen.

A vaquero with a tall, muscular build stepped down off his mount. With his European features, he looked more Spanish than Indian. He'd picked Maria off the ground after her shocking tumble. She hadn't seen the tree limb that knocked her from the horse. Before she knew it, she was on the ground, struggling to catch her breath. His big hands had been gentle but unbending as steel. Maria had seen a flash of compassion in his dark eyes as he'd helped her back into the saddle. She hoped he would feel sorry enough for her to help her escape. He walked past the soldiers without any fear.

All of Joshua's men exhibited an absolute disregard for any authority beyond Tyler's. Several of the soldiers moved to intercept the vaquero, but the soldier in charge waved them off. "Let him go. This is a civilian matter. Return to your posts."

The soldiers lowered their guns and slowly left the square. Soon it was only Maria, Joshua, and his cowboys waiting for the padre. He never came out of the church. Gavilan returned shaking his head.

"He refuses to do the ceremony?" Irritation edged Joshua's words.

"I could not find him." Gavilan spoke in English without much of an accent, which surprised Maria. "Nobody is in the church or the living quarters in the back."

Joshua looked at her. She met his eyes, a triumphant little smile on her lips. She would not marry him. Ever. He stepped down from his horse and walked to hers. Gripping her arm, he yanked her down from the saddle. "Find a place to see to your horses and get some sleep," he told his men. "Gavilan, come with us."

Leading Maria by the arm, he marched her into the sandstone chapel. Candles burned before an altar of a saint, but aside from that, the sanctuary was dark. "Wait for us here," he told Gavilan, motioning for the vaquero to sit on one of the long benches that seated the people. "I'll find the priest myself." He handed the vaquero the bag of coins he'd saved for the priest.

Maria attempted to pull away, but Joshua drew her closer to his side. "I realize you are young and unaware of what this war means for your family, but believe me, you will thank me for this marriage one day."

"I will never thank you." Maria spat in his face.

Joshua's mouth tightened into a grim line as he wiped the spittle from his cheek. He pulled her over to the candles and picked one up, then propelled her past the altar and through a door that led to the padre's private quarters in the back.

The modest chamber was empty. Joshua pushed Maria inside the small room and shut the door behind them. He forced her onto the padre's narrow bunk and then sat the burning candle on the little table in the center of the room. "I have wanted you for a long time," he said while removing his hat and gun belt, then his vest and shirt. He kept his pants on, with his long knife tucked into his waistband.

Maria couldn't believe this was happening. The last time she'd been in this church, her cousin, Donatella, was getting married. It had been a lavish affair with laughter and happiness and family and friends. Her mother's and father's funerals had also been held here. She was too young to really remember her mother's passing, but her father's burial she recalled quite well. It was his death that had stolen her freedom. He'd allowed her to accompany him all over the rancho as he worked the cattle and oversaw their vast sheep herds after her mother died from a fever.

Maria's childhood had been spent in a saddle, a sombrero pulled low on her brow to protect her fair, golden skin from the California sun, a riata in her hand just like the cowboys. Under her skirts, she'd worn pantaloons and boots like her father's, with spurs strapped on, just like every other man in California. She could rope as well as anyone, and during the *matanzas* could skin cattle better than many of her father's men. That had ended when her padre died one night during an Indian raid, lanced to the ground and left to perish when a handful of their horses were taken from the field.

"I will not marry you. I have no desire for this union." She looked around for a way to escape, but only the door he stood in front of offered any kind of exit. What was he thinking? Why was he undressing? Did he have marriage attire he wanted to put on? She didn't see how this was possible considering they'd carried nothing into the church with them but the bag of coins he'd left with his vaquero.

"Your uncle owes me a lot of money, more than he can ever hope to repay. If you do not marry me, I will take Rancho de los Robles, and your family will be destitute. The United States has run up her flag in every town along the coast. Soon more soldiers will arrive. Men with no regard for your welfare. Marrying me is the best thing to do, Maria."

She did not like the way he said her name. Like an endearment as he removed his spurs and boots. "What are you doing? Will you wear the padre's robes for our wedding? There are no other clothes in here."

"So you will marry me?" His smile returned.

She had no plans to marry him; she was only trying to discover why he undressed in her presence. Fear had begun to claw in her stomach, rising like a wild thing trying to dig its way out of a very deep hole. She knew little about men. Only a week ago, she'd received her first kiss from an American ship captain who had broken her heart upon announcing he had a fiancée back in Boston.

Looking around for a weapon, she rose from where Joshua had made her sit on the hard, narrow bunk the padre slept on. Perhaps with all these rough American soldiers in town, the padre had headed south. She saw nothing to defend herself with and turned her gaze back to him, measuring his size and strength against her own.

In his forties, Joshua was still a handsome man with a lean, hard frame and a thick head of blond hair that waved off his high, tanned forehead. Maria had never liked him, even though her brother, Roman had married his daughter, Rachel.

Joshua had asked for Maria's hand in marriage several years ago, but her Uncle Pedro had proposed her older cousin, Sarita, instead. Now Sarita was dead from a miscarriage. Even though she was older now, Maria had no desire to marry anyone yet, least of all this high-handed Yankee who'd always made her skin crawl.

"We should find the padre. He will want a confession from both of us before performing the marriage rites."

Joshua's lips spread into a wider smile. "I am planning my confession even now," he said, stepping toward her.

She finally realized his intent, and it sickened her. Her suspicion had been growing as he undressed, but she wouldn't accept it. He was a landowner. She was a daughter of the *gente de razón*. Things like this didn't happen in her world. She could see there would be no vows spoken tonight, but he intended to have her anyway. "I will not marry you, no matter what you do to me."

"You will change your mind after tonight." The confidence on his face struck her as insane.

"This is a holy place."

"I am not a holy man. I do not fear God."

"You will pay for this sin against me. This sin against God."

He laughed. "I have always liked this about you. Fire can burn a man up, but it also keeps him warm. Keeps him alive. Your fire will keep me young for a long time, Maria."

Desperate to stop this from happening, she dashed past him with the door her only hope. He grasped her wrist and yanked her back toward the bunk. Their tussle overturned the table and a chair, knocking out the candle. The room went dark. With every fiber of her being, Maria fought him. He was not violent, but he was very determined and very strong. He smelt of tobacco, sweat, and horses. By the time he pinned her on the padre's narrow bunk, her clothes were half torn off, and she was horrified and out of breath, but she was furious too. Enraged, really. The thud of his knife hitting the floor as he loosened his pants while straddling her stilled her spinning thoughts. He was focused on one thing; she became focused on one thing too.

No longer did she fight him. She reached for the floor, frantically feeling around in the dark for the dagger as he tore at her clothes.

The invasion of her body was more shocking than Maria could have ever imagined, but her fingers settled firmly around the hilt of the knife. It had taken too long to locate it on the floor without alerting him to what she planned. He was lost in what he was doing to her. She was lost in fury.

No longer was she frightened. There was nothing left to fear. Absolute rage overtook her.

She stretched out her arm as far as she could and, with all her might, buried the blade between his shoulders. His body went rigid with the impact of the blow. He grunted in surprise and then went still and became very heavy on top of her. Time had stopped the moment she realized he planned to have her without any vows. Now time began ticking again. She must go. She had to flee. Had to get away from here. Far, far away from California.

With all her strength, she pushed him off. He rolled onto the floor with a thud. The noise was explosive in her ears. She jumped up from the bunk, and pain pierced her where she was no longer a maiden. It was too dark to see anything in the room. She tripped over Joshua's body, sprawled at her feet in front of the bunk. She landed hard on her hands but didn't make a sound. At a very young age, Maria had learned not to cry. Her padre had not liked tears, so after her mother's death, she never cried again.

She swore she would not cry now. On her hands and knees, she crawled across the floor and found Joshua's gun belt in the dark. His shirt was there too, near the toppled table. She threw it on over her ruined dress. She still had her riding boots on. Her shock was abating, and a plan began forming in her mind. Searching the floor, she found his coin purse. For what he'd taken, he owed her much. Without her virginity, she was ruined.

When she reached the door, she rose to her feet. Finding the latch, she opened the door, and light from candles in the sanctuary spilled into the room. She wrapped the heavy leather gun belt around her waist and buckled it on. The thing was too big and slid down to where it settled with a pistol riding on each hip. She pulled one of the guns from its holster and cocked it. Then she walked into the church holding the gun ready at her side.

The vaquero sat there on the bench where they'd left him. His head rested in his hands as if he'd fallen asleep, but he looked up as soon as she approached. His eyes widened, but he didn't say a word.

"Take me to a ship," she said evenly.

Slowly, carefully, he stood up. "Where is the patrón?"

"He has decided not to marry me. Give me your knife."

The man removed his knife from his belt. Everything he did was measured, as if he knew she would kill him too if he displeased her.

"Bring it to me." She raised the cocked pistol at him.

He came to her slowly, handing her the knife by holding the blade between his fingertips and presenting the handle to her. It was a typical vaquero's knife, good for skinning cattle and shaving one's beard.

She took it, keeping the gun pointed at him. "Now give me your gun belt."

He did as she asked, unbuckling the belt that held his pistols. Many Californios did not carry guns, they relied on their lances and riatas, but Joshua had been a Yankee. In California, some Yankees carried guns. She tucked his long knife into her belt and held out her hand. "Back up," she told him after he placed his gun belt in her outstretched palm.

He stepped away, and she walked over to the candles burning in front of the statue of the saint. It was a woman, but Maria didn't know which saint she was. Her mother had been religious, but her padre had not, and when her mother died, her padre's need for religion had died too.

Her Aunt Josefa was a religious woman and made Maria say the rosary every night. Though Maria dutifully fingered the beads and moved her lips to please her aunt, she didn't always recite the prayers. Prayers had not helped her mother live, and to her deep shame and regret, her mother's death was most likely her fault.

Perhaps the little red-haired one is cursed. When she brought the feather, her mother died. In good hands, the sacred feathers always work. I have seen this before. In unworthy hands the feather brings death. The old Indian's voice sounded like rustling leaves as she listened outside the door that dark night.

Do not speak so loud. Someone might hear you, her father told the old Indian. The priest had already departed. Her father brought the Indian healer because he was desperate. Maria had searched the forest for the feather because she was desperate. The fever that killed her mother and so many others in California that terrible winter had been brought to California by Yankee sailors. She pushed the terrible memory aside. If she was cursed, the curse had helped her tonight, Tyler was dead and he deserved it.

After making sure the vaquero was far enough away that he wouldn't jump her and take her pistol, she put his gun belt on the bench and laid her cocked pistol there too. Then she pulled out his knife and began to cut off her hair.

"You should not do that," the vaquero said from where he stood across the aisle from her.

"It no longer matters." A knot formed in her throat, choking her, but she swallowed hard and kept sawing off her tresses. They fell at her feet near the burning candles before the saint, red, silky, and abundant.

"Your hair was very beautiful."

She met his eyes and, staring at him, continued to cut until all her hair was shorn above her ears. "Do you believe someone can be cursed?"

"What kind of curse?"

"With death?"

"Is the patrón dead?"

"He is asleep. Never mind. I speak and write in several languages. I will make a good cabin boy. Would you like to leave California with me?" She tucked the knife back into her belt and picked up her cocked pistol and his gun belt. Her eyes had been on him the whole time. Measuring him. Reading him. She prided herself on her intuition. She decided he had a good heart. It was a gamble, but she was willing to take it. He knew she'd killed Joshua. She could see it on his face. She also could see the compassion in his gaze she'd seen earlier when he'd helped her after her fall from the horse. He felt sorry for her. Never had she fallen from a horse, at least not since she was a very little girl. How had it happened? She'd been so sure of escape and suddenly she was hitting the ground so hard she saw stars. The fall had been her first humiliation, a shadow of the humiliations to come.

Walking over to him, she released the hammer on the gun and tucked it back into its holster. Then she handed him his gun belt. "Do you want to come with me or not?"

"Where would we go?"

"Far from here." She walked down the aisle away from him.

Strapping his gun belt back on, he followed her. "To go east, first you must go south to the Horn. I have sailed the Horn before. It's not as easy as herding cattle."

She spun around. "You have sailed?"

"I am not from California."

"Where are you from?"

"Valparaiso."

"Where is that?"

He smiled. "Far from here."

11

Chapter Two

Maria and Gavilan used Joshua's coins to purchase sea chests. Outfitted as deckhands, they rowed out to the ships and were turned down several times before being accepted aboard an impressive clipper with mountainous sails and a white angel on her helm. A burly, red-haired first mate hired them that afternoon, and by evening, Gavilan was on deck preparing the sails while Maria—Miguel now, having chosen her father's name—was in the captain's quarters listing everything taken aboard into the captain's logs. "I have a good memory and am good with numbers," she'd told the first mate, keeping her tarpaulin hat pulled low and her voice low as well. She'd bound her breasts and wore loose duck trousers and a baggy checked shirt, the typical sailor's apparel. Nobody expected a woman on board. Gavilan claimed she was his fourteen-year-old brother, both of them regular Jack Tars, and he did most of the talking when they'd reached the ships in the harbor. Before taking the job as a vaquero, Gavilan had been a deckhand for a number of years and knew his way at sea.

The captain had not yet boarded *The White Swallow.* Fortune was shining on them, for a cabin boy was needed on this brig, and one who wrote and spoke in several languages was unheard of in California, where most did not read or write. The first mate seemed thrilled to have acquired them to round out his crew before heading out to sea when the winds turned fair. Many sailors left their ships for pastoral California, and it was always hard to keep a full crew on board here.

As cabin boy, Maria would have her own room right beside the captain's quarters. She just hoped the captain would be like the first mate, unsuspecting of her gender. Really, it was Gavilan who convinced the first mate they were brothers searching for work aboard a clipper ship. Gavilan's quiet strength impressed the man, and the first mate had focused on him until Gavilan revealed she could write as well as speak Spanish and English and some Russian too. That had sealed their good fortune aboard the vessel.

So here she was writing down everything the ship would carry back to Boston. She also would translate records written in Spanish. The captain had a pile of these accumulated over several years of trading in California. This would take much of the voyage, Maria supposed. No wonder the first mate was so happy when Gavilan said she wrote and read in Spanish and English.

Gavilan brought her food later that evening. "The captain is on deck now," he said. "This isn't looking good for you."

"Why not?" Maria's hand cramped from all the writing, and she was running low on ink already.

"This captain isn't a fool. It won't take him long to see you are a woman."

"The first mate didn't see." Maria pulled her hat down lower on her brow.

"You will be under the captain's nose here in his quarters. He's a smart one. He will find you out soon enough."

Maria clenched her teeth. Her life depended on this ploy. Surely, they'd found Joshua's body in the church. Women were hanged for murder in California too. At least she supposed they were. She'd never heard of such a thing, but they hanged men for the offense. Surely, they would hang a woman as well. "I am a good actress. The captain won't discover me," she reassured Gavilan.

"You are a beautiful woman. How could he not see this for himself?"

"Nobody expects a woman on board. No woman has hair like this." Maria whipped off her tarpaulin hat, ran a hand through her very short hair, and then crammed the hat back on her head. She missed her long red hair. It had always been her crowning glory, but in a way, she felt free without it. She could hide without it.

"The first mate has already said you are pretty for a boy. He laughed when he said this, and does not suspect you yet. You are lucky this captain runs a tight ship. On other vessels, a pretty boy like you would not have an easy time of it with the men."

Maria's stomach knotted. She thought she'd nothing left to fear, nothing left to lose, but the thought of being violated again sickened her. She would die first. Or kill again. Pushing the terrible thought away, she focused on the list on the table in front of her.

"You worry too much. I have your knife." She pulled up her baggy sailor's blouse and showed Gavilan the hilt of his dagger. Gavilan had purchased a new knife in Monterey.

"This captain would take that from you in a minute. He is a formidable man and twice your size."

"So the captain has impressed you. Is he gruff and wind burnt with a cigar forever in his mouth?"

"No, you will see how he is." Gavilan set the plate of food before her on the table between the log books.

Her stomach grumbled. The fare looked better than she'd expected, though boiled, all of it, potatoes, cabbage, and poultry falling apart on her plate.

"I cannot protect you on this ship." Gavilan's dark eyes shined with regret. In the few days they'd been together, hiding in the pine forest that edged the town, waiting for their plan to come together, she'd grown fond of him. She knew he'd grown fond of her as well.

"I can protect myself." Maria had never been short on confidence. Most of her life, she'd feared nothing. Not the fierce grizzly bears they roped and speared to protect the cattle and sheep herds. Not the men who'd looked at her speculatively, the way Joshua had looked at her before she killed him. Not storms and not death. She was determined to sail away from California at any cost. She would not lose this opportunity aboard this ship.

"I think the captain is a good man. If he finds out you are a woman, he will probably just dump us ashore. Do your best to get us as far as Valparaiso."

"Do you have family there?"

Gavilan smiled ruefully. "I am the son of a wealthy man. You would be surprised at the life I left in Valparaiso."

Maria was intrigued. "Why did you leave this life?"

The smile disappeared from Gavilan's face. "I killed a man in a duel. A very important man. My father's friend. My father did not appreciate this."

"Was this your only duel?"

"The only duel that mattered to my father. My father's friend wasn't a good man." Gavilan's eyes bore into hers. "Many men are not good men. You are the kind of woman who attracts such men."

"I am not a woman," she reminded him. "I am your brother."

He laughed. "You are no more my brother than the sea is kind. You will find this out too. The Horn awaits us."

"You should return to your post on deck. We do not want to draw attention to ourselves down here."

"Wherever you go, you draw attention to yourself. Keep your hat on and your head low. I will do what I can to keep you hidden."

"Thank you, my friend. You are a good man."

Gavilan sighed. "You are not a good woman. You are like a wild mustang filly. Headstrong and determined to run free. Women do not run free. You will know this soon enough. Eat all your food. You will need strength if seasickness hits you."

"The sea will not make me sick. It will make me strong."

Gavilan shook his head, breaking into a little smile as he walked from the room.

The hand on her shoulder awoke Maria. She'd fallen asleep at the table writing in the logs. The brass lantern swung from the rafter, swaying to the rhythm of an ocean-going vessel. She could feel the sea rolling beneath the ship, carrying them away from California, she hoped.

"I see you are a hard worker. That is good."

His deep, melodious voice was so familiar. She glanced up as he walked over to his large double bed in a splendid room paneled in hardwood. He removed his overcoat and laid it on the bed. Even with his back to her, those wide shoulders and that sun-kissed brown hair curling jauntily over his shirt collar, she recognized him. Her stomach plunged to her feet, and she found it hard to breathe. How could this be? Of all the ships in the harbor, how could it be his ship they'd signed aboard?

"Nate tells me you speak several languages. I thought I would spend the voyage wearing out my hand without a cabin boy. I hate keeping records. If you serve me well, you will have a good future aboard *The White Swallow*. Nate started out as a cabin boy. So did I. You could become a first mate or captain one day, as we did."

Maria was speechless. She stared at him aghast. When he turned around, she ducked her head and furiously returned to writing. What she was putting down, she didn't quite know. Spanish was her native tongue. She realized she'd gone back to scribbling in Spanish when she was supposed to be copying the ledgers in English.

"Put your ink away. Go get some rest," he told her. "The weather is good now, and it is smooth sailing, but I didn't like the horizon tonight. There may be a storm brewing."

She kept her head low, deepening her voice. "What shall I do with these ledgers?"

"Leave them. You can start on them in the morn. Nate tells me you're just fourteen. Your mother didn't mind you leaving California?"

"My mother's dead," Maria mumbled.

"That's too bad. How long have you been sailing, son?"

She decided to be as honest as she could without revealing too much. She kept her eyes on the ledgers, her mind spinning with how to avoid recognition. Of all the ship captains on the California coast, it had to be him. "Not long, but your first mate said I won't be doing any deck work. My job is to translate your ledgers and do your bidding down here, according to Mr. Andrews."

"As you can see, I have plenty of translating for you. Look at all these books."

She glanced at him sideways, and to her relief, he was staring down at a box against the wall instead of looking at her. The wooden box held more ledgers.

"Go get some rest. You have a lot of work ahead of you, Miguel. Or should I call you Michael since were headed for Boston? Nate said you and your brother are from Valparaiso. I hope you don't plan on jumping ship when we stop there for supplies."

Her father's name sounded so strange on his lips. She decided she didn't like it. "Michael is fine," she mumbled, standing up and capping the ink bottle without looking at him.

"Are you afraid of me?"

"No, my brother says you're a good captain." She kept her head down and moved toward the door.

"You need to look a man in the eye when you speak to him." He removed his blue captain's coat and vest and pulled his white shirt over his head. Naked from the waist up, all muscle, he walked over to his washbasin. "Stand up tall and square your shoulders, my boy. And look me in the eye from now on."

"Yes, sir," she said, after clearing her throat, keeping her voice reverberating low. She stared at his naked torso with everything inside her unfurling. His muscles rippled across his back as he bent over the washbasin, splashing water onto his face and then wetting his hair and slicking it back as he glanced at her from the mirror hanging above the basin. He was such a handsome sight, but his disrobing reminded her of what had happened at the church with Joshua Tyler.

Life could be so cruel. A man like Captain Dominic Mason would certainly demand an unspoiled virgin for a wife. She was no longer that. Her maidenhead torn from her body. Her worth stolen away. Swallowing the lump in her throat, reminding herself to breathe, she walked from his room and found her own. Collapsing on her hard, narrow bunk, she wondered how she was going to remain disguised as a boy all these months at sea with the dashing Captain Mason. A man who moved her like no other, awakened every girlish dream she'd ever entertained for herself.

Her room was so tiny she could nearly touch every wall standing in one spot. It was a closet really, with a bunk and a chamber pot tucked under the bed and a whale oil lamp swinging from a rafter. It smelled musky. She didn't even see a washbasin. She could walk out her door and into the captain's chamber in one jaunt. That's how close she would live to Captain Mason for the next several months on the open sea. She tried not to think about what she'd once felt for him. How he was the first man to capture her youthful heart.

She felt old and used now. After what had happened in the church, the girl in her was gone. Perhaps her infatuation with Captain Mason would depart as well, though she doubted it. Seeing him stunned and thrilled her, if she were being honest with herself. But being honest with herself was not what she wanted to be any longer. She was a murderess and a soiled woman. A man like Captain Mason was beyond her reach. She wondered what his fiancée in Boston looked like? Probably pretty as a picture and pure as freshly driven snow. Maria rolled over on the bunk and stared at her sea chest.

Gavilan had deposited her chest there beside her bunk. Fortunately, they'd had enough coin to purchase what they needed from another ship in the harbor, though that ship hadn't hired them. She couldn't believe it was Dominic Mason's ship she was aboard. Had she believed in a good and faithful God, she would have laughed at his ways and thanked him, but after what had happened in the church, her belief in God's goodness had been crushed.

What kind of God would allow such a thing in his holy place? Her body had quickly healed, but not her soul. Something had been ripped away inside her soul when her maidenhead had been torn away. She'd had her revenge, but it did not taste sweet. The killing she'd done lay coiled like a poisonous snake down deep in her soul. It occurred to her that she was cursed now. Surely, she would go to hell for killing a man. But first she would live.

She pushed thoughts of God and hell from her mind. She would not think about God or hell or the loss of her virginity in a holy place. She wondered how Gavilan was doing with the crew. He was tall and strong and smart and usually didn't speak until spoken to. She liked his quiet strength. Certainly, he'd have no problem with the crew, especially since he'd been a sailor before.

Her eyes grew heavy, and finally she slept. It felt like only a moment before the knock came at her door. The portal cracked open, and his familiar voice stiffened her spine. She hadn't been dreaming. This really was Captain Dominic Mason's ship.

"Rise and shine," he said, and his voice sounded all business. "Looks like we'll be heading into that storm after all. Make sure you eat before the sea gets really rough. You aren't very sturdy for a boy of fourteen. You may regret signing aboard. Some people never find their sea legs. When the ship starts rolling, put the ink away. Nate found us some more ink, and we're gonna need it. I've neglected work on those ledgers for far too long. You did a right fine job translating yesterday." He left her door standing ajar and went on his way.

She rose and shoved her hat on her head. It was still dark out, but the blue light of dawn could be seen above deck. Opening her trunk, she was happy to find a pile of clothes there. Sailor's clothes, but at least she wouldn't be living in the same sloppy outfit day after day. She tightened the cloth binding her breasts and did her best to hide her feminine figure. So far nobody had really taken a second look at her. Why should they? Teenage boys were common on ships.

Closing her trunk, she walked from her room to his, where she used his washbasin to scrub her face. The water in a bota bag beside the basin was clean and fresh and cold. For how long that would last at sea, she didn't know. Staring at herself in the mirror hanging on the wall, she noticed something dark had crept into her face. She wasn't a bright-eyed girl any longer. Shadows deepened her eyes, and her gaze had grown hard and haunted, like the eyes of a prostitute she'd seen in Monterey when she'd accompanied her father there to sell hides. Joshua had taken all light and youth from her. She decided right then she would never say his name again, not in her thoughts nor out loud. The man who had ruined her deserved to be dead and forgotten, especially by her.

Gavilan brought her a plate of cold salt pork and biscuits not long after she'd settled down to work at the table with the ledgers. "This food will help if you get seasick. I see the captain hasn't gotten wind of you yet. I overheard him telling his first mate you're a right fine cabin boy with a real pretty hand putting ink to paper."

She didn't respond to his praise.

"What's wrong? You don't look proud of yourself, like I thought you would."

"I know the captain." She stared at the salt pork and biscuits without hunger.

"What do you mean you know the captain?" Gavilan's brow furrowed.

"I mean I know him. I've kissed him." Maria had never been one to hide anything. There'd never really been anything to hide in her life until now. Gavilan had risked his life to help her escape California. She wasn't going to keep secrets from him here on the ship.

He looked at her as if she'd slapped him.

"I know. I'm sorry. I cannot believe fate has put us on this particular ship."

"I knew you were something, but I did not think you were that kind of woman. I know the patrón . . . he . . . your dress was torn when I tossed it into the sea . . ." Gavilan broke off and uncomfortably looked away.

She could see he was disturbed. Did he harbor feelings for her? She hoped not. The last thing she wanted was for a man to press his suit on her again. "I have decided never to speak of your patrón. We must forget that ever happened. And I do not care what you think of me. I will kiss whoever I kiss. It will be up to me where I share my affections, and no man shall have a say in it. You hear me?"

Gavilan looked hurt and bewildered by her tirade. "You won't have to pretend you're a boy if you service the captain. The only work you'll do is over there." He pointed to the bed.

She blinked at him. Did he mean what she thought he meant? "You can go," she said abruptly, pulling the tin plate over and filling her fork with cold pork. Captain Mason said she better eat before the storm hit. It felt like a storm had already battered her life. It was true what Gavilan said. She could be any kind of woman she chose to be now that her body had been torn open by a man. Some women made a living this way. It wasn't a surprise to her.

Gavilan stood there staring at her for a moment longer. She could feel the disappointment radiating from him.

"Do you want to say something else?"

"I've said enough, I suppose."

"Then go."

"Mr. Andrews said I could bring your food to you here in the captain's quarters so you can keep after those ledgers. I think it best you take your meals down here instead of eating with the crew."

Swallowing that first bite of pork was hard. She didn't want to hurt Gavilan. He'd helped her thus far. Her feelings softened toward him. "Thank you for bringing my meals. I do not want to meet the crew. Dealing with the captain is trouble enough."

Gavilan nodded. "There should be some rope in here. If the storm gets really bad tie yourself into your bunk."

She returned her attention to her plate. Once he left, she made herself finish all of it. If nothing else, Maria was a survivor. And a hard worker. She got a lot done before the strengthening waves and rising and falling of the ship left her holding tightly to the ink quill and open ledgers. She corked the ink and secured it and all the ledgers as best she could in a box anchored to the wall. Everything in the room was fastened down one way or another. Only the swinging brass oil lamp moved on its own accord, her thoughts drifting on their own accord as well.

Captain Mason had been a guest at the rancho for several months. She'd dined with him, danced with him. The memory of his kiss wasn't ever far from her mind. Or what he'd said to her that night in the vineyard before leaving the next morning. The memory plagued her. Made her ache with what could have been. What might have been.

"I'm sorry. I cannot take you with me."

She'd moved closer to him until they stood toe to toe under the moon, tilting her head back to look up into his face, her hair rippling down to her waist. "Why not?"

"You have no idea what it's like to live at sea. A grand hacienda is the place for you, my lady. The wild ocean belongs to men who may live or die in every storm."

"Men such as yourself, Señor Mason?" She raised up on tiptoes to get even closer to him. "Why should I stay here? You won't be here." She draped her arms around his neck.

He took her by the waist, held her for a moment as if he might embrace her, and then gently but firmly set her away from him. "Because you are safe here with your family in California."

"I don't want to be safe." She moved right back against him, *dropping the shawl wrapped around her shoulders as she reached up and placed her arms around his neck, molding her body to his in a marvelous way. Though she had never kissed a man before, she boldly pulled his face down to hers. When she pressed her lips to his, he kissed her back, holding her snugly against his body, groaning in pleasure when she opened her mouth under his.*

Maria had seen the servants kiss. She'd been planning her first kiss most of her life. This was nothing like she'd planned. It was far more thrilling than anything she'd ever dared dream a kiss could be.

He finally tore his mouth from hers. "I'm sorry," he said. "I should not be out here with you. I have a fiancée in Boston."

That fiancée haunted her now. Her own past haunted her. And the coming storm made the haunting all the more awful. *Just keep working,* she told herself. *Translate the ledgers. If you do your job, he won't take notice of you.*

Chapter Three

Dominic was soaking wet, cold, and tired. What a way to start a voyage. With an unexpected storm. His crew had done a marvelous job keeping *The White Swallow* on course through high seas, but they appeared headed into the thick of it now. Most of his men had stayed with him as he sailed from California with his hold full of California banknotes—cattle hides he'd sell in Boston. He'd only lost two hands and his cabin boy to the golden shore, and he wouldn't miss that cabin boy one bit. Henry couldn't read or write, though he'd sworn he could back in Boston. The boy hadn't been of any help at all. Dominic had named California the golden shore because her hills were golden now as they left the coast. The hills had been lush and green when they arrived in the spring.

Sailing home without Steven left him sorrowful. He still couldn't believe Steven was buried on a hill overlooking the Vasquezes' hacienda. And California was at war now, though the war wasn't much to speak of so far, most of the towns along the coast having surrendered without any bloodshed.

The coast was really the only civilized part of California aside from the Sacramento Valley, where the rebellion had flourished with the American settlers digging in around Sutter's Fort. Dominic wondered what California would look like in a few years when he returned to San Francisco. He also wondered if he'd ever see Maria Vasquez again, though he reminded himself for the hundredth time to stop thinking about her. The last time he'd seen her, she'd stood on the upstairs porch of the Vasquez hacienda watching him depart. The wind had captured her hair, blowing it wild around her like flames. "You should wave good-bye to your sister," he'd told Roman, his closest friend in California, riding along with him.

"You should wave good-bye to her, amigo. It is you my sister watches ride away."

Dominic would never forget Maria's beauty or her fiery nature. She would not have made a good wife for him. He'd done the right thing in returning to Sally. Sally had waited five years already to marry him, and he knew she was the kind of wife he needed, steady and gentle as Sally was.

"Mr. Andrews, take the wheel. I'll be back shortly." He released the helm, and his muscles quivered after hours holding tightly there, with it only getting worse. Walls of water surrounded the ship. The vessel rolled in waves as high as Boston's brick buildings. This wasn't new to him. The Horn gave worse, but something felt sinister about this storm. Perhaps because it was so unexpected and fiercer than most gales here in the Pacific.

As he headed below deck, he passed his new deckhand. The young man from Valparaiso was strong and quiet and a hard worker. He was also very protective of his little brother. Dominic didn't know what to make of his cabin boy yet with that fair hand for writing. The boy had already accomplished more work in a day than his two other cabin boys had in the past several years. Never had he seen that kind of handwriting from a sailor before. It reminded him of a woman's hand, precise and flowing in perfect English. Of course, the boy wasn't really a sailor, and something about him didn't sit well with Dominic. For starters, the boy was far too educated, but he thanked his lucky stars the boy was aboard. Those ledgers had needed translating for a long time. The boy was also too pretty for ship life; Nate had pointed that out right off. "I didn't like how fair of face he was, Captain, but when I heard he could write in Spanish and English, I knew we needed him and his brother too. I'd say they don't have the same father by the looks of them."

"Well, we can't judge men by their looks," Dominic had told Nate.

Hopefully, the boy knew to tie himself into his bunk during the worst of the weather. He headed down to his cabin to check on him before grabbing a bite to eat and then returning to the helm in preparation for the worsening storm. But when he reached his quarters, Dominic couldn't believe his eyes. The boy was trying to work at the table with the brass lantern swinging overhead. He was lying across the table, holding the two ledgers down with his slender body, one hand clutching the inkwell, trying to write with his other hand and having a go of it. He had a plump, round fanny for a skinny lad. The thought unsettled him.

"Don't you know not to burn the lantern during rough seas?" Dominic strode into the cabin and stood there in amazement.

The boy didn't look up and kept trying to write.

Did he ever remove that darn hat? He couldn't even see the boy's face. Dominic was about to remove the hat from the boy's head himself when a large wave hit the ship. *The White Swallow* pitched straight up and then crashed down sideways. He let out a curse as he and the cabin boy went flying.

The ledgers rolled and so did the inkwell. The boy let out a yelp that sounded very feminine. When the ship righted herself, the boy was sprawled in Dominic's lap without his hat.

His first thought was to thank the Lord the lantern hadn't broken. The last thing he needed was a burning ship. The second realization was that he held a woman in his arms, a soft, curvy female. "Who the devil are you?"

She looked up, those green eyes of hers wide with surprise. She reached for the inkwell, righting it in her hand. Dominic held on to her, and ink ran down her wrist and onto his pant leg.

"Maria!" he said in disbelief. "What has happened to your hair? What on earth are you doing here?"

She closed her eyes for a moment, refusing to look at him as he held her in his lap, his arms wrapped firmly around her now. Was she frightened? Hurt? Had she run away from her family?

He put his hand to her hair, knowing something terrible must have made her desperate enough to cut it. Nearly all her beautiful hair was gone. This upset him almost as much as her being a stowaway on his ship. But the lack of hair didn't steal her beauty. Her face was even more beautiful without all that glorious red hair, if that were possible, her mouth lush and inviting, her cheekbones high and prominent. Her large almond-shaped green eyes when she met his stare stunned him.

"I killed a man," she whispered.

"You did what?" He held her more tightly.

"I buried a knife in his back. He deserved it." She shed no tears like another woman would have confessing murder. Her eyes were dry and haunted. She bit her lower lip to stop its tremble.

"Sweet Jesus," he said. It wasn't a curse. It was a prayer.

"I can't go back to California." She shook her head in despair. "Please don't make me go back. They will surely hang me."

Dominic took a deep breath and slid his fingers into her hair. Still so silky soft. He pulled her head down against his shoulder so he didn't have to look in her eyes and just sat there holding her, praying and holding her. *What will we do, Lord?*

Nothing came to him from his prayer, but a calmness settled over them as the storm lulled for a moment. Maria leaned against him, settling against his chest with a deep sigh of surrender. He could feel the tight binding under her blouse concealing her breasts in the oversized sailor's shirt. Her form was as fetching as her face. What was he going to do?

"I'm so tired," she whispered.

"Have you slept at all during the storm?"

"No." She handed him the inkwell. "I've been knocked around all day." She pulled up the sleeve of her shirt to show her bruises.

The brass lantern swung above their heads. Dominic stood up, picking Maria up with him, and both of them nearly tumbled into the bed when the ship plunged beneath their feet.

"I'm tying you in." He grabbed a rope near the bed. "Lie down and try to get some sleep. We'll talk after the storm abates."

She looked at him as if she couldn't believe what he was doing. "Raise your arms for a minute. We just need the rope over your body. I'm sorry, but this will keep you safe."

Thunder boomed. Lightning flashed against the cabin's windows before rain battered the ship. Dominic spoke louder to be heard over the squall. "I've got to get back to the helm." He knotted the ropes to his wooden bedframe, leaving her arms free and the binding loose enough so she could roll beneath the ropes.

In the short while he'd been down here with her, the storm had unfolded in earnest. Could things get any worse? What on God's green earth was he going to do with Maria? He reminded himself he wasn't on God's green earth. He was on the roaring sea, and by the sounds of his groaning ship, he knew things could get worse. A whole lot worse.

"How long will the storm last?" Maria's voice trembled. He'd tied the rope over her body several times as she lay on her back, looking up at him from the bed, her eyes wide and pleading. Maria Vasquez in his bed—Lord help him.

"I'm not sure, but I've got to put the lantern out. I'm sorry. I'll return as soon as I can to untie you."

"Please don't leave me in the dark alone."

"I'm sorry, I have to." Dominic reached down and cupped her cheek for a moment with his palm. Then he stood up and extinguished the lantern. In that instant, he felt the ship turn as a mighty wave slammed against her. In the dark, he dove onto the bed with Maria, holding on to the ropes, knowing things had just turned for the worst in earnest. Sailors called this a knockdown. Some ships never recovered from such a blow. Lightning flashed against the windows of his cabin once more. In that moment, he looked into Maria's desperate eyes and couldn't believe she lay beneath him. "God help us," he breathed as the thunder boomed.

"Don't go," Maria begged. "Please don't leave." He couldn't see her now that they were once again in darkness, but he could feel their bodies pressed together with only the rope between them, her hands clutching his shirtfront.

"I must go. My men need me on deck. They need their captain showing them this storm is nothing to fear."

"It is everything to fear. We are going to die, and I am going to hell!" Her voice rang with fear.

"We are not going to die. The Lord is our shepherd. We shall not fear."

"The Lord has cursed me. This storm is because of me!" Maria buried her fingers in his hair. She frantically pulled his face down and kissed him as if they were both about to die.

For a wild moment, Dominic kissed her back. Perhaps they really would perish in this storm. Death was a possibility in every storm. And the Good Lord help him, he wanted to kiss Maria. Had hungered for this girl from the minute he'd laid eyes on her in the spring, standing on that hacienda porch. Never had a woman set him on fire this way. He gave the kiss everything he had, and she did too. There was nothing between them, and yet everything was between them. Sally. The storm. This terrible desire blindsiding him as the ship rolled in the waves. He kissed her like this was his last kiss. Like she was the end and yet the beginning of everything he knew. When he couldn't take any more, he tore his mouth from hers. "Oh, Maria," he said, "We must stop this right now!"

"No!" she cried. "Please don't stop!" The desperation in her voice tore at his heartstrings. She arched her body up against him and sought his lips once more as the ship struggled to right herself on a mighty wave. Rain hammered the cabin.

Dominic wrapped one arm around the rope and the other arm around Maria, knowing the ship would plunge. She hung on to him with surprising strength and wouldn't give up on the kiss. It was like riding a tidal wave. Of desire. Of terror. It wasn't the storm that truly frightened him. It was his feelings for Maria. Something had come unmoored in him. The tight restraint he lived by. A captain must always remain in control. A captain must never give way to his passions. Never unleash his desires. Yet passion was overtaking him now. If he didn't put an end to this soon, there would be no end. In the midst of this madness, in some sane corner of his mind, he called on the name of the Lord and rolled away from her in the bed, begging God to help him.

He landed on the floor so hard it jarred his teeth and knocked some sense into him.

"Dominic!" she cried in the dark.

"I'm here," he said in his commanding captain's voice, doing his best to recover from what had just happened. Good Lord, what *had* just happened with her?

"I'll return for you when I can. Surrender to the rope, Maria. Do not untie yourself. Wait for me to untie you." Dominic was glad for the darkness as he crawled on his hands and knees across the cabin. A storm had put him on his hands and knees a time or two before, but a woman never had. Until now. And she was tied in his bed, headed for Boston or to the depths of the sea with him. A part of him wanted to return to that bed and let every ounce of good sense go. If they died tonight, they died together. But first they would love like he'd never loved before. Another part of him wanted to conquer the storm and conquer what he felt for Maria. Sally was his choice if he was going to remain a man of integrity. A captain who always did the proper thing. A captain who put everyone's needs before his own.

He had to get to the helm and assure his men all was well on deck. *The White Swallow* had been through storms before. Numerous storms. But never so early in a voyage had a storm caught them unaware, knocking the ship down.

Where had this fierce storm come from? He felt the door against his searching hands and rose up on his feet, yanking the portal open to step into the gale. In an instant, he was drenched and welcomed the driving rain and surf. Maria cried his name one last time before he threw himself against the door to close it.

Getting to the helm was not easy. He expected to find Mr. Andrews roped there, but instead his new deckhand was tied to the wheel, the young man's muscular arms straining to control the bucking ship. "Where is Mr. Andrews?" Dominic yelled over the fury of the gale.

"He hit his head!" Gavilan was big and strong but clearly having a difficult time steadying the ship in the raging sea.

"Do you know what you are doing?" Dominic grabbed hold of the wheel alongside the young man from Chile.

"I have sailed before, but never with a captain who abandons the helm in a storm."

The rebuke stunned Dominic. Probably because he deserved it. He was suddenly furious with this dark-eyed man holding the wheel alongside him. Both men strained to keep the ship upright in the waves dashing her. He hadn't given

Gavilan much thought until now. He should demand to know who he was to Maria. Certainly not a brother. The only brother Maria had was Roman. Perhaps a cousin, but he didn't think so. What he thought was a terrible thing. Had the girl already taken a lover? Was it possible she'd brought a lover on board his ship?

And where was Mr. Andrews? Nothing had ever felled Nate before. Nate was like a mighty oak. Dominic hadn't worried about the helm while in the cabin with Maria because Nate was always there. He trusted Nate with his life and his ship.

"Mr. Andrews was carried to his cabin, out cold and bleeding from the head. That rogue wave that knocked us down surprised us all. We've been fighting ever since to stabilize the ship. What have you been doing, Captain?"

"What I've been doing is none of your business." Dominic was ready to punch the man in the jaw. Instead, he grabbed the extra length of rope and tied himself to the helm alongside Gavilan. "Where is Mr. Jones?"

"The second mate helped carry Mr. Andrews to his bunk. I haven't seen him since."

The wind screeched. Dominic had a hard time hearing what Gavilan was saying over the weather. "Who turned the ship into the wind? I told Mr. Andrews we would turn away from the storm and run before it."

"Mr. Andrews attempted to turn the ship too late. The wave came out of nowhere. Mr. Andrews lost his footing and hit his head on the deck. Mr. Jones lost control of the situation. I stepped in to right things."

Dominic nodded and set his face like flint. He wasn't afraid of storms. But what he felt for Maria scared him to death.

For hours, roped to the helm with Gavilan, battling the fury of the squall, Dominic heard her calling his name before he'd shut the door against her pleas. Against the shocking desire he felt for her. It was like he sailed with a hold full of gunpowder instead of cattle hides. Something that would blow sky high if he ignited a spark. And before he knew what hit him, that spark had ignited. He'd set his mind to marry Sally. With the best intentions, he'd left the Vasquez hacienda determined to put Maria from his mind. Now here she was in his bed. He'd tied her there himself.

Why hadn't he ushered her to the cabin boy's bunk and tied her there instead? Why had he allowed her to kiss him? Allowed himself to kiss her back? Should he even call that kissing? Maybe he should call it losing his mind and morals and everything that mattered.

Normally, a storm like this would have him completely focused on his ship and his crew, but he couldn't focus. Nearly all he could think about was Maria.

He and Gavilan didn't talk at the helm. The dark-eyed man brooded beside him. Dominic estimated they were about the same age, nearly the same size and build as well, though Gavilan was darker with ebony hair and swarthier skin. A fine figure of a man. Jealousy reared its ugly head. Why was this man with Maria?

Chapter Four

Panic seized her. The dark was so dark. The screeching of the storm terrifying. The plunging and bucking of the ship beyond imagination. Maria considered crawling out from under the rope. It wasn't so tight she couldn't escape, but she kept hearing Dominic's promise to return and release her. She'd kissed him only wanting to make him stay, but it had turned into something more. Something desperate and primal that had nothing to do with fear and everything to do with how she felt about him.

She'd been a girl full of dreams the first time they'd kissed. Now she was a woman ruined by rape. Yet raw with hope. Would Dominic still want her? Was she still worthy of his love? Would she live to see his face again? In the dark, it didn't seem possible. She held onto the rope holding her in the bed and prayed for daylight. Prayed for the storm to pass. Prayed that she wouldn't go to hell. After what had happened in the church, she'd vowed to never pray again, but terror brought her to this place. Her grandmother's rosary was in her sea chest, a string of golden beads and a crucifix of solid gold that nearly filled her palm. She wished the heavy prayer chain was in her hand. From the time she could talk, she could recite the rosary. She'd done it every night before bed nearly all her life. Many nights she'd done it bitterly, longing to throw the golden rosary away from her. But the fear of God had kept it in her hand. The fear of God caused her to recite the rosary now, fingering the rough rope across her chest as she would finger the smooth golden beads running across her palms. The rosary was priceless, but that was not why she kept it.

Why did she keep it? Why did she want to hold it now? Why did she turn to God as if God was all she knew? The storm went on and on. To keep from going crazy, she focused on her favorite memories. Her first waltz. Her first horse. The waltz had been with Roman. Her father hadn't allowed her to waltz with anyone but her brother. Still, the dance had moved her. She was made for dancing. She had known this with every bit of her being as they swirled around the floor. How old was she then? Eleven? Twelve at her first waltz? Roman was five years older, and they'd wrestled as they danced over who controlled where they went on the floor. Of course, Roman won because he was bigger and stronger, and neither of them wanted to disappoint their father, so they danced politely but fiercely too. They were Vasquezes, a proud breed, the blood of Spanish conquistadores running through their veins.

Her stallion, Tonatiuh, had taught her how to master something much stronger than herself. Tonatiuh meant Sun God in English. Tonatiuh had been Junipero's horse. Junipero, her family's trusted *mayordomo* for twenty-eight years. After a bull had killed Junipero, nobody could get near his magnificent stallion, but Maria had been Junipero's little shadow. The old Indian cowboy, once the son of a proud Indian chief, had put her on Tonatiuh's back before he died. "I have had a vision of you becoming one with Tonatiuh. At first, I resisted this dream, but it will not leave me. Tonatiuh must know you are his master after I am gone. This is why you will feed and groom him from now on," Junipero had told Maria when she was six years old.

After that day, Maria took over caring for the stallion. Her father thought it a fine idea, so proud that his little red-haired daughter was chosen by Junipero to care for the highly prized animal. Junipero had been her grandfather's *mayordomo,* and the horse had been named after her grandfather, Miguel Roman Pedro de Alvarado Vasquez, a Spanish conquistador. The Indians called her grandfather Tonatiuh because of his blond hair.

"You remind me of your grandfather, so fierce and yet so tender and true to those you love," Junipero told Maria as he showed her how to brush Tonatiuh's golden hide until it glistened. "You are smart and loyal, and the gods favor you. Just as they favored your grandfather." Junipero had trained the stallion from when he was a colt first taken from his mother's side. Now Junipero trained Maria. She became a proud, bossy little vaquero, just as he was. Junipero was greatly respected and feared on the rancho. Maria decided she would be greatly respected and feared as well.

Lupe did not like Maria's attachment to Junipero. "He rejects Jesúcristo and follows the old ways that lead our people into darkness," Lupe said. "I do not understand why your father allows you to run with him and the vaqueros." When her father gave her the stallion, Lupe was furious. "That stallion will kill you! A little girl does not need a horse like that! You will break all your bones! He will tromp you to death!" Maria had never seen Lupe lose her temper before. The old Indian woman's tirade shocked her.

But Tonatiuh never tromped her to death as Lupe predicted, and as Junipero had prophesized, Maria and Tonatiuh became one, and the talk of the rancho. Little Maria was like a whirlwind of sun and flame on Tonatiuh. Her father made a lot of money gambling on her and the stallion when they visited other ranchos, where Maria raced the magnificent horse that never lost. When Tonatiuh died the month Maria turned fifteen, it felt like a part of her died with her beloved stallion. Tonatiuh was her first love. Her first war. And her first conquest.

In the beginning, the stallion hadn't wanted her for his master. Had even come at her, nearly stomping her in his stall one day after Junipero died. It wasn't until she denied the horse food for many days and then fed him by hand, day after day for weeks, that the horse finally turned to her in love and loyalty. Nobody could ride Tonatiuh but her. The stallion wouldn't let anyone else near him.

This had taught Maria to never give up and never give in to fear. She remembered this now, holding the rope across her chest, picturing herself holding Tonatiuh's reins as the ship bucked like a stallion. The storm was like Junipero's unpredictable gods, but Maria had learned a secret from Lupe when she was young. "Just believe and receive," Lupe always said. The old Indian woman meant believe in Jesúcristo and receive his grace and mercy, but Maria took it simply as the words came to her. Believe and receive.

In that moment, she believed she would survive the storm. The fear left her, and she grew determined to never fear a storm again. Never fear a man again. And never fear Dominic would not love her. She would make him love her. She had won Tonatiuh's love. Junipero's love. Maria had never lost anyone's affections in her life.

"You were made to be loved," Lupe had told her one night after they'd said the rosary together, when Maria was bruised and weary and discouraged trying to win Tonatiuh's love. Of course, Lupe was talking about being made to be loved by Jesúcristo, but as a determined little girl, Maria took it to mean she'd been made to be loved by Junipero's stallion. The next day she refused to feed the horse. And the next and the next. Tonatiuh would love her or he would starve to death. The horse grew weak, dropping a hundred pounds, before he learned to eat from her hand.

Before being taken and stripped of her virginity, she'd set her heart on Dominic. It wasn't even a conscious thought until this very moment. Of course he would love her. He had to love her.

When he had ridden away from the rancho without acknowledging her on the upper porch watching him go, she'd been stunned—but not defeated. Maria knew right then one day she would win his love. But after what had happened in the church, she'd lost all hope for a spell, believing a man like Dominic could only marry an unsoiled bride. Now, mastering her fear of the storm by remembering how she'd mastered other battles in her life, she realized she'd been made to be loved. All her life, Lupe had told her so. Junipero had told her so. Ultimately, Dominic must love her.

Chapter Five

In his cabin, Dominic took off his wet boots, undressed, and put on dry clothes. Maria slept soundly in his bed. He untied the ropes and removed them from the bed, thinking she would wake up, but she didn't stir. Morning light poured into the cabin through the windows in the stern. What a blessed relief to see the sunrise after the storm. He stared at Maria's face for a long moment, marveling it was really her in his bed. She was just as beautiful as he remembered. Her lips captured his perusal. Kissing her wasn't far from his mind. His muscles quivered with exhaustion after wrestling at the helm all night long. Certainly, he should wake her and send her back to the cabin boy's quarters, but the last thing he wanted was a conversation with her right now. He just wanted some sleep.

Quietly, he stretched out beside her on the bed. Though desperately tired, it took some time to fall asleep with her beside him. He stared at the rafters, wondering if Mr. Andrews would live. Mr. Curry, the ship's cook, had done all he could to save Mr. Andrews's life, but Mr. Andrews had slipped into a coma. It was in God's hands now. His second mate, Mr. Jones, was at the helm, and Dominic had sent Gavilan to his bunk to get some rest as well. The dark-eyed man from Valparaiso had probably saved the ship by turning her back into the wind and luffing through the squall after Mr. Andrews was injured.

Dominic didn't know how long he slept, probably not long, he decided, with Maria still sleeping soundly at his side when he woke up. Upon the realization she wasn't part of a delightful dream he was having, he sat up with a jolt and had to restrain himself from leaping out of the bed like a frightened schoolboy. Again, he chastised himself for not putting her in the cabin boy's quarters. Why on earth had he secured her in his bed? What was he thinking? Was he even thinking at all? Thus far, it felt like he was simply responding out of some deep, desperate need he harbored for Maria.

He left the bed and went to his washbasin. Standing before his mirror in just his pants, he realized how disheveled he was. The first thing he needed was a shave since he prided himself on always appearing the part of a perfectly put together ship captain. He knew the importance of appearance when it came to a crew. The eyes staring back at him in the mirror looked a bit beaten. Never had a storm blindsided him this way. And Mr. Andrews's accident was a bad omen for the voyage. He didn't believe in omens, he believed in an Almighty God, but his crew didn't share his faith. Sailors were a superstitious lot, and his crew had been badly shaken by the unexpected storm and Mr. Andrews's unfortunate injury at the helm.

A light knock fell on his door. Dominic quietly bid entry. The door opened, and Gavilan stepped over the threshold, carrying two plates of food. The man's gaze flew from him to

Maria in the bed, and then Gavilan set the plates down very purposefully on the table before pulling a rigger's knife out from under his shirt.

Dominic had a knife in his hand too, the one he shaved with. He stepped away from the mirror, raising his eyebrows and his knife in return. "I haven't bedded her," he said quietly, "if that's what you're thinking."

"But she is in your bed." Gavilan took a fighter's stance, pointing the knife at him.

"Yes, and we both know she's not your brother." Dominic couldn't help the wry smile that twisted his lips.

Slowly, Gavilan lowered his knife. "She is not my brother, but she needs someone to protect her."

Dominic glanced over at Maria, still sound asleep. "She must not have slept during the storm. Maybe she hasn't slept before that. She's exhausted. Tell me why."

Gavilan tucked the knife back under his shirt. "She hasn't slept much," he confessed. "Even before coming to your ship."

"Let's have your last name and your history with Maria." Dominic went back to shaving, keeping an eye on Gavilan standing beside the table with the two plates of cold salt pork and hardtack. It would take a while for Mr. Curry to right his kitchen and produce a warm meal for the crew.

"Gavilan Hernandez."

"So how long have you been protecting her, Gavilan Hernandez?"

"Not long."

"So you would agree your relationship with her has not lasted long enough for you to make another foolish move on my ship."

"I will not pull my knife on you again unless you harm her. She has already been harmed enough."

"I do not harm women." Dominic rinsed the whiskers off his blade in the basin.

"So will you tell the crew she is a woman?"

"No. We will hold to your plan. Or her plan. Whose plan was it to pretend she was your brother on my ship?"

"Her plan."

"Figures." Dominic finished shaving and rinsed off his knife one last time. He kept his voice low, hoping not to wake her. "How did you two meet?"

Gavilan fell silent.

"This ship keeps no secrets. Secrets are bad luck." Dominic didn't believe in luck, but he wanted to put some fear into Gavilan. Sailors were notoriously afraid of bad luck.

Gavilan grinned. "So we will keep the secret that she is a woman, but this will be your ship's only secret?"

Dominic smiled back. "You're a smart one. Did you know Maria before she arrived in Monterey?"

"I have known her since the spring. But she did not know of me until we rode into Monterey together a week ago."

"How did you see her in the spring?"

"She arrived at the patrón's hacienda for her brother's betrothal to the patrón's daughter. Every man lost his head over her. She was so beautiful and handled her golden stallion like a vaquero."

"Why did she cut her hair?"

Again, Gavilan fell silent.

"Come on, tell me, my friend. I will keep your secret."

"You said you do not keep secrets on your ship. Aside from your cabin boy being a woman."

"What happened to her?" Her confession of killing a man weighed heavy on Dominic's mind.

Gavilan hung his head as if it was his fault something terrible had befallen her.

Dominic dried off his knife and set it on the table beside the washbasin, waiting for the man's answer.

Gavilan finally raised his head. "I'm not sure what happened before she killed him. I wasn't in the padre's quarters with them. But I watched her cut her hair afterward. I think she cut it because he ravaged her. I could see it on her face."

"So you were there when she cut her hair?"

"After pointing a gun at me, she took my knife and cut off all her beautiful hair as she stood in front of an altar of a saint. I told her to stop cutting her hair, but she would not listen." Gavilan gave him a searching look. "Were you lovers?"

Dominic was taken aback. "No, why?"

Gavilan shrugged. "I'm not sure what kind of woman she is, but I have decided it does not matter. I will keep her with me."

Dominic raised his eyebrows in question.

"I am not a poor man. My father in Valparaiso is very wealthy. She will have the life she deserves there."

"And you were in California, why?"

"My father sent me away, but I can return to Valparaiso and live as a man of means under my father's thumb, if Maria will stay with me."

It was Dominic's turn to nod. "Fair enough. We will let Maria decide where she stays."

"Do you not want her?" Gavilan looked at Maria and then back at him.

"I am set to marry my fiancée in Boston."

Gavilan grinned.

Dominic's stomach knotted. He recognized a leader in Gavilan and had seen his determination at the helm. The man looked at Maria and then turned toward the door. Before going out, he said, "Why does she sleep in your bed? Why not in the cabin boy's berth?"

"The squall took us by surprise." Though Dominic knew he should never admit to a storm surprising the captain, for some reason he trusted Gavilan. He owed the man much for taking command of the ship after Mr. Andrews went down and Mr. Jones disappeared in the gale. He'd never liked Mr. Jones, but the young man was the son of one of his ship's benefactors, so he'd ended up second in command several years ago. Dominic had been looking for a reason to be done with Mr. Jones. Now he had it. The man was a coward. During the worst of the storm, Mr. Jones hid in Mr. Andrews's cabin and didn't return to the helm as he should have, leaving an untested crewman like Gavilan to command the ship.

But Dominic knew Mr. Andrews's injury, Mr. Jones's desertion, and the chaos that overtook the ship was ultimately his fault. He'd been with Maria when all hell broke loose on deck.

"The squall did come out of nowhere. I have never seen anything like it. I did not realize we were in trouble until the rogue wave hit us, but you should have been at the helm when it happened." Gavilan shut the door quietly in his wake.

Dominic sat down at the table and rested his forehead in his hands. Gavilan was right. He'd endangered his ship and his crew because of Maria. The thought of leaving her in Valparaiso left him cold. The thought of taking her to Boston greatly troubled him, but he couldn't return her to California. The war had everyone in an uproar in California, and Roman, newly married to Rachel in the wake of Steven's death, had enough to worry about without dealing with a sister wanted for murder.

Pushing away from the table as quietly as he could, he walked over and stared down at the young woman in his bed. Her hair was shorter than his and badly cut, but her skin was fair and golden and perfectly smooth. Long, dark eyelashes feathered her cheeks. Her lush mouth was so inviting; even now he longed to kiss her. He'd never felt this way with Sally, or any other woman for that matter. This desire for Maria was so reckless, and so unlike him.

Doing his best not to awaken her, he dressed in his captain's uniform and carried his plate out of the room with him, leaving her plate on the table. There was no doubt in his mind Maria could take care of herself, but she would need protection from men. How would he protect her and still marry Sally? If she preferred to stay with Gavilan, he supposed he could leave her in Valparaiso. He would write Roman a letter letting him know where his sister was and that she was well. In spite of just pulling a knife on him, he believed Gavilan was a good man.

He quickly ate his food as he headed for the top deck. The afternoon was very blue, bright, and fresh in the wake of the storm. He could see for miles across the ocean. If only he could see into the future and know which path to take. Did Sally really need him? Was need a good reason to marry someone?

Maria in his bed hadn't helped one bit. He could get used to her there. Everything about her tempted him. He'd tried to leave her in California. After spending several months with her family, watching Maria dance at the fandangos, getting to know the vivacious girl as they took their meals together, he found himself obsessing over her. She fired his blood and his imagination. Waltzing with her had left him feeling like a schoolboy. She was so bold, so beautiful, not just in her appearance, but in her spirit. Now her spirit was wounded. She tried to hide it, but he could see something broken in her. It made him want to take care of her. But he'd promised to take care of Sally for the rest of his life. And his parents would never approve of a Catholic girl. They would lose their minds over this. They were Ulster Presbyterians whose Scots-Irish ancestors had fled Ireland to escape the persecution from their Catholic neighbors, arriving in Boston in the 1700's.

"How did your cabin boy fare in the storm?" Mr. Curry approached looking weary from righting his ransacked kitchen after the storm.

"My cabin boy's fine. How's Nate?"

Mr. Curry's face fell. "I don't know if he's gonna make it."

In front of all the deckhands, Dominic always called Nate "Mr. Andrews." But alone with the cook below deck or at the helm with just the two of them, Dominic called him Nate. He'd confided in Nate that he wasn't sure about his cabin boy. He didn't like how the boy hid beneath his hat and wouldn't look him in the eye. He'd worried the boy might be a thief or a liar. Never for a moment had he suspected the boy might be Maria.

Dominic nodded, not knowing what to say. He blamed himself for Nate's injury.

The cook seemed to know that. "So is your cabin boy still wearing that tarpaulin hat, or did the storm knock it off?"

Should he tell Mr. Curry about Maria, or let things be for now? The cook wasn't as superstitious as most sailors, but a stowaway woman on board would make everyone uncomfortable. It would be like having a Jonah on board. The crew would consider her bad luck. Although their luck was in question already with the storm that came out of nowhere and felled the strongest man on the ship, Nate Andrews.

"The storm knocked his hat off, but I'm sure he'll put it back on. That boy needs a good haircut. His hair is awful."

"I'll cut his hair," Mr. Curry offered.

"I don't think he'd let you near his hair. He's a strange one. You probably won't see much of him up here on deck. Books seem to fit the boy."

"Well, we've needed a bookish boy on board for a long time. If he doesn't get under your skin, maybe we'll keep him. If he can read and write in several languages, he's worth his weight in gold. Maybe we should ask the brother if he reads and writes too."

"Yes, I'll do that." Dominic wanted to know if Gavilan was an educated man. Already he was impressed with Maria's protector. At least the man was willing to die for her. Threatening the captain's life was right up there with mutiny. Sailors were put to death for lesser offenses on the open sea. He wasn't about to tell Mr. Curry what had happened with the knife incident. His crew would throw the man overboard for something like that. He was thinking about making Gavilan his first mate until Nate recovered, if Nate ever recovered.

He needed to concentrate on getting his ship and his men back in shape after the storm. Half the crew was sleeping below deck right now, the other half dog-tired on their feet righting the ship, everyone battered and bruised. He probably should see to the animals too. Storms were hard on the livestock, just like they were on the men. Eventually, all the chickens, pigs, and sheep would be eaten on this voyage, but he didn't need them perishing too soon. Keeping himself and his men well-fed was always a priority. He didn't want a weak and diseased crew. They hadn't even taken on the Horn yet.

Chapter Six

Maria awoke in a comfortable bed. It felt like she'd been asleep for a lifetime. The sheets were soft against her cheek, the feather mattress beneath her so inviting. The large, stiff clothes she wore surprised her. She wondered what had happened to her sheer cotton sleeping gowns. She put a hand to her head and touched her short locks. With a groan, she rolled over and buried her face in the pillow. Memories flooded her. She wished to be lost in sleep again. The cabin door opened, and bootfalls approached the bed. Rolling back over, her gaze connected with intent dark eyes.

Gavilan stood there, holding a plate of food. "How did you sleep?"

Maria sat up, rubbing her eyes. She was in no mood to deal with this new Gavilan. She missed the old Gavilan who didn't speak unless spoken to. "You survived the storm." She hoped to change the subject.

"You survived the captain's bed."

"Please, Gavilan. Do not act like my dueña. I left her in California. I am my own woman now. I do as I please."

"How long have you pleased the captain?"

"That is none of your business." Maria crawled out of the bed and went to the washbasin with her thoughts spinning. She hadn't expected this from Gavilan. Water had been left in the bowl. She dipped her hands into the cool liquid and brought some up to splash her face. Then she did what she'd seen Dominic do, wetted her hair and slicked it back from her face.

"Did you only kiss him once? Or have you kissed him many times?"

She looked at Gavilan in the mirror. He stood behind her, still holding the plate of steaming food. On the table was a cold plate of untouched food. "I have already told you, who I kiss is no concern of yours."

"The captain has a fiancée in Boston." Gavilan dropped the plate on the table with a clatter. The sound jarred Maria's nerves.

"Yes. I know." She spun away from the mirror to put him in his place. "My life is my own. I will never be owned by any man. I will do whatever I please with whomever I please."

"You need a man to protect you. Doing what you please will get you in trouble."

"I don't care. I want—"

"A captain who will marry another?" he interrupted her.

Maria picked up the cold plate of food and handed it to him. "You can return this to the kitchen." She sat down and began to eat the warm food. It tasted surprisingly good, maybe because she hadn't eaten in two days.

"He will break your heart." Gavilan's dark eyes turned solemn.

When Maria returned her attention to her plate without answering him, Gavilan left the room. Captain Mason would not break her heart. She would win his love. Of that she was certain.

Maria awoke alone in the cabin. With the light coming through the stern windows, she suspected it was morning. She'd worked on the ledgers late into the night. Gavilan brought her breakfast. He took her empty plate from the meal the night before and left the room without a word. That was fine with Maria. She had little energy left to argue with him. She wondered where Dominic was. After quickly eating her food, she got back to work.

Hours later, when she decided Dominic wasn't coming back to his chambers, most likely because of her, she used his washbasin and then went to her own room and changed her clothes. She got rid of the binding around her breasts and wished for a soft chemise against her body. She'd never liked women's undergarments until now that she no longer had them. Donning a smaller pair of boy's duck trousers, the white ones meant for the Sabbath, and a checked shirt she wasn't swimming in, she tucked the shirt into the pants and no longer felt lost in sailor's clothing. That awful varnished hat she tossed into her sea chest with a relieved sigh.

It felt good to give up the ploy of being a boy, but she might as well do her cabin boy's job. What else was she going to do on this ship? She'd returned to the captain's bed because it was much more comfortable than her own, and she didn't want to be alone in the cabin boy's dark little quarters. Nightmares plagued her there. She didn't know where Dominic was or who had put out the brass oil lantern while she slept during the night, but she could still smell his presence in the bed, strong soap, wind, and sunshine. His smell pleased her. She didn't know what time it was, but realized she felt rested after two nights of solid sleep in his berth.

She got up, washed her face, and wetted her hair, tucking it behind her ears, and then went to work on the ledgers. At lunch, when the cabin door opened, she didn't look up from her work. "Thank you, Gavilan," she said kindly, continuing to translate from one book to the other.

"You're welcome." It wasn't Gavilan's voice. She looked up, and her eyes collided with a ship captain's uniform.

"Captain Mason . . ." She cleared her throat and tried to swallow her nervousness.

He had a plate too. "I thought we could take our meal together and talk about your future."

She pushed the ledgers away and made room for his plate and hers as he set them down on the table. He took a seat in one of the chairs anchored to the floor. She picked up her fork and began to eat because she didn't know what to say. He folded his hands and said a short prayer, thanking God for the food and a safe voyage with fair winds.

"You no longer look like a cabin boy." He put his fork to his food. "But I see you've continued in your work. I appreciate that. Where did you learn to read and write so fluently?"

She swallowed hard and tried to relax. "I had a very good tutor. Roman and I did lessons for years. I hated them when I was young, but I'm grateful for them now." He looked so handsome in his blue jacket over a white blouse tucked into buff britches. Tall leather boots shielded his feet from the elements. His hair was longer than hers and waved back off his tanned face. Those blue eyes were fastened upon her.

"Mr. Andrews and I didn't know what we were going to do about all those ledgers. I have not yet informed him you will not make a good cabin boy after all. He had high hopes for you considering this job falls largely to him if we can't find a qualified cabin boy to do it, and poor Nate can't speak a lick of Spanish."

"I don't mind doing it." Maria tried not to be distracted by how handsome he was.

"Gavilan is working out well with the crew. He has won the men's respect and is filling in as first mate until Mr. Andrews recovers. How did you two meet?"

Maria studied her food. "He helped me escape." She didn't want to say more. Didn't want to think about that night at all.

"What were you escaping from?"

"Tio Pedro betrothed me against my will. Gavilan worked for the man I was supposed to marry."

"The man you killed?"

"Can we speak of something else?" She looked up at him with her heart pounding in her ears. More than anything, she wanted to forget that night ever happened.

"All right. What do you plan to do with the rest of your life?" He quietly chewed his chicken.

"Live." She didn't know where and didn't know how, but she was on a ship. Dominic's ship. It was enough.

"Where will you live?"

"In a city beside the sea somewhere." She self-consciously tucked her short hair behind her ears.

"Your hair will grow out. You are still very beautiful." The admiration in his eyes turned something over deep inside of her.

"Does the crew know I am a woman?"

"No. And I'd like to keep it that way for now."

"Is the weather fair again?"

"The weather is lovely." He paused in his eating to study her. "Do you miss the sun on your face?"

She couldn't look away. He affected her so deeply. "I do. I grew up outdoors. It wasn't until my father died that I was made to sit in the *sala* and sew."

"I'm sorry about your father."

"Thank you. It feels like so long ago when it happened."

"How did you lose him?"

"He died in an Indian raid."

"That is terrible."

"Many rancheros were lost to marauding Indians in those days."

Dominic studied her. "You have grown up in a wild land. Nobody in Boston thinks about Indian attacks anymore."

"I do not fear Indians. Lupe practically raised me. She's an Indian. The vaqueros are Indians. Many of the Indians in California were tamed at the missions, and most of the wild Indians left only want to live in peace."

"They won't find peace with the war going on in California."

"No, they won't," Maria agreed, feeling sad for the Indians.

Dominic's gaze traveled over her as they talked. She'd left the top few buttons of her shirt unfastened. Without her binding, she was sure he could see the curves she'd done her best to conceal until now. She'd once been proud of her breasts and had flaunted her lush figure in low-cut gowns, but shame suddenly washed over her. She'd been soiled by a man. Her cheeks flushed under his lengthy perusal.

"You'll have to put your hat on and change back into a looser wardrobe if you wish to go on deck for some fresh air. We need to work out a time when most of the crew is below decks. Night would be best. I can't believe nobody realized you were a woman when you came abroad."

"I would like to see the stars," she admitted, dropping her gaze to the table.

"There is nothing like the stars at night on the open sea. Without them for navigation, we would be lost out on the deep." He turned his attention back to his plate.

"Perhaps you could teach me how to navigate by the stars."

He put his fork down.

She could feel his eyes upon her once more.

"Perhaps I could," he said thoughtfully. "Sally has always wanted me to show her how to sail by the stars."

Maria's throat tightened. She couldn't eat anymore. She raised her eyes to his, letting down the shield on her heart. "How long have you known Sally?"

"All my life. Her parents were close friends with my parents."

"So they betrothed you when you were young?" This made her feel better. A marriage forced upon him. She understood that.

"No. It doesn't work that way in Boston. I chose to marry Sally on my own accord."

Maria's hopes crumbled. "She must be very beautiful."

"She is pleasing to my eye."

"And you love her?" Maria could hear the blood rushing in her ears. She found it hard to breathe. Their eyes locked in something undeniable.

He paused for a moment and then nodded, "I do." A bittersweet smile twisted his lips. "There are different kinds of love. A steady love that sinks no ships is not a bad love to foster. Strong families are built on this kind of enduring love."

Maria couldn't bear to meet his gaze any longer. She looked down at her plate. Her appetite was utterly gone. A dull ache settled in the center of her chest.

"Sally is very kind and good. You will like her."

Maria pushed what was left of her food around her plate, pretending she was still eating. Perhaps she would never eat again. Not only was her virtue ruined, her heart felt ravaged too.

"We are Protestants. If you return to Boston with me, you'll find a very different life than what you're used to in California. Nobody in Boston dances like you."

"Do they dance in Boston another way?" She did her best to keep emotion from her voice.

"Yes, but my family does not dance."

"Do they throw grand parties?"

"Not the kind of parties you would enjoy."

"What does your family do?"

"They work. They go to church." Dominic's smile turned wry.

Maria gave up and pushed her plate away. She leveled her eyes on him, doing everything she could to bury her disappointment. "You do not like attending church with your family?"

"I didn't used to, but since Steven died, I've been reassessing my need for God."

"So you do not find it enough to simply follow the stars in this life?"

"I have seen too much of the Lord's handiwork on this earth to put my trust in mere stars."

Maria wanted to share his faith but could not. "I would not make a good Protester."

Dominic laughed. "You mean Protestant?"

"Protestants arose out of a protest against the Catholic Church. I have read the history of Martin Luther. He left the priesthood to marry a nun. My tutor was a Protestant, but my father didn't know this."

"So you are learned in the ways of Protestantism?"

"Yes, I could never be a Protester."

"My family is very devout in their religion."

"So you will marry Sally and lead a devout life?"

"I hope so." Dominic stood up and picked up both plates. "I will be sleeping in the cabin boy's bunk for the rest of the voyage, but I do not want the crew to know, so I may have to be in here from time to time to keep our secret. I'll also have to wash up in here. You can go into the cabin boy's chamber when I'm changing. I know we will be under each other's skin, but there's nothing I can think of to remedy this situation."

She pulled the ledgers back and looked them over. "I will try not to get under your skin," she assured him.

"What are you going to do about Gavilan?"

The question surprised her. "What do you mean?"

"The man is too fond of you."

She attempted a laugh, but it didn't come out like humor. "That is nonsense."

"He pulled a knife on me on account of you."

"What?" Maria's eyes widened. The thought of losing Dominic to Gavilan's knife shocked her.

"While you were asleep yesterday morning . . . your brother, shall we call him . . . pulled out his knife and threatened me for sharing a bed with you."

"I didn't know Gavilan was so hot-blooded."

Dominic laughed.

"What's so funny?"

"You calling someone hot-blooded. I find it funny."

"I do not find it humorous."

"You'll need to pace yourself on those ledgers or you'll wear out your wrist." He took her hand in his, studying the ink stains on her fingers and palms.

Her breath caught at his touch. "There is nothing else for me to do down here."

"You can read and rest if you'd like." He let go of her hand and pointed to his sea chest. "I have several fine novels in there. You should also take the time to write your family a letter letting them know your whereabouts. If you don't, I'll write to Roman myself."

"How will we send this letter?"

"When we reach Valparaiso, I will mail it for you on a returning ship." He walked to the door, carrying the plates with him.

"Thank you." Heartache struck her. She hadn't really thought about her family until this very moment. Isabella and Tia Josefa had wept as she rode away with Tyler and his army.

"You're more than welcome." Stacking the plates on top of each other, Dominic opened the door and went on his way, closing the portal behind him.

Maria stared at the door for several forlorn minutes after he was gone. How would she win his heart if he truly loved Sally? Neither had mentioned their embrace during the storm. They both pretended it never happened, which relieved and disappointed Maria at the same time.

She relived those wild kisses with the storm howling around them as *The White Swallow* sailed from summer into winter when they reached the Southern Hemisphere. It hadn't taken long to realize Dominic was an honorable man with a very strict set of rules he lived by. Every Sunday he led a Sabbath service on the deck. With a Bible in hand, he preached a sermon to his sailors in their white duck trousers. This practice had begun with Steven on their journey out to California, and Dominic wasn't willing to let it end because Steven was no longer on board, he told her.

It was on a Sunday when she first felt the sun on her face since boarding the ship. Dominic decided she could join them for the Sabbath service but told her to keep her distance from the men and keep her hat on. Of course, nobody else kept their hat on. Maria felt absolutely out of place, partly because she was the only one wearing a hat, and partly because the Protestant style of worship was foreign to her. The men didn't pay her any mind since they'd carried Mr. Andrews up from his cabin. The first mate looked like a dead man sprawled on the deck, practically dying before their eyes. Dominic knelt beside him and prayed over the man. A tear streaked his cheek as he pleaded with God to spare Mr. Andrews's life. Maria turned away and stared at the ocean, her throat so tight she could hardly swallow. Dominic's Protestant ways made her uncomfortable. God made her uncomfortable. She did her best not to think about God and not to remember she'd killed a man.

Chapter Seven

Maria and Dominic settled into a routine of sorts. When he came to his quarters to wash and change his clothes, she went to the cabin boy's room and waited on the bunk that smelled of him now. Sometimes she would lie down and press her face into the pillow where he laid his head. She loved the smell of him. Dominic was nothing but the perfect gentleman, and his sense of humor delighted her. He often made her laugh, and he began to teach her navigational skills, allowing her on deck at night, where he showed her how to chart their route by the stars.

Mr. Andrews never recovered from his coma in spite of Dominic's earnest prayers. On the day they buried the first mate at sea, Dominic led the sailors in a lengthy prayer and then several Protestant hymns that reminded her of Steven's burial. Rachel and Dominic had sung over the minister's grave too. Dominic had a rich, deep voice that carried over the waves and moved Maria to tears. They arrived in Valparaiso a few days after the funeral. Ships from around the world flew their flags in a brisk sea breeze inside the harbor. Snowcapped mountains seemed to rise right out of the ocean around the swarming seaport. Seagulls screeched and swirled overhead. Several landing boats ferried folks from the ship to the docks, where all manner of mankind in every form of attire unloaded the boats and transported wares to and from the ships. The harbor was ringed by steep hills, and beyond those higher mountains, the city busy and filthy and teeming with people, stray dogs, and squawking chickens. Little wooden houses covered the hillsides. Impossibly narrow streets of adobe twisted all over the city, and unfinished churches populated the place.

Gavilan was all smiles to be back in his homeland. He spoke easily with Dominic as the three of them climbed into a coach with two badly cared for horses. "My father's coach is much finer," Gavilan assured them. "He prides himself on his well-bred horses. These poor animals aren't fit to pull an ox cart, let alone a gentleman's carriage."

They passed through a labyrinth of alleyways and narrow streets before entering a plaza surrounded by finer buildings. On they traveled past residences surrounded by sprawling gardens and orchards, the winter day sunny and bright and not uncomfortably cold. Gavilan informed them the city experienced terrible rainstorms and earthquakes too, even icy winds this time of year, but today proved calm. Gavilan told Dominic of the large Protestant colony founded by the British there. When church bells began to toll at noon, everything stopped in the streets, men removing their hats, women crossing themselves. Gavilan crossed himself too and grinned at Maria sitting opposite him in the coach, shoulder to shoulder with Dominic.

She smiled back. Gavilan's happy mood was contagious. Being back on dry land with the sun on her face left her feeling lighthearted. Dominic remained in a somber mood since losing his first mate. He'd informed her the ruse of cabin boy would end in Valparaiso. He'd made Gavilan his first mate on the day Mr. Andrews passed away. Maria suspected it was to keep Gavilan bound for Boston with them. She knew Dominic worried Gavilan would choose to remain in Valparaiso and this would amount to a genuine loss for the ship. Gavilan was a worthy sailor and a natural-born leader among men, and a friendship was steadily building between Gavilan and Dominic.

Gavilan's father's mansion was situated on a hill overlooking the Pacific Ocean. The estate was of the strangest design Maria had ever seen. Balconies and towers and stairwells leading from one floor to the next on the exterior of a hodgepodge mansion. A male Indian servant dressed as a butler greeted them at the door. The servant's eyes widened in recognition when he saw Gavilan, and he shut the door in their faces.

"One moment please." Gavilan opened the door and stepped inside, leaving them to wait on the porch. He returned shortly with the butler, who apologetically took Dominic's and Maria's coats and then ushered them into a drawing room filled with priceless furniture and artwork. Maria was taken aback by the sheer volume of belongings in the house. A fire blazed in the hearth. It wasn't long before Maria grew overly warm. Apparently, Dominic did too because he loosened his shirt collar and rolled up his sleeves. In his blue captain's vest over his crisp white shirt, his hair curling around his ears and across his forehead, Maria found him irresistibly handsome.

A uniformed maid brought them wine on a platter. Gavilan had disappeared with the butler. The maid with black hair and fair skin stared wide-eyed at Maria in her white duck trousers and checkered shirt. Maria's hair had grown out some, but it was still very short and badly cut. She'd taken to wetting it each morning and slicking it back away from her face. She smiled at the maid, hoping to make a friend. The maid continued to stare at her with wide, unfriendly eyes, so Maria took a glass of wine from her tray and drank the whole thing in a very unladylike fashion to set the maid on her heels.

Dominic reached for his glass, giving Maria a warning look. "More please," she told the maid and held out her glass, waiting for the maid to refill it. With another full glass in hand, Maria walked over to a large window overlooking a lovely garden. She needed courage without her hair. On the ship it hadn't mattered. In fact, not having hair there had worked to her advantage. Here, with other women, she felt out of sorts and unattractive without her hair. The maid was young and pretty with long dark hair, and kept smiling at Dominic.

At the window, Dominic joined her. "Liquid courage in your cup?" he whispered near her ear, sipping from his wineglass.

The maid left the room. They were alone. The place reeked of wealth and refinement and a decadent air that surprised and somewhat unnerved Maria. She couldn't believe this was Gavilan's home. "Maybe," she admitted. "I could use a beautiful dress. Perhaps it would restore my courage."

Dominic tapped his glass to the side of hers. "To finding you some proper clothing, my lady."

Maria couldn't help but smile. She drank some wine and wiped sweat off the back of her neck. The room was blazing hot.

Dominic pressed his cool wineglass to his cheek and then to hers. "I think I might melt before this fire." His eyes locked with hers as he held the glass against her face. The urge to kiss him was suddenly so strong Maria began to tremble. He lowered his glass from her cheek and sipped more wine, staring at her intently. She drank the rest of her wine and walked away from him, her head beginning to spin.

When Gavilan entered the room, she was relieved. Somewhere along the line she'd begun to trust Gavilan and think of him as her protector at sea. After a few days of giving her the cold shoulder, he'd changed his ways and was warm and open with her now, bringing her meals in the cabin and often joining her and Dominic on deck under the stars. Gavilan made her laugh and treated her like a little sister, which put her at ease. As much as she didn't want to admit it, she'd come to rely on him to keep her safe.

"My father is getting used to the idea that I have returned. He has decided to meet you at dinner tonight. My brother, Romero, and his wife, Sofia, will also join us. I've asked Sofia if you may borrow a dress." Gavilan's happy mood was gone. He walked over to fetch the wine the maid had left on the platter on the carved mahogany table. Filling Maria's glass and then pouring himself a glass of his own, he raised a toast. "Viva Valparaiso."

Dominic and Maria joined him in raising their glasses, but wore concern for him on their faces.

"To tackling the Horn," Dominic said, searching Gavilan's eyes for an answer.

After downing his wine, Gavilan smiled without humor. "We shall see."

Maria hadn't had a real bath in far too long. Two Indian girls assisted her, carrying pail after pail of steaming water into the room decorated in red velvet curtains and a matching velvet bedcover where she'd slept off the effects of the wine that afternoon. The bedroom was crowded with priceless furniture and gaudy artwork. A gorgeous emerald gown was spread out on the bed along with a whalebone corset that looked uncomfortable after all this time without one. But Maria couldn't wait to wear the delicate undergarments. An old Indian woman came into the room with a pair of scissors. Maria nervously sat through a haircut. Mostly, it was just a snip here and a snip there to even out her hair.

The old woman soon departed, and washing her hair took only minutes in the tub, something Maria wasn't used to. Her hair had once been an ordeal. She also had never seen a bathtub in a bedroom before. The Indian girls weren't rude like the maid in the drawing room. The swarthy girls with long, straight hair and shy, dark eyes, didn't stare at her and worked unobtrusively, cleaning up Maria's bits of red hair around the chair and scenting her water with fragrant herbs after filling the tub. The maids were younger than her and had friendly eyes. Maria liked them.

The bath was an unbelievable luxury. She could have soaked there forever. The tub was certainly preferred over meeting strangers at dinner without her long hair. When she finally left the water and dried off, one of the maids returned just in time to help her dress. The Indian girl held a green satin ribbon in her hand. "For your hair," the girl explained in Spanish.

Maria smiled.

Slipping into the silky, soft undergarments made her sigh with pleasure. The other Indian girl had disappeared with Maria's sailor's garb. Maria hoped they were just laundering it and that the clothes would be returned. The whalebone corset was as uncomfortable as she remembered, but it cinched in her waist and enhanced her bust, not that she needed enhancement. The Indian maid towel-dried her hair and then combed it into several different styles before settling on a side part with bangs swept across her forehead. Maria hardly recognized herself in the mirror. The Indian girl then helped her into the emerald gown. The plunging neckline revealed far too much cleavage and left Maria feeling exposed.

"Your eyes are so green," the young maid said in Spanish. "This ribbon is perfect for you." The maid situated the ribbon in Maria's hair by tying it around her head. Maria was pleased with the look but had to learn how to breathe again in the corset. There would be no doubt in anyone's mind she was a woman tonight. She felt her courage returning and couldn't wait to see how Dominic responded to her appearance when she joined him for dinner.

Chapter Eight

Dominic stood in the drawing room holding a glass of wine. Thankfully, the roaring fire in the great stone hearth had been doused, and he wasn't sweating in his uniform as he had this afternoon. He'd rested, shaved, and bathed and felt like a new man, having brought along a fresh uniform to change into for dinner. The butler had taken his other uniform to be laundered. Dominic could get used to this kind of life in a mansion, but something about the place left him uneasy. He couldn't put his finger on it, but his intuition never failed him. Something was wrong in this strange, rambling house of wealth.

He met a number of refined people in the drawing room, but didn't find them genuinely friendly. Gavilan seemed to feel the same way and didn't try to talk to his father's guests. His sailor's uniform was gone. He looked every inch a rich man's son tonight, but he did not look at ease. He kept looking toward the door; watching for his father, Dominic supposed. Dominic wondered if Maria would find Gavilan attractive tonight. Apparently, the brother's wife found him appealing. She doted on Gavilan as if he were her husband instead of the brother across the room, speaking to an older gentleman who appeared Parisian. Everything in the room felt forced. The laughter. The small talk. Wineglasses were refilled again and again by uniformed maids. Dominic wondered when Maria would appear and what she would look like in her borrowed dress. He'd gotten so used to her in duck trousers and a sailor's shirt. Tomorrow he would escort her to a dressmaker's shop and acquire some gowns for her. He needed to start thinking about what he would do if she decided to stay here in Valpariso with Gavilan. It looked like Gavilan shouldn't stay either. He could already see there was bad blood between the brothers, perhaps due to history between Gavilan and his sultry sister-in-law. Like Gavilan, Dominic kept his eye on the door, watching for Maria. When Wade Reynolds stepped into the room, he nearly dropped his wineglass.

Wade. His worst enemy—if he had an enemy in the world. Captain of *The Sea Witch*, Wade was known for his breakneck speed in any kind of weather, his cutthroat dealings as a trading merchant, and his utter disregard for anyone outside of his crew and the ladies. A decade older than Dominic, he'd done his best to keep Dominic his first mate for the rest of his life. When Dominic left *The Sea Witch* to sail on *The Indiana* before acquiring his own ship, Wade's animosity became legendary.

Their eyes met almost as soon as Wade entered the room. Plucking a goblet of wine from a pretty maid's platter, and patting her behind without regard for anyone watching, Wade made his way directly over to him. They did not shake hands.

"Well, Dom, how long has it been? Two years? Three since I've seen you? I heard you'd sailed for California. How was the trading there with the war going on?"

Dominic drank some wine before responding. "My hold is full of California banknotes. I'm headed for Boston. Where are you headed?"

"California, naturally. I've heard it's a paradise just waiting to be plowed. Of course, I won't farm. I'll leave that for some other dumb New Englander. I plan on building a shipping empire now that California belongs to the United States."

"Really?" Dominic was surprised. "You've had enough of sailing?"

"I'm thinking of settling down. In a mansion like this, of course."

"There are no mansions in California. Only haciendas."

"Then I'll build myself a mansion," Wade said with a laugh. The mirth never reached his cool hazel eyes. The British man had a hawkish nose, heavy brows, and skin perpetually burned from sun and wind. The older captain kept a trim beard, and both his ears were pierced, like many sailors, but the rings in Wade's earlobes were solid gold and worth a small fortune, unlike most sailors' earrings. The ladies found him irresistible.

When Maria entered the crowded drawing room, Dominic would have gone to her, but Gavilan beat him to her side. Dominic was watching Maria when Wade said in his ear, "My lady for the evening has just arrived."

"That's my lady." Dominic spun away from Wade. He couldn't get to Maria fast enough. Gavilan was tucking her hand in the crook of his arm when he reached them.

"I bet tomorrow women will be taking scissors to their hair to achieve this new look Maria is sporting tonight," Gavilan told Dominic.

A nervous smile flowered on Maria's face. She'd worn daring gowns in California, but none like this. She looked stunning and far too seductive in the low-cut dress. Dominic wanted to whip off his coat and cover her up before Wade reached them.

"So, Dom, who are your friends?" Wade was right behind him, wineglass in his hand, his gaze thirstily drinking in Maria.

Dominic restrained himself from landing a blow to that hawkish nose. "My first mate, Gavilan." He did not introduce Maria.

Gavilan reached out to shake Wade's hand. He nudged Maria behind him at the same time, shielding her from Wade with his tall, muscular form. Dominic had never seen death in a man's eyes, but he saw murder in Gavilan's gaze as he stared at Wade. Taller than Gavilan, but not as powerfully built, Wade tried to smile at Maria over Gavilan's broad shoulder.

Dominic stepped shoulder to shoulder with Gavilan. The two men walled Wade off from her.

Wade laughed. "Well, boys, I see I've riled you. I'll wait till her hair grows out to bed her. I don't like short hair on a woman." Wade walked away, and Gavilan whispered a threat under his breath.

"Don't challenge him," Dominic said. "He's deadly with a pistol."

Gavilan and Dominic turned around to find Maria striding away, holding her gown in determined fists at her sides.

"Where is she going?" Gavilan seemed surprised.

"I don't want to see this," Dominic said.

They watched Maria fetch a glass of wine from one of the maids circulating the room with a tray. Snatching up a drink, Maria made a beeline for Wade. Gavilan was about to go after her when Dominic put his hand on his shoulder. "I've changed my mind. I want to see this."

Wade had found Sofia. Or Sofia had found him. Maria didn't pause with the other woman standing beside the ship captain, just went right up and threw the wine in Wade's face without fanfare.

Sofia let out a scream, covering her rouged mouth with her hand.

Wade slowly wiped the wine off his face. A wolfish smile curved his lips as he watched Maria stride away.

Chapter Nine

Gavilan was about to shake off Dominic's restraining hand to follow Maria when his father entered the room. They hadn't spoken yet. Hadn't seen each other in over five years. His father had made him stand outside his locked study this afternoon, pleading for entry to no avail. His father's butler, Mr. Rubino, came out of the study and assured him his father would speak to him after his dinner party this evening. "We will kill the fattened calf," Mr. Rubino told him his father said about his return. "Tell my son I am so pleased he is home, and the party will now be in his honor."

But when his father stepped into the drawing room that evening, he did not look pleased, he looked sick. Gavilan was stunned. His once robust father had lost weight, and his fine clothes hung on his bony frame like a scarecrow. A glass of brandy was in his hand and a slim Cuban cigar in his mouth, the kind his father had always favored. Gavilan nearly wept upon seeing him. He'd already talked to his brother, Romero, a short, tense conversation that left him feeling young and foolish, the way his brother had always made him feel.

Only Sofia greeted him warmly. Too warmly, which had always been a lance between him and Romero. He'd brought Sofia home to his family, and that was the end of their short but intense love affair many years ago. Romero had swept Sofia right out from under him, actually marrying her, which had stunned and infuriated Gavilan. But he was grateful for it now. After a few months of marriage, Sofia had done her best to return to Gavilan's bed, which fueled Romero's hatred for him. They'd been at odds ever since. The duel that made his father disown him had been fought over Sofia. She couldn't stay out of powerful men's beds. Romero would not protect her honor, so Gavilan had, much to his regret.

Without looking his way, his father invited the guests to follow him to the dining room as Dominic disappeared after Maria. Men in expensive suits filed down the hall. Gavilan walked over to the man who'd sired him. His father kissed him on both cheeks, and tears filled his eyes, but he didn't say anything. Nodding his head in approval, he motioned his son down the hall in front of him. Arriving in the dining room, his father told him to sit beside him at the head of the table and then saw to his guests. His father was always the most gregarious of hosts.

Dinner was a long, drawn-out affair in which his father displayed his wealth by presenting a king's feast served in course after course of delicacies from around the world. His father laughed often, conversed merrily with his visitors, and coughed from time to time, leaving Gavilan certain his father was deathly ill. Nothing had changed except his father's health. Gavilan found himself despising all these pretentious men, mostly foreigners, and worrying about his father dying. Dominic and Maria were seated at the far end of the enormous table and looked as uncomfortable as he felt sitting beside his father.

The ship captain Maria had drenched with wine found a place at Sofia's side. The two laughed and whispered throughout the meal. Romero pretended not to notice Sofia's flirtation. He spent the evening in deep conversation with a British diplomat seated on his left. Again, Gavilan was grateful his brother had stolen Sofia from him. The two had never had children, and Sofia seemed brittle and desperate now. She looked old and tired to him. He wondered if his brother regretted marrying her. What kind of life did Sofia have here? Endless hostess to his father's and brother's influential guests? Spoiled and pampered but apparently lonely. Romero barely spoke to her, and the couple hardly seemed a couple anymore.

Would that happen if he stayed here? He suddenly realized he liked his life at sea and had grown attached to the ship's crew. First mate fit him well. Captain Mason had won his loyalty and then some. And Maria was young and willful and needed protection in the worst way. He wasn't a religious man, but he believed God had placed him in Maria's life to watch over her, and he planned to do just that. He couldn't do that in Chile unless she stayed there with him.

The dancing commenced around midnight. Dominic wasn't about to let Maria wander from his side. Wade was wooing Gavilan's dark-haired sister-in-law, but Dominic didn't trust Wade. Maria was far too young and impressionable, keeping her away from Wade became his main concern. Gavilan, his tight-lipped brother, and his ill-looking father had disappeared from the party. He hoped for Gavilan's sake their meeting was going well in the study. The last he'd seen of Gavilan, he had a cigar in his mouth and was patiently listening to his brother as the emaciated father smoked his cigar and let loose a racking cough from time to time. Gavilan's father didn't look long for this earth.

Dominic just wanted to get through this party without Wade approaching Maria again. He figured the best way to keep Wade away was to whirl Maria around the dance floor. He held out his hand. "May I have the pleasure of this dance?"

She placed her palm into his with a pleased little smile. Never had she looked so beautiful, her eyes a striking green, highlighted by the emerald gown and the green ribbon in her hair. She'd been pensive since tossing the wine in Wade's face hours ago. He wondered what she'd been thinking all night.

"Tell me about that awful ship captain," she said as soon as they stepped into a slow waltz around the room and his wondering was over.

Other couples waltzed around them. A number of beautiful young women had joined the party in the ballroom after dinner. Dominic suspected they were high-class prostitutes.

"How do you know that captain?" Maria persisted.

He leaned in close to speak to her over the music. They were in a full-story ballroom on the top floor of the mansion, a huge open room with countless windows overlooking the city and Pacific Ocean. Lanterns lit the ornate ballroom, and the champagne and brandy flowed like a river. Most of the men were already drunk. The party was turning to debauchery. Dominic yearned to escort Maria back to the ship tonight. He'd done his best to frighten men away all evening long, behaving rudely to those brave enough to approach them. "Wade was my captain when I was young," he admitted. "Few can compete with him on the open sea."

"What kind of captain was he?"

Dominic did not like the curiosity in Maria's question. "Charismatic and cruel."

"How long did you sail with him?"

"Long enough to know you don't want to know him, Maria."

She looked at Wade dancing with Sofia, nuzzling the woman's neck as they waltzed, and then returned her baffled gaze to Dominic. "Why does her husband allow that to happen? She does not act like a married woman. She doesn't even act like a lady."

"These people are not the kind of people you and I are used to." Several couples were kissing on the dance floor. Dominic did not think they were married to each other. This kind of behavior didn't happen in civilized places, even among married couples. He held Maria with restraint in his own arms, keeping a tight rein on his emotions. Neither had imbibed much wine tonight. He was thankful for that at least.

"These people do not intimidate me. Wealth does not make one wise. And wine is making many act stupidly tonight." Maria frowned at him.

Dominic realized she'd misunderstood what he'd said. "I do not think these people are better than you and I. They are different than you and I. Their souls are empty. They're trying to fill themselves any way they can. Pleasure is their prize, and they do not practice restraint." He didn't tell her these wealthy people would probably end up in each other's beds before morning. Gavilan's father was a widower, and apparently a playboy, providing the rich with a place to carry out their indiscretions here in Valparaiso. He just wanted to get Maria back to the ship before the party deteriorated even further. His mind was spinning with thoughts of how to do this without insulting Gavilan and his father.

The waltz ended and another began. Wade and Sofia strolled over, and before Dominic could stop them, Sofia pressed herself into his arms and Wade whisked Maria away into a waltz. Placing both hands on Sofia's satin waist, he gently but urgently pushed her from him. He knew the kind of woman she was and would never allow himself to fall prey to her.

She laughed. "You need to loosen up, Captain Mason." She scooted right back into his embrace. "Waltz with me, love."

He did her bidding only to catch up with Wade and Maria twirling around the floor. Wade clutched Maria in his arms like stolen treasure. She looked so young in his embrace. Dominic was ready for a fight but still hoped he could get Maria away from Wade without any bloodshed.

"So tell me," Sofia pressed her bosom to his chest, "who is the striking young woman with the short red hair? I cannot tell if she is yours or Gavilan's."

"She is my charge." Dominic looked over the top of Sofia's perfumed hair, trying to keep track of Maria and Wade in the crowded, dimly lit ballroom.

"Your charge?" Sofia laughed. "Come, Captain Mason, you can tell me the truth. I doubt she is your charge."

"Where is your husband?" He tried not to sound as frustrated as he felt.

"I do not care where my husband is tonight. He does not satisfy me. You appear to be a man who can satisfy a woman.

We should find a secret place to get to know each other." She smiled seductively up at him.

Dominic wanted to escape her in the worst possible way. He felt like he held a puma in his arms. "Let's get you back to Wade. Maria is just a girl. It's past her bedtime. She needs to retire for the evening, as do I."

Sofia laughed again. A throaty purr that sounded more like a growl to Dominic.

"She does not look too young to me," she said. "At her age, Gavilan brought me here. And I have never left. Each week I meet men of means from every country. My father-in-law makes sure everyone has a good time in Chile. Relax, Captain Mason, I will not bite you. We call our home Casa de Placer. House of Pleasure. Everyone enjoys themselves here."

Dominic kept an eye on Maria. She was laughing now in Wade's arms. It did not surprise him. Wade could be quite charming. He decided right then he would not spend the night in this house of pleasure. These people were headed to the pit of hell and didn't even know it. He had to get Maria out of here. As the waltz ended, he made sure he and Sofia were next to Wade and Maria on the dance floor. Taking Sofia by the elbow, he swung her into Wade's arms and captured Maria's hand, dragging her back to his side.

Maria continued to smile.

Wade grinned at Dominic and put his arm around Sofia. He looked very smug. "You didn't tell me she was your cabin boy. What a smashing idea. I may have to find a cabin boy like Maria for my ship."

Sofia's face lit up. "I knew it! Her hair is short because she's pretending to be someone else. Gavilan tells me you are from California, my dear."

Maria's smile disappeared.

"I am taking Maria to Boston for finishing school," Dominic said. "Her brother, Roman, is a close friend of mine. We are like brothers. Which makes Maria something of a sister to me. There are no finishing schools for young ladies in California. The province is at war. It is a good time for a girl to leave California."

"Everyone is curious as to why Maria cut her hair. Wade and I made a wager. He assured me it would only take him one waltz to find out the truth about her."

Maria squeezed Dominic's hand and stepped closer to him. He sensed her nervousness.

"Cabin boys cannot have long hair," said Wade. "Sailors with long hair can be caught in the rigging or snared in a storm. Maria shared with me that she cut her hair to sneak aboard Dom's ship. Had it been my ship, I'd have known right off Maria was a beautiful woman, but you have always been blind, Dom. A good church boy from New England. You probably didn't even look at your cabin boy as long as he was industrious and kept working."

"Were you searching for an adventure?" Sofia asked Maria. "Is this why you snuck aboard Captain Mason's ship? Or perhaps you were on the run."

Couples began to swirl around them on the dance floor.

"How bold to disguise yourself as a boy," Sofia continued before leveling her gaze on Dominic. "You said you are taking her east for school. Did you decide upon this schooling after you discovered her stowed away on your ship or before that?"

Maria's hand trembled in his. "We had discussed her sailing to Boston with me well before she stepped foot on my ship," Dominic assured them. "A tragedy in California caused me to return to *The White Swallow* sooner than planned. I wasn't able to take Maria with me." Dominic drew her snuggly against his side. He did not like the way this conversation was spinning.

"What tragedy was this?" Sofia's dark eyes shone with interest.

"I took a minister to California from Massachusetts last spring. He was murdered there by an outlaw. Steven was an admirable man. We all felt his loss very deeply."

"Murder in California," Sofia said as if she knew something more. "Do you know women in some countries cut their hair when their husbands are killed?"

"Let's not ruin the night with such morbid talk." Wade stepped forward to put a finger under Maria's chin. "When you are done with finishing school, you must return to California and visit my mansion there, my dear."

"You have a mansion in California?" Maria's innocence with Wade infuriated Dominic. She had no idea the kind of man she flirted with.

"Not yet, but I will." Wade smiled at Maria, looking as if he'd like to devour her.

The urge to punch his old captain in the jaw nearly overwhelmed Dominic. Wade was nearly twice Maria's age and had ruined a number of decent young women back east, and in the Indies and the Sandwich Islands as well. Though most of the time, Wade found his satisfaction with women like Sofia.

"It is time for us to take our leave," Dominic announced, letting go of Maria's hand and putting his arm around her waist to sweep her away.

"I will see you in California," Wade called after her.

Dominic didn't turn around and was relieved Maria left the dance floor with him without an argument. He kept right on walking until they were out of the ballroom and down the stairs. He found the butler and informed him they would be returning to the ship as soon as they gathered their belongings. He was done being polite. He just wanted to get Maria back to the ship as fast as possible.

The butler looked horrified. "It is too dangerous on the streets of Valparaiso this time of night." He glanced at Maria and then back at Dominic. "You cannot take a young woman out there. That would be madness. You must stay the night here, sir, where you and the lady are safe."

The last thing Dominic felt in this house was safe. "Where is Gavilan?" he demanded.

"The last time I checked, he was speaking with his father and brother in the study. He has been gone many years. There is much to discuss between the family, sir."

"Please tell Gavilan that Maria and I have returned to the ship. If he wants to sail with us, we will depart the harbor tomorrow afternoon." Dominic hoped this would give him enough time to replenish his ship with livestock, fresh water, and everything they needed to journey around the Horn. Never had he been in such a hurry to leave a port before. Had he known Wade was here, he would have restocked his ship somewhere else.

"If you are determined to leave tonight, you must wait until the master's private coach is arranged for you. I will also see if I can gather some protection. We have men who guard Gavilan's father. I will see if they are in any condition to escort you to the harbor."

"Thank you." Dominic led Maria away with him. Most everyone was still on the third floor. Music could be heard two floors down. Lanterns lit the mansion's maze of hallways. Still holding Maria's hand, he went to the room where he'd rested that afternoon, hoping to find his other uniform there. Freshly laundered, it lay on the bed neatly folded. He scooped it up and turned to Maria. "Where is your room?"

"I'm not sure."

They prowled the mansion like thieves, searching for Maria's room for some time. Finally, they found her chambers on the second floor at the end of a strange hallway. When they stepped into the room, Dominic's gaze settled on the bathtub. It had been emptied of water. The room was spacious and fine but reminded Dominic of a bordello. Everything was in order. Maria's sailor's garb was neatly folded at the foot of the bed.

"I'll wait in the hall while you change your clothes." He went to the door, his eyes again settling on the tub in the decadent room. He couldn't help imagining Maria bathing there. Bewitching and beautiful. He needed to get himself and her out of this house of pleasure. Temptation was overwhelming in this place. Desire knifed through him every time he looked at Maria in her low-cut gown. He reminded himself she could never be his, but that didn't mean he'd ever allow a man like Wade to have her. Gavilan came to mind, but he pushed the thought away. He didn't want Gavilan to have her either. Thinking about Maria with another man left his insides knotted like the ropes that secured the sails on his ship.

Chapter Ten

"All hands ahoy!" Gavilan shouted. Sailors yelled in response and ran across the decks. A large black cloud rolled toward the ship. The crew did its best to haul down and clew up before the storm overtook them. "Double-reef the topsails," Gavilan bellowed as the ship slammed down and water plunged in, threatening to wash men overboard. Cape Horn was just as Gavilan remembered, the sea rough as ever, sleet icing the deck. Dressed in his foul weather gear, he knew it wouldn't be long before hail and snow overtook the vessel too.

Dominic was at the helm, smiling through much of the storm. Thunder boomed and lightning flashed. The squall worsened and continued for hours. Then days. Dominic's fortitude amazed Gavilan. He never wore down and remained lighthearted with the men despite the raging sea. When a line snapped and a sail flapped around so violently Gavilan thought it would bring the mast down, Dominic ran past him, rigger's knife in hand, and climbed the mast. He swiftly cut the rigging lines that held the flapping sail, saving the mast. Perhaps saving the ship.

Gavilan knew why the crew was devoted to their captain. Dominic was willing to die for each and every sailor and was the first to react with courage when other men froze or fled for their lives below deck in this awful place where the Atlantic met the Pacific. Several feet of water rushed across the decks. Dominic returned to the helm and drove the ship into the wind to relieve the pressure on the sails by letting them luff. It was an aggressive approach. Most captains chose to turn away from the wind and let the storm blow the ship along until the weather played out.

He'd done this same thing, driving the ship into the wind in the first storm during his trick at the helm. It was a gamble, but when it paid off the ship was still on course, and days—perhaps weeks—weren't lost getting back on track. Clipper ships were revered for their speed. If they had a captain who pressed through storms instead of running from them, they could get around the Horn much faster. Gavilan preferred Dominic's approach. He hated the Horn and just wanted to be done with this forsaken place at the bottom of the continent.

When the storm finally abated, Dominic took out his medical kit and began to tend the wounds the sailors had received during the storm. His medical book lay open on the steerage table, and Maria assisted him with the injured. Upon leaving Valparaiso, Dominic had revealed her identity to the crew. He'd somehow obtained a lady's wardrobe for her before leaving the harbor. The ship spent an extra day at anchor in Valparaiso, which had given Gavilan time to return, keeping his position as first mate after his father and Romero informed him he wouldn't inherit a thing. He could stay and enjoy his place as a wealthy son in Valparaiso, but he would be like Sofia, a host to his father's and brother's influential visitors. Basically a kept man. Gavilan wouldn't have it.

Blood soaked the bandage on his leg as he walked down the stairs into steerage. Many of the crew had slashed arms and legs. Some had suffered cuts on their heads and faces. Dominic and Maria were all business, working side by side, Dominic using a mending needle to sew up the worst of the injuries as Maria washed and bandaged the men. Whiskey was given to ease the crew's suffering.

As Dominic used the needle on him, Gavilan quietly watched Maria. Her hair was longer now, and she often wore the green ribbon tied there. Her gowns were plain and serviceable, covering everything but her hands and neck. She looked like the captain's wife. It alarmed him that she acted like a wife too as they doctored the sailors, anticipating Dominic's requests and meeting his needs as if she'd been at his side forever. The two hardly spoke but communicated on some other level of understanding. Their accord was uncanny. Sometimes they brushed against each other as they worked. Both would smile without realizing they smiled. For a man who was set to marry another in New England, Dominic was far too attached to her.

Maria handed Gavilan a cup of whiskey. He drank it fast, the throbbing in his leg beginning to wear on him. Dominic did a fine job sewing up the gash. They spoke of the second mate, Mr. Jones, while the captain closed Gavilan's calf wound. Of course, Mr. Jones wasn't injured in the storm. He never put himself at risk enough to be injured.

"After you get some rest, I want you to relieve Mr. Jones at the helm," Dominic said. "Once we hit Boston, I'll be replacing him. I don't care if he's the nephew of one of my partners. I can no longer take the worthlessness of that man."

"Anyone can be a fair-weather sailor like Mr. Jones," Gavilan agreed. "Maria could handle a trick at the helm in this kind of weather."

"I am a good sailor no matter the weather. I have never been seasick. Not once, even in the storms," Maria said.

"This is true. She is extraordinary." Dominic's eyes lingered on her. "She makes an excellent doctor's assistant. Now if we can only get her to master the game of chess." Dominic grinned at her.

"I do not have enough patience for chess." Maria wiped the blood off Gavilan's leg with a rag. She was smiling too. Gavilan had waited until all the other sailors were treated before limping down to steerage. He'd considered letting Maria beat him in chess, but he figured she'd know he was letting her win, and she wouldn't like that. He and Dominic often played chess in the captain's quarters, really Maria's quarters now, and took turns beating each other. Dominic was very skilled at the game, which was another reason Gavilan admired him. Sometimes Maria sat and watched them play, but more often than not she read one of Dominic's books, lying on the bed with her nose buried in the novel. For all her beauty, she had a very sharp mind. And her indomitable spirit delighted him.

"You are patient enough to work on my ledgers day after day," Dominic told Maria. "Certainly, you can master the game of chess before our voyage ends."

"I do not mind the ledgers." Maria wiped the blood off the table and then began to clean up the bloody bandages. "Chess is a game. I do not like games. They are a waste of time. Who cares if you win a game?"

Dominic raised his eyebrows at her. "You want to win at everything else, why not chess?"

"I don't care about winning a silly old game for silly old men. Chess bores me."

"A silly old game of chess? Gavilan, did you hear that? She called us silly old men!" Dominic laughed.

After battling some of the worst weather Gavilan had ever seen, and caring so tirelessly for his battered crew, the captain could still laugh. This amazed him. And watching Maria mop up the bloody bandages without batting an eye, Gavilan marveled she was so strong and capable, like a man, though she was a woman. Maria really would make a fine sailor. He hoped Dominic preferred a more delicate rose, but he couldn't deny how well the two operated together on the ship. Their accord left him feeling like the odd man out.

"Why don't you get some rest, Maria? You too, Gavilan." Dominic closed his medical book. Only the three of them remained around the table in steerage now. Maria had already wiped down all the medical instruments and tucked them back into the medicine chest.

"You need some rest too," Maria told Dominic. "You go to your cabin, and I will sleep where I should from now on in the cabin boy's berth."

"You are sleeping where I want you to sleep: in my quarters. I am the captain. I decide where everybody sleeps on my ship."

"You are not in charge of me. I am not one of your sailors." Maria's face turned stormy, but she lowered her voice. Men slept in steerage, the lowest-ranked sailors lying in their narrow bunks attached to the walls. Higher-ranking sailors bunked in the forecastle. Steerage belonged to the youngest, most inexperienced men on the voyage.

"I am in charge of you. I am in charge of everyone on this ship. You signed aboard as my cabin boy, remember," Dominic reminded her.

Maria placed her hands on her hips. "I am not your cabin boy anymore!"

Gavilan cleared his throat, hoping to cool their exchange. This was the thing about these two, one minute they were fabulous together, the next, fire flared between them. Everyone was exhausted from the storm. Tempers were short, but Dominic and Maria were never even with each other. It was always hot or cold with them.

"Come, Maria, I'll walk you to the captain's cabin." Gavilan no longer slept in the forecastle with the crew. Dominic had given him Mr. Andrews's private cabin. Gavilan now took his meals with Dominic, which often included Maria too. The three had become quite inseparable. He suspected Dominic made sure he only spent time with Maria in his quarters when Gavilan was there as well.

Maria handed Gavilan the last of the whiskey. "He won't drink it." She motioned to Dominic, standing there looking every inch the feared captain, though it was clear Maria didn't fear him at all.

Gavilan shook his head to the whiskey. He was the chief mate. He didn't need any more spirits than he'd already imbibed, just enough to dull the pain so he could get some much-needed sleep.

Raising her chin in defiance of them both, Maria threw back the cup and downed all the whiskey in one unladylike gulp.

Dominic stepped over and took her firmly by the elbow. "Well, it's bedtime for you, young lady." He propelled her toward the stairs.

"I am perfectly capable of putting myself to bed." Maria planted her feet in protest, unwilling to go with him.

"I am in no mood for this nonsense." Dominic scooped her up in his arms, carrying her. She did not seem all that displeased. Lowering his head and limping after them, Gavilan wondered what Boston would bring when they faced Dominic's fiancée.

Maria looped her arms around Dominic's neck and rested her head on his shoulder as he carried her to his quarters. With so many sailors injured and exhausted, the deck that night was empty aside from the roll of the ocean and a breeze sweeping *The White Swallow* up the continent now that they'd cleared the Horn and hit the Atlantic.

Dominic didn't put her down until they were well inside his quarters. After releasing her near the bed, he set about lighting the whale oil lantern, using flint and steel to ignite the wick. Maria's dress was soiled with blood, and she was too tired to care that Dominic was still in the room. Not to mention the whiskey had gone straight to her head on her empty stomach. Nobody had eaten much during the storm. She unbuttoned her gown and let it drop to the floor without a second thought.

In her undergarments, she walked over to the washbasin and scrubbed her hands and face. She remembered the luxurious bath in Valparaiso; how she longed to submerge herself in warm, scented water after hours tending to the bloody, battered men. Wearing just her bloomers and chemise, she leaned over the basin, splashing her face with the cool water, then slicking back her hair. It was long enough now to curl behind her ears.

When she turned around, Dominic was standing there as if he'd been thunderstruck. She'd gotten so used to him after months together that she really hadn't thought about what she was doing. She had hardly slept for days, and she could feel the whiskey in her limbs, making her arms and legs warm and heavy. It almost felt like she was dreaming. "My gown smells like the *mantanza*. I do not mind blood, but I am tired of smelling like a dead bull."

"You are in your undergarments." He looked so alarmed.

She laughed. "I never liked a woman's unmentionables until I became a sailor and didn't have them. Thank you for purchasing these for me. You got my size just right."

His gaze roved her body as if he couldn't help himself. Maria walked over to him. Without saying a word, she wrapped her arms around his neck and molded her body to his. Their lips met like lightning from the storm. Electricity shot through her. As they kissed, she helped him shed his vest and shirt, still damp from the pounding rain and soiled with sailors' blood. His bare chest and arms were all warm muscle under her hands as his clothes hit the floor.

She loved his amazing strength. Everything about Dominic was strong—his body, his mind, his heart. She knew she was taking advantage of his moment of weakness, but she was willing to do anything to win his love before they reached Boston. Her heart was racing. She realized she loved him. With all her heart, she loved this man. She wanted to carry his name and bear his children. She wanted to sail with him forever. How they ended up in the bed, she wasn't sure. Half-dressed and on fire for each other. Dominic's mouth slid down her neck onto her shoulder and back up to her mouth as if he'd never taste enough of her.

Neither heard the knock at the door.

"Captain," Gavilan called, and then louder, "Captain Mason, we are missing a sailor! Young Jamie isn't in the forecastle or in steerage. Nobody's seen him since the storm abated."

Dominic was out of the bed in a flash. He fastened his belt and threw on his boots, grabbing his shirt and vest off the floor. Jamie was only a boy of fifteen. He had visited the Vasquez hacienda with Dominic, and when Maria had pointed out that her younger sister, Isabella, favored the blond boy, Dominic told her he had promised Jamie's mother to get him back to Boston in one piece.

Maria threw the covers over her head, hoping Gavilan wouldn't step into the room and discover her in the bed without her clothes on. The lantern still burned, lighting the room with a soft, warm glow. Her face was aflame and so was her body. Something fierce and wild and wonderful had happened. Like they'd both forgotten everyone else in the world and all they knew was each other.

"How could we have lost Jamie?" Dominic was out the door with Gavilan.

The door slammed shut, and then rapid footfalls filled the deck. Sailors scrambling around above her head. Maria straightened her undergarments and tried to gather her emotions. The loss of another sailor would devastate Dominic. He still hadn't recovered from the death of Mr. Andrews.

She nearly got out of the bed to retrieve her rosary to pray but then reminded herself God certainly wouldn't heed her prayers. Perhaps this new tragedy was because of her. Perhaps

Mr. Andrews's death was because of her. Perhaps more men would perish because of her. She rolled onto her stomach and buried her face in the pillow, trying to turn off her terrible thoughts.

He is dead because of you.

Her father's voice haunted her as if he was speaking to her now. *You will no longer ride with my vaqueros. You will do as Josefa says and learn to sew in the* sala *as any good daughter should.*

The awful day returned so clearly in her mind. She was eleven years old and had insisted on hunting the bear with her father and his vaqueros. Why they'd split up, she couldn't remember, but Ricardo, a brave old vaquero, had volunteered to watch over her.

Her father had sent Ricardo and her in the opposite direction of where he thought the bear would be while the other vaqueros and her father followed the bear's trail through the brush. They'd boxed the beast into a canyon and planned on killing the grizzly there. It had taken many calves, and her father was set on destroying it.

As fate would have it, Maria and Ricardo, riding through the narrow canyon, came upon the bear first. She was not as brave as she pretended to be. When the bear charged their horses, she lost control of Tonatiuh and ended up pitched from the saddle. Ricardo leaped from his mount, knife in hand to protect her. By the time her father and his men galloped up to the clearing, the bear had Ricardo in his massive jaws, tearing him apart.

Ricardo was stabbing the bear with his knife. Maria couldn't look away from the awful scene. Before the vaqueros could get their lassos around the grizzly, Ricardo was nearly dead. He took his last breath in her father's arms with Maria sobbing over him.

And other men had died because of her. The storm that took Mr. Andrews's life had been a freak gale, arriving out of nowhere at the beginning of their voyage, probably because she was on board. Mr. Andrews had been at the helm in Dominic's place because he had been down in the cabin with her. Mr. Andrews had died because of her. She felt it. She knew it. She was cursed.

"Stop!" she ordered her thoughts out loud. "I am not cursed!" But even as she spoke against the dark voice hounding her, she believed the curse was still upon her.

Not long after the bear killed Ricardo, her father died in the Indian raid. Tio Pedro took control of the family, and the women were relegated to the hacienda. Maria was only allowed to ride in a sidesaddle for pleasure after that; she couldn't go near the vaqueros or the cattle. The decree had crushed her.

And the dark voice became relentless. Especially at night. *Your mother died because you are cursed. Your father died because you are cursed. Ricardo died because you are cursed. You are cursed with death. Those around you all die.*

She did her best to silence the dark voice, but never could, and for years she had nightmares of the bear killing Ricardo. She believed it was all her fault. As she grew older, she learned to silence the voice by saying the rosary. Tia Josefa insisted she recite it every night. At first, she had resisted this religious practice, but she soon learned reciting the rosary quieted her mind and filled her with a sense of peace before sleep.

There in the captain's cabin now, alone in the bed, she longed to get up and fetch her golden rosary from her sea chest. Dominic had carried her chest into the room not long after she'd taken over his cabin and placed it next to his larger sea chest against the wall. Both chests were roped down so they wouldn't be tossed around the cabin during storms. Just like every piece of furniture on the ship was secured in one way or another.

Of course, you are cursed. Ravished in a church. Murderess in a church. Do you feel guilty for killing Joshua Tyler in a church? Of course you do not feel guilty. You are cursed by God.

Maria covered her ears and began to sing a hymn in Spanish. Over and over, she sang the same hymn until she could no longer hear the dark voice.

The frantic footfalls eventually died away up on deck, but Dominic never returned to the cabin. Exhausted, Maria fell asleep, and the nightmares of bears killing those she loved returned with a vengeance.

Chapter Eleven

Boston, December, 1846

They arrived in Boston on a frigid night with ice clinging to the trees in the city. By the time they reached Dominic's parents' house, Maria was frozen. She shivered in the large cloak Dominic had draped over her shoulders as they departed the ship. In front of his childhood home, he helped her out of the carriage and paid the driver before the carriage rattled off, the horses' hooves clopping down the cobbled street, the sound of departing hooves leaving Maria strangely bereft.

Since Jamie had perished in the storm, Dominic had avoided spending time with her as much as he possibly could. He was polite, but no longer did he dine with her and Gavilan in the captain's quarters as he'd done before. He didn't come at night to see her, either. Maria grew so forlorn, if it wasn't for Gavilan, she'd have fallen into despair. She wished Gavilan was here now as they climbed the icy porch steps, but he'd stayed on the ship overseeing their landing in the harbor tonight.

"Please let me explain why you've come to Boston," Dominic told her as he let go of her arm and reached to open the door. "Do not say anything about being Catholic. Let's keep your religion just between us."

Maria didn't respond to what he said. A nervous lump was stuck in her throat.

Patrick Mason looked very much like his son, only older and gray-haired and more reserved than Dominic when he met them walking into the parlor. Mary, Dominic's mother, was a small, birdlike woman with keen brown eyes and gray-streaked brown hair who followed on her husband's heels. Both Dominic's parents greeted him with excitement and happy tears. His sister, Chloe, appeared as well, crying and smiling at the same time. Maria tried to step away from the family as they embraced, but Dominic put his hand on her back and firmly pressed her forward. "This is Maria, Roman's little sister from California. Did you receive my letters about California?"

"Just one," said Dominic's father, his gaze curious on Maria.

Mary and Chloe looked her over too. The smile disappeared from the mother's face, and her eyes narrowed in displeasure on Maria, before her gaze leveled on Dominic. "You didn't tell us you were bringing home a young woman."

Dominic cleared his throat. "Maria coming home with me wasn't in the plan, but circumstances made it impossible for her to stay in California."

"Impossible?" Mary kissed Dominic on the cheek, and then held his face in hands, as if chastising a little boy. "With God nothing is impossible. What kind of circumstances?"

"California is at war, Mother. It has become too dangerous for Maria there."

"Well, I'm sorry about California's war, but Sally has missed you so much. All your wedding details are in order. Sally received several of your letters and has planned accordingly. We are all so very excited to see you two settled down. Sally will be over the moon to see you in church tomorrow. We didn't expect you home before Christmas."

Maria clenched and unclenched her skirts in her fists. She stared at Dominic's mother, knowing she had made an enemy in Boston. Glancing at Dominic's sister, she didn't sense the same animosity radiating from the girl. Like her father, Chloe's blue eyes were simply full of curiosity, and a sweet smile remained on her face.

"It's late and Maria appears cold. Come warm yourself by the fire, my dear," Dominic's father said kindly.

Dominic's hand returned to her lower back. He propelled her further into the parlor ahead of him. He didn't take her cloak. Neither did he remove his own outer garment until the fire's heat penetrated their heavy woolen clothes.

Patrick asked Dominic about the voyage. Mary left the room and returned with steaming cups of milk. Wordlessly, she handed one to Maria and the other to Dominic. Maria watched the fire and sipped the warm milk, her mind whirling with worry.

Dominic's wedding was all planned? Had he been writing letters to his fiancée all this time? The ache in her chest spread throughout her body. Her head began to pound with a sudden headache.

"You're so beautiful," Chloe said. "Mama, isn't Maria lovely?"

Mary didn't answer her daughter. "I have prepared a bed for you in Chloe's room. Do you know how long you will be staying with us, Maria?" Mary asked, her voice clipped.

"Indefinitely," Dominic interrupted. "Maria cannot return home probably for several years, at least until the war is well over."

Mary's mouth fell open in surprise.

"She is welcome to stay here for as long as she likes." Patrick turned and smiled at Maria. "I have read all about California. I would love to sail there and see this paradise full of cattle, horses, and grizzly bears for myself someday."

"You are always welcome at my family's hacienda." Maria tried to smile. "We could plan a bull and bear fight for you."

"A bull and bear fight? You must be joking, my dear." Mary slipped her hand inside Patrick's elbow and tucked herself close beside him.

"Maria is a Califoriana. Her grandfather was a Spanish conquistador. The Californios slay bears with ropes and lances in California. It's certainly a sight to see."

"So, she is Catholic." Mary's voice grew even more strained.

Dominic took off his cloak. He helped Maria out of her cloak as well before answering his mother. For a moment, he met Maria's gaze, and in that instant, she knew their blossoming affair was over. He belonged to Boston, and to his family, and to Sally.

"The Catholics of Spain are not the Catholics of Ireland," he said quietly when he faced his mother.

"Well, in our home, Maria must accept our Protestant faith or she must leave." His mother sniffed and patted her nose.

"Mary," said Patrick, his voice holding a warning. "Our grandparents did not want Catholicism forced on them in Ireland. We will not force our Protestant beliefs on Maria here."

"But we will attend church in the morn. Will she lie in bed sleeping on the Sabbath?"

"I do not lie in bed on the Sabbath," Maria said.

Mary's mouth fell open once more at Maria's bold reply.

Dominic still held their damp cloaks. "Maria attended our worship services on the ship. And she finished translating all my ledgers on the voyage. I have never seen anything like it. Maria works harder than any sailor I've ever met. She never lies in bed. She's very industrious."

"Why was she working on your ledgers?" Mary's hand fell away from Patrick's arm. "You trust her with your ledgers? What would Sally's father say about that?"

Dominic cleared his throat again, obviously uncomfortable with the confrontation. "Maria's fluent in several languages. She reads and writes in Spanish and English, and even some Russian. Maria was a god-send for *The White Swallow*."

"A beautiful, young woman on your ship a god-send?" Mary's face was so pinched now she looked like she'd been eating lemons.

"That's enough," Patrick said. "Perhaps it is time we all found our beds. It's late and everyone is tired. We will speak in the morning."

"In the morning we have church. With Sally," said Mary.

Maria turned to Dominic. "I will attend church with you."

"Dominic will be sitting with Sally." Mary glared at her.

"You can sit with me," Chloe kindly offered. "I want to see California someday. Perhaps when you return to your home, I can go with you." The girl's smile was hopeful.

"Absolutely not," Mary was horrified.

Patrick turned to his wife and took her by the arm. "Come, Mary, it's time to turn in." He handled her gently, but his words rang firm as he ushered her from the parlor.

"Let's get you settled in with Chloe," Dominic said with a heavy sigh.

Maria heard the relief in his voice as his parents left the room. Tomorrow he would meet his fiancée in church, and so would she.

The next morning, Dominic sat beside Sally rather stiffly, looking as out of place as Maria felt in the small Protestant Church with stained-glassed windows and a tall white steeple. Sally's happiness was apparent to all. Maria kept staring at Dominic's fiancée because Sally was nothing like she'd imagined. Her gown was modest and simple, her long, dark brown hair rolled up into a tidy bun at the back of her slender white neck. She had the sweetest smile and the kindest eyes, large and dark and childlike eyes, but she wasn't beautiful. Not the way Maria had supposed she would be. Sally's real beauty came from within. There was a genuine serenity about the woman that fascinated Maria.

After church, Sally was nothing but kind to her when they met face to face. The family then spent the day together celebrating Dominic's safe arrival home. Gavilan joined them after the church service that was so foreign to Maria after growing up with only Catholic masses. They took a carriage to Sally's father's home, a grand mansion in the finest part of Boston. Sally's mother had died years earlier, and her father remarried a younger woman. Apparently, the younger wife had born him no children because none were around. Sally's father was one of the owners of Dominic's ship. It was all making sense to Maria now. Of course, he had to marry Sally. Being captain of *The White Swallow* demanded it. At least that's what she told herself as the day played out with Sally so happy at Dominic's side. Both Sally and her father were kind and gracious hosts. The younger wife was also polite, and to Maria's surprise, rather humble in appearance like Sally.

Once the meal was over, Sally made it a point to sit with Maria, asking her all kinds of questions about California. When she found out Maria had grown up with horses, Sally grew excited.

"I have always longed for a horse," she told Maria. "My mother died in a horse riding accident and Father sold all our riding horses after that. He has never allowed me to mount a horse on my own."

Sally blithely continued on about her childhood memories, so at peace about her mother's passing that Maria soon grew to envy her. Not once had she felt peace over losing her own mother to a fever. It wasn't even a shocking death like being flung from a horse, yet, Sally radiated a peace Maria found unbelievable. She'd never met anyone like Sally. Pretty soon Sally was treating her like her long lost friend, even a beloved sister. Maria was baffled.

"Oh Dominic," Sally said when he finally joined them in the parlor with all its wealth and privilege and warm, crackling fire. He'd been in the study with Sally's father for some time.

"Maria and I are going to be such dear friends, aren't we?" Sally turned to Maria, her face shining with pleasure.

How could Maria not nod and smile at Sally's unexplainable affection for her? Maria's gaze met Dominic's and he smiled too, a bittersweet twisting of his lips before his gaze sought out Sally's.

"Maria needs a friend," he told Sally. "She has no friends in Boston."

"Well, she has me," Sally said, happily patting Maria's knee. "We will become the best of friends, I just know it."

Chapter Twelve

Dominic spent most of his time seeing to his business as the weeks went by in Boston. His mother put Maria in school with Chloe. He hardly spoke to Maria in his parents' home. She wouldn't even look at him now, but she quietly did his mother's bidding, and was nothing if not polite to his family. His mother made sure she dressed just like Chloe, buttoned up to the chin every moment of the day. Still, the prim woolen dresses showed off her slender waist and lush curves. Maria had the finest figure he'd ever seen on a woman. Even modest gowns couldn't hide that, and of course he'd seen her in her undergarments on the ship. That image was branded on his mind forever. A vision he relived every single day of his life with a stab of longing.

When his ship partners, including Sally's father, suggested he return to California as soon as possible for another load of hides and pelts, he jumped at the opportunity. He couldn't wait to get away from Maria and his mother, but first he must marry Sally.

His wedding day had come like a storm he couldn't escape. He just needed to hold on tight and sail through it all. Deep down, he felt like he was going half mad. He wondered if Maria's emotions were a disaster too, though outwardly they both trudged through their days in dutiful silence. He pondered all this as he walked to the church on the day after Christmas for the ceremony that would make him a husband and Sally a wife.

It was a snowy afternoon in Boston, the streets nearly empty. He'd left the house in a somber mood, telling his mother he preferred to walk through the freshly fallen snow rather than ride in the coach with his parents, Chloe, and Maria. Only a few pristine inches of snow covered the ground. Just enough to crunch under a man's boots and whiten the afternoon. But the winter wonderland did nothing for his mood today. Lost in his thoughts, the muffled footfalls behind him came as a surprise. When he spun around, Maria grabbed the front of his cloak with all her strength.

"Please don't marry her," she begged. The look on her face froze him right on the sidewalk for all to see.

Shaken, he took her by the wrists and tried to loosen her hold on his jacket. "The wedding is in an hour. You must stop this, Maria," he said firmly.

The weight in his chest wouldn't lift. It felt like he carried a great burden. He knew what he had to do; he just couldn't look into Maria's eyes and then go do it. He had to marry Sally. He wanted to get his wedding over with as quickly as possible and get out of New England.

A hood covered Maria's head, her own black cloak as fine as his; he'd purchased it upon arriving in Boston. *The White Swallow's* voyage to California had been a great success, filling his pockets with a fortune and making his partners proud. Though the loss of Jamie and Mr. Andrews was keenly felt, after interviewing Gavilan, the partners agreed the young man from Valparaiso would make an honorable chief mate. Dominic was happy to sail with Gavilan again, and they spent nearly every day together preparing the ship for another long journey around the Horn after his honeymoon with Sally in New York.

But Maria wasn't about to let go of his cloak. "You must listen to me!" She clenched the fine woolen fabric in her fists, staring up at him with her heart in her eyes. The cold air made her breath frosty. "You cannot love her! How could you have kissed me the way you did on your ship if you love Sally?"

"Lower your voice." He looked around for others on the street but saw no one else. Tall trees, all naked branches like arms thrown out in a plea to the sky, harbored tiny birds. They hopped from branch to branch above their heads. Dominic felt as anxious and hungry as those little birds, but what he hungered for he could never have.

The small Presbyterian Church his family frequented wasn't far away. It seemed like his family was always at church, or industriously working. Life in New England was very different from life in California. Boston was freezing, busy, and full of stiff-lipped Yankees, Maria had said one day at the table. Nobody responded. He'd laughed when she said it, drawing a chastising glance from his mother, but he had to agree with Maria. Boston was so serious.

"So our kisses will forever be our secret?" She finally let go of his cloak.

Dominic was relieved she'd released him. He took a step away from her. "I have written Roman about what to do with you. Letters take time, Maria. We both know you can't return to California right now. I've looked into passage for you to Spain, but you cannot sail in winter. It's much too dangerous."

"You are sailing in winter." She moved closer to him and grabbed his hand, pulling him farther down the street, away from the tidy two-story cottage he'd grown up in.

Any moment, he expected to see his mother striding down the sidewalk, or his father sent by his mother to fetch them. He looked down at their clasped hands and saw Maria had forgotten her gloves.

"Here, take my gloves." He tried not to look into her eyes as he removed his gloves to give to her. He knew how she felt and certainly didn't want her knowing he was feeling torn between her and Sally. They could flee together right now. Sail away never to be seen again in Boston. For a moment, he pondered that, and then once again assured himself Sally was his best choice. His only choice if he wanted to continue to captain *The White Swallow* and remain on good terms with his family and Sally's father. And the truth was, he lost his head around Maria, which had to stop. Two of his crew were dead because of it. He didn't blame Maria for their deaths, he blamed himself.

"I do not need gloves," she told him. They came to a wooded lot between two houses and Maria led him into the trees.

He followed her because he was afraid his family would come along in the coach and see them together. Really, he should take Maria to the church. Gavilan was meeting him there, standing in for Nate, who would have stood by his side as his best man had he lived. Now Gavilan would fill Nate's shoes. He could ask Gavilan to take Maria somewhere else until she calmed down. He couldn't have her disrupting the wedding. It would be a small, quiet affair with only family and very close friends there. The quieter the better, he and Sally had agreed. Sally didn't want any fuss. "I've waited so long; I only want to be your wife," she'd told him sweetly when they decided on the simple arrangement.

He imagined what a wedding to Maria would have been like, a grand fiesta in California, no doubt. Dancing till dawn. Roman his best man. He tried not to think about that as they stopped in the trees and he pulled his hand away from hers. Then he handed her his gloves.

"I do not want your gloves," she said even more fiercely than before, and he regretted allowing her to hide them in the woods. "I want you," she whispered.

He took her by the shoulders, and she leaned into him. "Stop this," he said in his sternest captain's voice.

"I can't. I love you." Her declaration was breathless.

Dominic could hardly stand anymore. Their gazes met. He couldn't look away. "I'm so sorry, Maria . . ." He took a deep breath, fortifying himself for what he must say. "I don't love you."

It was a lie. He knew it was a lie the moment he said it.

"I don't believe you." Her bottom lip quivered.

Still holding her by the shoulders, he pulled her into his arms, pressing her against his chest so he didn't have to gaze into those green eyes that always beguiled him. "We are wrong for each other," he tried to explain. "You are barely older than Chloe. You're a girl. You need to go to school and discover what it means to become a woman—"

"In California, girls younger than me marry all the time," she interrupted.

"We are not in California. We are in Boston, and I have been pledged to marry Sally for a long time. She has waited years. I cannot break my pledge to her. Sally is a woman ready to wed. I have made her wait far too long already. You are a girl with all the time in the world to marry."

"I was not a girl in your bed! I was a woman in your arms on your ship. Are you marrying Sally so you don't lose your ship? Is her father the reason for this marriage?"

She tried to lean back to look up at him, but he kept one arm firmly around her waist and put his other hand on her head, holding her against his chest so he couldn't see her face. He could feel her heart racing madly against his. His heartbeat matched her own. "This is not about Sally's father. Please don't make this harder for me than it already is, Maria," he pleaded.

"Just tell Sally you've lain with me. Tell her you must marry me because you have known me as a man knows a woman."

"I have not lain with you!"

"But you have." Maria jerked back to look up at him. When she threw her head back, her hood slipped off. Her hair was growing out red and as beautiful as he remembered. It didn't curl now that it was longer, but fell in soft waves nearly brushing her shoulders. She often wore her hair tied in a ribbon as she'd done in Valparaiso. Today her ribbon was dark blue to match her prim woolen dress.

"I have not dishonored you," he insisted.

"She doesn't have to know everything. Only tell her I have been in your bed. This is not a lie. We have slept together."

Dominic grew frustrated. "She thinks you are her friend."

"I am her friend."

"If you were Sally's friend, you would not be here with me. You play with fire and you don't even know it."

"I know what I'm doing. You are the one who doesn't know the truth. We are meant to be together. I know we are."

"Oh, Maria, you must see what's best for all of us. It is best that I marry Sally."

He'd considered taking Sally with him on his return to California but decided it would be too dangerous a voyage for her in winter. Having Maria on board had made him anxious for many reasons, and Maria was so strong. He'd never met a heartier young woman in all his life. Sally wasn't like that at all. She was a delicate rose, tender and fragile. He had no desire to risk Sally's life when he didn't have a home prepared for her yet in California.

He still planned on building his mansion on San Francisco Bay. Now that California was in American hands, he knew others would take notice of the magnificent bay, and the province would boom. He'd purchased land in Yerba Buena and one day planned to make California his home, but that was still a far-off dream.

He'd toyed with the idea of making it a present dream. Running off with Maria and taking her as his wife. Returning with her to California, but she was a murderess there, and he'd been pledged to Sally for years. Breaking his pledge went against everything he believed in. He kept telling himself he only lusted for Maria, and lust he must conquer. Where she would end up, he didn't know. Spain would serve her well. She could dance there to her heart's desire. Wear beautiful gowns. Be herself all full of fair wind and fire.

He'd begun to think of Maria this way. As fair wind and fire. It still surprised him how smart she was. She'd finished all his ledgers and devoured every book in his sea chest during the voyage. Her mind was as magnificent as her body. He needed to get away from her. Far, far away. She was no more his than the sun was his. And like the sun, he would sorely miss her warmth. Perhaps he would live in a colder world for the rest of his life, always regretting he hadn't married her, but Sally remained his choice.

Maria stared up at him, her eyes filling with tears. "I know you are meant for me, but you refuse to believe it." She sounded so sad. He'd never heard her complain, never really seen her cry. She raised her hands to hold his cheeks. His face was very cold on this brisk New England day. So were her hands. "I will never stop loving you," she said.

"You should put on my gloves." He closed his eyes, allowing Maria to pull his head down until their lips met. Her kiss was so full of longing he could hardly stand it. It wasn't one of Maria's hungry kisses. It was a tender good-bye kiss. She was surrendering to his will, and he knew it. And he didn't want to accept it.

Instead, he suddenly, crazily wanted her to fight for him. He wrapped his arms around her fiercely and never wanted to let her go. Time stopped as his heart raced forward.

"Excuse me," Gavilan cleared his throat.

How Gavilan had ended up there in the trees without hearing him approach, Dominic didn't know. Perhaps the snow had muffled his steps. Maria buried her face against his chest, her body shaking with sobs. She'd been ravished and had killed a man in a church without crying, but now she fell apart in his arms. Dominic nodded at Gavilan, willing him to wait. He held Maria and kissed the top of her head. Any man would want her. She was a woman who would never be alone. Perhaps she and Gavilan would marry, though the thought pierced him, making it hard for him to keep breathing. Keep moving forward to his wedding today. Gavilan held his silence until he nodded to him over the top of Maria's head.

"Your mother sent me to find you," Gavilan explained. "I followed your tracks in the snow. Everyone waits for you at the church."

Waving his hand for Gavilan to come to them, Dominic gently pushed Maria into his arms. "Please take care of her for me."

"I will," said Gavilan.

It hadn't taken Dominic long to trust him with his crew, with his ship, and now with the woman he loved but could never have.

Maria sobbed even more when Gavilan pulled her away from him. "Are you sure?" Gavilan's voice was taut with emotion.

He smiled at Gavilan, a bittersweet twisting of his lips. His eyes burned with unshed tears. "I must stay the course with Sally."

Gavilan nodded and locked Maria in his arms. She fought at first, but he easily overpowered her.

When Dominic walked away, Maria wrapped her arms around Gavilan's waist and cried brokenly, her sobs in the woods accompanying Dominic to his wedding.

Chapter Thirteen

Boston, 1847

"You are so brave. Please stay here and help me be brave." Sally stared up at Maria from her bed of labor. Her brown eyes were filled with pain, her dark hair slick with sweat. It had been several days of struggling to give birth, and still the baby hadn't arrived. Sally looked exhausted. The doctor had come and gone, assuring them that first-time mothers often took days to have their babies, and he urged Sally to remain resting in the bed as much as possible until it was time to push.

Today, the doctor didn't look so confident that everything was going smoothly with Sally's labor. He was downstairs now speaking to Mary and Patrick. Mary had insisted Sally stay in the bed to reserve her strength for the actual birth. Now that

Mary and the doctor were out of the room, Maria urged Sally to get up and walk around for a spell.

"Indian women do not lie down until they are ready to give birth. Get up and walk." Maria braced a chair against the door under the door handle so nobody could enter the room.

"What are you doing?" Sally's voice trembled.

"I will open the door when it is time."

After making sure nobody could get the door open, Maria returned to Sally. "I know you are tired, but the baby will come faster if you walk around." Maria reached for Sally's hands and helped her from the bed. "I assisted Lupe with a number of births. She always told the women to walk to make the babies come faster."

Maria put her arm around Sally's waist and urged her to move around the room. They made the same loop many times, sometimes stopping in front of one of the tall windows for Sally to rest. It wasn't long before the door handle jiggled with someone trying to get in the room. Then a sharp knock.

"Open the door," Mary demanded.

Sally's eyes widened in distress.

"Keep walking. I will handle her." Maria walked over and spoke through the polished wooden panel. These doors were so different than California's thick plank doors in the hacienda. "Sally is sleeping," Maria lied, knowing Mary could hear her just fine though the thin door.

"Let me in," Mary demanded.

"Not now," said Maria. "I am watching over Sally. I will open the door when she wakes up."

Maria motioned for Sally to keep circling the room. Sally held her large belly and grimaced; she looked miserable walking.

"Open this door, Maria," Mary ordered.

"Come back later." Maria motioned again for Sally to keep walking. She rushed over to the windows and pulled the curtains closed so nobody could see in. They were upstairs windows, but still Maria didn't want Patrick or Mary to go outside and try to look up into the room. She wanted everyone to think Sally was really sleeping.

It was a beautiful September day in Boston, the sky clear and blue, a soft sea breeze blowing. For nearly an hour, Maria urged Sally to walk around the room as briskly as she could. Maria walked with her, half holding Sally up with her arm firmly around her waist. Before pregnancy, Sally was very slender, with narrow hips and not much of a bosom. She had porcelain skin, long dark hair she wore in that neat bun at the back of her neck all the time, and gentle brown eyes that were her finest feature. She was nearly ten years older than Maria, and Maria now she understood why Dominic had married her. Sally was special, the most kind and gentle woman she'd ever known. This past year, she'd become Maria's dearest friend.

"Do you suppose Dominic has received my letter about the babe?" Hope filled Sally's sweet, earnest voice, mingling with the pain of a contraction.

Maria didn't see how that was possible, but she wasn't about to tell Sally so. "Yes, I think he has," she said confidently. "I am sure he is on his way home this very hour, eager to meet his son or daughter."

Sally laughed, though Maria could tell it took nearly all of her courage to do so. "It could be another year before we see Dominic," she said. "By then our baby could be walking." Sally laid her head on Maria's shoulder. "I wish I was strong like you. Tell me again how you tamed that stallion when you were a little girl."

"You don't want to hear that old story."

"Yes, I do. I love that story. I see a little red-haired girl in California determined to win that wild horse's heart. I never realized a horse had a heart until I met you. I've never ridden a horse. Carriages have been my lot my whole life."

"When we get to California in a few years, I will teach you to ride," Maria promised.

"Do you think Dominic has started our house on the hill yet in Yerba Buena? We could build a stable near the mansion for our horses."

Maria tried not to think about Dominic's home on a hill overlooking San Francisco Bay. Sally just assumed Maria would live there too. It never occurred to Sally that Maria could be a threat to her happiness. At the wedding, Sally believed exactly what she'd been told. Maria had suddenly taken ill and had to remain at home. Nobody informed Sally that Maria had snuck out of the cottage and run after Dominic through the snow that day. That Gavilan had coaxed her to return to the cottage with him, where she sobbed until all her tears were gone. Gavilan had raced back to the church barely in time to stand by Dominic's side as the best man.

Their three-way friendship that had blossomed on the ship ended that day. Dominic and Gavilan grew closer than ever, spending most of their time down in the harbor readying *The White Swallow* for another long journey. Maria had struggled to adjust to sharing a room with Chloe and going to finishing school with Dominic's sister. It was Sally who finally put an end to Maria's miserable days at that awful school a few months after Dominic departed. "I do not like living alone in this big, dreary house across town, especially now that I am in a delicate way, and Maria does not like school," Sally had told

Mary and Patrick. "I want Maria to come and live with me and help me oversee the renovations. It is too much for me to handle alone."

When it was all said and done, Maria oversaw the renovations on Dominic and Sally's stately old home. Sally rested much of the time in her upstairs bedroom with several tall windows, where Maria constantly opened and closed the curtains for her. The pregnancy made Sally tired, and she was often sick, throwing up her meals until Maria grew concerned for her and the baby's welfare.

"She will be fine," Mary told Maria in her brisk, no-nonsense New England manner. "Just make sure she keeps eating, even if it makes her sick."

Maria did her best to convince Sally to eat, relieved she no longer had to live with Dominic's mother and father. The thought of losing Sally now terrified her. There was no way she could remain in Boston without Sally. Maria liked Chloe, but the girl was just that, a girl. They had nothing in common, and Maria wasn't about to move back into that snug little bedroom in the Masons' home and go to school each day with Chloe. But beyond that, Maria had never had a friend like Sally before. Perhaps had never been loved like Sally loved her. Unconditionally. When she was lonely, Sally loved her. When she was in a dark mood, Sally loved her. When she hadn't done a thing to deserve it, Sally loved her. Sally was kind of like Lupe, but young and Protestant instead of old and Catholic.

Maria wasn't used to being loved by a woman. Most women didn't take kindly to her at all. Many outright disliked her. But not Sally. From the moment they'd met, Sally loved her. Dominic had introduced Maria as his best friend in California's sister, and that was that. Sally immediately stepped right over and took Maria into her arms. She was the first woman who'd hugged Maria in a long time.

Sally read her Bible every day. She talked about Jesus like he was really there with them. Maria didn't have the heart to tell Sally she no longer believed in Jesus that way. But Sally's faith was so winsome that Maria had begun to think maybe it could be true.

"Please pray with me for this baby to come soon," Sally panted. "I'm so tired. When it's time to push, I won't have any strength left to deliver the babe."

"Yes, you will. Of course you'll be able to birth your babe," Maria said, swallowing her own fear.

Sally sagged against her, tears streaking her cheeks. A hard contraction hit her, and she let out a scream that startled Maria. Immediately, there was a pounding on the door.

"Let me in!" Mary demanded.

"You must let her in," Sally pleaded.

"You must walk some more," Maria insisted. The banging on the door infuriated her. "Stop knocking!" Maria yelled at the door.

Sally was horrified. "Oh, Maria, please don't fight with her. Dominic's mother means well; she's just stern, is all." At that moment, Sally's water broke and splashed down her legs and onto the floor, splattering Maria's slippers too. The urgent knocking on the door continued.

A man's voice demanded entrance. The doctor had returned. Such perfect timing.

Maria helped Sally into bed before going over to remove the chair from the door. When she opened it, Dominic's mother nearly plowed her over. Mary wasn't as big as Maria, but she was a force to be reckoned with. Certain the baby was now on its way into the world, Maria stepped aside and let the doctor and Mary do what they needed to do for Sally.

"Maria! Where's Maria?" Sally cried from the bed.

"Why is this water on the floor?" Mary's gaze leveled on Maria.

"Let's get to bringing this baby into the world," the doctor reminded everyone.

Sally's voice grew frantic. "Where's Maria? Please, I want Maria here to help me push."

"Maria can't help you push. She's going to get some towels to clean up the floor."

Maria could tell by the tone of her voice that Mary was angry.

"You clean up the floor. I need Maria!" Sally had never spoken harshly before. It stunned everyone.

Mary stepped back from the bed as if she'd been struck. Panting hard now, Sally was frantic for Maria.

Mary motioned Maria over to the bed. "You tend to her," Mary said shortly. "I'll be back with some towels."

"Hot towels," the doctor ordered.

The baby in Maria's arms was the most beautiful creature she'd ever seen. He had a head of fair hair and deep blue eyes. He blinked at her, and she blinked back at him. "Hello, young Nicky," she whispered.

The baby opened his rosy little mouth in response. A wave of true love washed over Maria. Sally had named the babe Dominic after his father, but they all agreed to call him Nicky. Sally was sleeping now. Mary had gone home for the night, along with Patrick and Chloe. Maria assured them she would take care of Sally and the baby. She wasn't even tired, though it was three in the morning, and nobody had slept much for the past several days.

As soon as everyone left, the baby awoke. Maria whisked him from Sally's side so he didn't wake her. Maria was worried about Sally. She'd had a very hard time of it, and even the doctor was concerned about her recovery.

"Your father is sailing the sea tonight. He's a very good captain," Maria whispered, gently rocking the babe, trying not to think much about Dominic. The size of the infant surprised her. Though babies were very small in general, the doctor said this was a large baby. Too big for his small, slender mother to deliver without injury.

"We are lucky to still have her with us," the doctor had said after Sally was asleep. "She shouldn't have any more children. I don't think she'll survive the next one. I'm not sure she'll survive this one."

"How can you say that?" Maria had tried to keep her voice quiet and calm. "Of course she will survive."

Mary, Patrick, and Chloe had looked at her with solemn eyes. The heaviness in the room didn't feel right with such a darling baby settled by his mother's side.

"Well, we are glad you feel this way," Mary said, giving Maria an even grimmer look. "Do you really have a brother in California?"

"What?" Maria was taken aback. "You are talking about Roman? Of course I have a brother!"

"Lower your voice." Mary stepped over to peek at the baby and Sally across the room in the bed.

The doctor finished tucking the last of his instruments into his bag. Maria had washed them for him without thinking about it. Cleaning up the blood and the medical tools and the mess reminded her of doctoring the sailors on the ship. She and Dominic had worked together so effortlessly. With this doctor, she felt on edge. He was old, and the way he looked at her over his eyeglasses made her uncomfortable. He'd brushed against her several times in the past few hours as they cared for Sally and the babe. Maria decided he was not a good man.

"If she survives the week, she should make it. But she won't be out of that bed for a long time. I'll be back tomorrow to check on her." The doctor gave Maria a lingering glance and then left the room.

"So you met our son in California? What part of California, did you say?" Patrick spoke kindly. Unlike the doctor, Maria knew Patrick was a good man. She could tell that the moment she met him. Still, Dominic's kind-hearted father looked at her suspiciously now.

"I did not say where I am from," Maria snapped. "Your son told you where I am from."

"So you two met at your family's hacienda near Monterey? You are a gently reared daughter of the *gente de* . . ."

"*Razón,*" Maria finished for her when Mary struggled with the Spanish.

"And this means . . . ?"

"People of reason." Maria propped her hands on her hips. Her skirt was stained with Sally's blood. She'd rolled up her sleeves and unbuttoned some of the top buttons of her confining dress to move more freely while assisting the doctor.

All three of Dominic's family members stared at her, listening raptly to what she was saying, as if trying to decide if they could believe her or not.

"So these people of reason . . . they are Catholics from Spain?" Mary's voice sounded strained.

"Yes, I am Catholic, but I was born in California. Only Spanish blood runs through my veins." Maria reached into the pocket of her skirt and pulled out her golden rosary. She'd retrieved it from her room on the second day of Sally's labor. By then, she was growing alarmed, watching Sally weaken with the baby still inside her.

"I do not approve of that pagan prayer chain." Mary raised her chin. To Maria, it appeared a challenge.

"Approve or not, I will not part with it. This rosary belonged to my grandmother, and yes, she lives in Spain. I hope to visit her there. Perhaps quite soon." Maria had no desire to leave Sally and the baby, but when Dominic returned she would have to go somewhere. Spain seemed good enough.

"We don't want you to leave," Patrick said in his firm, kind way.

Mary bit her lip. Maria could tell by the look on her face that she wanted her to leave and wanted to say so this very moment, but would not speak against her husband.

"Sally will need someone to care for the baby until she regains her strength. I could quit school," Chloe offered.

"You will not quit school." Mary folded her arms across her chest.

"Maria will continue to care for Sally and the babe as well," Patrick proclaimed.

"Have you cared for a babe before?" Maria detected fear in Mary's eyes, though her chin remained raised in righteous pride—or womanly challenge, Maria wasn't sure which was the case.

"I have cared for young lambs. And foals. And orphaned calves. A babe can't be much different." Maria raised her chin to match Mary's.

Mary turned to her husband. "Patrick . . ." Her voice was almost pleading.

"Maria will care for the babe and Sally. She is a strong and competent young woman, none of us can argue that." Patrick gave Maria a small smile. The slight twisting of his lips reminded her of Dominic. "So you're a farm girl?"

"I grew up on a rancho," Maria reminded them all. "I rode with the vaqueros for most of my life."

"What's a vaquero?" Chloe had her family's blue eyes and sun-streaked brown hair. She was a pretty girl in a wholesome way.

"A cowboy," Maria said.

"Oh, Patrick . . ." Mary breathed.

"Enough is enough." Patrick took Mary by the arm. "We all need some sleep." He turned to Maria. "You should lie down beside Sally and try to get some rest before my grandson stirs. He's a hearty boy. We all heard his lungs, and they are strong."

Maria glanced at the large, comfortable bed where the baby had been born. And conceived, she suspected. She didn't want to lie on that bed with Dominic's wife and child sleeping so sweetly there. That just seemed too cruel, if she were really truthful with herself. She decided not to be truthful. "*Sí*, we all need a siesta." She used the Spanish term just to spite Mary.

Chapter Fourteen

Boston, 1849

"Maria!" Nicky yelled at the top of his lungs, running from her for all his worth.

"Here I come, *chico!*" Maria yelled back, chasing the sturdy toddler across the sun-splashed yard, leaves flying up in their wake. It was their daily game. Nicky was very good at it. He loved running, and Maria pretended she couldn't catch him as they raced around the trees and rows of neatly trimmed hedges surrounding the old brick home. The estate was owned by Sally's father. Sally was already having her nap. She was stronger now and only spent the afternoons resting. Sally loved to sew and read when she wasn't resting. Maria usually entertained Nicky and kept him out of his mother's hair.

"Maria!" Nicky continued to yell for her. Her name was his favorite word besides "dog" and "Mama." Though he loved his mama, Nicky was more attached to Maria considering she had cared for him since the day he was born. Sally spent most of her time in the upstairs bedroom. For months, they didn't even know if she would survive, let alone live to raise her boisterous child. Nicky was a robust two-year old now with curly blond ringlets and dimpled arms and legs. He made Maria laugh all the time. Patrick kept saying they needed to give the boy his first haircut, but Sally and Maria wouldn't hear of such a thing.

"I'm going to get you," Maria called, darting around the hedge and nearly running into the man scooping the child up into his arms.

Nicky was laughing, and then he wasn't anymore. He stared wide-eyed at the man holding him in those strong, tanned arms. Identical blue eyes met and held between the boy and the man. Maria could no longer breathe.

"Is this my son?" Dominic looked at her and then back at the boy.

Nicky stared wide-eyed at his father in his ship captain's uniform a moment longer, and then began to wail, flailing to get out of Dominic's arms.

Maria moved forward and reached for Nicky. Her eyes met Dominic's, and for a split second she hated him almost as passionately as she'd once loved him. His arrival here had just ruined her life.

Regret in every line of his face, Dominic released the child to her.

Nicky wrapped his chubby arms around her neck in a death grip. "Do not cry, *chico*. This is your daddy. He has come home to you and your mama." It took everything in her to acknowledge that Dominic had every right to the child and she had none.

"How is Sally?"

Maria could see the fear in his eyes. He must have received their letters. At one point, the doctor told them Sally would not survive another week. Patrick had written Dominic a number of times. Maria wondered which letters he'd received, the ones that said Sally would die or that she would live.

"She is upstairs sleeping. Growing stronger every day." To Maria's utter surprise, Dominic covered his face for a moment, and his wide shoulders shook with emotion.

It was enough to immediately stop Nicky's crying. And constrict Maria's heart. She stepped up to him. Holding Nicky in one arm, she wrapped her other arm around Dominic. Nicky melted into her shoulder, perhaps afraid she might return him to his father's arms. Dominic wrapped his arms around both of them. In that moment of being in his arms, Maria's love for him came surging back with a vengeance.

"Sally is fine. She is going to be just fine," Maria whispered in his ear. "You have a handsome son and a wife without equal." She touched her lips to his wet cheek before untangling herself from his arms. She tried to hand Nicky back to his father, but the boy became an octopus. It seemed like he had ten arms hanging on to her.

"Let the boy alone." Dominic's tears turned to laughter. "By God, he looks just like me."

"He certainly does." Maria laughed too. "And he acts just like you. He will make a fabulous ship captain. His voice alone can still a storm."

Their eyes met and held. "Thank you, Maria."

"There is no need for thanks. Caring for your family has been my greatest pleasure." A lump grew in her throat until she could no longer speak.

"You've grown up." Dominic looked her over, sending a tidal wave of warmth coursing through her. "How old are you now?"

"I turn twenty this year."

"Twenty?" He captured her chin and raised her face to his. "Twenty," he confirmed, staring deeply into her eyes.

She came out of her trance and jerked her chin away from his touch. "Yes, twenty. Practically a spinster by California standards."

"Do you long to return to California?"

"No, I love Boston's balmy winters and your balmy mother too."

"Well, you still have your sharp tongue." Dominic grinned at her. "Every spinster needs a sharp tongue."

"Just like every father needs a sharp-tongued son." She shoved Nicky into his arms before either the child or he could react. Then she whirled away and ran.

Nicky went wild in Dominic's arms, wailing like a captured bobcat.

Before she cleared the front door, Maria was sobbing. She cried so hard she couldn't breathe. She had known this day would come, but still it had come like a thief in the night. Like the return of Christ. Like a judgment from the God who had cursed her. Her life was over here, and Dominic's life back with his family was just beginning.

• • •

With his son like a wild animal in his arms, Dominic watched Maria run away. Her hair was longer than he'd expected, but not as long as it had been the day he first met her. And to his anguish, she was even more beautiful than he remembered. "You want Maria?" He took a firm hold on his son. "If you want Maria, you must stop crying."

Nicky, is that what Maria called him? This boy, Dominic Steven Mason, howled all the more in Dominic's firm grip. "I will return you to Maria if you stop crying."

The toddler began hitting and screaming like a wild Indian with a tomahawk. Dominic was appalled. He did his best to get a good grip on the boy without hurting him as he walked around the hedge. When he cleared the tall green bushes, Sally was just stepping down from the porch.

In a simple white gown, she was pale and lovely, with her long, dark hair streaming down her back. The only time he'd ever seen her hair this way was when they'd made love.

"My goodness, he is throwing such a fit. I heard our son all the way from the bedroom. Where is Maria?" Sally began to laugh and cry at the same time.

Dominic took several mighty strides and swept Sally into his arms. They embraced and kissed with the toddler wrestling between them. It wasn't a passionate kiss. It was a careful kiss. Dominic worried they might end up with a toddler's fist between their lips. And he didn't want to hurt Sally. He always did his best to hold and kiss her gently. She didn't seem strong enough to withstand a man's passion.

"Nobody told me your ship had arrived in the harbor," she said.

"I swore everyone to secrecy. I wanted to surprise you."

They kissed again, sweetly, affectionately. The boy had settled down with his mother near, though the child was doing his best to lock his arms around his mother's neck. Sally smelled just as he remembered, like lavender. The slenderness of her body alarmed him.

"Are you well?" He tried to keep the fear from his voice. He'd lived in fear for nearly a year since he'd received the letter from his father saying Sally might not survive another month.

"I am well, praise our Lord," she said joyfully.

"Praise our Lord," he answered, beginning to smile.

"Where did Maria go? I can't believe you were able to pry Nicky from her skirts." Sally's brown eyes sparkled with love.

Dominic swallowed his shame. He suspected Maria had run off because of him. Seeing her with his son was too much. Like she was the woman who had borne him that hearty son. "Perhaps Maria disappeared to give us this time alone," he said, and his words rang hollow to his own ears.

Sally's brow furled. "Maria should be here now, sharing our joy. She is a part of our family. She is our sister."

"I think our boy's lungs scared her away. My ears are ringing from his screams."

"Maria is used to our son's voice." Sally happily took the boy into her arms.

The toddler grabbed hold of his mother's long, silky hair and wrapped it around his face, covering his eyes, trying to hide in plain sight. The attempt was so ludicrous, Dominic laughed. Yet inside he wasn't laughing. He knew just what it felt like trying to hide from something so impossible. Something right in front of you. His heart had soared when he saw Maria. Now it settled down with Sally. He couldn't wait to tell her they would be moving soon. By the time they reached their new home in San Francisco come summer, his mansion on a hill overlooking the bay should be finished. No longer would he live in a house owned by his father-in-law. His life commanded by the firm that owned his ship. Owned him, really. Every captain felt his ship belonged to him, especially on the open sea, but in reality, wealthy old men in business suits often owned the ships. Fortunately, Sally's father had always been more than supportive, giving Dominic nearly free rein as captain. But Dominic had settled things in California after deciding that's where his future lie. Now it was time to settle things in Boston.

Chapter Fifteen

Bound for San Francisco, 1849

Sally was heavy with child. Dominic worried about her. One morning, he finally confessed how concerned he was and told her they were sailing as fast as possible to get to California before the babe arrived.

"I have never felt stronger in my life," Sally assured him, and her serenity and happiness were a balm to his troubled spirit.

Chloe and Maria, on the other hand, continued to weigh on his mind. He'd pleaded with his parents to allow Chloe to sail to California with them because Sally needed her, and the girl was desperate to get away from their strict parents. Truth be told, Dominic had decided Chloe must replace Maria in

Sally's and Nicky's affections. When he returned to Boston, he was shocked to find his wife and son so dependent on Maria. It was "Maria this, and Maria that," every conversation about Maria. And her resentment toward him was staggering. Maria could barely be civil when he was around, and now that he was about to cut Nicky's curls here on the deck of his own ship, he thought Maria might stick a knife in him, she was so furious.

"What are you doing?" she said sharply when he sat Nicky down on a barrel and came at him with a pair of scissors. Sally wasn't happy about the boy's first haircut either, but she'd surrendered as soon as he explained it was time for their son to look like a real boy. And to start acting like a real boy too instead of a wild hooligan. Of course, as soon as Maria protested the haircut, Nicky jumped off the barrel into her waiting arms.

"Put him back on that barrel," Dominic ordered.

Every sailor on the deck quieted down. The sailors up in the rigging froze as well, staring down at them as if they had nothing better to do than gawk at their captain. "Get back to work!" Dominic boomed, and a flurry of activity followed amongst the sails and on deck.

"You will not cut his hair," Maria said with the boy firmly in her arms.

"Put him back on that barrel," Dominic repeated.

Crocodile-sized tears formed in Nicky's wide blue eyes.

"No." Maria narrowed her gaze on him and stood her ground.

Growing furious that Maria would defy him this way with his own son, Dominic looked around and found his man. He motioned Gavilan over. "Take the boy from her," he said evenly. Inside, he was on fire. How dare she create a scene like this in front of his crew? More than that, he'd had a devil of a time winning his son's affections thus far. He wasn't about to lose Nicky now over blond ringlets.

"Don't touch him," Maria said to Gavilan. She looked ready to kill someone.

Dominic stepped up and put his hand on Nicky's head. "It's time for you to become a sailor like my first mate, Mr. Hernandez." He pointed at Gavilan. "Look around, son. Don't you want to be like these sailors? Like Mr. Hernandez? We all keep our hair short because we don't want to get caught in the rigging. Getting caught in the rigging is very dangerous for a sailor."

Nicky looked torn between wanting to please him and his fierce devotion to Maria. Maria's eyes blazed with outright hostility.

Sally approached, laying her hand on Maria's arm.

The way Sally looked at him made him think she might side with Maria. The possibility infuriated him. He gave his wife a warning look and then gazed back at Maria, staring her down. He kept his voice low and steady and resolute as he addressed Gavilan. "Mr. Hernandez, take the boy from her. You will hold Nicky while I cut his hair." He'd never lost a battle on his ship with any man. He wasn't about to lose to a woman and a toddler he didn't quite know what to do with these days.

Nicky looked uncertainly at Maria. She smiled for the boy, a smile so full of love Dominic almost felt like a fool standing there.

"You must do what your daddy says," Maria told Nicky. "We don't want you getting caught in the rigging while you're working on the sails like a big boy, now do we?" She turned to

Dominic, her voice deceptively soft. "May I hold him?" Her eyes still blazed with fury.

"Please let Maria hold him." Sally released Maria's arm and placed a gentle hand on his hand that held the scissors.

"Sally, please," Dominic quietly said, "everyone must learn their place on my ship. I am the captain." He spoke kindly, but his ire was growing with Sally as well.

Every sailor within hearing distance was pretending not to hear a thing, but Dominic knew their ears were about to burst. He couldn't lose the respect of his crew over his son's haircut. Gavilan stood there not saying a word. His eyes were on Maria. Dominic could tell Gavilan felt sorry for her. He knew Gavilan would do whatever he asked, but the compassion shining in his first mate's eyes for Maria gave him pause. Perhaps he was missing something here. How could a haircut be so upsetting? It finally dawned on him that perhaps the haircut was bringing up memories of the night she'd shorn her own hair after being ravished.

"All right, you may hold him." He stared at Maria for a long moment, his wrath disappearing. He'd done his best to avoid any real interaction with her since he'd arrived back in Boston to find her playing so sweetly in the yard with his son.

"Thank you," Maria whispered.

Sally squeezed his arm in gratitude, and stepped back out of the way.

Gavilan helped Maria onto the barrel where she settled Nicky on her lap.

"You must not move," Maria told the boy. Nicky sat there like a little statue in her arms as Dominic went to work on his hair.

Sally gathered up a few curls as they fell, tucked them in her skirt pocket, and then walked away. Why couldn't she stay and support him so he could keep his mind on her instead of Maria right under his nose? What was the matter with these women? The boy was going to look like a real boy for a change.

Maria ignored him as he snipped off Nicky's curls. Gavilan returned to his post as silently as he'd joined the confrontation at the barrel. Dominic was thankful for his first mate's quiet strength. A profound difference from the roaring presence of his old first mate, Mr. Andrews, but when orders needed to be barked to the crew, Gavilan's voice fell like a guillotine. Nobody dared defy the dark-eyed man from Valparaiso.

Dominic hadn't been this close to Maria since greeting her that first day in Boston. Like Nicky, she sat very still, staring out to sea. She seemed so distant from him, even though she was so near. An ache flooded his chest. She smelled as he remembered, no perfume or rosewater like other women, but something so fair and sweet upon her skin. Her scent he could never forget. He caught himself glancing at her lush mouth, remembering her passionate kisses, so unlike the sweet kisses he shared with Sally. When he realized where his mind had drifted, disgust filled him. Sally was his beloved wife.

He quickly finished the haircut and told his son how handsome he looked. Nicky turned to Maria, waiting for her approval.

"You look like the captain of a grand sailing ship." She smiled so affectionately at the boy that the ache in Dominic's chest exploded into something he could hardly stand.

Where was Sally? Why wasn't she here to tell their son how fine he looked with a young man's haircut?

Maria hopped off the barrel and set Nicky's feet on the deck. She got down on her hands and knees and began scooping up every curl without a word, crawling around like a servant at his feet.

Dominic couldn't take anymore. He knelt down beside her. "The boy needed a haircut. I am sorry, Maria." He spoke very softly.

She pretended not to hear him, continuing to pick up every last curl, filling her pockets with the blond ringlets.

Nicky leaped onto his back while he was on his knees beside Maria. Dominic was relieved to focus on the boy. He stood up with his shorn son climbing atop his shoulders. This was the boy's favorite perch these days.

"Look at me, Maria," Nicky cried.

Maria gazed up at him. The wounded look in her eyes was nearly Dominic's undoing. He turned away and walked Nicky to all his favorite places on the ship, ending up at the helm, of course, where Gavilan stood watching Maria gathering Nicky's curls on the deck.

"I am surprised she let you win," Gavilan said with a twist of his lips.

Dominic took a firmer grip on his son's legs as Nicky leaned over, trying to get his hands on the big wooden wheel. "I would have almost preferred a mutiny."

"You nearly got a mutiny."

"This is why women do not belong on a ship," Dominic growled.

• • •

148

Watching Sally grow robust with the babe as they neared the California coast sent fear and anger coursing through Maria. Dominic had been warned another birth would risk his wife's life, but apparently he hadn't listened. Sally glowed with health and happiness these days as she strolled *The White Swallow*'s deck at Dominic's side. Nicky raced around his parents in his miniature captain's garb. Dressed just like his father, with his curls now shorn, the toddler spent most of his time mimicking Dominic and the sailors.

Every time Maria looked at the boy without his bouncing blond curls, she grew bereft. How dare he cut Nicky's hair off? Those curls represented the happiest season of her life. For the first few years, Nicky had been hers; now he belonged to his beaming parents. Maria was heartbroken.

"You still love him," Gavilan said when she joined him at the helm and he caught her watching Dominic and Sally at the railing with Nicky dancing around them. Gavilan was taking his trick steering the ship that evening as the sun went down in the Pacific. Dolphins swam close to the vessel. It was a beautiful evening.

Maria laughed. The sound proved hollow to her ears. "Hate is more like it."

"I do not believe you. Your heart is in your eyes when you look at him."

"It's the boy I love."

Gavilan stared at her for a long moment and then turned his gaze to the boy. "He's the spitting image of his father; of course you love him."

"I love the boy and his mother. The father I can live without."

"Because he married her instead of you?"

"I am glad he married Sally."

"Are you glad?"

"*Sí*, he makes her happy, God knows why."

It was Gavlian's turn to laugh. "You're a terrible liar."

"Where is Chloe tonight?"

"I told her passengers are not allowed to mix with the sailors. She went below. I guess I hurt her feelings."

"She's a lovely girl," Maria said.

"She is the captain's sister."

"I do not think the captain would mind you speaking with her. He holds you in high regard."

"This is precisely why I will not become entangled with the captain's delightful little sister."

"Entangled?" Maria grinned at him.

"I remember a cabin boy who became entangled with a captain several years ago. It did not work out so well for her."

"I do not remember this cabin boy."

"Are you enjoying being a passenger on this voyage? Do you miss writing until your fingers are numb and black with ink from the captain's ledgers?"

"I would rather be part of the crew than just a passenger."

"Yes, I know. I can tell by watching you. Would you like to steer the ship for a while?"

Maria stepped over and put her hands on the wheel. Gavilan kept one hand there himself and stood taller with Maria by his side.

"Do you not trust me to hold the wheel alone?" Her tone was teasing.

"Should I trust you?"

"Probably not."

"What will you do when we arrive in San Francisco?" Gavilan turned serious.

"I do not know." Maria leaned into the wheel, enjoying the pull of the ship under her hands.

"California has changed. You will not recognize her. Gold has made everyone *loco*."

"Do you plan on searching for gold too?"

"Perhaps. I'm not sure what I will do when we reach San Francisco." Gavilan smiled down at her. "Would you like to accompany me to the goldfields?"

"Do you think anyone will remember me in Monterey from that night?"

"Will they hold you accountable for the patrón's death? I do not think so. All they will remember is the gold in their eyes."

Maria did not want to think about that terrible night, but it had been on her mind more and more as they neared their destination. Sometimes she had nightmares of being hanged in California.

"The captain would not have brought you if he thought you were in any danger returning home. Nobody remembers California before the gold rush. Everyone has gold fever. Killings are commonplace in California now."

"I can't imagine that."

"It's beyond imagining. Gold makes men crazy. You won't have to worry about being hanged, but you will need a husband to keep you safe from all the men."

"I have no desire to marry."

"You are getting old. Practically a spinster." Gavilan grinned at her.

Maria laughed. "You are far older than me."

"But I am not a woman." His dark eyes bored into hers. "You would be safe with me. I would protect you with my very life."

"I know." She looked away, out over the vastness of the ocean, and then regretfully turned her gaze to the deck where Dominic and Sally watched the sunset as Nicky dragged a rope around in circles. "I do not long to be safe. I long to be . . . free."

"A woman cannot be free."

"I will find a way to be free in California."

Gavilan took control of the wheel. "You are still so stubborn. I thought perhaps the captain's sweet wife would rub off on you."

Maria watched Dominic take the rope from his son and then give Nicky a romping ride around the deck on his shoulders. Sally threw her head back, laughing. She'd taken to wearing her hair down, and it swirled around her like a velvet curtain. "You always wear your hair down, Maria and it looks so brave. I'm going to wear my hair down too on the ship," Sally had said. Her hair was much longer than Maria's. She touched her tresses in regret. Her locks were well below her shoulders now, but nothing like they'd been before she cut it all off.

Chloe appeared on deck and walked over to stand beside Sally, clapping her hands at Nicky's howling delight. Chloe had taken to wearing her hair down too. After months on the deck every day, Chloe's hair was bright with sun-streaks, just like Dominic's, and flowed below her slender waist. Her face was sun-kissed too because she refused to wear a bonnet. Since leaving her mother, the girl had blossomed into her own person. A young woman set on having her way, which was driving her brother crazy and keeping Gavilan on his toes.

"I think I have rubbed off on them." A little smile of pleasure lit Maria's face.

"I don't think the captain likes it." Gavilan looked the other way when Chloe turned toward them. The girl's gaze lingered on Gavilan and then on Maria, and then Chloe walked over and gripped the rail. Maria could tell she was upset at seeing them at the helm together.

"You must tell Chloe to leave me alone," Gavilan said.

"I will not tell her to leave you alone. You need a woman, and Chloe would be a wonderful wife for you."

Gavilan didn't say anything for a long time. He stared at the ocean out in front of them, all endless blue sea. Finally, he looked at Maria, and his dark eyes said it all.

Part Two

If I ascend to the heavens, you are there.
If I make my bed in hell, you are there.

Psalm 139:8

Chapter Sixteen

On a windy day, the sea spraying foam across the deck of the ship, *The White Swallow* sailed through the Golden Gate. John C. Fremont had christened the narrow, often perilous opening of San Francisco Bay the Golden Gate in his *Geographical Memoir upon Upper California* published in 1848, which Dominic read during the voyage at night in his cabin as Sally sewed. Fremont had been inspired by the Golden Horn, the entrance of the ancient city of Constantinople. San Francisco had the same great commercial possibilities with her magnificent bay surrounded by fertile forests and valleys stretching in the distance. Dominic agreed with the shaggy-bearded explorer and was settling here for this very reason. He wasn't sure exactly what he would do in California, but one thing he knew for certain, he was done being owned by the firm that controlled his ship. And also by his parents in Boston. He'd come to the realization he didn't want to sail the sea forever, and he could never live under the command of anyone other than himself on land.

When he'd sailed away from Yerba Buena in the summer of 1846, Lt. Washington Allon Bartlett was alcalde of the village. Bartlett changed the little village's name to San Francisco in January 1847. The city, as well as the rest of California, officially became a United States territory under the Treaty of Guadalupe Hidalgo, which ended the Mexican-American War in 1848.

Sally was up for any adventure as long as it was with him. He'd told her all about his plans for California, all the land he'd acquired, the mansion on the hill they would have overlooking the deep blue bay. He had hired his head carpenter and acquired the redwood lumber to construct his mansion before sailing for Boston. By then, he knew he had a son and couldn't wait to meet Nicky.

And in spite of his turbulent feelings for Maria, he'd found happiness with Sally. He longed to settle his little family in San Francisco, perhaps build his own shipping business, and then journey into politics.

Now, with the discovery of gold, sleepy little San Francisco had boomed from one thousand to twenty-five thousand inhabitants in less than a year, mostly men. Tents of all shapes and sizes covered the hills, and a number of buildings rose up amongst the tents. Plenty of buildings were down by the wharves as well now, and dockworkers frantically carried goods in all directions.

Abandoned ships and boats clogged the harbor. Dominic had never seen anything like it in his life. Passengers and crews stepped right off their vessels and onto steamboats and sailboats, heading up the Sacramento River to the Sierra Nevada foothills to chase the gold. They arrived on the Fourth of July with the whole city awash in wild celebration.

After discovering his mansion on the hill wasn't nearly finished, in fact much of his lumber had been stolen, and most of his builders had run off to the goldfields in the spring, Dominic settled his family in the nearest hotel. Just getting Sally, Chloe, and Maria to the hotel had been a nightmare. He may as well have had a wagon full of gold instead of a wagon of women. The fever on men's faces when they saw the young, attractive women alarmed Dominic. Chloe and Maria especially would not be safe in this strange city still being born—and messy as any birth could be.

The women took baths and changed into their finest apparel before walking down the street to a party they'd been invited to that evening upon anchoring in the bay. Sally dressed for the evening, then decided to stay in their hotel room right as they were leaving.

"I am fine," she assured Dominic. "Only tired carrying your babe." Sally smiled as she lay down on the bed in her beautiful dress.

Dominic wasn't convinced Sally was fine. He didn't want to attend the party without her, but she insisted they all go.

"You must take Chloe and Maria to the party," Sally said. "There will be military officers and important men of the city there. The sooner Maria and Chloe settle down with husbands, the better."

Dominic agreed with her and donned his captain's garb, escorting the two young women to the gathering. Maria and Chloe looked so lovely in their silk taffeta. Chloe's gown was lavender with lace trim. Maria's a dark, burnished brown with frills and bugle beads. Both girls had pinned their hair up.

Dominic tried not to look at Maria. She certainly wasn't looking at him. Since Nicky's haircut, they'd stumbled into a quiet truce of sorts, like the no-man's-land between two armies.

"Will Gavilan be coming with us tonight?" Chloe asked.

"I do not think so," Dominic answered, giving her a smile meant to comfort her.

"Why not?" Chloe sounded disappointed.

"Gavilan does not enjoy parties."

"Well, that is too bad. I love parties, and I love to dance."

"When have you danced?" Dominic raised his brows at her.

"Well, I haven't danced yet with a man, but I know I will love dancing. Maria has taught me how to dance."

Dominic took both women lightly by the elbows as they walked into the large building that had been adorned for the Independence Day celebration in Portsmouth Square. "Really?" He tried to keep his voice even as he turned to Maria. "You and Maria have been dancing on my ship, and I didn't even know it?"

Maria wouldn't look at him. Her gaze remained on the party.

"It's been our little secret." Chloe glanced past him and grinned at Maria, but Maria wouldn't make eye contact with her either.

Dominic wished Sally was here to keep the girls in line. Sally never chastised anyone, but her sweet, gentle presence helped people do the right thing.

A band began to play "Hail, Columbia," music composed by Philip Phile for the inauguration of George Washington. Many people still knew the song as "The President's March." Columbia was a poetic name for the United States. The song was practically the country's national anthem. The goodwill in the room became contagious. A young man carrying a tray of wineglasses stopped and offered them drinks.

After Maria and Chloe accepted their glasses, Dominic took a glass in hand, and his mood lightened. After the patriotic song, a rousing reel kicked in. Couples flowed onto the dance floor. A finely dressed military officer accompanied by his wife in a blue ball gown approached them. They introduced themselves as Captain John Matthews and his wife, Jane.

As Dominic spoke with Captain Matthews, Chloe fell into an eager conversation with Jane. His sister couldn't wait to meet people and appeared thrilled to have already made a friend in the city. Maria stood silently by watching the dancers.

Out of the corner of his eye, Dominic saw Wade. His old captain came right up to Maria with two glasses of wine in hand. Maria downed the wine she held and grinned at Wade. Dominic could hardly continue his conversation with Captain Matthews.

In his buff trousers, tall leather boots, vest, and dark blue jacket perfectly tailored to fit his tall, broad-shouldered frame, Wade looked every inch the dashing ship captain. He handed Maria the fresh glass of wine and took the empty one from her hand. Then he had the nerve to hand the empty glass to Dominic. "Hello, Dom. So good to see you in California, my boy."

Captain Matthews shook Wade's hand. "Hello, Captain Reynolds. I see you already know Captain Mason and his sisters."

Wade raised his hawkish eyebrows. "Yes, sisters," he said evenly, staring at Maria. He reached for Maria's hand, raised it to his mouth, and kissed it, letting his lips linger on her skin. Finally, he turned to Chloe, but only brushed his lips politely across her hand. "Miss Chloe, I haven't seen you since you were knee-high in pigtails. What a beautiful woman you've become."

Chloe blushed from head to toe. "Hello, Captain Reynolds."

Wade unabashedly looked her over, then returned his attention to Maria. "I've noticed you gentlemen discussing the future of California, and these two ladies having a jolly conversation, but Maria needs a companion for the evening. Come, my lady," he said, offering Maria his arm.

"We have just arrived," Dominic interrupted. "I was going to introduce my sisters around the room."

"Allow me to introduce Maria to the fine folks of San Francisco. You all enjoy your evening." Wade stepped right between Dominic and Maria and tucked Maria's arm firmly into his.

"Maria couldn't be in better hands," Mrs. Matthews gushed. "Captain Reynolds knows everyone in San Francisco and is quite respected here." She smiled at Wade, and he grinned back at her, making Mrs. Matthews blush too.

What a rake. Dominic was at a loss as to how to rescue Maria. He knew he could never outmaneuver Wade in public. Wade's charisma was unmatchable. He tried to catch Maria's eye to give her a warning, but she wasn't about to seek his approval. Her eyes were on Wade. A smile of pleasure curved her lush lips. She looked incredibly beautiful tonight and certainly all grown up. He almost missed the girl in the baggy sailor's clothes with the short hair as she diligently worked on his ledgers, pretending to be his cabin boy.

"Your hair has grown out," Wade said to Maria. "I like it." His gaze raked over her again, then he looked at Dominic.

"We'll see you on the dance floor." Wade winked before leading Maria away.

"Oh, let's dance too." Chloe enviously watched them go.

Captain Matthews laughed at Chloe's exuberance.

"By all means, dance with your sister, Captain Mason. Jane and I will make our rounds. Please pay me a visit soon so we can speak of your future plans. We are gathering delegates for our California convention, men of all walks of life willing to see California into statehood. The elections will be held next month. You should consider tossing your hat into the fray. You have a fine reputation, and you're a landowner here. I know, like me, you long to see California brought into the union as a free state. The Southerners want to bring their slaves here to work the mines. We can't have slavery in California, now can we, Captain Mason?"

"I don't believe in slavery," Dominic said. "And I'll do what I can to stop it from taking root in California." He reached for Matthew's hand, promising to pay him a visit soon. Then he whisked Chloe in the direction Wade had disappeared with Maria. But he didn't find them right away. The warehouse was filled with people. He danced with Chloe, and she was delighted he knew how to lead her in a waltz.

"Do you feel like we've missed out growing up without dancing?" she asked.

"I used to feel that way, but I don't any longer. Dancing is overrated."

Chloe laughed. "When did you become such a stick in the mud? You used to be fun. Now you're serious all the time."

"Am I serious?" Dominic was surprised, but then again, he really wasn't surprised. He hadn't felt carefree since Steven died. That day something monumental had shifted inside of him. He recalled cutting Roman loose from the tree, Roman confessing his belief in Jesus, and then together they'd taken Steven's body off the tree after gunning down Lopez.

In that moment of removing Steven's body from the tree, the image of Christ being taken off the cross had come to Dominic and never left him. Since that day, he'd striven to do what God wanted him to do, no matter the cost. Sometimes it felt like such a heavy burden.

"Yes, you are different. I don't like it one bit," said Chloe.

"Well, we will have to find you another dance partner, then." Shoving the uncomfortable thoughts from his mind, Dominic looked around for Maria. The men far outnumbered the women in the room. He recognized a few people. Ship captains like Wade. Truth be told, all he wanted was to find Wade and Maria and take the girls back to the hotel this very minute, lock both girls in their rooms, and check on Sally.

The dance floor was crowded with couples. With not enough whale oil lanterns in the building, the warehouse was rather dark. It felt like the building was shaking with the band's boisterous music. Considering the building had probably been thrown up nearly overnight, Dominic wasn't surprised it felt like the walls were about to come down around their ears.

"Do you think there is any chance of Gavilan showing me around the city? You could ask him to give me a tour. I won't be much trouble, I promise."

He was leading Chloe off the floor since he hadn't found Wade and Maria there.

"Gavilan is more serious than me. Why do you want to spend time with him?"

Chloe smiled sheepishly. "I like the strong, silent type. Not the strong, sad type."

"Are you saying I'm sad?"

"Maybe you are," Chloe said as if she didn't really care if he was sad or not. She was looking around at her first real party. Certainly, the first celebration with dancing and spirits and men smoking their pipes in plain sight of the women. Of course this would intrigue her. He just hoped to get her married soon to a good man in San Francisco—after she helped Sally get through having the baby, of course.

Was he sad? He didn't want to consider the state of his emotions. Not once did he believe he'd made a mistake in marrying Sally, but he couldn't remember the last time he'd laughed. Or even felt like laughing. And raising his son wasn't easy. Not a day went by he didn't think he needed to take a switch to that boy's backside, and some days he did.

It had taken him months in Boston to win the boy's respect. Now it was a constant battle to keep it. And he felt like he spent much of his life avoiding interactions with Maria. He didn't even want to look at her, let alone fight with her over his son, but finding Maria now in the boisterous Independence Day crowd was all he could think about.

"You are worried about Maria, aren't you?" Chloe squeezed his arm.

"You are too young to really remember, but I sailed with Wade for several years. He is not the man he appears to be."

"I remember when Wade was your captain. You told father he nearly killed a man by flogging him to death. That you deeply regretted not intervening in that beating. I listened at the door of father's study." Chloe shrugged. "I was a curious girl. I hope you don't mind."

The memory still haunted him. The sailor Wade had nearly whipped to death had begged for mercy when he could no longer stand the blows. When that didn't stop Wade, the sailor tied to the mast began yelling for Jesus Christ.

"I am your Jesus Christ," Wade had said, blood spattering his face from lashing the young man's back.

When Wade said that, Dominic's blood had run cold. The rest of the sailors had stood around silently watching the punishment. Wade wasn't afraid to use the whip. This sailor had stolen an onion from another sailor suffering from scurvy.

"I will have no thieves on my ship," Wade had breathed with exertion as he beat the young man nearly to death. The man had taken the onion because he too was coming down with scurvy.

That voyage had been unusually grueling due to Wade's unpredictable temper, the ship running out of provisions, and the voyage dragging on for weeks overdue. That day of the flogging Dominic decided he was done being Wade's first mate. He would take a position as second mate on another ship if he had to, but he hoped his ties in Boston and his loyal service on *The Sea Witch* had earned him his own ship.

A year later it had. Wade's favor had turned to disdain when Dominic stepped down as first mate on *The Sea Witch* and took a position as second mate on *The Indiana* until *The White Swallow* was ready for his command.

He finally spotted Wade and Maria in the crowd and grabbed Chloe by the elbow so he didn't lose her in the throng of partygoers.

Chloe said "sorry" and "excuse me" as they pushed through all the people talking and laughing and drinking by the barrelful.

Dominic had lost any urge to be civil. He all but dragged Chloe over to where Wade and Maria spoke to several finely dressed gentlemen in a corner of the room. The men were leering at Maria, it seemed to Dominic. He strolled right up and took her by the elbow.

"I'm sorry, gentlemen. My sisters and I must retire for the evening. My wife wasn't feeling well tonight and could not come along. We must get back to the hotel to see how Sally is faring. Thank you and good night." He pulled Maria and Chloe right along with him.

"Wait a minute," Wade said, striding after them. He caught up and captured Maria's hand. "My dear," he said, "you must allow me to call upon you—"

Dominic interrupted. "It will be a cold day in hell when you call upon my sister."

"She is not your sister." Wade's smile turned wolfish.

"She is my charge, and if you come around I will . . . do not come around."

Wade laughed in disbelief. "Are you threatening me, Dom?"

"Do not come around," Maria said, surprising everyone.

Wade raised his brows at her.

"I have a child I care for."

"A child?" Wade looked at Dominic and then back at Maria.

"My son," Dominic said as he ushered Maria and Chloe past Wade and out the door as fast as he could.

Outside, Maria jerked out of his grasp. "You have no control over me," she said.

"Don't I?" He glared at her as he released Chloe's elbow and began walking in the direction of the hotel, hoping they would follow. The streets were muddy and gouged by carts and carriages. The city was alive with raucous celebration. Out on the streets, all he saw were men. Large rats scurried to and fro with no fear of man whatsoever. He restrained himself from turning around to make sure Maria and Chloe trailed close behind him. Instead, he whispered a prayer for God's help with the women and kept on walking.

Chapter Seventeen

With Sally taken to her bed and Dominic overseeing the carpenters on the hill above Portsmouth Square, Nicky was once again Maria's charge. Sally was due to give birth in a matter of weeks, and Chloe couldn't handle Nicky. Only Dominic and Maria were able to control the rambunctious boy. The hotel was Nicky's playground. Up and down the stairs he went so many times Maria was ready to take a switch to his backside the way Dominic sometimes did.

"I've never seen such a will in a boy," Dominic said after breakfast in the hotel's dining room, where Nicky would not behave.

"He is just like you," Maria announced. "He will have his way, no matter the cost."

Chloe had gone upstairs to see Sally, who no longer joined them in the dining room mornings or evenings. Sally stayed in bed feeling unwell every day now.

"What's that supposed to mean?" Dominic asked. Together they trailed Nicky to his favorite set of narrow wooden stairs at the rear of the hotel. Up and down the landing the little boy went as Dominic and Maria stood nose to nose at the base of the stairs, both barely restraining their tempers. This confrontation had been coming for a long time.

"You know what it means!" Maria didn't bother to lower her voice. She didn't care who heard her.

"I have absolutely no idea what you're talking about, woman."

He really did seem confused, which made her even angrier. "Sally could die because of you!"

"Because of me?"

"Yes, you! Nicky's birth nearly killed her. But you don't care! You just take your . . . pleasure . . . and . . ." The matter was too delicate to even discuss. It wasn't very often something silenced Maria, but this conversation was too much for her.

Dominic looked as if she'd slapped him. "I was not taking my pleasure. I was loving my wife. But you know nothing about love, do you?" His blue eyes blazed with anger; his words were a knife in her heart.

"I know more than you think I know about love." She looked up at Nicky and knew she must part from him soon. She'd only stayed in the hotel to see Sally through the birth. After that, she wasn't sure where she would go, or what she would do, but she certainly wasn't going to live under Dominic's rule any longer.

"You have about ruined my son. You may call it love. I call it spoiling that boy rotten."

Maria swung her fist at his face.

He anticipated the blow and caught her wrist before she could harm him. His jaw turned hard and unyielding. "Sally adores you. My son adores you. I know you would do anything for them, and I thank you for that, but this can no longer go on. I have asked Gavilan to return you to Rancho de los Robles. You will leave at the end of the week."

It felt like he'd just knocked the wind from her. Leaving San Francisco was her decision, not his. She tried to yank her wrist from his hold, but his fingers were like a steel band around her arm. "You do not own me." She struggled to breathe. Her body shook from head to toe with fury.

Nicky noticed their confrontation and came slowly down the stairs, looking very concerned. "Daddy hurt Maria?"

Dominic dropped Maria's wrist as if he held a flaming stick.

"Daddy is not hurting Maria. Daddy and Maria are having an argument, but Daddy would never hurt Maria."

When Nicky reached the bottom step, Maria scooped him up, holding him against her, the agony of losing him driving away her rage. How could she live without this little boy? He'd become her whole world. She stared into his father's eyes and wanted to scream in agony. She considered begging Dominic to reconsider his decision, but her pride wouldn't allow it.

Nicky wrapped his arms around her neck and stared at his father too, as if challenging Dominic to remove him from Maria's arms. "Chloe can't handle him," Maria said quietly. Her mind spun with ways to stay with Nicky.

"Chloe must learn how to mother a child. She will have her own children soon enough."

"Sally needs me. She must get up and walk when it's time for the birth. If she lies in that bed like the last time . . ." Maria bit her lip. She didn't want to say Sally could die in front of

Nicky. "I made her get up and walk. The baby came because of me. Your mother and the doctor would have let her perish in that bed. Your son would have perished with her."

Dominic took a long, even breath. He stared at Maria, and his eyes turned sad. "You are not God, Maria. Nicky is here because the Good Lord brought him here. Sally is still here because the Lord has graciously allowed it. Life and death are in God's hands, not yours."

"God helps those who help themselves," Maria said stubbornly.

"That is not in the Bible. Ben Franklin said that. The Bible says God helps the helpless."

"Do not speak to me about God. He has done nothing for me."

"You did not see the hangman's noose. You are alive and well here, holding my son. Gold has erased every man's memory in California." Dominic attempted a smile. "You have been given a second chance." Their gazes locked in combat. And something more. Something neither of them would ever give in to.

Tears flooded Maria's eyes. "He should have been ours," she whispered, and then she whirled away with Nicky clinging to her for all his worth. The two headed down the hall toward the hotel's lobby, where she knew Dominic would not cause a scene by yanking his son from her arms.

San Francisco was often foggy at this hour. This morning's sun was a rare treat. Had Maria taken the stairs, Dominic would have followed her. He would have snatched his son from her arms and sent for Gavilan immediately to escort her to Rancho de los Robles today. For everyone's sake, especially Maria's. He'd sent Roman a letter, paying a Californio on a fast horse to let Roman know they'd arrived safely in San Francisco and that he would be sending Maria home shortly.

He could no longer stand looking at her. On the voyage home, she'd kept her distance, allowing Nicky time to bond with him and Sally. He even thought that perhaps she and Gavilan were falling in love. Maria was always at the helm when Gavilan was there. Dominic wondered if they would ultimately marry and raise a family of their own in California. He tried not to think too much about it. The last thing he needed was to dwell on his feelings over Maria and Gavilan together.

Gavilan was a fine man. After spending the past several years with him at sea, he trusted Gavilan with his life. He knew Chloe had grown sweet on Gavilan, but Gavilan always did his best to keep her at bay. If Gavilan didn't change his mind, Chloe would find someone else for her affections. With twenty thousand men in the city, there certainly had to be a good man here for his sister to marry.

Dominic walked up the stairs and down the hall to Sally's room. He needed to see her smiling face before heading over to their half-finished house on the hill. He'd paid a small fortune to replace the stolen lumber, and finding more carpenters proved difficult. Most able-bodied men were headed for the Sierra Nevada foothills, hoping to strike it rich in the snow-fed streams before winter returned.

As soon as he walked through the door, he knew Sally was in trouble. She moaned in the bed, curled onto her side with her arms wrapped around her belly. Chloe was racing around the room in a panic. "Where is Maria?" Chloe was nearly hysterical.

Striding over to the bed, Dominic took his wife by the shoulders. Gently, he pushed her back on the pillows so he could look at her face. Sally's dark eyes were full of pain. "I'll fetch the doctor," he said.

"We have already sent for the doctor. One of the maids went. Where is Maria?" Chloe asked frantically.

"Outside with Nicky."

Sally was panting hard. "Send Chloe . . . to fetch Maria."

"Chloe, go get Maria." A sense of dread filled him.

Chloe ran from the room. He sat down on the bed beside Sally, and they spoke of the babe, trying to comfort each other. "Just think, our son or daughter will be here soon. I sure hope he or she is more docile than Nicky."

"I want to name her Maria," Sally said between contractions, and Dominic was taken aback.

"What about your mother's name?" He held her small, pale hand in his. "Elizabeth Mary Mason is a fine name."

"I have set my heart on Maria."

"We might have another son." Dominic tried to smile. He didn't want to quarrel with her at a time like this. Truth be told, they had never quarreled. Not once. He wasn't about to start now.

"I do not think it's a boy. In fact, I know it's a girl. Promise me we will call her Maria."

"Why Maria?"

"I want a daughter like Maria. She is strong. And brave. And beautiful. Maria could have had any man in Boston, but she chose our son instead. I thought I would die after Nicky was born, but Maria helped me live. She raised Nicky and took care of me until you returned. We must name our daughter Maria." Sally's eyes were so guileless, so full of love and admiration for Maria. Did it ever occur to her why Maria had taken over their lives the way she had?

He didn't want to think about why Maria had done it. Sally was waiting for his answer. How could he tell her no?

The door flew open. Chloe returned with Maria and Nicky in her wake, saving him from an answer. Dominic kissed Sally's clammy forehead and then strode over and snatched his son from Maria's arms. Maria didn't seem to mind. She hurried over to Sally, reassuring her all would be well.

Watching Maria tenderly stroke Sally's hair back from her face, speaking urgently yet confidently to his wife that she would be fine, the baby would be just fine, steadied Dominic too. The unusual bond between his wife and Maria had surprised and unsettled him in Boston. Now he was happy for it. It was clear Sally needed Maria, and he needed to get over how he felt about her. He didn't even know how he felt about Maria anymore. They'd become more enemies than anything else.

"Mama okay?" Nicky asked anxiously, and Dominic bounced the boy in his arms, giving his handsome son a reassuring smile.

Looking at the boy was like looking in a mirror. "Your mama's just fine. Maria's going to take good care of her. Let's go check on the carpenters."

Nicky enjoyed watching the carpenters work on the house. Taking his son along meant he would not get an ounce of work done with the boy at his side, but with Sally in labor, he doubted he could accomplish much of anything beyond removing his son from underfoot. The last thing he wanted was to leave his wife at such a perilous time, but birthing was women's work.

He would not be welcomed back into this room until the baby was swaddled at his wife's side.

It comforted him to know Maria was in charge. She was an excellent nurse with a steady hand and a sharp mind. He recalled on the ship how they'd doctored wounded sailors together. Her confidence filled others with confidence. Skillfully tending their wounds, she would tell the sailors they would be just fine, and they believed her. Listening to Maria assure Sally all would be well nearly convinced him all would be well.

He left the hotel and headed for the stable to fetch his horse. San Francisco was changing by the day. Buildings going up faster than lightning, and tents everywhere. Mules and horses pulled carts and carriages down the muddy streets. No sidewalks yet. Men from all corners of the world scurried about. Orientals with long pigtails. Mexicans in sombreros. Irishmen with red beards. Frenchmen and Englishmen and Italians. Frontiersmen. Occasionally, a woman in a sunbonnet strolled past, but this was so rare that men stopped what they were doing to stare at her.

Folks were turning abandoned ships in the harbor into gambling dens and houses. General stores charged far more than provisions were worth. This really was the wild and wooly west compared to Boston. He hoped more women would come. The city desperately needed their civilizing influence. Men were now appearing at the hotel asking to court Chloe and Maria. Dominic impatiently turned them all away.

He'd thrown his hat into politics and had a good shot at being chosen as one of the delegates from San Francisco for the California convention to be held in the fall in Monterey. Captain Matthews was introducing him around the city, and because he was a landowner here, and a man of integrity with a fine reputation, his prospects of getting elected were very good. It helped that he was antislavery. One of the big concerns was Southerners bringing their slaves to work the mines, which alarmed the other miners already here. Dominic had no desire to mine for gold, which also made him a desirable delegate, considering he would be around for the convention instead of off at the mines seeking his fortune. He couldn't wait to get his house on the hill finished. At least there he'd feel more in control. And of course, by then Maria would be gone. The thought left him staring at his son, aching with regret.

Chapter Eighteen

Maria held the baby swaddled in her arms, staring down at her in wonder. She had a rosebud mouth and a lovely little face. Her hair was dark and abundant. She looked like a perfect little doll.

"She's too small," said the doctor, holding his spectacles on his face while shaking his head as he gathered up his instruments. An Indian woman assisted him. Her arrow-straight black hair was pulled neatly away from her face into an English hairstyle. She wore a white woman's clothes. Her round, brown face was tightly drawn, as if the baby didn't please her either. Maria tried not to pay them any mind.

"We have named her Maria," Sally said, and tears rushed to Maria's eyes at the shock of it. "Has Dominic returned yet?" Sally's voice was so eager for her husband.

"Chloe is downstairs on the porch waiting for him. He'll be here any minute now." Maria couldn't stop staring at the tiny baby bundled in her arms.

"We wanted to name her after you. I know we haven't found a church here yet, and you aren't a Presbyterian, but when we baptize her, I want you to be her godmother."

Maria swallowed the lump in her throat. How could Sally trust her to be the child's godmother? They'd talked about God, and Sally always spoke as if Maria shared her great faith. Even when Maria voiced her doubts about God, Sally would always say, "But, Maria, you know the Lord loves you! You know our Lord died for you and I on that old rugged cross. Of course, you have faith like a mustard seed, Maria. A mustard seed of faith is faith enough!"

There were times Sally's unshakable faith infuriated Maria. But other times that unbending faith filled Maria with such hope. A terrible, awful hope because she'd remember what happened in the church. Staring at the baby girl who bore her name filled her with staggering hope and happiness. Nicky was the light of her life. This baby girl would be the same. Somehow she would convince Dominic to allow her to go on minding the children. Sally needed her. The children needed her. All Chloe cared about was finding a husband, going to parties like the Independence Day one, and mooning after Gavilan when he was around. Maria had enjoyed the party. Wade was a gallant escort and could dance like a Spaniard, but in the end, she was more than happy to return to the hotel and tuck Nicky into bed.

Sometimes Maria let her mind wander to Wade, the rakish ship captain Dominic didn't like. She'd asked Sally about him in Boston, and all Sally said was, "Wade is not a good man. If you ever see him again, you must stay away from him, Maria." It was the only bad thing Sally had ever said about anyone.

But Sally telling her to stay away only made Maria want to see Wade again. All her life she'd been told what she couldn't do. As soon as someone told her not to do something, she wanted to do it. When Tia Josefa told her she could no longer ride with the vaqueros, Maria had snuck out of the hacienda and done just that. Her rebellion riding with the vaqueros didn't last long. Tio Pedro beat her backside with the rod until perspiration covered his brow and Maria was so sore she could hardly walk for a week. But she had done what she wanted to do.

When she had seen Wade at the party, she'd known she would dance with him. In his dashing arms, with his golden earrings sparkling in the lantern light and his gaze hot upon her, she felt so beautiful. So desired. So wanted. She hadn't truly felt wanted since she'd been taken from the hacienda like a captive. That was something she never allowed herself to think about anymore. Why it crossed her mind now as she stared at the tiny babe in her arms, she didn't know. But for a moment it was like her whole life flashed before her eyes as she stared at the baby, and she wasn't proud of what she saw.

She wasn't worthy of this tiny babe named after her. The baby's eyes were a deep blue, like the ocean far away. Dominic's blue eyes swam in her mind's eye. She didn't know how to measure what had happened with him on the voyage to Boston several years ago. She couldn't define those moments in his embrace as desire. It was so much more than desire. She'd decided never to allow herself to think on it again because of Sally. She and Sally were more than friends. Sally had become a mother and sister rolled into one for Maria. Sally always saw the good in her and insisted it come out. Never had a woman encouraged Maria this way. Loved Maria this way. Her devotion to Sally ran deep. Deeper than her feelings for Sally's insufferable husband.

The Indian woman changing the bedding beneath Sally began to shake her head at the doctor. The woman's gaze met the doctor's across the room, and both grew anxious. The woman folded a sheet tightly and tucked it between Sally's legs. "Clamp down on that," the doctor said as he came to stand beside the bed, staring down at Sally's pale, blood-spattered legs.

Maria was sitting beside Sally on the bed, and she stood up with the babe in her arms to see what concerned them. It didn't take long for the sheet to turn bright red between Sally's legs. Fear filled Maria, but she wasn't about to let Sally see that. "She needs labor tea," Maria said, and both the woman and doctor looked at her with blank faces. From the moment they'd walked through the door, Maria had doubted their ability to see Sally safely through this birth.

"She needs to bear down on that cloth," said the doctor. "You must will your body to stop bleeding, Mrs. Mason."

With as much calm as she could muster, Maria settled the baby beside Sally on the bed. Sally was growing paler and sleepier by the minute. Her eyes had closed while the doctor examined her. Maria put her hand on Sally's cold, damp forehead. "Sally, look at me."

Sally opened her eyes, and they were more serene than Maria had ever seen them. "I am going to be fine," Sally whispered, then she looked around the room. "Where is Dominic? I need my husband."

"Go find her husband," Maria snapped at the woman standing there looking utterly useless with that dispassionate, Indian face. She had that stoic, stiff-lipped demeanor Maria had seen all her life on so many Indian faces. Most of the Indians in California had settled for their lot as servants to the wealthy class of landowners and wore their surrender on their countenances. The missions had done this to the Indians, everything about God was about surrender, Sally said. Maria wasn't about to surrender to losing Sally.

"You must live," Maria told her, and Sally smiled.

"I have lived, Maria. Never have I been so happy as I have these past several years. I have Dominic. I have Nicky. And I have my Marias." Sally turned her head to look at the babe beside her. "I knew she would be beautiful. She has her father's eyes and your brave spirit. I just know it."

The last thing Maria felt was brave. The doctor rolled up another bedsheet and replaced the saturated one between Sally's thighs. He threw the bloody sheet on the floor and walked over to his medical bag. Surely, he had some ergot in there. Sally needed labor tea, and she needed it badly.

"I will fetch tea," Maria gently told her. "You must drink it all before you fall asleep."

Sally grabbed Maria's hand with surprising strength. "Don't go until Dominic gets here." Sally's face was so radiant Maria was taken aback. "I feel the presence of our Lord, Maria. Do you feel his presence in the room?" Sally squeezed her hand.

Maria longed to scream no, she did not feel the Lord's presence in the room. She did not want God here. If God was here, he'd take Sally away.

"Oh, Maria, don't you feel him? I can feel Jesus here with us," Sally insisted.

"It is the blood loss," the doctor said without emotion.

"Do you have the powder to make the labor tea?" Maria tried to keep her voice soft and steady as she squeezed Sally's hand. The baby slept so peacefully at her side, her tiny face on the pillow beside her mother's face. A face so pale now that Sally looked like a doll, just like the babe.

"I have no powder," he admitted. "There are so few women in San Francisco. She is only the third birth I have ever attended in my life. The other two happened in New York."

Maria longed to fly at the doctor and scratch his eyes out. Certainly, he'd take the money Dominic would pay him for his service, even though he had no labor tea to stop the bleeding.

"You should have sent for a midwife." Maria glared her wrath at him. "She would have made labor tea, maybe even before the birth to stop the bleeding."

"Finding a midwife here is like finding gold in the street. Why do we need midwives when mostly men are here?"

Maria was about to tear the doctor apart with her tongue when the door flew open. Sally had closed her eyes, but now they popped open. "Dominic," she called, and he strode right over to the bed the way Maria had seen him stride across the deck of his ship. His powerful presence in the room settled everyone.

"Look at our Maria," Sally said so proudly when Dominic leaned over them.

Maria tried to let go of Sally's hand, but Sally wouldn't release her.

"Oh, Sally," he said, and Maria could hear the love in his voice.

"Isn't she beautiful?" Sally reached her other hand out to capture her husband's hand.

Maria tried to pull away once more, but Sally held her fast. Dominic stared at the baby and Sally as if Maria wasn't there.

"She is perfect." Dominic smelled of wind and sunshine and was the only powerful presence Maria wanted in the room.

"She won't let go of my hand," Maria whispered to Dominic. The emotions flooding her with him so near caused tears to course down her cheeks.

"Sally," Dominic said tenderly, "Let Maria go make you some tea."

"How do you know she needs tea?" Maria said.

"The Indian woman assisting the doctor told me." Dominic's shoulder pressed against her as he leaned over the bed. Maria longed to just sob in his arms. She knew. They all knew. Even Sally knew she wasn't long for this world.

"I don't want tea," Sally breathed. "I want you and Maria with me. Where is Nicky?"

"He is outside enjoying the sunshine with Chloe," Dominic said.

Sally smiled. "Chloe can't handle him. That's why God gave us Maria."

Maria wept harder. The baby slept on, oblivious to her mother slipping away on the pillow beside her. The infant and Sally were nearly cheek to cheek. Neither looked fully human. Both appeared like something from another world. A holy world. Maria tried to rise; she needed to fetch her rosary. It was in her sea chest in her room, but when she tried to move, Dominic put his hand on her shoulder, firmly holding her there.

"I must get my rosary," she whispered to him.

His eyes met hers for only a moment. "No, you are needed here."

"I will pray with my rosary." Maria's whispered words turned into a sob.

"Maria." Sally squeezed her hand. "Feel his presence, Maria. Our Lord is with us. He loves us."

Dominic squeezed Maria's shoulder. "Easy, Maria. Let's not wake the baby with your tears."

"Don't cry," Sally said. "I am not sad. I am happy. We have a daughter. A beautiful baby girl who will grow up to be just like you, Maria."

"She is delirious from blood loss," said the doctor.

Dominic straightened up beside the bed. "I must speak with the doctor for a moment."

Sally let go of his hand, but not Maria's. As Dominic stepped away from the bed, Sally closed her eyes and rested. Dominic walked over and put his hand on the doctor's shoulder, speaking so low Maria couldn't hear what he said. But the doctor rolled up one more piece of bedding, came over to remove the blood-soaked sheet from between Sally's thighs, and replaced it with the tightly wound one.

"Keep that there. Perhaps her bleeding will stop," he said before leaving the room.

Dominic returned and sat beside Maria. Never in her life had Maria felt so utterly forlorn. Not even when the bear killed Ricardo right in front of her. Dominic seemed to sense her tenuous grip on reality. He leaned against her, steadying her with his big, warm body as he leaned over to look at Sally and the babe. "We will pray for God to bless us," he said. "Heavenly Father, thank you for our beautiful little Maria. And thank you for Sally. Strengthen her, Lord. Please let Sally stay here with us. Please, Lord, we plead for your mercy."

"Please, Lord," Maria begged, and everything inside her howled for mercy.

"The Lord gives and takes away. We bless your name, Oh Lord," Sally breathed. "I love you," she told Dominic. "In heaven, you will be my brother." Then she squeezed Maria's hand. "I love you, my sister."

Maria could hardly stand this agony. They could not lose Sally. They just couldn't. What would Nicky do without his mother? What would Dominic do without his wife? What would she do without this woman who'd believed in her, loved her for no reason at all? "I love you, Sally," Maria said on a broken breath. "Please don't leave us."

"Maria," Sally whispered. "I can see the light from here. It's getting lighter still. It's so beautiful, Maria."

Maria's world was getting darker. Sally could not die. Anger rose up in her. "You will not die!" Maria cried.

Dominic took her firmly by the shoulders and all but lifted her off the bed. "Sally does not need this," he said quietly, his face close to hers.

"Please don't be harsh with Maria," Sally pleaded as her grasp was jerked from Maria's hand. With a sudden burst of energy, Sally focused on Dominic and Maria. "We all must surrender to the will of God. Nicky needs you. And our little Maria needs you both. You must do what's best for the children. Promise me you will think of the children."

"We promise to do what's best for the children," Dominic assured Sally, nudging Maria out of the way and touching Sally's cheek so tenderly.

The baby began to stir beside her mother. The infant didn't cry. Hadn't cried when she was born either, but made a kittenish sound. Dominic picked up the babe and held her in his arms.

Sally smiled. "Maria belongs in your arms," she whispered, closing her eyes. Dominic stood up and turned to Maria. She was standing behind him with tears streaming down her cheeks. He handed her the baby and then returned to Sally.

But Sally was gone.

Maria knew she was gone. It almost felt like her sweet spirit flew away right in front of them. Taking a seat beside his wife on the bed, Dominic lay his body over Sally's and wept.

Chapter Nineteen

"She is the only wet nurse I could find. My daughter must eat." Dominic ran a hand through his hair in vexation. He and Maria were about to kill each other, and they'd only buried Sally this morning. In San Francisco, everything moved fast, including death.

"Her lips are rouged." Maria placed her hands on her hips.

"Most of the women in San Francisco rouge their lips."

"You could not find an Indian mother at the mission?"

"I did not go to the mission." Dominic strode past her.

She trailed him down the hotel's upstairs hallway, grabbing him by the arm and halting him there. "That soiled dove will poison Maria Elizabeth."

Dominic spun around. "Maria, so help me, I am at my wit's end with you! My children are not yours! They are mine!" he yelled in her face.

Maria let go of his arm. "Find an Indian wet nurse!" she yelled back.

"You find an Indian wet nurse!"

"I will!" Putting both hands to his chest, Maria shoved him as hard as she could.

Dominic barely moved. He clenched his fists at his sides.

With a will, Maria swept around him and swooshed down the hall to her room. There she threw open her sea chest and pulled out her white duck trousers and a striped sailor's shirt. Dropping her dress and bloomers to the floor, she threw on the pants and shirt over her chemise. She absolutely hated the tarpaulin hat, but she gathered up her hair, tucked it all under, and resolutely stuffed the hat on her head.

By the time she reached the stable, her anger had cooled some. Both she and Dominic were growing desperate. The babe hadn't eaten yet.

Without a word to anyone, she took Dominic's horse from the stall. She didn't bother to saddle the big roan gelding, knowing she could ride the animal faster without a saddle that didn't fit her. As soon as she led the horse out into the fog, she swung onto its back like any vaquero would and kicked the gelding into a gallop. Her tarpaulin hat had blown off by the time she'd cleared Portsmouth Square with the animal running full speed.

Men yelled as she raced past late that afternoon. The fog was rolling into the city like a gray beast, consuming the place. She veered around mule-pulled carts and carriages led by horses. An Oriental man with a long braided pigtail yelled after her in a language she'd never heard before when she nearly ran him over as he crossed the street. Large tents lined the plaza. Already they were filled with men and laughter and banjos and fiddles banging out lively music. The night hadn't even begun. A woman garbed in sailor's gear riding a horse as if the very devil was on her heels wasn't the strangest thing anyone would ever see in San Francisco. Strange goings-on were commonplace. Dominic did not allow them to leave the hotel after the noon meal. Mornings were safest in San Francisco. Chloe loved the colorful chaos of the city, but Maria found it disconcerting. Too many men. She'd never been out in the city alone, but nothing mattered now except finding a suitable wet nurse for Maria Elizabeth. The baby still hadn't cried or eaten, and she slept most of the time.

Nicky had howled his head off from the moment he'd left Sally's womb. His wet nurse said she'd never seen a child so robust. So thirsty. When the rouged woman said Maria Elizabeth wouldn't eat, Maria wanted to take a rod to the woman's back. Instead, she'd walked out of the room and gone straight to Dominic's room. When she barged into his room without knocking on the door, he'd captured her by the elbow and marched her right back out into the hall, where they'd had their argument. He'd taken off his jacket and his shirt was unbuttoned, leaving his chest exposed. This came to her as she raced across the scrub hills on her way to the mission several miles away. She'd felt those muscles under her hands. Had she embarrassed him by catching him in a state of undress? He didn't seem embarrassed, he seemed exasperated.

Everything felt raw and unreal. It still seemed impossible that Sally was gone. Had they really laid her to rest in the Sailor's Burial Ground on Telegraph Hill, where new graves appeared daily? Because she wasn't Catholic, Sally couldn't be buried in the mission cemetery. Nicky had clung to Maria during the ceremony, utterly unlike his unruly self. Dominic had paid a hotel maid to sit with Maria Elizabeth. Chloe had stood there weeping alone until Gavilan wrapped a protective arm around her shoulders. The girl had turned and sobbed against his chest. Maria hadn't cried at the funeral. She had no tears left after weeping all night in a chair in Sally's hotel room with Maria Elizabeth asleep in her arms.

Dominic had sung one of Sally's favorite hymns after the minister finished reading about a woman more precious than rubies from the Bible he held in his hands. The minister had tried to sing along but hardly knew the words. Maria wasn't even sure he was a real minister since he'd taken the money Dominic offered him to come to the cemetery on the hill. When Dominic began to sing with all his heart after the minister closed in prayer, it had stunned her. Nicky had raised his head from her shoulder and stared at his father too. The fog above their heads hadn't interfered with the view where the ocean met the horizon. The water had been so blue this morning and so close to this place many simply called "Yerba Buena" now that more than just seamen were laid to rest there in a city no longer predominately Catholic.

Dominic had sung at Steven's funeral with Rachel, their voices intertwining in worship. On the ship, he'd sung by himself when Mr. Andrews died, and then again when Jamie perished overboard during the storm. Dominic's deep, baritone voice always soothed Maria's soul, but something was different today. His voice had grown stronger and sweeter until it felt like the heavens were standing still just to hear him sing. Nicky had stared at his father in wonder, and so had Maria.

She remembered all this as she raced to the mission where she wished Sally could have been buried. A gray wolf trotted across the dunes, and several deer were running ahead of the wolf. More birds than she could ever count filled the sky. Mission Dolores, when she arrived, was deserted, the once sturdy buildings lapsing into decay. The pitiful sight of the religious outpost stunned her. Sally was better off at the Sailors Burial Ground. A rancheria of half-civilized Indians encamped nearby, but they pretended not to understand when Maria pleaded for a woman willing to suckle a babe. She offered the Indians money, and they stared at her wide-eyed and unresponsive, the Indian women nearly naked, the men dressed practically in rags. Everyone wore beads. The naked, dirty children hid from her in their huts. These weren't the mission Indians she'd expected to find here. Cursing them in Spanish, she spun her mount around and kicked up dust in their faces as she rode away.

As evening cast shadows across the sandy hills covered in brush and wild rosebushes, she raced back to San Francisco, her horse foaming with sweat, her hair whipping in the breeze off the ocean. As she neared the city, the tents looked like lanterns on the hills, the gambling halls alive with men and music and raucous laughter.

Desperation was a living thing in her now. Maria Elizabeth needed a suitable wet nurse. She galloped through the streets and didn't stop until she slid to a halt at the stable. Jumping down from her mount, she threw the reins at the Mexican stable boy, who looked at her in her sailor's garb as if she'd lost her mind.

Maria ran to the hotel. She didn't knock on the door of Sally and Dominic's room, just plowed right in, hoping the trollop had managed to nourish Maria Elizabeth. The rouged woman was gone. Dominic sat in the chair holding the baby. He looked up at her, and the resignation on his face nearly stopped Maria in her tracks.

"Where's the painted woman?"

"She's gone. The baby won't eat."

Maria clenched her fists. "Of course she won't eat from that . . ."

Dominic raised his brows.

"That immoral woman." Maria stopped beside the chair and stared down at the tiny face looking up at her from Dominic's lap. The baby's eyes were half-closed. Her breathing was rapid, her chest rising and falling much too fast, like the beating of hummingbird wings.

"The doctor says she's not ready for this world. In a matter of hours, perhaps a day or two at most, she'll be gone."

"No," Maria breathed. She knelt down beside the chair, placing her hand on the baby's silky head. Her hair was dark, like Sally's, and soft as goose down. "She must live," she said vehemently as she stared at the china doll baby. That's what she looked like, a beautiful little china doll. The tears flooding Maria's eyes surprised her. She didn't know she had any tears left after all she'd cried for Sally.

"Nicky has looked everywhere for you. He has run Chloe ragged searching for his Maria. They finally fell asleep in Chloe's bed. You should go check on him."

"We need to find a wet nurse," Maria stubbornly said.

"The wet nurse is no use."

Maria's eyes locked with his. "Of course she is of no use. You brought your daughter a dirty harlot."

"Harlot or not, Maria Elizabeth cannot eat because she is struggling for breath. Put your hand on her chest." Dominic captured Maria's hand and gently placed it on the baby. Her breathing felt shallow and quick, just like those hummingbird wings Maria had imagined. He took her hand off the baby and laced his fingers through hers as he looked into her eyes.

"Nicky needs you. I will take care of Maria Elizabeth until our Heavenly Father takes her home."

Maria tried to pull her hand away. Dominic wouldn't release her. "Accept this, Maria."

"Never," she whispered.

"Sally was right. We must surrender to the will of God."

"I will never surrender to the will of God. Give me Maria Elizabeth. I will see that she lives."

Dominic clenched his hand, squeezing Maria's fingers. His grip was painful. "Life and death do not belong to you."

Something she could no longer deny rose up in her as the dark voice filled her thoughts. She repeated what she heard in her head. "Perhaps I do hold life and death in my hands. People die because of me."

Dominic's eyes widened and then narrowed on her. "Do not believe the devil's lies. God gives and takes life. You do not."

Though she tried to pull away, he would not let go of her hand. His grip had grown so tight her fingers were starting to go numb.

"Was it God who plunged the knife into the man who raped me? Where was God in the church that night?"

For a moment, Dominic closed his eyes. When he opened them, he let out his breath wearily. "I have no idea where God was that night. I have no idea why God took Sally. All I know is God gives and takes away, and we must bless his name."

"I will not bless his name!" Maria was finally able to jerk her hand free. "Give me Maria Elizabeth. I will not let you just sit here and watch her die."

"It is not up to you." Dominic returned his attention to the babe. "She is my daughter, not yours. Maria Elizabeth will be buried with her mother."

Maria knew she could never wrestle the babe from him. Her mind began to spin a plan. "I am sorry she is not mine. I will see to Nicky." She walked from the room without looking back.

Chapter Twenty

Morning dawned in a blanket of fog. Maria had convinced Dominic to find the wet nurse harlot. He didn't think it would do any good, but he walked several blocks, roused the woman out of bed, and came back to the hotel with her. When he walked through the door of his room followed by the wet nurse, he immediately knew he'd been fooled. The room was empty.

He shoved money into the woman's hand and told her to go home as he strode down the hall to Chloe's room. She and Nicky were asleep in the same bed, but both of them awoke when he barged into the room. "Where's Maria?"

"I don't know." Chloe's hair was a mess, and she looked like a shadow of her usually vibrant self.

"Me want Maria," Nicky said stubbornly, and the look on his little face reminded Dominic of the rebellious look Maria had mastered in his presence.

"I want Maria too," Dominic said, trying to sooth his son. He turned to his sister. "Maria has taken the babe. I must find her. Do not let Nicky out of your sight."

He strode out and returned to his room, where he threw on his cloak and packed a few things. He didn't know what he needed or where he was going, but his first stop was the stable. Sure enough, he found his gelding gone.

"Did she have a babe with her?" he asked the stable boy.

"Maybe, she did not swing onto the horse as I've seen her do. She asked me to help her into the saddle, and she held on to a bundle under her cloak. She never has me saddle a mount for her—she always rides bareback—but she wanted a saddle today."

"Get me another horse. A fast one. Did she say where she was going?" Dominic followed the boy as he rushed to ready another animal.

"She mentioned that she hadn't seen her family in a long time."

That was enough for Dominic. He'd suspected Maria might try to get to Lupe after telling him this morning that Lupe would know what to do for Maria Elizabeth. Against his better judgment, he'd left her sitting in the chair cradling his tiny daughter. The baby hardly seemed conscious.

The stable boy selected a big black horse. The horse was more wild-eyed than Dominic would have liked, but there was no doubt this horse was fast. The boy had him saddled in seconds, and they were out the barn door in no time at all.

The fog-shrouded city was just coming alive. Mule-drawn carts pulling loads of every kind of ware filled the streets, including lumber. It wouldn't be long before his mansion was inhabitable on the hill. There was still much work to be done on the dwelling, but it would be livable soon. Several other homes on the hill above Portsmouth Square were already finished. Dominic couldn't believe Wade owned one of those dwellings. A few weeks ago, he'd found several of the carpenters he'd originally hired working on Wade's house. He hadn't known it was Wade's place until he spoke with the head carpenter.

"Captain Reynolds doubled our pay. Eggs are selling for a dollar a piece. Potatoes a dollar fifty a pound in the city. We couldn't turn down his offer to finish his place first. We'll get back to yours soon as we're done here," the head carpenter had told him.

"I'll find another crew," Dominic had informed the man. He hadn't yet seen Wade on the hill. The whole thing frustrated him to no end. He kept a tight rein on his high-headed horse until he left the plaza. It was unbelievable that Maria had taken his daughter and fled the city. At least he suspected she'd fled the city. He really wasn't sure where she'd gone, but his guess was Rancho de los Robles. Perhaps he was even more surprised Maria Elizabeth was still amongst the living this morning. He'd thought the babe would slip away in his arms during the night. After praying for hours while holding her, mostly that he would accept the Lord's will in the taking of his wife and daughter, he'd drifted to sleep in the chair.

Maria had awoken him that morning. "Let's see if she will eat." Her hand was eager on his arm, her gaze on the babe filled with desperate longing.

Dominic unwrapped the babe and saw her chest still rose and fell with breath.

"Please let me hold her," Maria pleaded.

He could not stand the grief he saw in Maria's eyes. She wore her cloak, the same one he'd purchased for her in Boston several years ago. He'd thought she wore her nightgown underneath it, but when he looked down at her feet, he saw boots. "Are you going somewhere?"

"I was going to look for the wet nurse with the rouged lips," she'd said very submissively. "Perhaps Maria Elizabeth will suckle today."

Dominic had looked at his daughter and known she wasn't long for this earth, but Maria sounded so hopeful he wasn't about to tell her that. "I'll go fetch the wet nurse." He'd wrapped the baby back up in the blankets and handed her over to Maria.

The smile that slipped onto Maria's lips was worth his efforts. He'd felt absolutely helpless watching Sally die. He felt the same now with the babe. He understood the desperation on Maria's face. If he could make his daughter live, he would. He'd give his own life in place of Sally's. In place of his tiny daughter's. If he could barter with God, he would. But the hand of the Almighty was heavy upon him. *Accept this,* he heard in his spirit. Each time he asked for mercy, pleaded for mercy from God, *accept this,* returned to him.

Maria had settled herself in the chair and cradled the babe to her chest. When he'd returned to Boston, Maria's great love for his son had stunned him. He'd never expected this maternal bent in her that just seemed to grow stronger each day. Sally had loved their son, but she hadn't cared for him. Maria cared for Nicky. The boy ate with her. Slept with her. Played with her morning, noon, and night. The two were always together. Dominic couldn't get over it. Maria didn't look like a mother. She looked like an actress born for a stage, but her mothering instincts were the strongest Dominic had ever seen in a woman.

"Do you want to remove your cloak?" he'd asked, watching her settle herself with his daughter.

"No, I am cold. San Francisco is always cold."

"Do you miss Rancho de los Robles's sunny hills?"

"I miss Lupe. She would know how to save Maria Elizabeth."

Dominic raced his wild horse in this direction now because of those words. If Maria wasn't headed for Rancho de los Robles, he would eat his own hat. Fortunately, he'd packed a sack of food, enough for himself and Maria if he found her, so he wouldn't have to eat his hat.

Once the stallion was worn down after hours on the trail, he became a good, strong mount. The horse was certainly faster than the gelding Maria rode, but he suspected Maria was a better rider than him, though she did carry his babe, which would slow her down quite a bit. The El Camino Real was worn enough by other travelers to easily follow between San Francisco and Monterey. Most of the way to Rancho de los Robles was on this ancient road. Surely, Maria would know to follow The King's Highway, as the Americans called it.

After leaving the foggy San Francisco Peninsula, he rode south for the Santa Clara Valley, where the sun shone down and he paused to secure his cloak to the back of his saddle. He turned toward the coast once more in the direction of Monterey that evening. Around every bend in the road, he expected to find Maria riding ahead of him, but on he went through redwoods and oak groves without a glimpse of her. Farther inland, the weather was beautiful, warm and sunny and perfectly enjoyable without the fog. Sometimes he wondered if he should settle farther from the ocean to take advantage of California's mild climate, but he had no idea how he'd make a living out here in one of these fertile valleys. He wasn't a farmer. All he knew was the sea, but he'd just made a fortune in real estate, selling much of the land he'd purchased several years ago in sleepy Yerba Buena. Never had he dreamed a gold rush would send San Francisco's real estate sky high, men paying in handfuls of gold since coin was still scarce in California.

He had Gavilan down at the wharf running his new shipping business. Already they'd hired a new captain and first mate for *The White Swallow*, and sent her off to Boston with a load of hides and a plan to bring mining supplies and passengers around the Horn. His partners back in Boston would certainly approve of that. They'd be surprised to see a new captain and first mate, but what could they do? Dominic had his own fortune now. He was negotiating the purchase of several more ships in the harbor abandoned by their crews, but not by their captains and officers. Sending these ships back to Boston stocked with hides and then returning them here full of mining supplies and passengers willing to pay a fortune to get to the goldfields would be a lucrative business. For now, he was done sailing. He wanted to stay home in his mansion on the hill, return to his family each night after working in an office down at the harbor, but he no longer had a wife to return to, and soon his tiny daughter would be gone as well.

Sally had made him and Maria promise to do what was best for the children. No longer would he have to answer to his parents or worry about Maria not being Protestant here in San Francisco. He couldn't see why he shouldn't marry her, considering that would probably be best for Nicky. Nobody in the city would question a quick union if he and Maria didn't kill each other first. Last night had been a full moon so Dominic decided to ride on as long as he could see the road. The moon didn't disappoint him. It illuminated the path, and he moved his horse along more carefully after sunset. He couldn't stand the thought of Maria and his daughter alone in a country with bears and wolves and panthers aplenty, and perhaps outlaws as well. The last time he'd ridden this road, he'd come upon the scene of Steven's murder.

A small fire alerted him to a camp along the road. He knew it was Maria before he rode up to the fire. He didn't know how he knew, he just knew. Stepping off his horse, he led the stallion over to a tree and tied it there. His gelding stood nearby, tied to another tree. His heart pounded as he walked over to Maria. She sat crossed-legged on the ground beside the fire, rocking something in her lap. He knew she rocked his daughter. By the look on Maria's face, his dead daughter.

"Maria," he said gently. She looked up at him, the firelight illuminating her beautiful face. The agony in his soul matched hers. Never had he seen that kind of look in someone's eyes before. He worried for her sanity. "Maria," he said again, kneeling beside her. She leaned over and fell right into his arms. It knocked Dominic onto his back on the ground, with her on top of him, the baby pressed between them. The little body was already stiffening. His daughter had looked like a doll when she was born. Now she felt like a doll between their bodies. "Oh, Maria," he said, wrapping his arms around her.

She began to howl like a wild animal. He rolled onto his side so he could see her face, holding her tightly in his arms. He didn't try to take his daughter from her. In death, the baby belonged to both of them. Maria screamed for several minutes and then began to sob. Her sobs were so violent Dominic worried she would injure herself. He held on to her as best he could, wondering if she'd lost her mind. It struck him that he needed to pray. Fervently, he began to pray. Soon he was praying out loud for God to deliver Maria from this awful spell.

It seemed like hours before she quieted. The grass was soft and smelled sweet under his cheek as he laid his head to rest once she'd fallen asleep against his chest. The fire was only embers now, and he wondered if he should stoke it back up to keep the wild animals at bay. He was grateful Maria's wailing hadn't drawn any predators into their camp. He tried not to think about bears as he closed his eyes. After his encounter with the grizzly in California a few years ago, bears were what scared him the most.

How long they slept, he didn't know, but Maria awoke before he did. He felt her moving against him when he came awake. She was sitting up, staring down at the baby she held. Lying beside her, he sat up too. "Please, may I have her?" he asked softly. The sanity had returned to Maria's eyes, but she still looked shattered.

Wordlessly, she handed him Maria Elizabeth. Dominic kissed the baby's cold forehead and then gently rolled her up in her blanket. He stood up and carried the baby to his saddle. He had another blanket tied there under his cloak, and he pulled that loose and rolled the baby in that too. Then he tied his daughter on top of his cloak. What else could he do? He wasn't about to bury Maria Elizabeth here alone in the wilderness. He'd already decided she would be laid to rest beside Steven at Ranch de los Robles, which was far closer than traveling all the way home to San Francisco.

He walked back to Maria. He hadn't realized she was dressed like a sailor until that very moment. Her cloak was folded near the fire, which smoked just a little now, nothing left of it but warm ashes. She had no bedroll, no saddlebags that he could see. "Have you eaten?"

She shook her head. He went back to his horse and pulled some bread and dried beef out of his saddlebag and a bota of water. Returning to her, he offered her the food and drink. She wouldn't take it. Sitting down beside her, he offered it again. She refused.

"I'm sorry," she whispered. "Everybody dies because of me." Her eyes were so haunted.

He put the food and bota down on the grass and took her face in his hands. "Maria Elizabeth died because she came too soon." Maria shook her head, and he held her face more firmly. "Believe me, Maria, her death belongs to God, not to you."

"I am cursed," Maria whispered, and tears spilled down her cheeks.

Dominic used his thumbs to gently wipe the tears from her face. "You are not cursed." He kissed her forehead, and she turned her face up to his. Oh so sweetly, he kissed her mouth. A kiss to remind her she was alive. And he was alive. And life would go on. She began to cry again and leaned against him. He lay back on the grass, holding her. They both fell asleep again, having gone days with very little rest.

He awoke staring up into the endless blue sky of mid-morning. His body responded to Maria pressed against him in spite of himself. Determinedly turning his thoughts to Nicky, he wondered how his son was faring with his sister. Surely, Gavilan would come to the hotel when he didn't show up today at the office building they'd purchased at the wharf. He'd told Chloe to ask Gavilan to sleep in one of the hotel rooms until he returned so his first mate could watch over her and Nicky at night if he did not return with Maria right away. San Francisco at night was a dangerous place.

Should he leave Maria at Rancho de los Robles? Perhaps that would be best, but he didn't want to face his son without her. No other woman would love Nicky the way Maria loved him. The boy had lost his mother. He didn't need to lose Maria too. And Maria certainly didn't need to lose Nicky. The realization that it wasn't really up to him alarmed Dominic. Once he took Maria home, she would be under her Uncle Pedro's and Roman's authority. Californian women were ruled by their men. She might even be put back under a dueña. And constantly chaperoned. Spanish families did that. He pressed his cheek against her hair as she slept. It had grown out and smelled so sweet. Felt silky-soft against his face. He tried not to think about her body pressed against him. Once they returned to Rancho de los Robles, he might never get to touch her again.

Maybe they shouldn't ride on to Rancho de los Robles today. Maybe he should take Maria back to San Francisco. Bury the babe with Sally and get Chloe, Maria, and Nicky moved into the mansion as soon as possible. Go on with life on his terms.

His terms.

Was anything on his terms anymore? Had life ever really been on his terms? In the past several years, he'd buried four people he dearly loved. Steven, Nate, Jamie, Sally, and soon he would bury his daughter. Had he lost all these people because of his terms?

Is this my punishment for desiring Maria?

He didn't want to think this way, but he couldn't help himself. The sky was so blue as he looked into the vastness of the heavens. Absolutely endless blue with no answers. In his arms,

Maria fit so perfectly, like her body was made for his. He'd tried to leave her in California. Tried to never think about her again. Tried to do the right thing. He'd married Sally and done exactly what he thought the Lord would have him do. Yet here he was with Maria, the two of them alive while Sally was dead. And they both were so wounded. Their hearts so ravaged. Perhaps they both were cursed. The spoiled girl Maria used to be was gone. The flirtatious girl gone too. The spitfire in her was still there, but she fought now for others. Maria had fought for Sally. And Nicky. And Maria Elizabeth. Would she ever fight for him?

Since he'd walked away on that snowy street several years ago on his wedding day, he could do nothing right with Maria. He'd denied his love for her and married Sally. Was this why Maria seemed to hate him now? Yet she mothered his children more than his wife had. Maria's love was so fierce. Could she ever love him with this fierce love again? He longed to just get lost in her. He was tired of doing the right thing. He just wanted to let go of everything else and hold on to Maria.

Chapter Twenty-One

Maria hadn't said a word since she woke up in his arms. She untangled herself from him and walked into the trees. When she returned, he handed her food and water. She ate and drank just a little, then went to saddle her horse. He walked over and put the saddle on for her. When he turned around to see what she was doing, she was standing at his saddled horse with her hand on Maria Elizabeth rolled up in the blanket. "Do you want to ride with the babe?" he asked.

She nodded and bridled the black horse herself. After mounting the stallion, she untied the babe. Taking the lifeless bundle into her arms, she rode that way, holding his daughter for the rest of the day. It was the most poignant thing he'd ever seen. He'd never met a woman like Maria. As the sun set that evening, she rode into the rancho's yard ahead of him, carrying his dead daughter home with her.

Roman was the first to greet them. He swept Maria off the horse and held her in his arms for a long time, the babe wrapped in the blanket between them. Rachel came out onto the porch with a dark-haired child in her arms and another one holding on to her skirts. When she recognized them, she took the older child's hand and hurried down the steps. Dominic got off his gelding and embraced her. The children were smiling because their parents smiled.

"Oh my goodness," said Rachel. "You've brought Maria home!" Rachel and Roman traded places, Rachel hugging Maria as Roman stepped over and captured Dominic in a bear hug.

Dominic could hardly swallow. The emotion swelled in his throat till he found it hard to breathe. Roman squeezing him so tight added to his lack of oxygen.

"Dom!" Roman clapped his hands on Dominic's cheeks after squeezing him. "So good to see you, *mi amigo!*"

"Yes, it is good," Dominic said, turning his gaze to Roman's children, a boy and a girl. The boy was the oldest, standing at his mother's side, looking like a miniature Roman.

"This is Estéban. And here is Maria Domitilla. We call her Tillie." Roman took the little girl from her mother's arms. "She has your eyes and your spirit," he told Maria. The child was perhaps close to two years old with her father's black hair and those green Vasquez eyes.

"She's beautiful. You have named her after me and our mother?" Maria smiled at the child and then at Roman.

Roman put his arm around Rachel. Now that she wasn't holding her daughter, Dominic could see she was expecting again, the gentle swell of her abdomen revealing another babe on the way. He laughed in spite of himself. In spite of his own babe they would bury tomorrow. He kneeled down to stare at Roman and Rachel's son. The boy also had his father's raven hair, green eyes, and swarthy features. He was a handsome boy, a year or so older than Nicky. "Hello, Estéban. You are named after Steven, I suppose."

Roman smiled proudly, as did Rachel. "Yes, and he is a sensitive boy who loves Jesúcristo."

Dominic put his hand on the boy's head. "You are a fine lad," he said.

Estéban grinned at him.

Maria was staring at the bundle in her arms as tears streamed down her face. Dominic stepped over to her, wrapping his arm around her waist. "God has given us another Maria," he said, feeling a swell of intense sweetness rising up in him. "Your niece, Maria Domitilla, does have your eyes."

Roman and Rachel stepped in close. Roman put his arm around his sister too. His other arm was wrapped around Rachel. Estéban had returned to his mother's skirt, anchoring his small brown hand on her blue dress.

"We must say a prayer of thanksgiving," Roman said, bowing his head. "Heavenly Father, thank you for bringing Maria home to us. Thank you for *mi hermano*, Dom, being here. We see Dom and Maria are hurting. You are the great healer. You see all and know all. Bring healing to your people, Jesúcristo. We pray in your name, amen."

Dominic opened his eyes and laughed through his tears. He laughed because God had done this thing. Taken a Maria and given a Maria. Hope for the future hit him like a fresh wind after a terrible calm. He saw hope on Maria's face too. Her eyes were still on the beautiful niece named after her.

"When you disappeared from California, we did not know if you were alive or dead," Roman said to Maria. "We did not get Dom's letter for several years."

Maria's gaze flew to Rachel, and Dominic could see the weight of killing Rachel's father lay heavy upon her. He pulled Maria snugly to his side. "I cannot say Maria enjoyed Boston, but my son cannot live without her, and I have lost my wife, so Maria must return to San Francisco with me soon." He said it with authority, with confident hope, his gaze firmly on Roman.

Roman looked from Dominic to Maria, then back again. "I am sorry your wife is gone. She was a believer?"

"More so than most," Dominic assured him.

"Then she is in heaven with Steven, where we all hope to be someday." Roman smiled, and his eyes shone with light. Dominic could not get over the change in his friend. They'd once beat each other senseless, killed a bear and an outlaw together. The man standing before him now appeared a gentle father and adoring husband, and a strong man of God.

"Yes, that is our hope." Dominic squeezed Maria's waist. What was she thinking? Her eyes were still on the little girl in her brother's arms, her cheeks wet with tears. "Maria holds my daughter, Maria Elizabeth. I'd like to bury the babe next to Steven in the morning."

Dominic turned to Maria and took the bundle from her arms.

The smiles slipped off of Roman's and Rachel's faces. Roman handed his own daughter to Rachel. "Take the children and Maria into the house," he gently told Rachel.

"Of course." Rachel swept the children toward the porch.

Maria remained rooted at Dominic's side. "I will stay and help with the babe."

Roman looked at his sister and then put his hand on Dominic's shoulder. "I am sorry, amigo. Christ has called you to suffer. May he strengthen you as well."

"Thank you." Holding the bundled babe cradled in one arm, he kept his other arm firmly around Maria.

"Let's put the babe in Steven's room. The room with the heavenly painting." Roman's eyes lingered on Maria. She still appeared in a state of shock. Dominic was just glad she'd found her voice, once more proclaiming she would stay beside him.

"I will see to the horses," Roman offered.

Right away, Maria led Dominic, carrying the babe, to the room where he and Roman had carried Steven's body several years ago. Dominic placed his tiny daughter on the bed, rolled in the blankets, and looked up at the painting of heaven above the bed. It had so comforted him when he and Roman laid Steven there. Without faith in heaven, he wondered how people went on after losing a loved one.

Maria lay down on the bed beside the babe. She curled into a fetal position alongside his daughter and closed her eyes. Dominic took a seat on the bed beside her. "They really are in heaven," he said softly. "We will all be reunited there one day on those golden streets."

A sob shook Maria's body. Dominic put his hand on her shoulder. "Oh, Maria."

"I am not going to heaven," she whispered with her eyes still closed. "I am bound for hell."

"No." Dominic lay down beside her, pulling her into his arms. "Please, Maria, surrender to God. Ask his forgiveness for your sins. Jesus died on a cross so you can go to heaven too. We are all sinners in need of the Savior. I too have killed a man."

Maria opened her eyes and looked at him. "Who have you killed?"

"I shot the outlaw who murdered Steven."

"I thought Roman killed him."

"Roman's arm was damaged. He was weak with blood loss. I knew the shot was mine to take. I have asked God to forgive me for killing that man."

"I am not sorry for killing Rachel's father. I will not ask God to forgive me." The look in Maria's eyes frightened Dominic. She wasn't ready to surrender to God. After all she'd been through, he thought she'd turn to God, but he could see her turning away.

"We all must ask for God's forgiveness."

"I will not ask." She closed her eyes.

He put his hand on her face. There was a sad and haunted beauty about her now that deeply unsettled him. How could he reach her? How could he change her heart that was growing so hard?

Nicky. It had to be Nicky. "We will return to San Francisco. Nicky needs you."

Maria opened her eyes. A vulnerability was there that he hadn't seen since his wedding day. "I need you," he whispered. He heard the door open as if from a great distance.

A young woman stood in the door frame. She had long, straight dark hair and blue eyes. Her skin was darkened by the sun. "Isabella!" Maria cried and jumped up from the bed. The sisters flew into each other's arms.

"We thought you were dead." Isabella's words were filled with joy. "When the letter arrived that you were with Captain Mason in Boston, it was like you'd been resurrected. We had a grand fiesta in your honor."

"Where are Tia Josefa and Tio Pedro?"

Isabella's joy turned to sorrow. "Mama passed last year."

"No," Maria breathed.

"She did not suffer. She died in her sleep. We don't know why. Mama went to bed one night after praying her rosary and did not wake up the next morning."

"And Tio?"

"Papa has gone to Monterey. To find out about the gold. Gold is all he thinks about these days."

Maria cupped Isabella's face in her hands. "I am sorry about your mama. My goodness, you have grown up," she said with a laughing sob.

"Are you Captain Mason's wife?"

"And still speaking your mind." Maria tweaked her sister's cheek. "Sally is Captain Mason's wife."

Dominic joined the sisters where they stood by the door. "Sally is in heaven with Steven. And your mama. And my daughter, Maria Elizabeth." He pointed to the bundle of blankets on the bed.

Slowly, Isabella realized what was on the bed wrapped in the blankets. "Oh no, you've lost a child? I was out riding when you arrived. Roman told me you were home, and I ran to the house. Roman called after me to wait, but I just had to see you." Tears filled Isabella's blue eyes.

"Well, here I am," said Maria, and the change in her demeanor made Dominic smile.

Californio funerals always turned into fiestas. They buried Maria Elizabeth beside Steven that morning, and by evening, the Indians were playing their instruments in the courtyard with gusto. The music of her childhood filled Maria with unexpected pleasure. Everyone feasted and danced. Tio Pedro had returned from Monterey with a party of men on their way to the goldfields, all Californios looking for a way to win back their wealth and honor and their old lives of parties and gambling and a relatively carefree existence. Many Californios had lost their livelihoods during the American takeover, Roman explained that night at dinner.

Her brother's great faith unnerved Maria. He reminded her now of Steven, the minister, always speaking of God. The men with Tio Pedro, on the other hand, were as thirsty for brandy as her uncle. They weren't bad men, but they were getting drunk, and that made Maria nervous. They had not been there that morning for Maria Elizabeth's burial. Some of them were young, some middle-aged, some old. Gold made men forget their age, forget everything but the promises of riches in the goldfields. They'd arrived with several horse-drawn wagons loaded down with mining supplies. Maria could see Isabella was overcome with the gold-seekers' excitement, and there was no fear of men in her. She laughed and danced with Tio Pedro's friends and looked so grown up and beautiful and vivacious. Maria wondered, had she ever been like that?

Of course she had. Californiana girls were known for their vivaciousness, their sparkling eyes and dexterous dances. Of course she'd once been like that when she was young, but no more. When she finally took to the floor to dance at Tio Pedro's insistence, all her agony came out. She could no longer dance with joy. She danced with sorrow. The musicians caught on, and their music turned dark and grieving, like Maria's soul. Before she'd finished dancing, Tio Pedro had gone to the Indians and made them stop playing. They struck up a waltz, and Tio Pedro led Isabella onto the floor.

Roman headed for Maria. "Do you remember how to dance with me, *hermana*?" he asked. "Tio is not going to let you ruin his party, you know." Roman smiled at her.

"Do men of God dance?" she asked.

Roman threw back his head and laughed. "There is a time to dance. You should read the Bible."

"You read the Bible," she said with some of her old fire. "That's not for me."

Roman took her in his arms. "You will follow me," he said, and for a moment she felt like a little sister in his arms again.

"I will make you follow me," she challenged.

"Well, we will see." He swung her around the courtyard as the stars came out.

For a while, they settled into a battle of wills over who would lead. Of course, Roman won because he always won; he was much too strong to overpower, and neither of them wanted to miss a step in the dance and look stupid and less Spanish. In his arms, the sadness left her, and she was transported back to the carefree girl she'd once been. The girl who not only wanted her way, but demanded her way. Pretty soon Roman was laughing.

"You always do this," he said.

She grinned at him as they swirled around the floor. "Do what?"

"End up having your way."

"Am I having my way?"

"I am leading, but the dance is yours."

They swirled around the floor and came upon Dominic and Rachel standing together watching them. The children had been handed off to dueñas. Roman stopped right in front of them and swung Maria into Dominic's arms. "She is yours," he said with a laugh. "I can do nothing with her. You try, amigo." Roman swept Rachel, in a beautiful ball gown the color of her blue eyes, into a waltz, and off they went.

Dominic wasted no time following them around the floor with Maria in his arms. She was wearing one of her old dresses, a striking gown. During the siesta that afternoon, Rachel, Isabella, and Maria had all gone to the creek together to swim and bathe. The day was sorrowful but also full of rejoicing. It was good to be home. Maria had always loved swimming in the creek on a warm summer day. They'd washed their hair, and Indian maids had styled it for them when they returned to the hacienda. Maria hadn't felt beautiful in a long time, but she did tonight with Dominic's gaze upon her.

"If I could take your sadness away, I would," he said as they danced.

"It is a sadness we share." There wasn't another place on earth she'd rather be at that very moment than in his arms.

"One day all our tears will be washed away."

"Perhaps." She smiled into his eyes. "Are you leading, or am I?"

"Of course I am leading." He grinned.

"I am not so sure," she challenged.

He tightened his hold on her. He was not Spanish, and he was not Roman, but he could dance better than any American she'd ever seen waltz—except Wade. The roguish ship captain came to mind, but she pushed him from her thoughts. She'd only given Wade the time of day because Dominic didn't want her. The older ship captain made her tremble and made her feel like a desirable woman. But nobody made her feel like Dominic made her feel.

He will die because of you.

The dark voice descended out of nowhere. It so shocked and unsettled her that she stumbled in her steps. Dominic looked at her in surprise, nearly picked her off her feet, carrying her through the dance before she recovered in his arms.

"What's wrong?" Dominic held her more tightly now.

The dark voice was gone as quickly as it had come. "I am thirsty," she lied. "And tired."

He walked her off the floor and took her over to the table that held wine and brandy decanters. Maria ignored the men nearby who refilled their glasses again and again.

"Would you like to go for a walk?" Dominic handed her a glass of wine. He took a glass too and reached for her hand. Roman had put no restrictions on them, and Tio Pedro was too drunk now to do so. He was speaking with the men as they gulped down their brandy, every word about the gold rush.

Dominic didn't understand this lust for gold. He had no desire to see the elephant for himself. This is what everyone asked in California these days. "Have you seen the elephant?" They were talking about the gold in the goldfields. The elephant story came from an old farmer who longed with all his heart to see a real elephant. When a circus came to a nearby town, he took his wagon, loaded for market, by way of the circus, where the elephant led a parade. The farmer was spellbound by the elephant, but his horses were terrified of the giant beast. They bucked and pitched and overturned the wagon, scattering the farmer's vegetables to the four winds. But the farmer was so pleased having seen the elephant that he looked at his toppled wagon and proclaimed, "I don't give a hang! I have seen the elephant!"

Having seen the elephant summed up the lure of gold in California, the thrill of discovering wealth, as well as the disappointments and hardships most miners faced along the way. "Men are losing their minds over gold," Dominic told Maria as they stepped out into the darkness with a thousand stars overhead.

"Isabella said Tio Pedro was a shell of himself after Tia Josefa died, and then he heard about the gold. Gold has brought him alive again."

"Gold is a terrible thing to live for." Dominic took her hand and tucked it into the crook of his arm.

"Men have lived for lesser things." She savored being close to him.

"And men have lived for greater things. What do you think of me becoming a delegate for the California convention, and then perhaps a senator? I'd like to help California join the Union."

"A senator?" Maria smiled. "You would make a fine senator, Captain Mason."

But he won't live that long. The dark voice suddenly came and filled Maria with dread.

Chapter Twenty-Two

In bed that night, Maria could not escape the dark voice. She tossed and turned, but it would not leave her. She shivered in her bed, cold when she shouldn't be cold. When she finally fell asleep, she dreamed of bears killing Dominic. The following morning, she walked the vineyard alone. At the height of summer, the vines were green and lush, bearing tiny grapes. In September, the grapes would ripen, but she didn't plan on being here for the harvest. The August day was already warm. She continued down to the creek and removed everything but her chemise and bloomers. Wading into the stream, she stared down at the clear, cool water swirling around her legs. She didn't care that her bloomers got wet. She sat down and let the water carry her into the bathing hole, a wide pool surrounded by boulders and trees, the sky so blue overhead. The water was warmer in the pool. She swam around as she had when she was a girl, savoring the tranquil beauty of the small paradise.

Doves cooed in the trees, and a deer coming down for a drink bounded back into the undergrowth when it saw her. The water was more than refreshing. A bit numbing. She wanted to be numb. She wanted to stop thinking. Stop wondering if Dominic would die because of her.

"You should not swim alone," he called when he stepped out of the trees. "I've been looking for you."

She watched Dominic strip off his shirt and swiftly remove his boots. Before she knew it, he was in the pool with her, diving under the water, then rising to the surface and swimming toward her in his britches. This would be the perfect dream if it were a dream, but it wasn't a dream. She could not escape the fact that he might die because of her. A bittersweet smile flowered on her face as he swam to her. She stood shoulder-deep in the water waiting for him. The creek flowed into this wide area, where it settled and swirled before narrowing into a flowing stream again and disappearing around a bend.

Dominic stood up when he reached her. His bare chest took her breath away. He was as muscular as she remembered, with golden-brown chest hair that matched the hair on his head. She found it hard to breathe; he was so handsome.

"I sure hope nobody finds us out here," he said, and it struck her that she really didn't know this side of him. The respectable Yankee ship captain she knew would never swim in a stream with her in her underclothes.

"Have you lost your mind?" She could not stop smiling now.

"Maybe I have. I'm tired of doing the right thing. I'm letting myself do what I've always wanted to do with you."

She could reach out and touch him, but she didn't. She stepped back, away from him in the water, stopping when her chemise plastered to her body in the shallows of the pool. The chemise stuck to her skin, revealing her curves, and she quickly stepped back into deeper water for modesty's sake.

Dominic was not deterred. He came until he stood within arm's reach of her. "Let's make a life together, Maria." His blue eyes were so full of longing that she closed her own eyes so she didn't have to look at him.

He will die . . .

She shook her head at the dark voice, willing it away. Willing hope into her heart as his hands settled on her shoulders. He pulled her to him, and water rippled out from between their bodies. Then he kissed her liked she'd always dreamed he would kiss her. Without reservation. Without restraint. Without anything between them. Not even the water. She put her arms around his neck, molded her body to his, and savored this surrender.

He kissed her for an endless time there in the water. It wasn't cold with his warm body pressed to hers. Nothing had ever felt so delicious, Dominic's big, hard frame molded against her soft curves.

"I trust I will be attending your wedding soon, amigo," Roman called from the trees.

When they heard his voice, Dominic immediately released her. She quickly swam away from him.

Roman was astride his golden stallion. "I am headed for the roundup. You two should come and help."

Dominic swam to shore and walked from the water. He pulled on his boots and donned his shirt as he spoke with Roman about the roundup.

Maria stayed in the pool until Roman waved his arm, and then rode off into the trees.

"Should we marry here or in San Francisco?" Dominic called to her with such happiness.

Her eyes widened and her heart stopped. He truly wanted to marry her?

"I'm not leaving until you give me an answer." His smile was brilliant.

Tears filled her eyes. "We should marry here on the rancho," she managed to call back.

"I'm going to help Roman with the roundup. Do you want to ride along?"

"I will meet you at the stables as soon as I dress for the day. Will you saddle a horse for me while I change into my riding habit?"

"I'll be waiting for you, ready to go when you get there."

Dominic had never felt so happy in his life. Perhaps all the pain of losing Sally and his daughter made his joy more intense. A conviction overcame him that God was rewarding him for doing the right thing by Sally. He had kept his word. Been a faithful husband to a godly woman. Now finally, he would have Maria. Sally had been an obedient wife. He didn't think for a minute Maria would be an obedient wife, but he couldn't wait to marry her. Absolutely couldn't wait to join Maria in the marriage bed.

He walked to the stable in his wet britches. His shirt was damp now too, sticking to his wet body. The day was only getting warmer. He enjoyed his cool clothes. Half his life he'd worn wet clothes. Life on the ocean was always wet. And often turbulent. He realized he enjoyed the excitement of the deep.

Testing himself on an unforgiving ocean. Conquering what seemed unconquerable, the sea that killed more men than she blessed.

"Where is the patron?" he asked the Indian boy he found cleaning a stall when he got to the stables.

"*El patrón* headed for the roundup."

"Are you going?" The Indian boy grinned like he couldn't believe it.

"Of course I'm going."

"Let me saddle a horse for you."

"I can saddle my own horse, thank you. Two horses. I need one for Maria."

Dominic still felt on fire for her. Mercy came with the realization she would soon become his wife and he wouldn't have to fight his feelings for her anymore.

Maria, his wife. A mother to his son.

His smile widened when he realized she was already a mother to Nicky. Where had she put all those golden curls she'd collected on his ship? Probably with her golden rosary tucked in her sea chest. One day curiosity had gotten the better of him, and he'd opened her sea chest after months of it so tempting beside his own in his cabin. He found nothing personal in the chest except her rosary, a golden crucifix worth a small fortune attached to a chain of golden beads. And her knife, reminding him she was made of sterner stuff than most women. At the time, he'd wondered if she'd ever stick that knife in him. It surprised him that life and death lay side by side at the bottom of her sea chest, under her sailing gear. The weapon she'd used to kill and the image of the Savior on the crucifix, offering forgiveness for that sin.

Would she ever accept the Lord's forgiveness? Sally had treated her like a beloved sister in Christ. He knew Maria had some faith, but her faith seemed to be placed in the golden rosary, not in the living God.

Show her who you are, Lord, he prayed as he saddled the horses the Indian boy brought to him. *Do what you must to open her eyes to you.*

He realized the boy was leading the black stallion along with his gelding. "I don't trust that horse," he told the boy.

"Dona Maria will have no problem with this one," the Indian boy said with another surefire grin that rankled Dominic. Obviously, the boy thought he wasn't much of a cowboy.

"You know I'm a ship captain. Have you ever sailed the high seas, son? Ever been around the Horn? Fought a raging storm on the ocean?"

The Indian boy understood he was being put in his place. He stopped smiling. "No, señor, but you need to watch yourself at the round up. A bull killed my grandfather."

The Indian boy handed Dominic a red saddle blanket.

"I'm sorry about your grandfather," he said, feeling foolish now. "The life of the vaquero isn't an easy one. I've seen those wild bulls. They're something fierce." He slapped the red blanket on the black stallion in a hurry, and then cinched on the saddle fast, wanting to get out of the stables and be on his way with Maria. As he saddled his gelding, the boy bridled the black stallion for him.

Maria soon appeared wearing a brown sombero with a bright red braid and an attractive brown riding habit. How beautiful she looked. She spoke kindly to the Indian boy, grinned at him, and swung up on the black stallion in one

226

fluid motion that looked effortless and didn't displace her hat. Dominic felt like a lesser man having to use a stirrup to mount his own horse.

Riding into the sunshine alongside Maria, he realized Rancho de los Robles's fields were no longer full of palominos, as they'd been before the war. The Vasquezes had lost most of their golden herds to the soldiers, but some palominos remained. Such beautiful horses. Golden horses for a golden land. He looked toward the two-story hacienda with her double porches, remembering exactly what Maria felt like pressed against him in the pool. Thankfully, Roman was still the protective brother he'd always been. When he heard Roman calling, for a moment he wondered if Roman would lasso him and drag him to shore. Drag him senseless behind his horse for bathing with Maria. But instead, Roman had basically ordered them to marry. It was exactly what he wanted; Maria would make a fine senator's wife. She was as bold and beautiful and wild just like California.

He was woolgathering since Maria seemed more intent on riding fast then talking to him. Instead of daydreaming about her, he needed to think about his shipping business. Gavilan was stocking a crew even now on the clipper ship *Raven*. The *Raven* still had her captain but had lost the rest of her crew to the gold rush. Fortunately, a few sailors were already returning from the snow-fed Sierra streams, having seen the elephant, no richer for it, and ready to return to their lives at sea. Each day, Gavilan combed the streets for these returning sailors, offering them twice the pay to board the ships headed for Boston with holds full of cattle hides.

Dominic had found the California *mantanza* that often followed a roundup utterly wasteful. Hundreds of dead cattle stripped of their hides, most of the meat left to rot in the fields. Vultures, ravens, coyotes, wolves, and bears feasting together on all the wasted meat. He must speak to Roman about this since the beef could be sold to the miners. A fortune to be made by supplying the men in the goldfields with this meat. Most men saw fortunes to be had in the gold itself. Dominic saw profit in supplying the miners with what they needed. The men also had to get to the goldfields. He and Gavilan already had two ships stocked and headed for Boston. The *Raven* would be their third clipper acquired after being abandoned in San Francisco. These ships would return full of eager passengers paying a pretty penny to get to California and her gold.

He wondered if he and Maria would have green-eyed children. Roman had stamped his offspring utterly Vasquez with those green eyes and ebony hair. The only thing he saw of Rachel in the children was their sweet dispositions. Perhaps God would bless him and Maria with sweet, green-eyed children too. He pictured a green-eyed daughter they could name Sally. Hopefully, she would somehow be blessed with Sally's sweet spirit. Raising a daughter with Maria's indomitable spirit did not appeal to him. He was mad about her, but he didn't want a daughter full of fire like she was. A wife full of fire was enough to handle. He laughed out loud thinking about green-eyed daughters. Maria, riding beside him, looked at him strangely.

"Sorry, I was woolgathering about our wedding."

She smiled but didn't say anything. Was she nervous about lovemaking? Would she really marry him? He wasn't sure what she would do. He was never sure of anything with Maria. The horses were at full gallop now, but Dominic could tell she was holding the black stallion back because of him. All Californios rode this way. Everywhere they went, they raced like the devil was on their heels. Dominic's backside wasn't enjoying the beating.

"We must have a stable so Maria can teach me to ride," Sally had said on the voyage to California. At the time, he thought Maria hated him, and the battle not to gaze at her, think about her, or allow himself to dream about her had made him act sternly, even with Sally. He smiled now remembering Sally's happy words on the ship. Sally had been way ahead of them. Surely, it was the Holy Spirit in Sally knowing the things to come. They would certainly need a stable and he would have to get used to riding like a Californio to keep up with his Californiana wife.

Chapter Twenty-Three

When they reached the roundup, Dominic lost Maria in the sea of cattle and vaqueros. It was nearing noon, the day already growing hot. Dust swirled and filled Dominic's nostrils with dirt and the smell of lumbering animals. Sweat ran down his back. The cows bawled and tried to flee, but the swarthy-skinned vaqueros just whooped and whistled and moved them expertly along. Dominic joined in the exodus of pushing the cattle across the rolling hills as summer waned. These cows looked very little like those in the East. Dominic was used to quiet-eyed milk cows. These California cattle had wild, rolling eyes and long, sharp horns. They didn't look much for producing milk or decent meat that he could see, with their wiry frames. No wonder their hides held most of the value. He kept an eye out for Maria and Roman, but didn't find either of them, so he just rode on with the nearest vaqueros.

Maria finally galloped up with a happy smile on her dusty face several hours later, clearly in her element herding cattle.

He noticed her red saddle blanket hanging down well below her saddle and chided himself for doing a poor job saddling her mount. Maria realized she was losing the blanket as she approached him and slowed her horse, leaning over to grab the flapping blanket. How she planned on fixing it while riding, Dominic didn't know. But when she leaned sideways, reaching for the blanket, her saddle swept sideways too. She landed on the ground, having ripped the blanket right off with her. The black stallion circled around her with the saddle hanging from its side.

A lumbering bull saw Maria with that red blanket in her lap. The horned beast stopped. Snorted. Pawed the earth. And then charged her.

Vaqueros yelled in Spanish. All hell broke loose.

Dominic spurred his gelding over to her and jumped down beside Maria on the ground. Yanking the red blanket from her lap, he took off running, waving the red blanket for all his worth.

The bull turned away from Maria and honed in on him, just as he'd hoped.

He zig-zagged because he knew he couldn't outrun a bull in a straight dash. Two vaqueros raced up behind the bull, twirling their lassos above their heads.

"Drop the blanket!" Roman yelled as he arrived at breakneck speed on his palomino.

As he ran, Dominic looked to see if Maria was safe. Thank God, she was! It was the last thing he remembered before the bull plowed him over.

● ● ●

Dominic was about to die. Because of her. Maria sprang to her feet and ran after Dominic as the bull pursued him. Vaqueros raced past her on their horses with their riatas whirling in the air. Roman rode into the fray, yelling for Dominic to drop the red blanket, but Dominic bravely held onto it, and kept running away from her. Away from the raging bull.

Oh no! Roman wasn't going to reach him in time.

One of the vaqueros roped the bull, but too late, it overcame Dominic in a cloud of dust, and he crumpled beneath its hooves.

Maria screamed in terror and kept running toward him.

Another vaquero roped the bull's hind leg. A third vaquero galloped in and roped the bull's other hind leg. The three horsemen quickly took control of the bull.

Roman jumped off his horse where Dominic lay sprawled in the dirt. He wasn't moving.

Maria ran up and fell to her knees beside him.

He was bleeding from his forehead and out cold.

The vaqueros dragged the bull away.

Maria took Dominic's head into her lap. Roman went to his horse and returned with a bota. He poured water on Dominic's face. To Maria's vast relief, he came to with a groan.

"Oh, Jesucristo! He's alive," she breathed.

"Thank the Lord!" Roman smiled at Maria and offered Dominic a drink of water.

Dominic swallowed the water and then smiled up at Maria. "I'm so happy the bull didn't hurt you." He sounded so grateful. "I think he mostly missed me."

"You foolish man!" Maria wiped blood from his forehead. "He didn't miss you. He nearly killed you!"

"He could have killed *you*. That saddle blanket was my fault. I saddled your horse carelessly this morning. I'm so sorry."

"No, I am sorry. This happened because of me." Maria knew the curse upon her had caused this.

"Let's get you both home." Roman waved a vaquero over who was leading Maria's horse. It no longer had a saddle on it. Another vaquero led Dominic's gelding. Roman helped Dominic up into his saddle. "You can ride behind me," he told Maria.

"I will ride my own horse." She impatiently wiped tears from her eyes. She took the reins of the black stallion from the vaquero and swung up onto his bare back.

"Is she safe riding that way?" Dominic asked Roman.

"Safer than you," Maria said, feeling heartsick. Because of her, Dominic had almost died. She had to do something. She had to get away from him.

"I am sorry my father took you from your home during the war," Rachel said to Maria at the hacienda later that afternoon. "We were so worried about you. For a long time, we didn't know what had happened to you."

Maria had dreaded this conversation for years. Now it was here. Of course it was here. Could her day get any worse? Her reckoning had come. Looking into Rachel's soft blue eyes, she remembered her father's passion-filled blue eyes in the candlelight before she killed him. Holding Roman and Rachel's small daughter in her arms, Maria walked beside Rachel, who led her son by the hand, to the cookhouse. Lupe had promised treats for the children. Dominic was with Roman bathing down at the stream. Aside from the scrape and bump on his forehead, he seemed fine.

"You should not have worried about me. I can take care of myself," Maria told Rachel, not knowing what else to say to her. This conversation made Maria feel even worse. Watching Dominic nearly die had left her shaken. Not only was she cursed, she'd killed Rachel's father. These children would never know their grandfather because of her.

"Did my father hurt you?" Concern shined in Rachel's eyes.

Maria could tell her sister-in-law had mustered all her courage for this difficult conversation. Maria just wanted to get it over with and get away from everyone she cared about. Everyone she loved. "No," she lied. "I escaped your father in Monterey. He didn't harm me one bit."

"Oh, I'm so thankful my father didn't hurt you. We don't know who killed him in Monterey, but with the war going on, it was not a surprise."

Maria glanced around the yard where she'd spent many happy days as a child. The hacienda was as peaceful and inviting as she remembered. Rosebushes bloomed, and towering trees cast shade between the big house and the cookhouse. The magnolia tree they walked under now was in full bloom. How could she keep the secret of killing Rachel's father forever? Regret gnawed at her. She needed to see a priest to confess the murder. She could never tell Rachel, but she could confess to a priest. Perhaps a confession to a padre would end the curse.

"Do you believe a person can be cursed with death?" Maria's heart sped up as she waited for Rachel's answer.

"We are all under God's curse if we do not accept the Savior's death on the cross for our sins."

The little girl in Maria's arms began to fuss. "I think she is hungry." Maria handed Tillie back to her mother.

Rachel took the child and kissed her plump little cheek. Estéban clung to Rachel's skirts, looking so much like Roman. Maria had been about his age when their mother died. Was this when the curse of death took hold? With her failure to save her mother with the sacred feather?

The death curse will never leave you. The dark voice whispered with a vengeance. Maria longed to cover her ears so she couldn't hear it.

"Are you all right?" Rachel looked at her in concern.

"Perhaps I should go lie down for a while. I am tired."

Rachel gave her a gentle smile. "I will pray for you. God loves you, Maria. Don't ever doubt the Savior's love for you."

Maria turned away so Rachel couldn't see the tears burning her eyes. She did not feel loved. She felt cursed by God.

She went to her bedroom upstairs in the hacienda and opened the trunk that had been in her room for as long as she remembered. Her gowns were still there from several years ago. She packed three of her most beautiful dresses and her finest undergarments, knowing what she must do. Knowing she would need beautiful gowns to begin a new life. Not the life she longed for, but the life she must face with the curse upon her.

More than anything, she wanted Dominic to live. She tried not to think about what he would do when he found out she was gone. He would not understand and certainly would not desire her anymore. Which was exactly what must happen. Dominic must live. The only way to guarantee he lived was for her to leave him.

• • •

The black stallion appeared happy to see her early the following morning. He lifted his head in his stall and stared at her with large, intelligent eyes, nickering softly when she approached. "You are such a dark beauty. You and I were meant to be together," she told him. She saddled him without any mishap, rejecting the sidesaddles Tia Josefa always insisted she ride in, and taking a man's saddle from the tack room instead. Deserting Dominic while he slept left her heart unbearably heavy. She could never be his wife. Could never taste his love. To think she might have married him was madness.

She could no longer risk loving Nicky either. Sally and Maria Elizabeth were gone. Perhaps on account of her. For a moment, she leaned against the black horse and allowed herself to sob without measure. The stallion didn't move as she cried on his neck. Just stood there and absorbed her tears into his long, black mane. How would she go on without Nicky? For the past several years, he'd been her whole world. She couldn't think about what she was doing. She just had to do it. Tears pouring down her face, she strapped her bundle of gowns on the back of the saddle and led the stallion out into the predawn darkness. When she climbed upon him, she put her heels to his flanks. "Run, Dark Beauty," she urged. The stallion now had a name, and she had a desperate plan.

Chapter Twenty-Four

Wade smiled when he saw her riding up the hill to his freshly painted mansion. He could smell the new paint and imagined he could smell her as well. From the moment he'd first met her in Valparaiso, he knew he must have her.

"I told you the red-haired woman would arrive today." Mr. Guzman stood at his side dressed in a dark suit and black top hat. The clairvoyant from New York always wore black and charged too much for his services, but the man with fathomless gray eyes never got things wrong. Wade was convinced he talked to the devil himself. Mr. Guzman claimed he conversed with the dead. Whoever he spoke with, the man knew the future better than other men knew their own mothers. Wade believed everything the man said.

"Should I bed her tonight?" Wade smiled when he asked the question. He certainly didn't need a fortune teller's guidance for this, but it amused him to hear what Mr. Guzman would say.

"Most certainly bed her." Mr. Guzman pulled a tiny bottle out of his vest pocket. "But she will need this medicine with you. She does not really want you. She is running from her fate."

The smile disappeared from Wade's face. "What is her fate?"

"A man with blue eyes."

"My eyes are not blue."

"Exactly." Mr. Guzman pressed the tiny bottle into his hand. He stepped off the porch, tipping his hat to Wade. "Good day, Captain Reynolds."

"I'm not sure it's a good day." Wade was no longer amused. He squeezed the tiny brown bottle of laudanum in his fist.

"She won't need much. Just a few drops at night to sleep." Mr. Guzman thought of himself as a physician too.

Wade did not return the man's smile.

Maria rode up to the mansion, and Mr. Guzman turned his smile on her. He tipped his hat again. "Mighty fine horse you're riding there, miss."

She climbed down from the saddle and allowed Mr. Guzman to kiss the back of her hand.

Wade wondered if Dom was the blue-eyed man Guzman spoke of. He stepped down from the porch and took the reins of Maria's horse. A fine animal. The kind of horse he would own for himself. "Is this your horse, my dear?"

"He belongs to the stable down in Portsmouth Square." Maria seemed nervous.

"Well, we must remedy that. Where is your child?"

She acted surprised that he remembered the child she'd mentioned at the Fourth of July party.

"Her child is dead," Mr. Guzman said. "The babe was the blue-eyed man's." Mr. Guzman donned his hat and walked down the hill, whistling as if he hadn't a care in the world.

Wade and Maria stared after him. "How did he know about the babe?" Maria looked trail weary now that he really studied her. He noticed his butler standing quietly on the porch, waiting for his orders with a new guest's arrival. "Fetch a servant to take this horse to my stable."

The butler hurried back into the house to do his bidding. Wade looked at the bundle tied to the stallion's saddle and then back at Maria. "Do you plan on staying with me?"

Her eyes widened at his forthrightness, and then she turned her gaze to the ground as if he'd shamed her. She didn't strike him as the kind of woman easily shamed. He reached out and put his hand under her chin, raising her face to his. He found her utterly beautiful. It galled him that Dom had her first. "Why did you leave my friend?" Neither mentioned Dom's name, they didn't have to. Both very well knew the ghost between them.

Her green eyes flashed with pain. "He was not meant for me," she said softly.

"Did he cast you out, or did you leave him?"

"I left him."

"And you think I am meant for you?" He couldn't help the wry smile that twisted his lips. It gave him some comfort to know she'd chosen him over Dom.

"Maybe." She smiled just a little.

"Maybe?"

"I came here to find out."

He handed the reins to the servant boy who came running from behind the mansion. "Find a stall for this fine animal, William."

The Oriental boy would have led the horse away, but Wade stopped him. "One moment please." Wade untied Maria's belongings from the saddle. "Come, my dear, we must find you a stall as well."

Maria did not take the arm he offered her. "I do not need a stall. I am a woman, not a horse," she said hotly.

Wade nodded for William to go on, and the boy led the black horse away. Wade had named the boy himself because he didn't like his Oriental name when he acquired him in China.

"I don't like to ride horses that have already been ridden, but I will make an exception for that one." He nodded after the horse and his servant disappearing behind the mansion. "I will name him and keep him because I fancy him. Just as I will make an exception for you."

"Because you fancy me?" She did not look pleased.

"I have always fancied you, my dear. It's unfortunate you bore Dom a child, but I'm willing to overlook it if you are willing to forgo propriety. If you please me, you can live here. I understand Dom recently lost his wife. Did she know about the babe between the two of you? I was told Mrs. Mason died in childbirth. Poor Dom." He couldn't help the smile that twisted his lips. It was about time Dom experienced some bad luck.

Maria's eyes widened. "I do not desire to become your wife."

"Well, that makes it easier between us. I'm sorry we're off to a bad start. You look tired and hungry. Have you been on a long journey?"

The wind was rising off the bay, blowing Maria's hair around. She had such fine red hair; why she'd ever cut it was beyond him. He was happy to see it had grown out in the past several years. He longed to twist his fingers in her locks and force her to say his name in pleasure. She always called him Captain Reynolds rather coldly. That must change. "Come, I will have my cook prepare a meal for us, and we can talk about your future here."

She finally relented and took his arm. Carrying her bundle, he led her up the steps of his mansion and into the grand foyer, freshly painted a golden hue. A crystal chandelier hung from the high ceiling, sparkling in the sun shining through the second-story windows. "Mrs. Mueller," he called, his voice echoing through the house.

The gray-haired German woman who ran his household appeared almost immediately. She wasn't old, just gray before her time. Perhaps the death of her husband in the Sierras while seeking gold had turned her hair completely silver. Mrs. Mueller was stern and sturdy and ran his household the way he'd always run his ship. With an iron fist.

"Have the cook prepare a special meal for us this evening. We are celebrating tonight." He looked at Maria and then back at Mrs. Mueller. "And bring some wine to my chambers." He turned to Maria. "Come, my dear."

Her hand trembled on his arm as he led her through the foyer and up his sweeping staircase. For a woman who'd already borne a child out of wedlock, she seemed inexperienced and uncertain, though she did her best to hide this from him. He was surprised Dom would take her for his mistress. The first mate he remembered wouldn't have done any such thing, but California allowed men to partake in desires they'd never sample back home in civilized society. Wade knew Dom had fancied Maria three years ago in Valparaiso. Dom never could hide anything from him, and his desire for Maria had been written all over Dom's face. Apparently, Dom had still married his fiancée in Boston in spite of his feelings for Maria. That was the Dom he knew and admired, always doing the honorable thing, no matter the sacrifice.

Wade wasn't surprised Dom wasn't the perfect gentleman anymore here in San Francisco. The city was a lawless place with murders every night and thievery every day. Men walked the town armed and in pairs, with pistols and daggers thrust into their belts. Even respectable women left their husbands here, and nobody thought twice about it. Bonnets—that's what good women were called in San Francisco—were so scare that if a bonnet didn't like the husband she had, she was welcome to choose another man, and nobody blinked an eye. Most of the women in the city weren't wives anyway. They were harlots. Wade had never been interested in harlots. He'd paid Mr. Guzman to tell him if Maria was in his future after seeing her at the Fourth of July ball. Guzman had called her the woman with red hair. Wade had never told Mr. Guzman Maria had red hair.

He led Maria straight to his quarters and placed her bundle on the floor beside his bed. It was a grand four-posted canopy bed shipped from China. A dragon was carved into the mahogany headboard and footboard, the dragon's hind legs and tail wrapping around the footboard, the front feet all claws, with the head fierce and breathing fire across the headboard. The magnificent bed covered in red silk dominated the room. For years, he'd sailed the China trade route, and his chambers showed his love of the Orient. "Do you know Oriental women shave their bodies? They don't have much body hair to begin with, but they're a very clean race," he told Maria. "I like clean. I expect you to keep your body shaved for me."

She stepped away and strode to the window, keeping her back to him. She stood there silently, staring at the wide blue bay in the distance. The afternoon was waning, and the wind filled the bay with whitecaps. Wade didn't have to see this for himself. He knew the ocean better than he knew anything else. Wind made waves. Just as women like Maria were made to pleasure a man.

"Take off your clothes."

She spun around. "What?" The shock on her face delighted him.

"You heard me." He could smell her fear, and he liked it. "Don't play coy. We both know why you've come here."

"I've been riding for days. I'd like a bath." She raised her chin, locking eyes with him.

A knock at the door ended their staring contest. "Come in," he called to the servant.

A maid carried a platter that held a decanter of wine and two crystal goblets.

"Have a bath drawn for my guest in the bathing room," he told the maid, his eyes returning to Maria.

She spun back to the window, presenting her stiffened spine to him. He'd never seen a finer figured woman, even in her dusty riding habit that was well out of style. He wasn't about to let her defy him. As soon as the maid shut the door, he walked over to the window, taking her by the shoulders and pulling her against his body. "You will take off your clothes for me," he breathed in her ear.

Her body went rigid. Pressing his lips below her earlobe, he slid his mouth down her slender neck. She was frozen in his arms, reminding him of the sheep he'd sheered on his uncle's farm when he was a boy. Sheep did not fight the shearer, they froze instead. This had always made him despise sheep. "You are not a sheep, so do not act like one, my lady."

"You are not a wolf, so do not act like one, Captain Reynolds," she returned.

He laughed at her spunk. "I may not be a wolf, but I am ravenous for you." His lips descended on hers, and he kissed her the way he'd wanted to kiss her in Valparaiso. He didn't like that she'd bore Dom a child, and he needed to make it clear he would breed no bastards with her. Ending the kiss, he pushed her away. "I never knew my father. My mother's brother raised me and never allowed me to forget how fortunate a bastard like me was to have a place at his table. His sons rode fancy horses, chasing foxes across the countryside, while I sheared their father's sheep and fed his hogs until I was old enough to sign myself aboard a ship leaving England. Do not think I will marry you or allow you to bear me any bastards. I do not want a wife and children. I am not that kind of man."

"Perhaps I am not that kind of woman." Her green eyes flashed with challenge. She no longer seemed afraid. She appeared quite determined.

He threw his head back and laughed. "I don't know what to make of you. Let's get to know each other. Take off your clothes."

Her eyes locked with his. "No."

"No?" He wasn't used to hearing that word from anyone.

"I would like a bath first. And some wine. And then food."

"I suppose a woman like you is used to certain luxuries."

She walked over and poured two glasses of wine, returning to him with the goblets. "If you have whiskey, I'd prefer that."

"Where did you acquire a taste for whiskey?"

"At sea."

"On Dom's ship? That surprises me. I've never seen him drink whiskey."

"Neither have I." She closed her eyes and drank the whole glass in one long gulp.

"I don't like my women smelling of wine when I bed them." He took the glass from her hand.

"It's up to me when and if you bed me."

"Really?" He looked at her for a long moment, downed his wine, and dropped the empty wineglasses on the floor where they shattered at their feet. He scooped her up and tossed her onto the bed rather roughly. "You have a lot to learn, my dear. We'll start your lessons now."

Chapter Twenty-Five

Dominic climbed the porch steps and knocked on the door of Wade's mansion. It had been over a week since he'd returned to the city. Riding home alone to San Francisco without Maria, he'd prayed the whole way. He had no idea why she'd run away on the black horse, and he kept asking God to help him find her. Now he was about to learn where she'd gone and why. He'd discovered just an hour ago at the stable that Wade had paid an outrageous amount of money for the black stallion, telling the stable owner the horse was a gift for his mistress. Dominic's blood ran cold when he heard this, and he gave himself time to gain his bearings and cool his temper before walking up the hill to Wade's house.

Truthfully, he was sick inside. Utterly ill at the thought that Maria could be with Wade. He'd walked past his own unfinished mansion before reaching Wade's grand estate farther up the hill. Wade's home looked barren on the treeless hill. Bushes and wild strawberries grew on the ridges, but there were no trees here where rich men's homes were sprouting up from redwood lumber acquired across the bay. The wind howled across the empty hills, echoing the howling in his soul.

At his knock, a butler came and opened the door. "I'm looking for Maria Vasquez." He unclenched his fists, trying to relax. Perhaps she wasn't really here.

"One moment please." The butler waved Dominic into the foyer. He braced himself and looked around as the butler disappeared down a hall. Of course, Wade's mansion was grander than his own with real crystal chandeliers hanging from the ceiling and pricey paintings already hanging on the walls. Oriental artwork depicting scenes from China, a crouching tiger approaching a young woman barely clothed in one large piece of art, a dragon menacing another scantily clothed young woman in another painting in the foyer. Had Maria entered this house, she would have had to walk past these paintings. Wouldn't she have known then what kind of man Wade was? Maria couldn't be the mistress Wade bought the black horse for, but in his heart, Dominic already knew she was. What he didn't know was why. The why was tearing him apart. He smoothed his hair down where the wind had blown it astray and tried to calm his pounding heart.

Footfalls came down the hall. Dominic could tell it wasn't a woman's walk. He expected to see the butler, but Wade entered the foyer with a smile on his face. "Dom," he said with pleasure, stepping up as if they were best friends, reaching out his hand for a shake.

"Where is she?" Dominic did not reach for Wade's outstretched hand. He kept his hands loose at his sides, restraining himself from falling into a boxer's stance and beating Wade senseless.

"Is that any way to greet your old captain?" The smile remained on Wade's face, but his eyes were cold and mocking.

"I want to see Maria."

"Come, I'll pour us a drink." Wade turned to head down the hall.

Dominic had no choice but to follow him. Wade took them to a parlor outfitted in the finest Oriental furniture and more paintings no woman should have to look upon. It reminded Dominic of sailing with Wade on the China trading routes. He tried to still his memories. The last thing he wanted to remember was his time on Wade's ship, the beautiful young Asian women Wade brought aboard in port that sometimes left the captain's cabin in tears. He could hardly stand himself, wondering if Maria was in this house. And if he could get her out without a fight.

He looked at Wade's belt, noting he didn't carry his pistols in the house. Certainly, he had a knife in his boot; Wade always kept a knife there.

"If you're looking for weapons, I assure you, I don't wear them in the house." Wade walked to a side table and poured two glasses of wine. "I'd offer you whiskey, but Maria favors it. She drinks too much, but I've overlooked this for now on account of her lost child."

Dominic felt like he'd been punched in the gut. How could she tell Wade about Maria Elizabeth? Or Nicky? Which child was he referring to? Perhaps Wade knew Maria had loved both his children as if they were her very own. Dominic couldn't believe she'd abandoned Nicky for the likes of Wade. Riding back to the city, he kept hoping Maria had headed back to Nicky. But when he returned to the hotel, no one had seen Maria, and the boy was a wreck without her. So was Chloe.

The only thing holding Chloe together was Gavilan, who'd stepped in to help with the boy. When Dominic returned to the hotel, Nicky wouldn't let him out of his sight. For the past week, Dominic had carried his son around in his arms when the boy wasn't in Gavilan's arms. And Nicky would not stop asking about Maria, and sometimes his mama, but mostly it was Maria that Nicky cried about.

The nights were the worst. Dominic hadn't known until they boarded the ship for California that Nicky always slept with Maria. He'd insisted the boy stay with him and Sally in his captain's quarters until Nicky drove them crazy asking for Maria at bedtime, so he allowed the boy to return to Maria's bed. Now Chloe slept with Nicky, and his sister looked like a haggard mess because Nicky awoke all night long, crying for Maria. Dominic decided he wasn't about to leave this mansion without her if she was really here.

He refused to accept the wine Wade offered him. "Go fetch Maria, or I will find her myself."

Wade set Dominic's glass of wine back on the table and settled himself in a nearby chair with his own glass of wine. "You'll have to rouse her from my bed." Wade smiled wolfishly and raised his glass in a toast. "I'm surprised she knows so little in the boudoir, but maybe I'm not surprised, knowing you."

"What's that supposed to mean?" Heat crept up Dominic's neck and settled in his cheeks, burning there with a vengeance. It was a good thing he'd left his pistols at the hotel. Had he a gun on him, he'd shoot Wade between his mocking eyes.

Wade leisurely sipped his wine. "Really? Must I tell you? Fortunately, she's the finest looking woman I've ever seen because she knows nothing but what I've taught her so far in bed. I'm used to a woman who knows how to pleasure a man . . ."

Dominic came at Wade with his fists flying. Wade let out a yell for assistance, slamming his wineglass down on the arm of the chair, breaking the goblet to create a deadly crystal shard. Wade came out of his chair with the crystal knife in hand. Dominic tackled him as two burly sailors from the Sandwich Islands raced into the room. The Kanakas tackled Dominic as he dove at Wade. Glass slashed through his shirt, slicing open the flesh above his ribs, but he didn't care. He was going to kill Wade or die trying.

The Kanakas pulled him off Wade, and Dominic fought like a madman as Wade rose to his feet, holding his bloody crystal knife. When Maria entered the room and began to scream, Dominic stopped fighting. The Kanakas grabbed him by the arms and held on to him as he did his best to gain his footing and stand on his own.

"Let him rise." Wade dropped the crystal knife and walked over to Maria.

"He is bleeding." Maria tried to get to Dominic.

Wade restrained her, taking her in his arms. "He is all right. It's only a flesh wound, my love."

"Let her go!" Dominic tried to shake loose of the burly sailors.

They tightened their grip on him.

Wade led Maria over to Dominic. "Make your choice, Maria. Him or me?"

Wade let her go, and she slapped one of the Kanakas restraining Dominic.

The Kanaka seemed shocked by the blow, but he didn't let go of Dominic.

"Release him," Wade ordered.

The Kanakas stepped back, the one rubbing his dark cheek. The burly sailors seemed more afraid of Maria than Dominic or Wade.

Maria tore at Dominic's shirt until she could see the wound for herself. What Wade had said was true. He wouldn't die from the wound. In a week or two, it probably wouldn't trouble him at all, though now it spurted blood, turning his white shirt red. Maria reached down and yanked up her skirt, removing her white cotton bloomers so fast Dominic couldn't stop her. She wrapped the bloomers around his midsection, tying the legs of the bloomers around his ribs to stop the bleeding.

Wade laughed. "She's never removed her bloomers that fast for me."

Dominic stepped toward Wade, but Maria pressed both hands to his chest to halt him. Her wild gaze captured his. "Please don't fight for me. Wade is my choice."

"What?" Dominic couldn't believe it. How could she be here in this Oriental palace with the man he despised most in the world?

"He is my choice," she said again, so very clearly.

Dominic blinked hard, his eyes burning. Just a week ago, he thought Maria would be his wife, the mother of his children. Nicky and more little ones to come, God willing. Now here she was, Wade's mistress. How had this happened? Why had God allowed this terrible thing to happen?

"I don't love you." Her voice trembled.

She was lying. She had to be lying. "I don't believe you." Dominic took her hands, still pressed against his chest, and pulled her against him.

"Easy, Dom. You heard her: I am her choice." Wade nodded to the Kanakas, and they stepped closer to Dominic and Maria.

"Tell your men to back off." Dominic didn't look at Wade. He kept his gaze fastened on Maria. "Say it again. Tell me you don't love me."

"I don't love you." Tears filled her eyes.

Tears flooded Dominic's eyes too. "I don't believe you," he whispered. "Please come home with me."

"This is my home." Tears coursed down her cheeks.

Dominic glanced around. "Wake up, Maria!" he cried. "Look at this place. You are in the devil's lair!" He was ready to lose it again. He was about to kill Wade or be killed by Wade's henchmen. He glanced at the paintings on the wall. Tiger paintings. Dragon paintings. "The devil has blinded you. Listen to me! Listen to God," he ended with a heartfelt plea.

"I don't believe in God anymore." She tried to step away from him.

He wasn't about to let her go. "Oh, Maria, don't give up on God. Don't give up on me. Don't give up on Nicky," he finished, tears streaking his cheeks now too.

Wade began laughing. "Get out of here, Dom. You're embarrassing yourself. You're embarrassing me, your old captain. Act like a man, for God's sake."

Dominic ignored Wade. This *was* for God's sake. He knew it so clearly. This was bigger than his love for Maria. He felt God's love for Maria pouring into him. Knew it was God's love because his pride vanished. Utterly vanished at this very moment. Maria's mouth had fallen open when he said Nicky's name.

Dominic knew he'd pierced her heart with his son. He'd promised himself he wouldn't use Nicky to win her away from

Wade, but now, in desperation, he'd used his son. He realized God had used his own Son as well to save him. Along with this realization came peace. A warmth and peace washing over him like nothing he'd ever experienced before.

He let go of Maria's wrists as that heavenly peace flooded him. Her eyes, wide and haunted, locked with his. She began to shake her head. She backed away from him, adamantly shaking her head.

"No," she whispered. "Nicky is better off without me. You are better off without me. That's God's truth."

Dominic knew she was making her choice. And it wasn't him and Nicky. It was Wade and the devil.

"You're believing lies, Maria. The devil is filling your heart with lies. God is real, and he loves you. He sent his Son to die for you."

"That's enough." Wade stepped between him and Maria.

Dominic looked Wade in the eye. "God sent his Son for you too, Wade."

"Get out of here," Wade breathed. "Get him out of here," he hissed vehemently to the Kanakas. He turned and pushed Maria away.

The sailors grabbed Dominic by his arms. He didn't fight them. He looked at the two young, muscular men. "God sent his Son for you and you." He locked eyes with each sailor as he said it. "You know it. The missionaries taught it to you on the islands."

"Get him out of here," Wade snarled.

"Let him walk out on his own. Mister, walk out on your own," the Kanaka with the softest eyes replied, releasing his arm. The other Kanaka propelled Dominic from the room and down the hall toward the foyer and front door. The second Kanaka remained rooted where he stood in the parlor.

"Get out of here!" Wade shouted at the frozen young man.

Dominic could hear Wade cursing the Kanaka in the parlor as the other one hauled him away. He went willingly. He knew with all his heart Maria was in God's hands. She'd made her bed in hell. Only God could help her now.

Chapter Twenty-Six

Maria allowed Wade to lead her to his chambers. He slammed the door and locked it. She'd seen his bad temper in the short time she'd been here, but never this seething anger. Most of the time he wooed her with champagne and kisses and expensive gowns. Each night they dined on delicacies from all over the world. Wade purchased his food from the ships as soon as they hit the harbor. She knew he was in a rage right now, but she ignored him, hurrying over to the window, hoping to catch a glimpse of Dominic going down the hill.

Wade stalked after her and yanked her away from the tall glass pane. "I know you want him!" Wade grabbed the front of her dress and tore it down the center, exposing her chemise. He slapped her hard enough to split her lip open. "You're still in love with him. Why did you come to me if you love him?"

"I don't love him," Maria lied.

Lying to Wade was easy. Lying to Dominic had nearly shattered her.

"Don't lie to me. You're a terrible liar, Maria."

"So I love him!" she screamed in Wade's face.

He slapped again, this time so hard her neck cracked and she landed in a heap on the floor. He yanked her to her feet by her hair. "Don't ever raise your voice to me," he snarled.

She spit in his face. It was the last thing she remembered.

When she awoke, she couldn't open her eyes. They were swollen shut, and her head pounded madly. Mrs. Mueller ordered her to drink a bitter syrup, holding the small bottle to her bleeding lips. The syrup burned fiercely when it hit the cuts on her mouth. She recognized the laudanum Wade doled out to her at night to help her sleep.

Since coming to the mansion, she had a hard time sleeping. When she did finally sleep, she had terrible nightmares about bears and tigers trying to kill her. In only a week, she'd come to rely on Wade's opium-laced syrup. How thankful she was Mrs. Mueller poured it into her mouth now so she could return to the darkness of oblivion.

How many days passed in bed, she didn't know. A doctor came to see her, a strange man with cold hands and a voice that unsettled her. Mrs. Mueller nursed her slowly back to health. Wade wasn't around. When she was finally able to open her eyes again, she noticed flowery wallpaper of vines and blossoms covering the walls. The room was feminine and lovely, done in green and rose colors. An Oriental air was here too.

When she finally looked in a mirror, she was horrified by her bruised and swollen face. A large gash split her cheek. Breathing was hard as her broken ribs mended. She spent at least a month recovering. When her face finally healed, a large scar below her eye marred her left cheekbone. She'd become dependent on the laudanum Mrs. Mueller ministered to her several times a day. "Don't take much," Mrs. Mueller always said, "or you'll end up worthless to yourself and to others. Just sip enough to see you through the pain."

The pain gradually subsided, but her dependence on the laudanum intensified. Mrs. Mueller began to make her bathe, dress, and style her hair each day, sending an efficient young maid, a girl named Fang from China, to help her prepare for the day, but the days led nowhere. Mrs. Mueller made her get out of bed, gave her a few drops of bitter syrup that softened everything, and then Fang took over cleaning her up. After that, Maria sat for hours staring out the window at the bay.

When she finally dared another look in the mirror weeks later, she no longer recognized herself. A mysterious woman stared back at her. The scar on her cheek was terrible. Maria stopped looking at herself in the mirror from that day on.

Still, she wore the finest gowns sent to her room by Wade, and each day her hair was artfully curled by Fang and pinned up on her head as if she were the grandest lady in San Francisco. But she wasn't a lady. She was Wade's harlot, though she hadn't seen him since he'd beat her senseless and left her nearly dead. Only Mrs. Mueller and Fang came, Mrs. Mueller to bring her meals and the medicine, and Fang to help her dress.

Finally, one morning Mrs. Mueller gave her a syrup that wasn't bitter and didn't soften her day. It still came in the little brown bottle, but Maria knew almost immediately the syrup did not contain the opium she needed. Getting through her bath and dressing ritual was torture. "I'm sorry," Fang said several times. "Please just try to hold still. I am almost finished with your hair."

As soon as Fang left the room, Maria ripped all the pins from her hair and threw herself onto the bed. A pounding headache set in, and before long she felt like she was coming out of her own skin. She got up once and went to the door, but of course it was locked. Returning to the bed, she buried her face in the pillow and for a while allowed herself to remember her old life.

She imagined she could smell Nicky's soft blond curls again under her chin and feel his chubby arms locked around her neck. His laughter echoed through her mind. Her heart ached so badly she thought she might die of a broken heart. She did not allow herself to think about Dominic. Each time he entered her mind, the ache that filled her rendered her nearly numb.

When Mrs. Mueller finally brought her noon meal, Maria begged for the laudanum. Mrs. Mueller allowed her only a few drops after she ate all her food. "Captain Reynolds says it's time you return to the land of the living. He wants you out of this room and riding horses with him come Sunday."

"I am not ready to ride a horse." Maria's legs felt weak, and she still had pain in her ribs.

Mrs. Mueller looked at her with the closest thing to compassion Maria had ever seen on her stern German face. "I thought you would have learned your lesson after nearly dying. Captain Reynolds never takes no for an answer. You'll ride with him on Sunday."

That night after dinner, Mrs. Mueller again gave her only two drops of the bitter syrup. Maria didn't think it would get her through the night. She went to the chest in her room and dug through it until she found her golden rosary. Carrying it back to her bed, she lay there squeezing the crucifix in her hand, but she did not recite the prayer. Mercifully, she fell asleep and slept all night, but when she awoke in the morning, all she wanted was more laudanum. She stared at the golden rosary beside her in the bed for a long time.

Fang came and made her bathe and dress and sit for the styling of her hair after she ate her breakfast. "These eggs cost a fortune. And if the city knew bacon was served in this house, they might rob us blind. Captain Reynolds has guards accompany the grocery deliveries so our butter, cheese, fruits, and vegetables aren't stolen."

Maria did her best to remain still, listening to Fang go on, though every stroke of the brush through her hair was torture, and her head pounded painfully.

At lunchtime, Mrs. Mueller gave her two drops of syrup, but it did not taste bitter. "Please, I need the real medicine. I won't make it through the day without it."

"Captain Reynolds will see you this afternoon. Ask him for your syrup." Mrs. Mueller hurried out the door.

When Wade stepped into the room several hours later, Maria could hardly stand herself. She wanted to plead with him for the laudanum but couldn't bring herself to grovel at his feet. How long had it been since she'd laid eyes on him? More than a month, of that she was certain. She thought he would close the door behind him, but a man followed him into the room. The man in the top hat she'd met when she first arrived here. The man's strange gray eyes made her uneasy.

"Mrs. Mueller tells me you're having a hard time getting off the medicine."

Maria did not answer Wade. Her eyes were on the man trailing him into the room. Something cold came into the room with the men. Perhaps it was air from the hall. Winter was nearly here, and the small stove in her room was lit with a fire these days. Today it hadn't been lit yet. She missed the fire's heat.

"Hello, my dear, remember me? I'm Mr. Guzman." She recognized his voice as the doctor who'd cared for her when her eyes were swollen shut and she thought she might die.

Wade walked over and tenderly took Maria by the arm. "Come, sit over here, my love." He led her to a chair in the corner of the room like a tender husband.

Mr. Guzman followed them over. He pulled out a gold watch hanging on a chain from his coat pocket. "You will feel much better after I reset your mind," he said. "You won't need the medicine anymore. You'll be much stronger. I promise."

Wade pushed her down in the chair more gently than she was used to from him. He watched her closely as Mr. Guzman began to swing the golden watch in front of her face.

"Keep your eyes on the watch. That's it, my dear. Keep following the watch with your eyes."

Wade kept his hand on her shoulder, standing at her side as she sat in the chair. She grew colder and colder until she began to shiver. Her head pounded, and she longed to close her eyes.

"I know you're getting sleepy, but don't close your eyes. Keep following the watch, my dear. Stare at the watch."

Mr. Guzman began to softly chant in a language Maria had never heard before. The sensation of something slithering up her spine came over her. Her skin actually crawled.

"I need laudanum," she whispered.

"You do not need laudanum," said Mr. Guzman. "Your spirit guide will strengthen you."

"I don't want a spirit guide." Maria felt tired, so tired, but also alarmed. "I want medicine."

"It's a free spirit. A strong spirit. It will help you overcome your need for the medicine."

Maria closed her eyes just for a moment, but when she did, Wade squeezed her shoulder.

"Don't close your eyes," Mr. Guzman ordered. "Keep staring at the watch." He began to chirp in that strange language.

The slithering sensation on her spine intensified. It crawled up her back and seemed to spread through her neck and then spill over her head. The pounding eased and something popped. She wasn't sure she actually heard the pop, but she felt the pop. Something popped right out of her head. Her eyes widened when she realized her headache was gone and she no longer hungered for the bitter syrup.

Mr. Guzman stopped swinging the watch. He smiled. "I can see it's no longer in your eyes, my dear. You've been a perfect patient. Thank you." He pocketed the watch and looked at Wade. "That should do," he said quite confidently.

Wade let go of Maria's shoulder and walked Mr. Guzman from the room. At the door, he handed Mr. Guzman a sack of coins. In that instant, as Wade dropped the sack of coins into Mr. Guzman's hand, the flashback hit her. Tyler dropping the coins in Gavilan's lap in the church. She felt so cold she thought she would never, ever feel warm again.

Closing the door, Wade walked back over to her. "Are you feeling better?"

She looked at him and wondered if she could kill him too. How hard would it be to obtain a knife and bury it in his back?

"Yes, I think I am feeling better," she said, rising from the chair.

"Would you like to accompany me on a horse ride tomorrow?"

"Yes, I think I would." Her legs felt much stronger. All over, she felt stronger.

"I'd like to start again with you." Wade stepped up and tenderly ran a finger along the scar beside her eye. "I am grateful I didn't completely ruin your beauty. I am a jealous man, Maria. Don't ever tell me you love someone else."

He was dressed rather fancy, as always. His tall leather boots and buff trousers made him look like a ship captain on deck, but his white shirt was unlaced, and she could see brown hair curling on his chest. He was roguishly handsome in a dangerous way. Now she knew just how dangerous he really was, but she wasn't afraid, perhaps because she no longer cared if she died. Dying would end her pain and heartache, and she found that inviting.

"Would you rather I lie to you about who I love?"

"Lie if you must, but never, ever say you love someone else again. If you say it again, I won't kill you, I'll kill the man you love."

The bottom dropped out of Maria's stomach. She did her best not to show how stricken she was. "Perhaps the lie I told was about loving him. If I truly loved someone else, would I be here with you?"

"I've thought a lot about that." Wade turned from her and walked over to the window. The day was absolutely gray, fog thick as a blanket over the city and rain drizzling down.

Maria could hardly breathe. He could kill Dominic. She knew it. Knew it so clearly. She stood there commanding herself not to move a muscle. Never could Wade know she really did love Dominic. Loved him so fiercely she would kill a hundred men for him. She would kill herself to keep him safe.

After staring out the window, Wade turned around to face her. "You could prove your love to me. You've never kissed me on your own accord. I've always been the one to kiss you."

Maria stood there feeling that tingle return to her spine. Feeling her body growing stronger in a room growing colder. Maybe she would kiss him. Maybe she would kill him. But never would she ever allow him to hurt Dominic.

"Come to me." Wade reached out his hand to her.

"Prove your love to me, Maria." He pulled her into his arms in front of the window, closed in by fog and riveted with rain.

She draped her arms around his neck and kissed him, and she became something else, something darker than herself.

Paula Scott

Part Three

*If I rise on the wings of the morning
and dwell on the far side of the sea,
even there your hand shall lead me,
your right hand shall hold me fast.*

Psalm 139:9–10

Chapter Twenty-Seven

In August, Dominic won the election for delegate to the California convention. In celebration, he took Nicky out for a horse ride across the hills. The little boy loved horses and pleaded for Dominic to take him riding every day. Most days he did just that, enjoying these outings with his son in the midst of enjoying little else in his life without Maria. By September, he, Nicky, and Chloe were settled down in Monterey for the length of the convention. He set up a house in the seaside village with a small staff of trustworthy servants. Gavilan resided in the mansion in San Francisco with a larger staff while Dominic was in Monterey and had become very good at running their shipping business.

In the first weeks after discovering Maria was living with Wade, both he and Gavilan kept an eye on Wade's place, always watching for Maria, but they never saw her. Finally, they surrendered to the fact that she'd made her choice, and they must live with it. Wade was their main competitor when ships sailed into the bay and lost their crews to gold fever. Both Wade's company and theirs rushed to secure the abandoned brigs. Usually, the captain remained aboard. Convincing him to allow them to outfit his ship with a brand new crew before sailing the ship back to Boston and then returning her to San Francisco with men and mining supplies was relatively easy. Getting to the captain before Wade got to him was the real challenge. Nothing pleased Gavilan more than beating Wade out of a new ship.

Dominic preferred to spend his time taming California's wild and wooly ways instead of overseeing the ships. San Francisco troubled him greatly. No one was safe after dark in the city, and even in the daytime men were slain in the streets over so little as a bag of onions. Bordellos were popping up everywhere, and gambling halls overran decent hotels. The city was sectioned into quarters like Chinatown and Little Chile, with Ireland, Germany, and nearly every other nation under the sun accounted for in men warring over race, creed, and color. Never had he seen a city so divided. Vigilantes ruled the muddy streets. Men were strung up and hanged without trials. Trying to civilize California and bring her to statehood kept Dominic from dwelling on Maria. He'd found a fine little church in Monterey and enjoyed Sabbath services each week with Chloe and Nicky. Sitting in church listening to the sermon fed his hungry soul. He read his Bible every day and prayed for Maria to return to him and Nicky, but more than that, for Maria to return to God.

Something deeply profound had changed in him that day in Wade's mansion when he realized the depth of God's love. Dominic couldn't imagine turning his son over to die on a cross for sinners, but that's exactly what God had done for him. It still brought tears to his eyes when he thought about it. Each night he and Nicky kneeled beside the bed and said their prayers. Nicky prayed for Maria to come home and for his mama to be happy in heaven along with his baby sister. His son's earnest prayers tore at Dominic's heartstrings. He longed to do something, anything to rescue Maria. But every night he felt the Lord's hand restraining him from any human effort. He must wait and pray for God to bring Maria home.

For now, he threw his passion into saving California from the ruthless masses bent on turning her into the wild west. Every man walked the streets of San Francisco with pistols and knives in their belts. Just getting men out of the mud and darkness was a worthy endeavor. San Francisco needed sidewalks and streetlamps like Boston. And something really needed to be done about the fearless rats that were overrunning the city.

But in the meantime, forty-eight delegates from all walks of life were shaping the future of California in the quiet village of Monterey at the new Colton Hall. Only six delegates had been born in California. Like Dominic, nineteen had lived there for less than three years. The two youngest delegates, J. Hollingsworth and J.M. Jones, men in their twenties, came from Maryland and Kentucky. At fifty-three-years-old, the oldest delegate was José Carrillo, a Californio representing the Los Angeles district. The men crafted the constitution based heavily upon the constitution of Iowa, and to a lesser degree, the constitution of New York. John Hamilton, a young man who graduated from West Point just two years earlier, and on his first tour of duty in Monterey, spent three days and nights steadily writing the constitution on parchment. It was decreed all laws must be published in Spanish and English. It took thirty-seven days before the constitution was approved by the delegates in October. One month later, they ratified it by electorate. The first legislature met on December fifteenth in San Jose and petitioned Congress to admit California to the Union. By then, Dominic couldn't wait to get back to San Francisco to find out if Gavilan had seen Maria.

"She has taken to riding with Reynolds around the city and across the dunes on horseback," Gavilan told him, and his hopes plummeted.

"Does she look well?" Dominic wondered if Gavilan could hear his heart pounding. It felt like his blood roared in his ears.

"There is a scar below her eye."

"A scar?"

"A bad scar." Gavlian shook his head. "I went to the mansion when I knew Reynolds was down at the wharf. I spoke with Maria. She denied he'd hurt her."

"How did she get the scar?"

"She says she fell down the stairs. I don't believe her. Had she admitted Wade did it, I would have killed him. I still might kill him."

Dominic poured both him and Gavilan a cup of coffee. "Killing Wade is not the answer."

"Why not?"

"Because the Savior says we are to love our enemies."

Gavilan nearly spit out his coffee. "Is that what you gathered down at that convention these past few months?"

"No, I gathered that before I left here."

"I think he gave her that scar." Gavilan's dark eyes were hard as onyx.

"Wade is the man she has chosen." Dominic accepted the burn in his mouth as he gulped down his hot coffee. Every day he told himself Wade was Maria's choice, and every day it hurt him. Human beings were given a choice. God didn't force humans to love him. He sacrificed his Son and let man choose. That was true love.

"He's the devil," Gavilan said.

"I think I'll take Nicky on a horse ride this afternoon. If Maria sees Nicky, perhaps she'll change her mind and return to us." He hoped Nicky could handle seeing Maria riding with Wade. The boy no longer asked for her during the day, but he still prayed for her to come home every night and refused to sleep with Chloe, though he'd finally accustomed himself to his aunt. But Nicky was no longer the boy he once was. The exuberant child was gone. He now minded his manners and obeyed his father and Chloe, but his son was often a sad, quiet little boy, which grieved Dominic. The best way to put a smile on Nicky's face was to take him horseback riding.

"Nicky might not even recognize her. She wears fancy hats that hide her face now," Gavilan said.

"Because of the scar?" Alarm shot through Dominic. How bad could it be?

"Maybe it's her face or maybe she just doesn't want to be seen as his mistress."

"You think she's ashamed?"

"I think she doesn't want to show her face to the bonnets." Gavilan finished his coffee and sat his tin cup down.

"There aren't many bonnets in San Francisco."

"More women arrive every day, most by ship, but some by wagon train too. In the time you've been gone, the Bonnet population has tripled.

"So there are a hundred bonnets instead of thirty?" A smile tugged at Dominic's mouth. "Any of these bonnets pleasing to your eye?"

Gavilan didn't return his smile. "I don't want a bonnet."

"What about Chloe? She's sweet on you."

"She's far too pure for the likes of me."

"Maria has chosen Wade."

"I haven't given up on her."

"And you think I have?"

"You've changed."

Dominic rubbed his chin, whiskers prickling his fingers. He needed a shave. And a bath. And a meal. He'd taken Chloe and Nicky to the mansion and come straight to the wharf upon arriving from Monterey this morning. "What's that supposed to mean?"

"You're a man of peace now. Maria needs a man of war."

"The real war is for Maria's soul." Dominic looked deeply into Gavilan's eyes. "And maybe your soul too, my friend."

Gavilan picked up his tin cup and studied it. "I know my soul. It may be empty, but it's honest."

"The Good Lord loves honest men."

"You think the Good Lord will bring her home? Because if he doesn't, I'm going to do something about it."

"The Good Lord lets us choose our way."

"So we're supposed to let her choose that devil?" Gavilan threw his cup down in disgust.

"Folks choose the devil every day."

"You don't know how many times I've nearly stuck a knife in Wade down at the wharf on a misty morning. I could toss him in the ocean with no one the wiser."

"I want Maria to choose me not because Wade's dead, but because she truly wants me. The same reason God wants us to choose him. He wants our love."

"I'm not sure I believe that." Gavilan rubbed the back of his neck.

"Will you spend Christmas with us? Chloe has her heart set on you being there."

"That reminds me, there's a holiday party at the Henry House. Why don't you take Chloe, and I'll stay home with Nicky."

"Chloe loves parties, but she'd want you there too."

"I don't like parties. I'd much rather mind Nicky. We'll sit in front of the fire on your bearskin. Tell me again how you came across that grizzly so I can tell Nicky the story of how his father killed the bear."

"I didn't kill that bear. It almost killed me."

Gavilan laughed. "For a captain, you're kind of soft."

"You ever faced a grizzly before?"

"Not on my knees. I stay on my horse and keep a gun in my hand." Gavilan laughed.

"Speaking of guns, I see you have acquired the habit of wearing one." Dominic nodded at the pistol strapped to Gavilan's belt.

"I've always worn a gun in California. A man's a fool not to."

"I hope to civilize this city."

"Well, until you do, I'm keeping my gun."

"You're welcome to keep your room in the mansion. You don't have to sleep with your gun up there."

"Down here at the wharf, I get to the ships faster. My room here suits me just fine."

"There's more to life than business, Gavilan."

"Perhaps, but with a lady in the mansion, I feel more comfortable living here."

"Are you ever going to give Chloe what she wants?"

Gavilan smile ruefully. "I don't understand your sister. There's far better men out there for her than me."

"You underestimate yourself."

"I know where I've been. Your sister needs someone like you. A churchgoing man who lives without a gun. You've got the Good Lord. I've got my gun and a lot of blood on my hands."

"You've killed men?"

"Too many."

Dominic nodded in understanding. "Every man is offered forgiveness. Even men with plenty of blood on their hands."

"I'm not ready to change my ways."

"That is part of forgiveness." Dominic looked at the paperwork scattered across his desk. "Sometimes I miss the sea."

"Will you ever return to her?"

"I would if a certain woman would sail away with me."

Gavilan's smile turned crooked with regret. "I have those thoughts too."

"Thoughts of red hair and green eyes?"

"Why do you think she chose that devil?"

"Why do any of us choose the devil for our master?"

"It's not the same."

"Isn't it?" Dominic leveled his gaze on Gavilan. He was headed for the door now. Out into the fog and rain of a muddy San Francisco morning.

"You could have given her a mansion too," Gavilan said.

"Do you think it's his mansion she wants? Wade's life of wealth and privilege?"

Gavilan shook his head. "No. I think she's riding a horse she never meant to saddle."

"Did you ask her why she chose Wade when you spoke with her?"

"She said Reynolds was the man she deserved."

Dominic closed his eyes, said a prayer for Maria, and then focused on Gavilan. "It's the lies that get us. The lies we believe about ourselves. About God. I used to believe I deserved God's grace. I mostly did right and good in my life. I was a good person. Hell wasn't for me. The truth is hell *was* for me. Hell is for any of us unless we meet the Savior face-to-face and meet our dirty, rotten selves in the process. I never really saw my dirty, rotten self until the day I saw the Lord when I tried to use my son to make Maria return to me. That's what God did. He used his Son to win us back from the devil."

Gavilan didn't say anything else, he just bowed his head, and walked silently out the door.

Chapter Twenty-Eight

Maria stared at the scar on her face in the mirror. Usually, she avoided mirrors. When she went out, she wore elaborate hats that hid her face. Tonight was her first party since the Fourth of July, when she'd danced with Wade to punish Dominic. Wade had always been her way of hurting Dominic. A way to show him she didn't love him. But she'd always loved him. Even after he'd married Sally, she still adored him, and hated him for walking away from her that snowy day in Boston. But she loved him for that too. He'd done the right thing. Dominic was a good man. Sally had deserved him.

Oh, how she missed Sally. There was nobody in this world now to tell her she was worth something. Looking in the mirror, all Maria saw was a worthless woman. A prostitute. A slave. That's what she really was, a slave to Wade's dark passions. Some days she pondered killing him. Burying a knife in his back as she had Tyler, but then her suffering would end, and she hadn't suffered enough yet.

She raised her hand and traced the scar down her cheek. It started just below the outer corner of her eye and ran several inches down her face in a crooked line. Once red and inflamed, it was now turning white, like lightning slashing her countenance. Her cheekbones were more prominent, her features sharper than ever. She'd lost the girlish fullness in her face. Every innocent line was gone. An older, wiser woman stared back at her. Eyes haunted by all she knew, all she'd lost. Not a night went by that she didn't miss Nicky. His warm little body curled against hers. His breathing soft and steady somewhere near her cheek or in her hair.

Instead, there was Wade's hard body, having his way. She'd learned to go somewhere else in her mind. Sometimes she'd relive the conversations she'd had with Sally about God. Sally's faith had been so winsome. So filled with hope. Sometimes she imagined playing with Nicky in Boston, when the trees were turning on a crisp autumn day. Sometimes she dared dream of Dominic. The way he smiled. The way he laughed. The way he prayed. How good he was.

All goodness was gone from her life. It showed on her marred face. She dropped her hand from the scar. "No makeup," she told Fang, who'd come to help her dress for the party. "And I will not wear my hair up tonight. I will wear it down with that dress."

"You wear it up," Fang argued as she laid the red-and-black satin and lace dress on the bed. Where Wade had found Fang, Maria didn't know, but she was an expert with hair and makeup. Fang could take a sow's ear and turn it into a silk purse, but Maria refused to be a silk purse. Let them see the sow's ear. Let them see the scar in all its terrible glory.

Like all her other dresses now, the exquisite red-and-black gown was brought to her room and laid out on her bed by Fang. The bodice and sleeves were fitted black lace, the skirt blood-red satin. Red satin bands split the black lace sleeves just above her elbows, after that, the lace flared out, loose and flowing on her arms. A striking dress. A dancing dress. Did she even feel like dancing anymore?

Would people admire her dancing as they had when she was young and beautiful, or would they be too horrified by the scar on her face to even admire her dancing?

Fang helped her into the gown and then fussed over her hair. "It looks lovely up. You're a lady. Ladies wear their hair up."

"Am I a lady?"

Fang looked at her with those dark, almond-shaped eyes that held their own painful secrets. "The captain says you are his lady."

"Captain Reynolds is a liar. I am not his lady. I am his whore."

Fang became upset. "Please let me pin it up. Captain will be mad if I not pin your hair up."

"I will tell Captain Reynolds I would not let you touch my hair tonight." Maria smiled at the girl. "If I wear my hair down, it covers my cheek. See?" Maria brushed her hair over to the side of her face that was scarred. "I want to cover the scar."

"You survive something fierce. A tiger." Fang smiled, trying to cheer Maria.

"Captain Reynolds is the tiger."

The smile disappeared from Fang's face.

Maria moved her hair around, letting it drape her scarred cheek. "There, that's better, don't you think?"

"I fear him," Fang confessed.

"You don't have to be afraid, but never make him angry."

Fang kneeled down and slipped red satin slippers on Maria's black-stockinged feet. The slippers were expensive, the same color as the blood red of her skirt. "The captain own me," said Fang.

"Owns you?" Maria stared at the slippers, wondering if they could survive San Francisco's mud.

"Pay money for me." Fang rose to her feet. "Mother sell me."

"Your own mother?" Maria felt sick for the girl.

"Not really my mother. She buy me as a baby. Raise me and other girls to sell to men. We call her Mother."

So Fang came from a madam. Maria had suspected as much. "Is it better here than where you lived before?"

"Oh, so much better! I only serve you now."

Maria touched Fang's slender arm in affection. "I'm glad you serve only me, but I cannot wear these slippers. I must have my boots. How do I look in this dress?"

"Like a grand lady." Fang smiled.

"I am not a lady." Maria returned her smile and stood up, kicking off the red slippers. She went to the end of her bed and pulled out her favorite pair of boots. "Slippers are for ladies." She bent over and put on her boots and then fluffed her skirts out to cover them.

It was almost Christmas and cold outside. As she donned her cloak, she wondered how to get the wooden box of painted tin soldiers to Nicky. She'd purchased the box weeks ago and had it hidden under her bed. The bed she didn't sleep in anymore. Wade insisted she sleep with him. But during the day, this was her domain. She went over to the bed and kneeled down, pulling out the box, then carried it over to Fang. "I need you to give this to Bao. Tell him to deliver it to the green-and-white mansion down the hill while we are at the party. It is for the boy who lives there." Maria knew Dominic and Nicky had been gone for months in Monterey but were to return to the city any day now.

Fang looked frightened.

"The captain won't know. He will be with me," Maria assured her. She suspected Fang was falling in love with Bao. The young, muscular Chinese man was new here and handsome; the maids liked him.

The girl nodded and took the box into her trembling hands.

"Thank you." Maria squeezed Fang's shoulder, and the girl smiled. Maria pulled her hood up over her hair and left the room.

Wade waited downstairs in the parlor. He already had a drink in his hand and was holding a crystal glass for Maria. "Some whiskey to warm you before we step out?" He offered the glass to her.

She accepted the whiskey and downed it without removing her hood from her head.

"You have done nothing to conceal your scar." His eyes were intent upon her.

The whiskey flamed in her belly. "It is your scar. I wear it for you."

"Careful, Maria. I am not in a festive mood."

"Then why are we going to this party?"

"Everyone who is anyone in the city will be at this party tonight. Where's Fang? Perhaps there's still time for her to do something to conceal it."

"Fang says it's the mark of the tiger."

In spite of himself, Wade smiled. "I have always been fond of tigers." He looked at the heavy gold ring on his finger, at the head of the tiger that had cut her face, leaving the scar.

Maria glanced around at the paintings on the walls. Dragons and tigers all over Wade's house. She walked to the door and was relieved to see Wade's carriage with its matching black horses waiting in front of the mansion. She quickly went out, and the coachman opened the door for her. One of the horses snorted in impatience. They were well-bred animals, sleek and strong and fast. But, as always, the roads were a muddy mess. Men often went out and cut brushwood and limbs off trees in the surrounding countryside to throw in the streets. Everything was dumped in the streets—broken barrels, tobacco boxes, planks of every shape and size—in an attempt to overcome the mud. It made for a bumpy, boggy ride in the carriage.

Wade climbed in behind her as they boarded the coach. Stars filled the night sky, blanketing the velvety blackness like diamonds as they slowly rolled through the muddy mess at a snail's pace. The Henry House sat on a hill overlooking the bay, the three-story dwelling lit up by whale oil lanterns. Very few men lived in houses such as these. Most dwelled in tents and shanties, hotels and boardinghouses in the city. People eagerly streamed into the fine mansion tonight, mostly men, well-dressed gentlemen, San Francisco's finest. The coachman released them practically on the front porch so Maria didn't have to wade through the mud. Men parted the way to allow the coach to deposit a lady right on the doorstep. When a lady arrived anywhere in San Francisco, it was cause for celebration. Wade swept in behind her, his black cloak swirling around them like the wings of a great bird of prey. His possessiveness showed. He followed her closely into the house, where a butler took their cloaks.

"Your hair does not please me," Wade whispered as the servant stepped away.

Maria ignored him. She walked quickly into the sea of men, leaving Wade no choice but to follow her. A woman wearing a fashionable green dress stepped up on the arm of a distinguished-looking gentleman. "Captain Reynolds," the woman said with pleasure. "You have a lovely guest with you tonight."

The woman stretched out her hand to Maria. As she did, her gaze lingered on Maria's scar. Her mouth fell open, and her welcoming words disappeared.

"Maria suffered an unfortunate accident on a stairwell several months ago," said Wade.

The woman recovered and squeezed Maria's hand. "A blessed Christmas to you, my darling. Where are you from?"

"Maria and I met in Chile, Mrs. Brewster," said Wade. "Maria stole my heart in Valparaiso, and I have never been the same. Good evening, Colonel Brewster." Wade shook the distinguished-looking man's hand and then put his palm on the small of Maria's back, pushing her firmly through the receiving line.

The house was packed with people. A smattering of women and more than a hundred men. Wade led Maria over to a refreshment table, where they picked up glasses of champagne before walking up several sets of winding stairs to the third-story ballroom. They settled in with several ship captains Wade had known for years. Everyone spoke of the gold rush, snow in the Sierras making it impossible to mine right now, but that didn't quell the men's excitement.

Still feeling the effects of the whiskey, Maria sipped her champagne, wishing she was somewhere else. Anywhere else. A place where people didn't stare at her scarred face. The night wore on, champagne flowing like a rain-swollen river, men's laughter loud in her ears. A band kicked in, and music enlivened the party. Perhaps there was one woman for every ten men in the room. Maria didn't meet anyone. Wade didn't even introduce her to the ship captains. He kept her close and avoided making introductions.

When the dancing began, Wade swept her around the crowded dance floor but soon went back to discussing the gold rush with men who snuck curious glances at her when Wade wasn't watching. Maria sipped champagne and was grateful for the courage it gave her. After several drinks, she didn't care about her scar or Wade or anything else. She daydreamed about Christmas, imagining Nicky's face when his toy soldiers arrived. Would he be there to accept his box? Would he wonder where it came from? Did he ever think of her? Did Nicky ache with missing her as she ached so terribly for him?

Did his father ever ache with missing her? Or did Dominic hate her now?

She recalled the last time she'd seen him. The day was hazy in her mind on the account of the beating. At first, she didn't even remember he'd come to the house, but slowly bits and pieces of the day returned to her. The fight between Wade and Dominic. The look Dominic gave her before Wade's men escorted him from the house. What was in that look? Resignation? Release? The ending of all things that mattered to her?

It was for the best, she assured herself. The dark voice rarely came anymore. The curse of death was gone from Dominic because she was gone from him. Her gaze scanned the room, searching for him in a sea of faces she didn't recognize. The oil lanterns burned, but not brightly. The ballroom was full of windows, some moonlight spilled in, but not enough to bring much light to the celebration. She'd heard Queen Victoria's husband, Prince Albert from Germany, had installed a Christmas tree at Windsor Castle again this year and that many upper-class homes in America had Christmas trees now too.

Sally had talked about Christmas trees with a sparkle in her brown eyes, saying they would certainly have one next year. Last year, they'd read Charles Dickens's *A Christmas Carol* out loud beside the fire on the long winter nights leading up to Christmas. And on Christmas Eve, the famous poem *A Visit from Saint Nicholas,* which Dominic recited, having arrived home from the sea to find himself a father to Nicky. Even now she could still hear his melodious voice reading the whimsical poem, Nicky on his knee, but not exactly happy to be there, with Maria trying to blend into the background and allow Sally, newly pregnant with Maria Elizabeth, all the happiness in the world.

Maria's eyes filled with tears. Had she only known last year's Christmas would be a lost portrait of brilliance. The glow of everything she wanted. Sally's life. Sally's son. Sally's husband. And Sally's faith.

For Christmas, Sally had given her a psalm embroidered on a handkerchief. At the time, it hadn't meant much to Maria. Now the memory of Sally's face shining with love as Maria unwrapped the embroidered handkerchief caused tears to flood her eyes. She quickly closed them to stop the tears, and her head spun with champagne and regret.

Did she really want Sally's faith? Did she really believe in a God who died for her sins? Would she ever understand this

God? She remembered the knife in her hand on the night she'd killed Joshua Tyler. Did she regret taking his life? Perhaps she did now. It had led her down this very dark road. She wouldn't leave Wade because she deserved his beatings and his beddings that tortured her soul. She remembered Dominic's warm, muscular body against hers in the swimming hole. The delight on his face. She'd chosen to run from him not in spite of love, but because of love. If she had to die every day to ensure he lived, she would.

Opening her eyes, she focused on the face right in front of her. Dominic's face. "Hello, Maria."

She blinked hard, barely able to comprehend he was really standing there. Smiling at her. Her throat tightened, and she couldn't speak. Wade's voice droned on in her ears. He was in deep conversation with his back to her in the crowded room. She tried to return Dominic's smile but couldn't. Oh God, how she wanted to throw herself into his arms. Beg him to take her out of here. To take her far away from Wade and all she'd become with him. She'd thought she was ruined after the rape in the church. Now she was beyond ruined. Beyond any kind of redemption she could ever imagine for herself.

"Gavilan told me you'd been injured." He reached out and gently ran his fingers down her scar.

Maria shivered, closed her eyes, tried to breathe. Was it really Dominic's fingers on her face? Opening her eyes, he was still there, his gaze upon her so tender.

"Did you really fall down the stairs?"

"Yes," Wade said in a voice so deadly Maria stepped away from him. Wade grasped her arm and yanked her back against his rigid frame.

Dominic stepped even closer amid the laughter and the music and the party swirling around them. "I don't believe it." He captured Wade's wrist, raising his hand in front of their faces. "I believe it was this ring that scarred her face. I've seen what this ring can do to a man's face on *The Sea Witch*."

Wade jerked his hand away. "Don't tempt me to kill you, Dom."

Maria stepped between them, Wade's breath huffing through her hair, Dominic so close she wanted to die if she couldn't escape with him.

"At least I would be a worthy opponent," said Dominic. "A man strapped to the mast and a woman at your mercy in your own mansion. What kind of monster are you, Wade?"

"I fell down the stairs," Maria insisted, pressing her hands against Dominic's chest, feeling his heart pounding fiercely there.

He looked down at her, and she pleaded to him with her eyes. "I really did fall down the stairs." *Don't cry!* she commanded herself. *Smile like you mean it. You must convince him it was an accident.*

Dominic searched her face. "Oh, Maria, what are you doing?"

I'm saving you, she longed to say. *You stupid man! I am a cursed woman!* "I am dancing," she suddenly said instead, pushing past him and Wade, before either could stop her.

She rushed across the dancefloor, straight over to the musicians. A waltz was ending, and Maria begged the men to strike up a Spanish tune. A song that took her back to the girl she could hardly remember. The girl she'd once been. The girl who could dance like no one else in Monterey, or anywhere in

California for that matter. She would show them. She would show them all.

The musicians were delighted by her request. They didn't know the song she suggested, but said they'd do their best to accommodate her. She didn't recognize the tune they kicked up, but it was Spanish, and it was danceable.

She spun out onto the floor, her blood-red skirts swirling about her. Raising her arms above her head, the black lace sleeves flowed down, spilling over her face. Hiding the scar. The floor cleared, and soon she was alone. And she danced like she'd never danced before.

Her gaze swept the crowd as she stole their adoration. It took a few minutes of turning and dancing before she found Dominic standing at the edge of the floor with Wade right beside him, both men looking like they'd charge the dance floor at any moment. She smiled for Dominic and imagined every kiss, every touch she would never have from him, and then she danced with that in mind. With lost lovemaking in mind.

Her longing was tangible, and the room swelled with awe and wonder. The crowd's hunger hit Maria and fueled her dancing. Fueled a fire burning through her. She danced until the fire consumed her. When the music finally ended, she swirled off the floor in the opposite direction of Dominic and Wade. She rushed through the crowd with all eyes upon her.

"Who is that dancer? The woman with the scar?" She heard again and again before she found the stairs and flew down them. And then another set of stairs, and another, until she was on the bottom floor and out the front door, running into the cold, dark night.

Chapter Twenty-Nine

In the stable of a hacienda near the Henry House, Maria hid in a tack room. She used a saddle as a pillow, which she'd done many times in her life. Winter in San Francisco felt warmer sometimes than summer with the night clear and no fog shrouding the city. Just stars and moonlight and Maria knowing she would rather die than go on living without Dominic. Getting through Christmas seemed impossible now, having seen him. Her heart felt decimated at the end of her dance for him. She'd put all her longing into that dance. When it was over, the thought of returning to Wade had been unbearable. How could she go back to the two of them standing there at the edge of the dance floor? Good and evil. Both wanting her. She saw it in Dominic's eyes. Knowing he still wanted her made her all the more determined to disappear. She could not endanger his life.

She remembered the ocean cliffs she'd passed on rides around the countryside with Wade. Before first light, she left the warmth of the stable and began walking toward the ocean. She didn't want whoever fed the horses in the morning to find her in the tack room. The sea wasn't far, and nobody was out this early on Christmas Eve morning.

She shivered in her lace and satin dress, but more from what she was about to do than from the cold. Mud stuck to her boots, and the hem of her gown grew muddy as well. She reached the rocky cliffs sooner than expected, in time to watch the dawn break on the far side of the sea. That's what Dominic called the line where the horizon met the ocean, the far side of the sea. She wondered if her spirit would fly there when she died. Or would her spirit go directly to hell?

She didn't want to consider where her spirit would go. She just wanted to end her life. She wasn't afraid of dying. After Wade had nearly killed her, fear of death had vanished, perhaps because she remembered nothing at all from almost dying. The pain came when she lived.

She didn't look to where the surf broke against the rocks far below. She looked straight ahead. Did Nicky have the toy soldiers yet? Nicky had always risen early in the morning, long before Sally. Maria had often awoken to find him crawling out of the bed when he wasn't even old enough to walk yet. "Come back here, you little coyote," she used to tell him. That was her name for Nicky when he was small, "little coyote." He reminded her of a sneaky little wild dog, so smart, so determined, so fierce. Nicky would be fine without her. He was a strong, sturdy boy.

She closed her burning eyes, remembering his soft curls, and tears coursed down her cheeks. Why she thought of those silky blond curls now, all over the deck of Dominic's ship, surprised her. She'd hated him that day for cutting Nicky's hair.

Those curls were still in her sea chest, along with her knife and rosary.

She knew why the knife reminded her of death, but why did the rosary remind her of life? Jesus dead on a cross, that golden crucifix fitting perfectly into the palm of her hand. How did that cross signify life? Lupe told her it did. The cross was life for death. The only true sacrifice, Lupe had said.

It occurred to her she was offering her life for Dominic's this very moment, dying so he could live. Breaking the curse of death by breaking herself against the rocks.

The wind off the ocean whipped her red skirts and billowed them against her legs. She shivered again, suddenly truly cold. How could a soiled woman be a sacrifice for such a good man? She wasn't good enough to be a sacrifice. Still, dying would end her heartache. And perhaps keep Dominic alive. At least Wade wouldn't kill him on account of her.

She must stop thinking.

Must stop waiting.

A raven lit in a nearby tree, a twisted cypress, the big black bird watching her. The raven seemed to know what she was about to do. Waiting there to fly down to the rocks and peck her bones clean.

Just do it! Jump!

The dark voice came with a vengeance, startling Maria out of her grief. The raven squawked in the tree. Seagulls screamed in the distance. The pounding waves far below matched the roar of Maria's heart.

She looked around as she always did when the voice hit her. She saw no one, but in the distance, above the city, smoke rose in a billowing cloud. Some houses in the city had chimneys, and many tents had woodstoves, but this smoke was different.

It looked like a large fire near Dominic's house. Wade's house too, but Wade's Oriental palace could burn to the ground for all she cared. But not Dominic's beautiful mansion. Nicky lived there. Dominic lived there.

Before she knew it, Maria was running back to the city. Shrubs on the sandy hills tore at her skirts. How glad she was to have worn her boots! By the time she got to the plaza nearly an hour later, Dennison's Exchange was gone. The gambling house on Kearny Street between Clay and Jackson, overlooking Portsmouth Square, had been solidly built and was now a mighty heap of rubble. The fire spread in both directions away from the incinerated gambling hall, consuming the line of buildings on the south side of Washington Street. With no fire department in the city, frantic men with mining tools were tearing down tents and temporary structures and blowing up sturdier houses with gunpowder in an attempt to halt the flames.

The noise was terrible. Maria covered her ears as explosions rocked the plaza. Smoke made her cough. She didn't know where to go. Utter relief filled her that up on the hill, the mansions were safely standing.

"You need to get somewhere safe, miss!" a man shouted. His face was covered with black soot, and the whites of his eyes gave him a wild look. He was running down the street with a shovel in hand.

Maria realized he was yelling at her. Men rushed everywhere. Some carried belongings, others tools. An Oriental man with a long pigtail ran past her carrying a chicken under each arm. The scene was surreal. And then out of the smoke and chaos, Wade appeared on the black stallion. The horse she considered her own. She saw him too late. He galloped right up to her and slid to a stop, nearly running her over. "Get on!" he ordered.

She longed to defy him, but he looked like the devil himself. He kicked free from the stirrup so she could climb aboard. Without a word, she grabbed the hand he stretched out to her and hoisted herself up behind him in the saddle. They raced out of the burning plaza and looped around the flames before riding up the hill to Wade's mansion.

Tears filled Maria's eyes as they passed Dominic's home. Everyone was standing on the porch watching the city burn. Nicky spotted her and began yelling her name. The moment was so awful Maria buried her face in Wade's back and wished she'd died at the cliffs.

Nicky howled her name all the more.

Wade laughed. She raised her head long enough to see him waving to them. She wanted to die and be done with it.

Dominic did not return Wade's greeting. He scooped Nicky up into his arms and held his son close. Maria squeezed her eyes shut again.

"Merry Christmas, my love," Wade said. "I searched all night for you. Did you think I would let you go that easily?"

Maria didn't answer him. She wondered if he'd kill her for running away. A part of her hoped that he would. She should have thrown herself onto the rocks. It would have spared Nicky the shock of seeing her. And spared her from having her heart ripped out as he howled her name in longing.

Dominic had gotten home in the wee hours of the morning. He'd searched for Maria nearly all night long. *Why God?* he whispered as she rode up the hill with Wade. She still wore the black-and-red gown of the night before. He could see her boots and black stockings covered with mud. Where had she gone? Had she spent the night outside? Obviously, she'd been walking somewhere through the mud.

He hadn't wanted to return home without her, but he knew Nicky would awaken, and he wanted to be there so Nicky wasn't frightened. He'd watched the fire overtake Dennison's Exchange an hour ago. He considered going down there to help put it out, but a part of him reckoned the gaming hall needed to burn. All the gambling halls in the city could burn, along with the brothels. The city would be far better off without the deplorable places.

By the time he realized the fire wasn't going to stop at Dennison's Exchange, Nicky and Chloe were frightened and didn't want him to leave. Then Maria rode up the hill with Wade, and now Nicky was beyond consoling.

He understood his son's grief. He felt like screaming his anguish too, seeing Maria's arms around Wade as she hid her face against his back. The fire ravaged the city, and it felt like his heart was burning down as well. He carried his wailing son into the house.

"Maria," Nicky sobbed. "I want Maria!"

"I do too," Dominic said. "But she lives with Captain Reynolds now."

Nicky fought to escape him. "I go see her!"

"You cannot see her."

"I see Maria!" Nicky wailed, kicking like crazy.

The boy's lungs had always taken Dominic aback, though Nicky had not thrown a temper tantrum like this in a long time. Now the boy raged in his father's arms until he was exhausted. Dominic sat down in a chair and held the boy until he cried himself to sleep. The ordeal reminded him of a storm at sea, when all he could do was hold tight to the wheel and do his best to steady the ship. In all his years on the sea, he'd learned so much about holding on when all seemed lost. So many things at sea were out of a captain's control. The weather. The waves. The wind every ship needed to go anywhere. But there were also many things a man could do to keep on. Like every day plotting his course, taking out his instruments, looking up, and determining his way by the sun. Using heavenly lights instead of earthly ones. The sun was there, never changing. And so was God, never changing. A steadfast love he could count on, no matter what. He counted on that love now. For him. For Nicky. For Maria.

He sat there holding his son and praying for Maria. Praying for Nicky. Praying for himself. He was afraid to release his emotions. Maria should have been his wife. Should have been a mother to Nicky. It made no sense that she had gone to Wade.

Seeing her on the back of that horse with him, the same black stallion Dominic had ridden to catch up with her when she took Maria Elizabeth to Rancho de los Robles, about gutted him. Not only was she riding that horse with Wade, she was in his mansion, in his bed. The thought of Maria in Wade's arms was worse than anything he'd ever imagined.

He looked down at his sleeping son, and tears flooded his eyes. Nicky didn't look a thing like Sally. He could have been Maria's child. The boy loved her like she was his mother. Second-guessing himself had never been his nature. Making decisions and living with them without looking back had always been one of his strengths. But now he couldn't help wondering if Maria had gone down this dark path with Wade because he'd married Sally instead of her.

His mind went back to that day in the vineyard when she'd kissed him. Maria's first kiss. He'd known it was her first kiss, even though she'd acted like she'd kissed a hundred men. He'd wanted her so badly then. Wanted to throw every good intention to the wind and sweep that Spanish girl up and carry her away on his ship.

Had he ever considered God might have brought Maria into his life to be his wife instead of Sally, and he'd missed that turn on the road? Tears rolled down his face, dripping onto Nicky in his lap. He hadn't cut the boy's hair in quite a while, and his golden curls were back. Couldn't Maria see this? He'd allowed Nicky's curls to grow back hoping she would come back as well.

The pain in his chest felt physical. Tracing the scar on Maria's face last night left him aching inside. Her beautiful face marred by evil. She didn't fall down the stairs. Wade had done that to her with his tiger ring.

He wanted to kill Wade. Get his pistol, walk up the hill, and shoot him between the eyes right now.

Vengeance is mine sayeth the Lord.

The thought silenced his own thoughts. He recognized the Shepherd's voice.

The Lord will repay the righteous.

"I'm not righteous, Lord," he whispered out loud.

My blood shed for you makes you righteous in my sight.

"Yes, Lord." Dominic nodded his head, tears splashing down his face.

Trust in me.

"Yes, Lord." Dominic felt so broken. Utterly broken, like Maria was broken. Wade, of all men. His worst enemy. The man he'd once admired more than he'd admired his own father or any other man in the world.

He remembered the first time he saw Wade standing on the deck of his ship in the Boston harbor, commanding men as *The Sea Witch* prepared to set sail for China. Sunlight had flashed off Wade's golden earrings. He'd looked like a god of old, tall and handsome as the devil. The man had turned out to be a devil indeed. But in the beginning, when Dominic was sixteen years old, he'd idolized the older ship captain. Dominic had already been a cabin boy aboard another ship, and quickly moved up the ranks to sailor on *The Sea Witch*. Wade made him second mate after just a few months. Dominic was only seventeen when he became an officer.

"You're a leader, Dom. We're not going to waste that ability," Wade had said. Everywhere Wade went, Dominic went too for several years. Wade often ribbed him for being a "wide-eyed *church* boy." At sea, Wade didn't touch drink, but in Shanghai, he preferred whiskey in a crystal glass. In Shanghai, Wade had handed Dominic his first drink and his first woman, making sure Dominic didn't leave China without losing his virginity. And not with just any woman. Wade had found the most beautiful prostitute in the city and left him with her for three days in Shanghai. "You won't come back to my ship until you're a real man," Wade had told him.

When Dominic had returned to *The Sea Witch* that Sunday after three days losing his way, drowning in sin and pleasure and unspeakable things, Wade made him first mate. "It's good to see you know what you're made of now," Wade had told him. "I couldn't have a boy for my first mate. I needed a man." Wade had smacked him on the back and headed for the helm with a grin on his face.

Dominic stared down at his precious son sleeping in his lap and couldn't stop the tears rolling down his face. "I'm such a sinner, Lord," he whispered, wiping his nose. The thought of Nicky on a ship under a man like Wade horrified him.

Of course, Maria would lose herself to Wade. Hadn't he done the very same thing? It was different because he was a man, but still, everyone fell under Wade's spell. Wade had a way of enthralling people. Seducing them so easily. Leading lambs astray and then to slaughter.

Bring her back, Lord. You made the heavens and the earth; certainly, You can bring Maria home to me. To You, Lord.

If I say, "Surely the darkness shall cover me,
and the light about me be night,"
even the darkness is not dark to you;
the night is as bright as the day,
for darkness is as light to you.

Psalm 139:11–12

Chapter Thirty

Maria could feel the rage radiating out of Wade like the flames licking the city as she rode behind him on the black stallion. What would he do to her once they were alone in the house? The servants wouldn't dare intervene. There was nobody to help her. Wade dumped her near the porch steps and rode off toward the stable. Hurrying into the mansion, she raced up the stairs to her room. Going straight to her sea chest, she threw open the lid and reached inside for the knife. She had killed before; certainly, she could kill again.

Pick up the cross. Trust me. I will help you.

Maria stared at the knife in her hand, wondering where those words had come from. It wasn't like the dark voice. This voice descended on her calmly, with authority, radiating peace.

She gripped the knife more tightly, resisting the urge to put it down.

Not the knife. Pick up the cross.

Did the words come from inside her? She didn't think so. She wasn't sure where the strange thought came from, but it stopped her in her tracks. She stared at the rosary lying in her sea chest, Jesus on the cross. She'd seen it all her life, but suddenly she really looked at it.

Wade's boots thudded in the hallway.

Put down the knife. Pick up the cross, my beloved.

Tears filled Maria's eyes. She held tightly to the knife. It was the only thing she had to defend herself. She pushed away from her sea chest and stood up on her feet as the door handle rattled.

"Jesúcristo, help me," she whispered, squeezing the hilt of the dagger in her hand.

Wade threw open the door. He was wearing the same clothes as the night before. So was she, her dress muddy and torn and smelling of smoke. "My love," he said with a slow, wicked smile, "I see you are ready for me."

She raised the knife. "You will not touch me."

"Oh, but I will." He walked into the room with all the confidence in the world. "You give me such pleasure, Maria."

"You are the devil!"

"And you are my prize. Put down the knife. I'd hate to break your pretty hand."

"You underestimate me."

He raised his eyebrows. "Do I, my darling?"

"I have killed a man before. I am not afraid to kill again."

Wade stopped in the middle of the room. "Really?" The smile on his face grew. "You must tell me about this killing."

"The man took my honor. I took his life." Maria raised her chin, resisting the guilt she felt for killing Joshua Tyler.

Wade watched her intently, like a bird of prey watches the grass for a mouse. "Mr. Guzman says you have the gift."

"What gift?"

"You hear voices. You speak to spirits."

"No," she said, even though she knew it was true. Mr. Guzman must hear the spirits too. But this didn't seem to bother him.

"You are a clairvoyant, my dear." Wade looked so pleased.

"I am not!" Maria tried to keep her voice calm. The knife trembled in her hand.

"Do you know where you get the power?"

"I do not have power."

Wade smiled. "Of course you do. You talk to the spirits in the night. In your sleep, you speak to them."

The hair on the back of Maria's neck rose, as did the hair on her arms. "You're lying."

Wade slowly walked toward her. "Put down the knife."

Maria raised the knife. "Don't come any closer."

"I wish you could see how beautiful you are right now. So wild, my love. Like St. Elmo's fire."

Maria's hands trembled. So did her legs. "You ruined my beauty," she accused.

"Oh, Maria, I didn't ruin your beauty. I marked you as mine. You are now the tiger's lady." Wade raised his hand, showing her his ring, the head of the tiger with its ruby eyes pointing at her. "Do you know where I got this ring?"

The knife began to feel slick in her hand. Her palms were sweating. "Where?" She wanted to keep him talking. If he was talking, he wasn't beating her.

"Shanghai. The man who made this for me had a beautiful daughter. A woman of the night. She made a boy into a man for me."

Warning rippled through Maria. There was a reason Wade was telling her this story. Not a good reason. "I do not care," she bluffed.

"You will care." Wade motioned for her to sit down in the elaborately carved chair nearby. It was covered in red velvet and had come from China, like Wade's other furniture.

"I don't want to sit down."

Wade walked over to the chair. "All right, I'll sit down."

Maria moved away from him.

"Dom owes everything he's become to me. I made him into a first mate before he was eighteen years old."

"I don't know what you are talking about."

"You know exactly what I'm talking about. Dom, who you played the whore for in front of every gentleman in San Francisco last night."

"I danced for no one but myself."

Wade laughed. "Do you think I am stupid, Maria? I know exactly who you danced for last night. Was that even dancing? It looked like you were making love to him."

"I have never made love." Her lips twisted in distain.

The smile disappeared from Wade's face. "You will pay for that remark."

"It's true. I have only been taken by men. I have never been loved."

Wade squeezed the woodened arms of the chair, his knuckles turning white, before he stood up. "Put down the knife. I'm afraid if I take it from you, I will kill you with it."

It was Maria's turn to laugh. "I hope you do. Take my life. Put me out of my misery."

"I don't want to kill you. I want to finish my story. The man who made this ring for me had a beautiful daughter. A woman of the night."

"Stop talking!" She bit her lip, trying to keep her wits about her.

"That ring maker's daughter made Dom into a man for me. I tried to turn that church boy into my equal but never really succeeded. I loved Dom once. Now I hate him even more."

"You are wicked!" she cried, longing to silence him.

He lunged at her, grabbing her wrist, twisting hard.

Pain pierced her arm. Maria screamed but didn't drop the knife.

He twisted further until she fell to her knees, dizzy with pain, but she wouldn't drop the knife.

"This is why you are my woman," he said right before he broke her wrist. He took the dagger and stuck it in her skirt as she lay on the floor. The blade brushed her thigh before he shredded the length of her skirt between her legs.

The shredded skirt gave her the ability to kick her legs free. Her boots were still covered in mud. When she kicked Wade in the face, mud smeared across his cheek. He fell backward, hitting the floor with a thud.

Pick up the cross.

Maria quickly crawled to her sea chest, following the calm, authoritative voice. Her arm throbbed. Pain filled her shoulder, flowering through her chest. Her broken wrist hung limp at her side. Using her other hand, she reached into the chest and grabbed her rosary. The heavy golden cross filled her hand.

"You shouldn't have done that." Wade stood over her, dirt smeared across his cheek from her boot. His lower lip bled. He grabbed her by the hair and yanked her backward.

"Jesúcristo!" she cried, holding the cross up to his face.

Wade stared at the cross, the golden chain of rosary beads dangling down her arm, swaying in the silence. Wade let go of her hair and took a step away from her.

"Where did that come from?"

Maria steadied herself on her knees beside her sea chest. She felt sick from the pain in her wrist. "My grandmother."

"You think a cross can stop me?" Wade tried to laugh, but the laugh didn't come out.

Maria wrapped the chain of beads around her arm. She kept the cross raised against him. "God has stopped you."

He used his shirt sleeve to wipe the blood off his lip. Something happened in the room. Light poured through the windows. A peace Maria didn't understand descended upon her. She felt protected by great power. Wade walked over and stared out the window with his back to her.

The sound of a distant explosion rocked the city.

"They're using gunpowder to stop the fire." Wade's voice was quiet and calm.

She cradled her throbbing wrist in her lap, holding on to her rosary, staring down at the cross in her hand in a kind of wonder. *Jesúcristo,* his body carved in gold. How had this cross stopped Wade?

She realized how weary she was. The few hours of dozing in the tack room hadn't done her much good. The long walk to the cliffs and then running back to the city had left her spent. The searing pain in her wrist traveled up her arm and crippled her shoulder. Her knife lay on the carpet. She scooted across the rug as quietly as possible to pick it up. Scooting back, she dropped the knife into her sea chest but didn't put down her rosary. Her wrist hurt so bad she could hardly stand it.

"Could you fetch me a doctor?" she dared ask Wade. He was standing so still by the window; she wondered what was going through his mind.

Slowly, he turned around. There was no anger on his face now. He walked over to her and knelt down, taking her wrist gently into his hands.

She cried out in pain at his touch.

After examining her for a moment, he released her.

Sitting on the floor beside her sea chest, she tucked her broken wrist against her stomach, cradling it there with her other hand that wouldn't release the rosary.

"I may have trouble finding Mr. Guzman in the middle of the fire. I'll send Mrs. Mueller to help you for now." Wade stood up and left the room. He was like a different man. Calm. Controlled. Even kind. The change in him stunned Maria.

"Thank you." Her own words surprised her. Why was she thanking him?

He turned and looked at her. "You always fight me," he said sadly. "You are mine, Maria. I will not share you with any man. Especially not Dom." He stared at her almost tenderly and then left the room.

From the moment she'd picked up the rosary, everything had changed. She should have listened to the voice that told her to pick up the cross and not the knife when Wade was coming down the hall. Something supernatural had happened that she couldn't explain. She did hear voices, had spent her entire life trying not to listen to them. The voices frightened her. Especially the dark voice. It had been gone since she'd left

Dominic, but she'd clearly heard it telling her to jump off the cliff this morning. And the raven waiting for her death. Closing her eyes, she willed herself to stop thinking. From the time she was a little girl, she'd lived with dark spirits. Tears filled her eyes. She'd been born with spirits. Good spirits. Bad spirits. She never saw the good spirits, but sometimes she sensed they were trying to protect her. Sometimes when she awoke in the night, she saw one of the bad spirits. A dark shadow passing before her face or lingering in the corners of her room, terrifying her.

When Isabella had joined the family and grew old enough to share a room with her, Maria complained to everyone, but secretly she loved Isabella sleeping with her. Isabella was always scared in the night too. The girls huddled together, reciting the rosary on the really bad nights.

"Do you think it's the devil?" Isabella would ask in her little girl voice. "Lupe says the devil is real."

"Don't listen to Lupe," Maria would say. "That old woman is just trying to scare you into believing in Jesúcristo."

"I do believe in Jesúcristo," Isabella would insist. "You should believe too!"

When she was small, Isabella had been so full of faith. Everything had been real to her. Everything true. Maria had outgrown that, and now everything had become half-truths. She began to question the voices. The battles in the night. They'd only made her stronger. She'd learned not to cry in the night. Learned how to keep Isabella from crying too.

"We live in a land of spirits," Isabella had said. "They are all around us. Tempting us to do good or evil."

"Nobody can tempt me to do anything," Maria had said.

"You should do what Lupe tells you to do," Isabella had said. "Believe in Jesúcristo and pray his angels chase away the bad spirits."

"I believe in myself," Maria had said. "I don't need angels to protect me. I can protect myself."

But she couldn't protect herself. She'd been raped by men. Beaten by men. Tears slipped down her face. She was growing weak in her mind and heart. She felt it. She knew it. Was it Wade's cruelty? The voices returning? Going crazy over losing Sally and Maria Elizabeth? Since the baby died, she hadn't been the same. She had known the moment Maria Elizabeth's little spirit left her body. It was almost as if she felt a little pop, a kind of release while holding the infant that dark, terrible night in the wilderness. The baby had been breathing in her arms, and then she wasn't, she was flying away.

And all those spirits flying around the campfire. Dark spirits. Mocking spirits. Spirits full of glee and mirth swirling around her. Maria had curled into a ball around Maria Elizabeth's limp little body. Holding a tiny human being that was no more. She hadn't saved Maria Elizabeth. Hadn't saved Ricardo from the jaws of the bear. Hadn't saved her own mother with the woodpecker feather from the sacred oak grove. Everybody died.

Maria longed to stop the flood of memories. The old Indian woman telling her the woodpecker feather could heal her mother. Perhaps this was her first memory. Her worst memory. Searching forever, it seemed, for the special feather in the forest. A little girl alone and frightened out in the woods. She'd finally found a woodpecker feather and rushed home to her mother's bedside. Her mother had been sleeping when she tucked the feather underneath her pillow. Her mother died that night. Maria didn't remember weeping with the rest of her family. She remembered her heart hardening. God had not accepted her offering of the woodpecker feather. Maybe it was the feather that had killed her mother.

She began to sob and couldn't stop. She didn't hear Mrs. Mueller open the door and come into the room. The German woman knelt down beside her on the floor and pressed the little cold bottle to her lips. The bitter syrup to make her forget the pain. Oh, how she wanted to forget not just the pain, but everything. Maria thirstily drank the syrup. The bitter liquid slid across her tongue like saving grace. Softening her memories. Softening her pain. Softening everything but her heart.

I own you, the dark spirit had said when she was seventeen years old. The night she'd returned to her bed after kissing Dominic in the vineyard. She'd fallen asleep, refusing to cry over him admitting he was set to marry another, even though she loved him. When he confessed he had a fiancée in Boston, it was a knife in her heart. The spirit came while she slept. She awoke with the dark spirit on top of her. A weight like a man, pressing her into the mattress.

She couldn't breathe. Couldn't move. *I own you,* the spirit had whispered, and a scream had gathered in her throat. A wild scream of resistance. Isabella had flown from the bed screaming too. Tia Josefa had run down the hall holding her rosary. Her aunt had burst into the room and taken Isabella into her arms. By then Maria was out of bed, shaking all over. The heavy weight holding her down was gone. The dark spirit gone from the room.

The bitter syrup trickled down her throat now. "More," Maria whispered. "Please give me more."

"Just a little more," Mrs. Mueller said. "We don't want you to become addicted again to Mr. Guzman's medicine."

Mr. Guzman had put a spirit in her that hated the medicine. How he did it, Maria didn't know. It had happened during the hypnotism. Even now her body tried to resist the medicine, but she willed the resistance away. She just wanted to forget everything. She just wanted to die.

"Mr. Guzman says you have the gift," said Mrs. Mueller, and Maria heard fear in that stern German voice.

Mrs. Mueller was afraid? Of her?

Maria began to laugh. It started low and came alive in her. Such awful laughter.

"Stop laughing," Mrs. Mueller ordered.

Maria could not stop laughing. Tears rolled down her face, and still she laughed.

"You're crazy." Mrs. Mueller backed away from her.

Maria kept laughing until Mrs. Mueller was gone, and then she wept.

Chapter Thirty-One

Dominic picked up one of the toy soldiers and turned it over in his hand. It was beautifully crafted and carefully painted by a steady hand. All the little soldiers were designed this way. Nicky loved them. His son sat on the bearskin rug before the flickering fire in Dominic's chambers, quietly playing with them. Dominic sat in a chair watching him, missing Maria so much. It was Christmas. Half of Portsmouth Square was in ashes. His heart was in ashes too. He just couldn't forget Maria behind Wade on that horse, riding up the hill with San Francisco burning. Nicky howling her name. Why hadn't God let him find Maria? Why had Wade found her instead?

He told himself that at least he knew where she was, safe from the fire. He suspected the toy soldiers were from her. Chloe said a young Oriental servant had brought them to the door while he was at the Henry House.

"A gift for the boy who lives here," the young man had said. Wade employed Orientals. The Chinese were his servants of choice.

"They're earnest workers and give me no lip," Wade had said years ago when Dominic visited his home in Boston and noticed all the servants were Chinese. "But they don't make good sailors like the Kanakas. The Orientals are land slaves."

Wade's voice rang in his ears. *Land slaves. Ship slaves.* Wade enslaved men. And women as well. He seemed to have no conscience, but he was the best ship captain Dominic had ever known. It was almost as if Wade walked above other men. Had tapped into some kind of power beyond mankind. Just like finding Maria when he couldn't find her. Everything went Wade's way.

Dominic squeezed the soldier in his hand. What a Christmas. The Lord's birthday. *Birth something new, Lord. Whatever you're doing, please get it done. Make me your soldier. Let me fight for Maria.* He suspected this battle for Maria had much to do with him. It was his choices that had led them all here to this awful place.

Gavilan would be here shortly. Chloe was overseeing the servants preparing Christmas dinner. Everyone was in a solemn mood with the fires of yesterday and Maria returning with Wade. As if he'd conjured up Gavilan's arrival, he walked through the door dressed in a gentleman's attire, holding a gift. "I see you've already opened your gifts," Gavilan said to the boy, dropping the wrapped package beside Nicky.

"Just this one," said Nicky. "We don't know where it came from." Nicky pointed to the finely carved wooden box that housed the soldiers neatly in several rows, the little metal figurines lying in satin, shining from the fire's glow. Most of the soldiers remained in the box. Nicky played with only two. Dominic had stolen one, and Nicky hadn't missed it yet.

Gavilan looked up. Dominic winked, wishing with everything inside of him that Maria was there, a part of their quiet celebration.

Ruffling the boy's curls, Gavilan came over to Dominic. Standing up, Dominic dropped the little soldier into his breast pocket and then shook Gavilan's hand. "Merry Christmas, my friend."

"Merry Christmas to you."

"Is it a nightmare down there?"

Gavilan knew he spoke of the city. "Nobody knows it's Christmas. They're already rebuilding, stripping the latest ships in the harbor as best they can for lumber and whatnot. I've posted guards on our ships. They won't be getting anything from us."

"Maybe we should help rebuild."

Gavilan shook his head. "They're throwing up shacks. Just enough shelter to get them through winter. As soon as the snow melts in the mountains, they'll return to the goldfields. I'm all for rebuilding the city, but not like this; these men live like animals. I was hoping the fire would bring them to their senses, but it hasn't. They're so sick with gold fever they can't even think straight."

Dominic put his hand on Gavilan's shoulder. "Thank you for all you do. I hardly ever see you anymore. You're always at the office running our business."

Gavilan smiled. "What else is there to do?"

"You could run off to the goldfields."

"Breaking my back digging up gold dust to spend on whiskey and women isn't for me."

Dominic laughed softly. "Instead of working so hard, you could court my sister."

Gavilan smiled. "Maybe someday."

"Why not today?"

"I heard Maria was riding through the city on the back of a horse with Wade yesterday. What kind of man takes a woman for a ride through a fire?"

That's why Gavilan wasn't ready to court Chloe. *Maria.* Dominic made sure Nicky wasn't paying them any mind. He hadn't spoken to Gavilan since before the party. He lowered his voice. "Maria ran away from us at the party. Wade found her first."

Gavilan's jaw hardened. "Ran away from us? Who is us?"

"I ran into them at Henry House. You're right, that's a terrible scar on her face. I tried to speak with her, but Wade got in the way. She danced. Wade and I stood there watching her, then she was gone."

"So you and Wade went after her together?"

Dominic lowered his voice even more. "Wade went his way, and I went mine. Wade found her, I didn't."

"A little help from the Almighty might do some good." Gavilan's eyes narrowed in anger and frustration.

"Were you listening in church last Sunday?" He was pleased Gavlian had recently taken to attending church with them. Gavilan came to the church tent late and left early, but at least he came. Chloe was beside herself with delight about it.

"I'm always listening. If God can part the Red Sea, he can certainly bring that redhead home, if he wants to."

"Home to you or to me?" For some reason, he suddenly felt like teasing Gavilan a little bit.

"I don't care if it's you or me. As long as she's back with us, I'm willing to step aside and let you wed her if you're willing. If you're not, I'll wed her."

Neither mentioned the awful truth. Wade was most certainly bedding Maria. "If God brings her home, I'll wed her."

"Even if she carries his child?"

"She won't."

"How do you know she won't?"

"Wade won't sire any children. He has his way of stopping that."

"What kind of man doesn't want a son?" Gavilan looked at Nicky. Dominic realized for the first time Gavilan longed for a son of his own.

"Wade isn't like other men."

"Now that's the truth. I'm just waiting for my chance to get rid of him."

Dominic put his hand on Gavilan's shoulder. "That isn't the answer."

"It may not be your answer, but it's mine."

"Dinner's about ready," Chloe said from the doorway.

Nicky tucked his two soldiers back into the box. "Where's my other soldier?" He looked around for the one Dominic had in his pocket.

"We'll find it later." Dominic let go of Gavilan and walked over to Nicky. "I'm sure it's around here somewhere." He scooped Nicky up into his arms. The boy was getting so big.

"Is that the bear that nearly killed you?" Gavilan pointed to the bearskin rug.

"That's him." Dominic grinned. "I won."

"Looks like he was about nine feet tall." Gavilan stepped across the bearskin rug and walked toward Chloe, standing in the doorframe. "Have you ever seen one of California's grizzlies, Chloe?"

A smile blossomed on Chloe's face. "No, I haven't. Maybe if someone would take me for a ride across the hills, we could spot a grizzly."

"I don't want to see a grizzly unless it's a skin on the floor," said Gavilan, "but a ride across the hills with you might be nice come spring."

Gavilan followed Chloe down the upstairs hallway. Dominic carried Nicky in their wake. He suspected Gavilan had been wanting to speak to him about Maria since he'd returned to the city from Monterey. Now that Gavilan knew where things stood, maybe he'd pay more mind to Chloe. Dominic hoped so. Men were always trying to capture Chloe's attention, but she seemed to only grow more determined to get Gavilan to see her as more than a little sister.

The toy soldier was heavy in his pocket. Somehow he wanted Maria to know he knew the soldiers had come from her. And he wanted her to know today. On Christmas. He could take the soldier to Wade's stable, ask a stable hand to walk it up to the house. Pay the stable hand to make sure it got into Maria's hands. *If there's a better way to get to Maria, show me, Lord.*

They were all sitting down to dinner when guests arrived. Dominic rose from his chair, told the servants to set places at the table for the guests, and went to the foyer to greet their unexpected visitors.

"Don Pedro," he said happily. "Merry Christmas, *mi amigo*. My home is your home."

"*Feliz Navidad*! You have a magnificent hacienda, Captain Mason," Don Pedro replied.

"Please call me Dominic." He hugged Don Pedro and then turned to Isabella. "You grow more beautiful every time I see you, Isabella."

She smiled, her almond-shaped blue eyes shining in her olive-skinned face. Those clear blue eyes with thick black lashes were so surprising on her. Dominic hugged her, his hopes soaring. With Maria's sister and uncle here, certainly he could get the soldier to her now. Even more, maybe he could get Maria away from Wade.

"Where's Maria?" Isabella had the prettiest smile, perfect teeth very white against her tanned skin.

"She lives just up the hill." Dominic tried not to show how much this hurt him.

"Since when does a man not live with his own wife?" Don Pedro shrugged out of his once-fine cloak that had seen better days. He'd lost some weight and looked more fit and healthy than Dominic had ever seen. The hard work of the goldfields must have done the old Spanish don some good.

"Maria and I aren't married." Dominic realized Maria's family's arrival could become a real problem. What would Don Pedro do when he discovered Maria living with Wade without the sanctity of marriage?

"Why not?" Don Pedro looked confounded.

"When we returned to San Francisco, Maria decided . . ." Dominic wasn't sure how to delicately describe her present situation.

"She isn't here for Christmas?" Isabella intervened. The girl seemed to sense his distress and was trying to help him. "That is so like Maria. Always running off somewhere when the best thing is right in front of her."

"Running off? Why would she run off, Captain Mason?" Don Pedro persisted.

"Please," Dominic sighed. "I am a captain no longer. Call me Dominic. And come, let's discuss this over our meal."

That took some of the steam out of Don Pedro's questions. "A meal? Looks like we arrived just in time, Izzy." Don Pedro handed his cloak to Mr. Miller, the butler. He helped Isabella out of her cloak, practically yanking it off the girl, and pushing it at Mr. Miller in a rush to get to the table.

Don Pedro apparently wasn't leaner because he liked to eat less, or drink less for that matter. As they all sat down, Dominic said a quick but heartfelt prayer over the food, then Don Pedro commenced to eat like a sailor and drink like one on shore leave. Dominic did his best to answer their questions about Maria without telling them she'd become Wade's mistress.

Nicky took a liking to Isabella, and by the end of the long celebratory meal, he was all but in her lap. After dinner, they went to the parlor and sat by the fire, where Don Pedro continued to drink brandy and tell stories of the gold rush. He seemed to have forgotten all about Maria.

Dominic quietly excused himself and spoke with Mr. Miller, instructing him to send one of the servants up the hill to announce to Maria, if possible, that Don Pedro and Isabella had arrived and wanted to see her. He took the toy soldier out of his breast pocket. "Please give this to whoever you send and tell them to put it in Maria's hand, and if they can't put it in her hand, to do their best to see she gets it. Tell her it's from me." His throat tightened.

"Certainly," said Mr. Miller, looking a little perplexed with the soldier in hand.

Dominic spun away and returned to the parlor, where Gavilan and Chloe were doing their best to be polite hosts as Don Pedro drunkenly proclaimed that as soon as the snow melted in the Sierras, he would be a millionaire. Nicky had disappeared with Isabella. Dom suspected the two were upstairs on the bearskin rug with the soldiers.

"We came to the city to restock our mining supplies, only to find her burned to the ground," Don Pedro informed Dominic.

"It's the worst fire I've ever seen," Dominic agreed. "You can't throw up a bunch of shacks and tents and live like varmints, drinking and gambling all night long, without something like this happening."

Don Pedro didn't take the hint about drinking all night long. He refilled his glass with the last of the brandy in the decanter. When a servant hovered at the door, ready to bring more, Dominic waved her away. He wished Roman and Rachel and their children had come as well. Next Christmas, he must invite them all to the city. Perhaps by the grace of God, Maria would be here too, and San Francisco would be a more civilized place. Next month, the province was holding elections for senators. Dominic had hoped to throw his hat in the mix, but without Maria by his side, he didn't want to become a senator. Maybe he would just spend his time trying to clean up the city and figuring out a way to win Maria back.

Show me the way, Lord, he prayed as Don Pedro ranted once more about the gold rush. Chloe sat there sweetly with her hands in her lap while Gavilan rolled his eyes at Dominic when Don Pedro wasn't looking.

Dominic half listened to Don Pedro while imagining what Maria's Christmas looked like in Wade's Oriental palace. Then he stopped himself from imagining. It was too painful to think of Maria celebrating Christmas with Wade.

Had Gavilan really thought he'd reject her because she'd been in Wade's bed? As much as this hurt him, and it hurt him deeply, hurt him more than just about anything ever had, he wasn't about to give up on her. He'd gone astray before too. When he was young and proud and under Wade's spell.

Maria was young and proud and under Wade's spell. Though she didn't look nearly as young and proud anymore. She looked wounded. And older, with that scar on her face and pain in her eyes. Yet when she'd danced, he saw the girl she used to be, the passionate Spanish beauty a stage couldn't hold. A man couldn't hold.

Oh, Maria, come home to me. Come home to Nicky. His son wouldn't have a full set of soldiers until Maria returned it to him. Dominic just hoped she'd return the little soldier in person.

Chapter Thirty-Two

Maria awoke alone in her room, her arm strapped to a board. Mr. Guzman and Mrs. Mueller had put her through terrible pain trying to set her broken bones the week prior. Before leaving, they'd given her the bitter syrup. She hadn't seen Wade since the day of the fire. How many days ago that was, she didn't know. Christmas had come and gone in a haze of pain. The holiday seemed like a long time ago. She reached under her pillow and pulled out her golden rosary. And then the toy soldier. How the soldier had ended up on the table beside her bed, she didn't know. When she found it there, she'd been half out of her mind from the laudanum. She slept with it now, wishing the little soldier was Nicky . . . or Dominic. To be with both of them was all she wished for anymore. She tried not to dwell on these thoughts because they were so torturous.

Rain pounded the window. Was it January? Had the year 1850 arrived already? Fang told her Tio Pedro and Isabella had shown up at the mansion wanting to see her on Christmas.

Wade had turned them away. Fang didn't know what Wade told them. She didn't even know it was Tio Pedro and Isabella, just a Spanish man and a beautiful blue-eyed Indian girl claiming to be Maria's sister. That could only be Isabella.

Had they seen Dominic? Had they lodged at his house just down the hill? Fang came every day to help Maria dress and bathe and keep her company. Maria only used the bitter syrup to sleep at night. It didn't have the hold on her it once had. Whatever magic Mr. Guzman had worked months ago still lingered, giving her strength to not become enslaved to the laudanum again.

Fang helped with the mystery of the toy soldier one of Dominic's servants had delivered without Wade knowing. So Dominic knew she had sent the soldiers for Nicky. And he'd sent one back to let her know he knew it was her. She wondered if Nicky was missing the soldier. He was smart enough to realize it wasn't in the box with the rest of them. It bothered her that Nicky might be missing his soldier, but the last thing she wanted to do was send it back. The little soldier gave her hope that she wasn't alone.

Today Fang brought her a small leather Bible and another toy soldier along with it. Maria recognized it as the same Bible Sally had given to her back in Boston. Dominic had her sea chest delivered to Wade's mansion not long after she'd settled there, but the Bible wasn't in her sea chest. When it came, she wasn't sure how Dominic had ended up with it, but now here it was, along with the brightly painted little soldier Fang placed in her hands.

"You read book to us?" Fang said as she picked up an ivory-handled brush and began to comb Maria's hair, without mentioning the soldier Maria quickly tucked away.

Maria was surprised the Oriental girl wanted her to read. "I'm not sure I can read this book, Fang."

"Why not?"

"It's a holy book. I am not holy."

Fang stopped combing Maria's hair. "The man who sends the soldiers thinks you holy. He give you book. You talk in your sleep about this man."

"How do you know I talk in my sleep?"

"I stay with you because you drink too much syrup. Mrs. Mueller afraid you die. I stay with you. Keep you breathing."

"When did you stay with me?"

"I stay with you only first nights after you do this." Fang pointed at Maria's arm wrapped to the board. "How you do this?"

"I fought with the tiger again."

Fang shook her head. "No! You no fight with tiger. He kill you one day!"

"I don't care if he kills me."

Fang shook her head even more. "You no say! You my mistress. You die, where I go? You die, I must go back to men." Fang was getting upset.

It dawned on Maria that Fang's life revolved around hers now. Certainly, Wade wouldn't send the girl away if she was gone, would he? He wouldn't return Fang to prostitution? Maria knew the Chinese prostitutes in the city led terrible lives. Out of all the prostitutes in San Francisco, they were the most abused. Many died quickly. She'd grown to love Fang. The girl was her only friend here.

She looked at the Bible in her lap. The Word of God. Sally always called it the Word of God. She'd said it so reverently, as if it was true, as if God himself had written this book. Sally had read the Bible every day. Sometimes she made Maria sit down and read it with her. Back then, in Boston, it never occurred to Maria that she wasn't worthy to read the Bible. She wasn't even sure she believed what Sally believed, that it was really the Word of God. Sally would hold the Bible, and Maria would hold baby Nicky. Maria was much more interested in Nicky than the Bible.

He'd been such a precious baby. Sally hadn't seemed to mind that Nicky preferred to be in Maria's arms instead of hers. Sally would lie in bed reading the Bible while Maria walked Nicky around the room, cooing to him, loving him. She'd barely heard what Sally read, but some of the words returned to her now.

Where can I go from your Spirit?
Where can I flee from your presence?
If I ascend to heaven, you are there.
If I make my bed in hell, you are there.

Why did she remember the words so well? *I think this is your psalm, Maria. Psalm 139. Let me read it to you again.* And Sally had read it again, her sweet voice washing over Maria as she carried Nicky to the bed and laid him down beside his mother. Maria had lain down alongside Nicky, tickling his belly. Kicking his little legs, Nicky had smiled his gummy smile at her. All three of them in the bed as Sally read the psalm. Maria remembered the psalm because it had struck her so strangely that God could be in hell with someone. *If I make my bed in hell, you are there.* The words came back to her so clearly in Sally's voice. Maria's heart began to pound. She had made her bed in hell with Wade. Could God really be with her here in Wade's house?

Sally had stitched Psalm 139 onto a handkerchief for her at Christmas last year. Where was that handkerchief now? Suddenly, desperately, Maria wanted that handkerchief. She jumped up from the chair. She had to find that handkerchief with the psalm stitched on it.

"What wrong?" Fang asked.

"I need to find something." Maria went to her sea chest, threw it open, and began digging through it with one hand. She couldn't use her broken wrist.

Fang came over to help her. "I look for you." Fang bent down beside her, peering into the trunk.

"It's a handkerchief. A white handkerchief with colorful stitching."

Fang used both hands to move clothes around. Mostly it was apparel in the trunk. She found a folded white handkerchief, but when Fang opened it, Nicky's silky blond curls were nestled there. Tears filled Maria's eyes. She reached out and touched the curls. How soft they were. How much she missed that little boy. Using one hand, Maria tenderly folded the handkerchief back around the curls.

Fang tucked the handkerchief aside and continued to search for the other handkerchief. Maria really didn't know if the psalm handkerchief was even there. She hadn't cared much about it after Sally gave it to her. Back then, her mind had been full of Nicky. The baby was all she really cared about, and of course, his daddy.

Oh Sally! Where is the handkerchief!

A smile spread across Fang's face as she pulled a white handkerchief from the trunk. She used both hands to hold it up for Maria.

Where can I go from your Spirit?
Where can I flee from your presence?
If I ascend to heaven, you are there.
If I make my bed in hell, you are there.
If I rise on the wings of the morning
and dwell on the far side of the sea,
even there your hand shall lead me,
your right hand shall hold me fast.
Psalm 139:7–10

The text was neatly stitched in many colors. Sally's needlework was the most beautiful thing Maria had ever seen. Tears splashed down her cheeks. She read the psalm out loud to Fang. When she came to the verse, "If I rise on the wings of morning or dwell on the far side of the sea, even there your hand shall lead me, your right hand shall hold me fast." In that instant, she felt God there. Maria grew warm. Peaceful. Certain she was held in everlasting arms.

Fang handed her the handkerchief and began to cry too. Both women were weeping on their knees beside the sea chest. Maria put her uninjured arm around Fang and held the girl as best she could, still grasping Sally's handkerchief in her hand. Fang began to cry harder and soon was sobbing. Maria wasn't sure how to pray, or what to pray, but in her heart, she cried out to the God who promised to be with her even if she made her bed in hell. Fang had known a bed of hell too. Perhaps many hellish beds with many hellish men. How could God be with women who slept in these hellish beds? Fang had probably never had a choice the way Maria had chosen Wade. She should never have come to Wade, but deep down inside, she didn't feel worthy of a good man. A man like Dominic, who prayed and sang so beautifully to God. She'd been ruined in a church by a man who didn't fear God. She'd killed and for a long time didn't feel bad about taking a life. What kind of woman was she? The kind of woman who made her bed in hell, that's what she was, and God was with her. She wasn't too ruined for God.

Jesus loves you, Maria. He loves you so much he died for you. Sally's voice came back to her.

Fang lay her head in Maria's lap. Maria put down the handkerchief and stroked Fang's straight, dark hair with her uninjured hand. How old was the girl? Probably not that much older than Isabella. Fang's hair reminded her of Isabella's hair. The girl's dusky skin was like Isabella's too. "Jesus loves you so much he died for you, Fang," Maria whispered, stroking the girl's long hair. Fang cried softly. Quietly. The rain had stopped, but wind still rattled the upper-story bedroom windows.

If I rise on the wings of morning. The wind sounded like wings beating the glass. Maria smiled. Fang needed her. And they both needed God. Had Dominic sent the Bible? Of course he had. *Oh, Jesúcristo, guard Dominic's life. Guard Nicky's life. Guard Fang's life and my life.* The more she prayed, the more she wanted to pray.

Fang finally sat up, wiping her eyes. The girl seemed embarrassed by the emotions that had overcome her.

"Will you help me put all this back?" Maria motioned to the belongings they'd removed from the sea chest while searching for the handkerchief.

Fang was happy to return everything to proper order in the trunk.

Maria picked up the handkerchief and walked back to the velvet chair. She sat down and read the words of her psalm again. It wasn't the whole psalm. She remembered Sally saying this particular psalm was very long. Aside from hearing the Bible read in church, and by Sally, Maria knew little about the holy book. She retrieved the Bible and searched through it until she found Psalm 139. She felt like she could read it now that God had touched her and Fang. She was reading while Fang arranged her hair when Wade walked into the room. Maria shut the Bible and hurriedly hid it under her bandaged arm.

"I've arranged my coach to take us to the polls," Wade said. "It's election day. Of course, you can't vote, but I will."

So January was here. Maria looked toward the window, rattling with the wind. The rain came and went, sometimes pouring down in torrents. "Won't the roads be impassable?"

"It will take us awhile, but we'll get there. You'll stay in the coach, but I want you to look presentable."

Maria could feel Fang's fingers tense in her hair. The girl was still trying to do her job, carefully pinning up her tresses. Wade walked over and handed Maria a small bottle of medicine.

"Drink this."

Maria looked at the little brown bottle, and dread flooded her. It was birthwort, the medicine women took to stop a child from forming in their womb. Wade himself had never given birthwort to her before. It always came from Mrs. Mueller, who acquired it from a midwife somewhere in the city.

Wade smiled. "I've missed you." He spoke as if it was only the two of them. He didn't acknowledge Fang. It was like the Oriental girl wasn't even there. "Before we leave, Mr. Guzman is coming to have a look at your arm and see that you no longer need your medicine at night. I do not think your weaning will be as traumatic as before. You look clear-eyed this morning." Wade touched her cheek, tracing the scar.

Maria shivered.

"It's whitening nicely. I kind of like your scar now, my love."

Maria dropped her gaze from Wade's. Underneath her bandaged arm was her Bible. She'd never wanted a Bible before, but the thought of having to part with it now, especially knowing Dominic had somehow delivered it to her, upset her.

Wade put his finger under her chin and lifted her eyes to his. "It's a new year. California will be a state soon. Perhaps we should marry."

Fang dropped the pins in her hand. Wade ignored the girl. Fang got on her hands and knees and crawled around the floor, picking them up. Maria could hardly breathe. The thought of marrying Wade was too awful. She closed her eyes, unwilling to look at him any longer. He was being tender with her, but she knew his tenderness wouldn't last. It was only a matter of time before his rage rose again. *If I make my bed in hell, you are there.* The words of the psalm whispered through her mind unbidden. God was with her. In this hell with Wade, Jesúcristo was here.

Tears flooded her eyes and leaked from her closed lids. They trailed down her cheeks, and Wade's thumbs wiped them away. He held her face in his hands. The hands that had nearly killed her.

"Look at me, my darling." Wade's voice was thick with emotion.

Maria had never heard his voice this way before. Soft and tender and a bit uncertain. Opening her eyes, she could see love in Wade's eyes. Could a man like Wade actually love her? She doubted it.

"You're crying with happiness?" He ignored Fang crawling around on the floor at their feet.

Her head was swirling with what she could do to escape him. She would not marry him. She'd killed once to escape marriage to a man she despised. If she had to, could she kill again?

If you dwell on the far side of the sea, even there your hand shall lead me, your right hand shall hold me fast. The promise from God filled her mind, easing the desperation in her heart.

"I'm having a ring made for you. A ring like mine." Wade put his hand right in front of her face. The tiger ring with its ruby eyes staring at her. "You must have your own tiger ring. When the ring is finished, we will wed."

Maria looked down at the floor, and Fang glanced up at her. The girl's dark, almond-shaped eyes proved fathomless. A tear left a wet streak on Fang's cheek too. Fang had been bought and paid for. Maria had not, but the two of them were both Wade's slaves. At least Fang didn't have to share his bed. Or did she? Where did Wade go on the nights he didn't satisfy himself with her? She'd not been in his chambers since before the Christmas Eve party.

Fang broke eye contact with her and reached under Maria's chair to sweep up the last pin.

"Would a tiger ring please you, Maria? Perhaps we should make the tiger's eyes emerald in honor of your green eyes?"

As Fang scooted away with her handful of hair pins, Wade knelt down, putting his hands on Maria's knees.

Maria mustered a smile. "Emeralds would be nice."

"Done!" Wade's voice rose with excitement. "I never thought I'd marry, but you have changed my mind, my dear. Perhaps we will even do away with this after a ring is firmly on your finger." He touched the bottle of birthwort in Maria's hand. "Do you know how many women here marry and they are already with child? Of course most of the females in San Francisco live on birthwort and are making a fortune plying their trade. The morals of this city are deplorable. This is why I am casting my vote today. I want sidewalks and clean streets. Tossing garbage in the streets the way men do is beyond me. It's not helping the mud. It's only turning it to sewage. Men live like animals here. If California is to become a state, we need men in the legislature who will clean up the city. And men need wives to civilize them. I never wanted to be civilized until I met you." He leaned in and kissed Maria.

When she didn't respond, he plowed his fingers into her hair and kissed her until she accepted his passionate assault. The pins in her hair fell to the floor, her hair tumbling down.

"You make me happy," he said after ending the hungry kiss.

Maria's cheeks flamed with shame. Poor Fang. She would have to gather the pins back up and start over again.

Wade's face was wanton with lust. "We will celebrate the election tonight with champagne and your return to my chambers, my dear."

Chapter Thirty-Three

Dominic slogged through the mud to get to the polls. The weather was fierce, wind howling off the bay, rain pouring in torrents. The streets were a muddy river, yet the neighborhood polls were crowded all day long with men eager to promote the public welfare. Getting to the polls was a real challenge with rough-looking men thrusting their favorite tickets into new-comer's hands, demanding a vote for Geary of the old council or a plea to vote in a new council.

"The old council has made money enough! Let's give a new council a chance at the public crib!" cried a ticket holder.

"No. Geary is our man!" cried another.

The shouts deafened Dominic. He was relieved that he'd removed his name from the ballot. It wasn't his time to run for senator or anything else. Maybe it was time to return to the sea. He missed the mighty blue ocean rolling under his ship and being in command of his whole world. San Francisco didn't seem to be under anyone's command. Dominic hoped this election would bring more law and order to the city.

Every citizen of the United States was entitled to vote, men from every part of the earth claiming to be an American citizen today in San Francisco. Frenchmen doing their best to speak without an accent. Brawny Irishmen insisting they were born in America. Italians shouting in broken English that they were from New York. A swarthy-skinned Sandwich Islander in line in front of Dominic held up his ticket, swearing to the judge he was born in Boston.

"Where was your father born? What street did you live on in Boston?" the judge inquired.

The poor fellow didn't know how to respond.

"Turn him out, he's a Kanaka!" yelled a challenger behind Dominic.

The prompter alongside the man did his best to offer instruction, but the Sandwich Islander's vote was quickly rejected, and he was pushed aside.

After casting his ballot at the polling desk, Dominic waded back through men and a sea of mud to head for his office down at the harbor. He couldn't believe it when he saw a black gentleman's coach pulled by two black horses parked up the street. The coachman was laboring to place boards under the wheels to keep the coach from sinking even more and tipping over in the mud. The fine horses were up to their knees in mud. Dominic pressed his hat down more firmly on his head to keep it from flying away. He'd walk right by that mired coach on his way to his office. Perhaps he could help the poor coachman steady the vehicle. Where was the rich man who owned the coach? Down at the polls no doubt, wading through the chaos of men and mud, trying to cast his ballot. He hurried his step to aid the laboring coachman when one of the coach's dark window panes suddenly raised and a woman leaned out the window of the tilting carriage. Wind immediately captured her bright hair and blew it loose from its pins. Only Maria Vasquez had that hair.

Elation shot through him. Had she received the Bible he'd sent her yesterday? Had the toy soldier made it to her several weeks ago? Don Pedro and Isabella had returned to Rancho de los Robles, disappointed at not seeing her, Don Pedro grumbling that the fire had ruined his plans to restock his mining supplies. Dominic was practically running when he reached the coach. Thunder cracked and the sky opened once more, pouring down rain.

Maria pulled her head back in the window without seeing him. He stopped momentarily at the coachman's side. The Oriental man was covered in mud, straining to get a board securely under the coach's left tire. He was a young, strong fellow. Dominic worried less about him upon examining his sturdy constitution there in the pouring rain. "Where is Captain Reynolds?" He raised his voice to be heard over the slosh of the storm.

"At the polls." The coachman kept after his muddy business with the boards.

"I am Captain Reynolds's friend, and I must have a word with the lady."

The coachman looked up in surprise. That very morning Dominic had tucked another toy soldier into his breast pocket, promising Nicky these soldiers had a mission to accomplish and were headed off to war on their behalf.

"What war, Papa?" Nicky's blue eyes had widened in wonder and adventure.

"A war for love."

Nicky had blinked. Confounded. The boy was young and didn't understand. Dominic had ruffled his blond curls. "Someday you'll fight your own war for love, my boy. This is my fight. Now you mind Aunt Chloe while I'm off today."

"Yes, sir," Nicky had answered, picking up his soldiers and returning them to the battle he imagined on the bearskin rug. His father's chambers were Nicky's playroom. Dominic didn't mind. He loved having his son close by. The boy now slept in his own room just down the hall, but as soon as he awoke in the morning, Nicky padded down the hallway to Dominic's room and settled himself before the fire on the bearskin rug.

Dominic rose early each day, stoked the fire, and then settled down to read his Bible in the early hours before the sun rose over the sand hills above his mansion. Above Wade's mansion and the other grand houses being built on the hill above Portsmouth Square. The square was already rising out of the ashes from the Christmas Eve fire, buildings going up in a matter of days, many saloons, gambling dens, hotels, and boardinghouses to shelter the tide of immigrants. Some thirty thousand souls had poured into the city in 1849. Dominic suspected 1850 would see even more. Fortunately, as soon as the snow melted in the mountains, many of these men would head for the goldfields, leaving the city to gain its bearings without the flood of virile young men struck senseless by gold fever.

"Sir, you're a six-footer and solidly built, perhaps you boarding the coach and sitting on the right side until I steady her with these boards would help."

"Perfect, my good man! I'm happy to help!" Dominic strode around the coach and opened the right door. Yanking off his hat, he leaped up into the interior in a gust of wind and rain. He slammed the coach door closed and plunked down on the seat beside Maria. She was leaning to the right, trying to right the carriage with her body weight. He dropped his hat on the floor and took her in his arms, placing her on his wet lap. He was soaked from the rain and laughing.

She let out a surprised yelp, and he laughed all the more. "I didn't run for senator. I've decided to roam the streets helping carriages in distress."

Maria looked at him as if he'd lost his mind. He took her face in his hands and kissed her. For a moment, she resisted, and then she was kissing him back with all the passion he felt for her. Rain and wind rocked the coach. A small carriage lantern cast a warm glow. She was on his lap, her hair tumbling down. He threaded his fingers into her silky locks. She trembled in his arms. He kissed her and wanted to go on kissing her forever. She pushed his heavy woolen cloak away from his shoulders, and he removed hers. The cloak landed on the floor of the carriage on top of his drenched hat. Her gown was elaborate and laced all the way up her back. When he found himself undoing her laces, he came to his senses. "Maria," he breathed, "my love, we must stop."

"I don't want to stop," she murmured against his mouth. "I don't ever want to stop. I will die before I stop!"

"We both might die." Dominic took her by the shoulders and pressed her gently but firmly from him. "Wade will kill us if he finds us together."

"I don't care." Maria was breathless.

"I care. We must think of Nicky."

A stunned look came over Maria's face. Tears filled her eyes. "How is Nicky?"

"He loves the soldiers you sent him." Dominic's eyes dampened too.

"He does?"

"Yes, he certainly does."

Tears trickled down Maria's cheeks. Dominic touched her tears, traced the scar below her eye, down the curve of her cheekbone. "Oh, Maria, why did you leave us?"

"I had to," she said, closing her eyes as if in agony.

"I don't understand." He felt her agony but had no idea where it came from.

"I know you don't understand. I'm not sure I understand anymore. It seemed so true. Now I don't know what is true." She opened her eyes, crying harder now.

"What don't you know?" All the hurt he'd felt when she left him came rushing to the surface. He thought they would marry and finally build a life together. Finding her at Wade's mansion when he returned to the city had torn him apart, even more than his infant daughter dying. At least he understood dying. He didn't understand Maria's leaving him to become Wade's mistress.

"You must know I love you. I've always loved you, Dominic."

She so rarely said his name. It was always Captain Mason. Usually Captain Mason with a vengeance. Now it was Dominic, with such love. He could hear love in her trembling voice. Feel that love in her trembling body. Taste that love on her trembling lips. She pressed into him so eagerly, opening her mouth under his. This woman who fit him perfectly. Like God had made her to fit him. He drank in her sweetness. Wanted to lose himself in her. She was still so very beautiful, even with the scar. Perhaps more beautiful to him for having survived the battle that left the scar. She smelled like a spring breeze. Tasted like honey. Oh Lord, how he loved her. He felt something hard on her arm pressed between them. As he kissed her, he moved his hand, running it along whatever was keeping her arm stiff.

She had a broken arm.

He didn't stop kissing her, but he vowed he would not leave this coach without her. He wouldn't ever let Wade hurt her again.

She seemed to sense the change in him and pulled away. "I am too ruined for you, aren't I?" The hurt in her eyes pierced his soul.

"You could never be too ruined for me. I would wash you with my own blood if I could, but I can't. Only God can do that."

He'd just read this morning in his Bible about being washed in the blood of the lamb.

She sighed in wonder. "He hasn't left me. Even though I made my bed in hell, Jesúcristo never left me." Her laughter turned to sobs. She leaned against him, crying great sobs that sounded like relief.

"Of course God never left you. How could Christ leave you? How could I ever leave you, my love? I have loved you since the moment I saw you standing on that porch with your family at Rancho de los Robles. Why did you leave me?" He spoke against her ear, pressing his face into her silky hair. He didn't want to know, but he had to know, why had she turned to Wade?

She pressed her tear-soaked face against his damp neck. They were both wet from the rain on him, but steamy warm, the coach incubating them against the storm and the reality of Wade returning at any moment. She said something against his neck he wasn't sure he rightly heard. He took her by the shoulders, setting her upright on his lap. "Say that again."

"I am a cursed woman."

"Is that what you believe?"

"It's true. Men die because of me. I don't want you to die. I couldn't bear it." Her face was full of grief and regret.

"That is the devil's lie, Maria." He didn't mean to say it so sharply, but righteous anger flooded him. "Did Wade break your arm?"

She opened her mouth, but he stopped her from speaking. "The truth, Maria. We are done with lies between us."

"I wouldn't let go of the knife."

"Why did you need a knife?"

"I danced for you at the Christmas ball. Wade was furious."

"And the scar, he did that to you too?"

"On account of you. That day you came for me, I told Wade I loved you. He nearly killed me."

He hadn't known. How could he know Wade would treat her so poorly? *Oh Lord, help us. Free us from this devil. Show me what to do.*

They had to get out of the coach. He knew this with certainty. Dominic picked her up off his lap and put her down beside him on the seat. He grabbed their cloaks and then his hat. Pushing open the coach door, he stepped out into the pouring rain. His boots sank deep in the mud. The horses stood with their heads nearly touching the mud, their tails tucked tightly against the rain and wind. The animals looked miserable. The coachman was walking up the street, carrying another board. His head was down, and he was fighting the wind and mire. He didn't see them departing the coach.

Dominic helped Maria down out of the carriage. "I'm sorry about the mud. There's no help for it." He threw her cloak around her shoulders and sat his hat on her head. "Let's go."

He grabbed her uninjured hand and led her as fast as he dared down the mired street. Around the corner was a new hotel. The fire hadn't burned this part of town, and this brick hotel hadn't been hurriedly thrown up with timber and canvas like so many others. It was a well-crafted building, reminding him of hotels in Boston.

They walked right into the hotel like a married couple, Dominic's arm around Maria. "We are fresh off the ship," he told the man at the counter. "And weary from our voyage. We need a room. Your finest, please."

"Well, sir, you sailed in on a gale," the man said pleasantly.

"Yes, and my wife is cold and wet. I'd like to order a bath for her as well. Do you have a room with a fireplace?"

Maria looked at him, her eyes wide but trusting.

The man smiled. "I see you are a man of means. My best room is pricey."

"Does it have a fireplace?"

"Yes, sir, and it overlooks the bay."

"We'll take it." Dominic reached under his clock and pulled out his billfold.

"I usually deal in gold, but since you are new to our city, I'll accept American dollars only. No foreign currency."

"We're from Boston." It felt like the same conversation from last July, when they'd first arrived in the city, only this hotel was newer and grander, and not located near the plaza like the last hotel. Hopefully, Wade would never think to look for Maria here.

She remained quiet at his side.

"Was your wife injured in a storm?" The man behind the desk tried not to stare at Maria's face and bandaged arm, but he wasn't doing a very good job of it. "Those storms at sea can be fierce, especially this time of year. I busted my head open in a storm at sea. Lost a year of memory because of it. Do you and your wife sail much?" The man looked a bit perplexed by Maria's injuries.

"Yes, I'm a ship captain. We've weathered many storms together." Dominic tenderly touched Maria's cheek. "My wife is the strongest woman I've ever known."

The man behind the counter smiled in relief. "Well, you, sir, have a beautiful wife. You're a lucky man."

"Yes, I am." Dominic handed the man the money for the room and received a key in return.

"Will your trunks be along shortly?"

"We've hired a man to transport them from the ship, but not in this weather. We'll wait till the rain abates to bring our trunks here."

"Very good, sir. Enjoy the warmth and beauty of the city's finest lodging. I'll send a boy right up to light your fire, and my servant girls will draw your wife's bath. If you remove your boots and leave them with me, I'll have my servants clean them and deliver them up to your room."

"That's a fine idea." Dominic smiled. "The mud out there could bury a mule."

The man laughed. "It's buried several, and horses too. Have a seat right over there to remove your boots." The man pointed to a bench covered in green velvet and pushed up against a wainscoted wall. "We don't let dirt go up those stairs. Our new establishment strives to be the cleanest and finest in the city."

"You're off to a dashing start. I'm glad to see you have no gaming tables in here," Dominic said as he looked around the lobby.

"My fine Christian mother would roll over in her grave if I let such vice through the door. The Baptists raised the first Protestant Church in California a few blocks from here this past summer. The Episcopalians, Congregationalists, Presbyterians, and Methodists are building too, and all have Sabbath schools established in the city. What strain of faith are you and your wife, sir?"

"Presbyterians."

"Very good, sir. I'll send your boots upstairs promptly, and the bath too."

Chapter Thirty-Four

The room was on the fourth floor of the tall brick hotel and was spacious and lovely. Maria felt like she was dreaming. The rain had only strengthened, beating the windows, rattling the glass windowpanes. Dominic helped her out of her cloak and then removed his. A boy came and lit the fire in the fireplace. Few hotel rooms had fireplaces, but this hotel room was a suite with a parlor just off the bedroom and tall windows that overlooked the city. Maria's arm ached. Down in the lobby, Dominic had removed her boots for her. She couldn't dress without Fang's help and didn't know how she'd remove her gown and undergarments tonight, or even what she'd sleep in. The promised bath soon arrived, a wooden tub lugged into the room by a sturdy young man followed by servant girls carrying pails of steaming water. Neither Dominic nor Maria spoke to each other. Reality was setting in, and certainly by now Wade was combing the city for her.

What had they done?

Did Dominic really want to be here with her? He'd paid a small fortune for this room. He was milling around now, looking out every window, studying the locks on the door before he went and squatted down in front of the fireplace to warm his hands. His clothes were soaking wet. So were hers. They had no shoes. And the hotel owner thought they were married. Would she even be able to sleep tonight without any laudanum? Where was her pride? Her courage? She felt so weak and vulnerable right now.

The servants set up the wooden tub in front of the fire in the parlor. After filling the tub with water, they quietly left. Maria stood in front of a window watching the rain pour down. *He will die now,* came the dark voice. *Because of you, Dominic will die.*

She longed to cover her ears. Retrace her steps. Return to Wade's carriage mired in the mud. It was a bed made in hell, but at least it didn't terrify her. Being with Dominic terrified her. The dark voice wouldn't stop. She began to recite her psalm in her head. *Where can I go from your spirit? Where can I flee from your presence?* She wanted to flee. It was the same overwhelming feeling she had at Rancho de los Robles after swimming with Dominic in the pool. After being filled with absolute love for him and then convinced he would die because of her love.

His hands settled on her shoulders. Dominic leaned down and pressed his lips to her temple. She could feel the warmth of the fire on his damp clothes. He smelled of wood smoke and something sweet and spicy. It wasn't his ship captain's smell, but it was close and deliciously familiar.

"What are you thinking?"

The urge to lie was so strong, she forgot to breathe. How could she speak when she couldn't breathe?

"You're thinking of a way to get out of here. A way to run from me again." He pulled her back against his chest and wrapped his arms snugly around her. "Where can you go from me, Maria? I will follow you wherever you run."

"What if I go to the far side of the sea?" she whispered.

"I will find you there."

"Would you sail us there?"

"Maybe." He ran his fingers along her bandaged arm. "You will need help bathing."

Everything inside her melted. She turned in his arms, looked up at him. Noted the restraint in his eyes, his grin of regret. "But you won't help me bathe."

His smiled widened. "Unfortunately not. Unless I can find someone to marry us right now."

She couldn't keep playing along. "How can you marry me? I'm not worthy of your love. I will never be worthy of your love."

"Must we go over again what makes us worthy?"

"My past is hardly behind me."

"I never look back, Maria. You should know this about me by now."

Tears filled her eyes. "I don't know why Sally had to die. I should have died instead of her."

"Don't do this." Dominic pressed a finger to her lips to silence her.

She reached up and pushed his hand away. "I've been so proud. So stubborn all my life. Sally was none of those things."

"The Lord took Sally for his own reasons. And Maria Elizabeth too. The Lord gives and takes away, and we will bless his name."

"I wish I were her."

"You could never be Sally."

Maria spun back around in his arms, trying her best not to cry anymore. She could not look at him. The words he said were so true and painful. She could never be Sally. A lance sliced her heart.

"It is you I have always been mad about, Maria," Dominic whispered in her ear. He pressed his body against hers, the hard, muscular plane of him molding to her smaller frame. She remembered the first time she'd felt the length of him upon her. The night he fought with Roman and she'd sprung upon him, all fury, ready to scratch his eyes out. He'd rolled her over on the dance floor and carefully held her down, his big body all muscle and heat, his intent blue eyes searching hers as every part of his body touched hers. And she was lost, utterly lost in his conquering. She'd never forgotten that night.

"You can't keep running from me, Maria."

She leaned her head back against his chest in surrender. She was so tired of running. "How can I stay? Wade will kill us."

Dominic rested his cheek on top of her head. "The Good Lord holds our lives in his hands. I do not fear Wade."

Maria's heart raced. "I fear him," she admitted.

"I'll take care of Wade when it's time. Let's have a look at your arm." Carefully, he removed the bandage from her wrist. He took off the splint and then another layer of cotton. "Did a doctor care for you?"

"Wade's clairvoyant set the bone."

Dominic's eyes widened. "You're kidding?"

"Wade thinks Mr. Guzman's better than a doctor."

"Wade's crazy. He's always been crazy."

"Mr. Guzman speaks to spirits. He says I hear spirits speaking too."

Dominic took Maria by the shoulders. "Do not listen to any spirit but the Holy Spirit. Demons are full of lies. Clairvoyants speak to demons."

"I've heard voices all my life." Maria's heart was pounding so hard now.

"Don't listen to those voices. Listen to God. Read the Bible. Did you get the Bible I sent you? Ask God to send the voices away."

"I did get the Bible. I read from it this morning. Thank you. So you do not think I am a cursed woman? A crazy woman?"

"We are all under a curse until we accept Christ's death on the cross for us. Have you accepted his death for you?"

"I don't know. How do I accept it?"

"Believe it," said Dominic. "And love God with all your heart."

"I believe it," she whispered.

He smiled, kissed her lips.

She smiled and kissed him back.

He swept her up into his arms and carried her over to the bath in front of the fire. She held her broken wrist with her good hand to keep from bumping it. It didn't hurt as badly now and wasn't all that swollen. It must be mending. Dominic set her feet on the floor and turned her around so her back was presented to him. He loosened the laces on her dress.

"What are you doing?" Her heart continued to pound, speeding up even more. She felt a bit light-headed.

"Undressing you." He undid her gown, pushed it carefully off her shoulders and down her arms, especially her injured one, until it whooshed to the floor in a hiss of satin.

She stood there in her chemise and petticoat beside the tub. He stood behind her. He undid her petticoat, and it whispered down around her feet as well. He then loosened the strings on her bloomers. And her chemise strings. She wrapped her arms around herself to hold what was left of her clothes on. Her injured hand worked better than expected.

"That should do it." He took her by the shoulders and turned her around to face him. His eyes locked with hers. "I wish I could stay and be your lady's maid."

Her chemise strap fell off her shoulder. He didn't look down. Kept his eyes on her face.

"You're leaving?"

"I'll be back, but I'm taking this with me." He left her petticoat on the floor but scooped up her gown.

"You can't take my dress."

He smiled. "Oh yes, I can. And your cloak too." He walked over and lifted her cloak and his off the chairs near the fire. "You're not getting your boots back either anytime soon. No more running for you."

"What do you expect me to wear?"

"I expect you to rest. After your bath, take a nap. I'll bring back some dry clothes for you when I return."

"When will you return?"

"Soon, I hope."

"What if you don't return?"

"Don't listen to that voice, Maria. The devil is a liar. God has numbered my days. Hopefully, he's given me a big number so I can spend the rest of my days with you." He stepped back over to her and kissed her on the forehead. Reaching into his pocket, he pulled out Nicky's toy soldier, handing it to her, and then he walked swiftly to the door. At the door, he slipped into his cloak and held up the key. Her dress and cloak he carried under one arm. "I'm locking you in. Wish me luck in finding our boots."

"Why should you have your boots when I am standing here in my unmentionables?"

"May I mention how lovely you look in your unmentionables?"

She did her best not to return his smile, though that smile filled her belly with warmth. "Please don't be long." She tried to sound brave, squeezing the toy soldier, warm from his breast pocket. It wasn't her life she worried about. It was his.

Chapter Thirty-Five

Down in the lobby, Dominic pulled on his freshly shined boots and left the hotel after paying the hotel owner to dry Maria's clothes. "My wife will be getting some sleep, so please do not disturb her. I'll pick up her apparel on my return."

"Very good, sir." The hotel owner was eager to please, Dominic's billfold apparently his inspiration.

The rain had eased, but the streets were rivers of mud. Choosing his way carefully, Dominic journeyed to the harbor and sought out Gavilan at the shipping office.

"Are you sorry you did not make a bid for senator today?" Gavilan asked when he walked through the door.

"After wading through the mudslinging at the polls, not to mention the actual mud, not an ounce of me is sorry." Dominic removed his hat and hung it on a hook beside the door.

Gavilan gave him a half-cocked grin. "Perhaps you miss the sea. No mud there. Just waves.

"Perhaps I do." Dominic walked over to the table where Gavilan was taking inventory of their shipping logs.

"I need you to stay at the mansion with Chloe and Nicky for a while. I have some business to attend to and don't want them left alone."

"What kind of business?" Gavilan's grin evaporated.

Dominic pulled up a chair and sat down on the other side of the table. "Maria."

"Maria?"

"She was at the polls today in a mired-down carriage. I persuaded her to take a walk with me."

"A walk in this weather?"

Dominic leaned forward in his chair. "I left her at a hotel. She's got a broken wrist."

Gavilan came out of his chair. "I'm going to kill that—"

"I'll deal with Wade," Dominic interrupted Gavilan's fury. "This is my fight, not yours, my friend. Right now Maria needs to know she's safe. Needs to know . . . I love her."

"So you're hiding from that dandified devil." Gavilan sat back down.

"I don't see it that way."

"What way do you see it?"

Dominic didn't like what he saw in Gavilan's eyes. Murder occurred daily in San Francisco, and very few were brought to justice for it, but that didn't make it right. "Vengeance is mine sayeth the Lord," he told Gavilan.

"I sayeth dead men tell no tales."

"I'm going to be patient and see how this plays out. Perhaps Wade will come to his senses and let her go without a fight."

"Perhaps you'll come to your senses and give that devil his due."

"I'm not that man anymore." Dominic leaned back in his chair.

"I know." Gavilan sighed. "I wish you'd wear your gun in the city. Most men do."

"I've got the Good Lord and you watching over me." Dominic grinned.

Gavilan pulled the revolver out of his gun belt and placed it on the table. "Want to take that with you today?"

"I've got one at home."

"At home, it won't do you no good when Wade comes calling."

"He won't know where to find me. My fear is he'll come calling at the mansion and I won't be there. Chloe and Nicky will be there."

"I'll be there." Gavilan took the gun and tucked it back into his holster.

"Thanks, I knew you would." Dominic stood up and headed for the door. He couldn't go to the head magistrate's office yet since he was just elected today, but soon he would seek him out. The long walk through the muck and rain back to the mansion gave him time to consider what Wade might do and how he'd react. All was quiet when he walked through the door. Nicky ran into the foyer and begged to go for a ride in the rain. They'd done this a few times, saddled up their horses and rode out into the storm just for the adventure of it.

"I'm sorry, not today, my boy." Dominic ruffled Nicky's golden curls. "It's election day. I must return for the celebrations." In truth, he couldn't wait to return to the hotel to celebrate his reunion with Maria, but he couldn't share that with Nicky. Not yet. He hoped to bring Maria home with a ring on her finger in a few days, but not until he knew Wade's next move. "Gavilan is coming over to stay with you and Aunt Chloe. Perhaps you can entice him to take you out in the rain or play soldiers with you here."

A grin split Nicky's face. He adored Gavilan. The boy galloped off, most likely to gather up his soldiers for a game of war with Gavilan.

Dominic went upstairs to the bedroom, where a trunk held most of Maria's wardrobe. Before leaving Boston, the women had visited a seamstress to update their dresses. Nobody had really known what to expect from San Francisco, so Sally, Chloe, and Maria had packed a half dozen trunks with everything they thought they'd need for life in their new city. Opening Maria's trunk, he found exactly what he searched for, a lovely gown for speaking their vows. He gathered up the yellow satin and lace frock, along with other articles of clothing, undergarments, and another more practical dress and sunbonnet for Maria. Respectable women all wore bonnets on the street, no matter the weather.

In his room, he shrugged out of his wet clothes, dressed in gentleman's attire, and packed into a valise what he thought he would need for a few days. He figured he'd return to the mansion tomorrow to check on everyone if he felt Maria was safe alone at the hotel. His gun belt and revolvers were on his bureau. He'd taken to only using them when he traveled, but heeding Gavilan's advice, he strapped the pistol around his waist now. It might be dark when he arrived back at the hotel. The winter days were short, and the storm would darken the sky all the more quickly come evening. The best way to return to the hotel was on foot. A carriage would be impossible with the streets so mired. Even a horse would have a hard time of it getting through today. Plus, he'd look the least conspicuous on his own two feet. Men scurried all over the city clothed in apparel from every country. Workers hauled lumber on their backs to fire-ravaged Portsmouth Square. The plaza had practically returned overnight, the city being rebuilt in the blink of an eye.

By the time Dominic left the mansion to return to the hotel, the rain and wind had stopped, though clouds remained as thick and threatening as when the storm rolled in off the ocean several days ago. Dominic made his way back down the hill to the hotel near the harbor, lugging several valises. Beyond the harbor, coastal range mountains rose. Snow was falling steadily in the higher elevations beyond those mountains. Every day ships from all over the world sailed into the harbor with men raring to get to the goldfields. They sloshed through the muck and slime of low tide, carrying their trunks on their shoulders, only to find more muck in the city and a snowpack in the Sierras that had buried the goldfields. This left the gambling halls, saloons, and boardinghouses packed with boys and men whittling away the hours with gambling and not much else because they only wanted to get rich quick.

Gambling didn't just infect the miners—merchants, lawyers, judges, politicians, and even governors were ensnared by the faro tables. Dominic was grateful he'd found a hotel that didn't cater to gambling or any other noticeable vice that he could see. On his way to the hotel, he did his best to avoid the rats that plagued the city streets as music drifted out of the saloons and gambling dens, and laughter and loud voices filled the air with night approaching. The city was always boisterous, but even more so this election eve. The polls closed early with Col. John W. Geary's name shouted in the streets as First Alcalde. Geary was a mountain of a man at six feet six and well over two hundred pounds who'd earned his fame in the Mexican War. Geary would now govern the city. Dominic hoped to pay him a visit in a day or two with Maria at his side, ready to become his bride.

David C. Broderick was elected senator, and Samuel J. Clarke became a member of the Assembly. By the time Dominic reached the hotel, he knew every result of the election just by word in the streets. He walked over countless broken bottles and trash. The truth was that something desperately needed to be done to clean up the city—not just the garbage, but the overwhelming tide of sin taking over. Even respectable men lost their way in San Francisco. He hoped Geary, with all his strength and mental toughness, could bring some law and order to the city. And certainly, they could erect more planked sidewalks so a man didn't have to wade through the mud and trash and respectable women could venture out without finding themselves bogged down in a carriage, though he'd thanked God for that bogged-down carriage today. He couldn't wait to hold Maria in his arms again. He was going to do everything he could to persuade her to marry him as soon as possible.

Chapter Thirty-Six

Without her outer clothes, Maria felt so vulnerable. After bathing, she put her drawers, corset, and chemise back on, which wasn't an easy feat with her broken wrist. The undergarments were silk and held in place with ribbons. It proved nearly impossible to get herself resituated in them. She couldn't tighten them on her own with just one hand. Wade had purchased the undergarments. They were lacy and expensive and certainly not the least bit modest. There'd been a time when she would have felt proud and beautiful in these unmentionables, but now she just felt shame for all she'd done and all that had been done to her. She had hours alone in the hotel room to think about her past, and it wasn't pretty.

She rebound her wrist to the board because it ached and sat in front of the fire, wrapped in a blanket from the bed. Without Dominic there telling her the voices she heard in her head were lies, the dark doubts returned with a vengeance. If only she had her golden rosary, or Sally's psalm handkerchief, or her Bible to read from, anything to still the onslaught of punishing thoughts. It was almost as if demons were howling on some dark hill of her heart.

This awful darkness is in me, she whispered to God. *Help me, Lord! Deliver me from this evil.*

She began to feel sick after her prayer, her insides swirling and pitching and turning over with a vengeance. She ran for the chamber pot and threw up. Again and again, she threw up until she was spent. It felt like some supernatural cleansing had come over her, something terrible emptying out of her body. Afterward, she lay on the floor, praying for mercy. For healing. For God's forgiveness. And finally she felt forgiven. She truly did.

When a knock came at the door, she covered herself with the blanket and unlocked the portal. The two maids who'd filled the tub stood there holding her scrubbed boots. She welcomed them into the room, and they emptied the tub and the chamber pot. Together the maids lugged the wooden tub into the hallway, where the boy who'd carried the tub into the room came and retrieved it.

Once the maids were gone, Maria laid down on the bed and fell asleep. When she awoke several hours later, Dominic leaned over her. A tender smile softened his freshly shaven face. He was dressed so handsomely and appeared so pleased.

"I've brought you some gowns. Would you like to get dressed and go to dinner?"

She sat up but quickly lay back when her loosened undergarments slid down in a rush of silk.

Dominic kept his eyes on her face. "Roll over, I'll help you."

She turned onto her stomach, and he tightened up the laces. He was as practiced as a lady's maid, which gave her pause. "I guess you're not as pure as freshly driven snow either," she said, her heart pounding. She felt so different now. So humble and uncertain, so not like herself.

"Your drawers are lovely." She could hear the pleasure in his voice.

"You shouldn't be looking at my drawers."

He gave a tug, lacing her tighter. "I should tie you in knots. That might help both of us tonight."

When he finished, she rolled back over and sat up, crossing her arms over her chest, holding her bandaged wrist like a shield across her breasts. His smile stole her breath away.

"I find you so beautiful." He didn't touch her, but he looked like he wanted to.

She raised her uninjured hand to cover her scar. How she regretted her months with Wade.

He reached out and took her hand, pulling it away from her cheek. "I don't mind your scar. It reminds me that I have won you in a great battle. You are more than your scar, Maria. More than what's been done to you and what you've done in the past. None of it makes me want you any less. You are more than your body. More than your beauty. You are the one my soul loves."

She did her best to swallow down the tears choking her. "I'm sorry for running away from you." When she said it, she realized she was even more sorry for running away from God. The tears then came. Oh, how they came.

Dominic pulled her into his arms and sat down on the bed, holding her. He cupped her face and kissed her lips. "You taste like the sea," he whispered against her tear-drenched lips. He smiled. "Perhaps we should dwell together on the far side of the sea."

Maria began laughing and crying at the same time. "I just read that this morning. 'If I dwell on the far side of the sea, even there your hand will guide me, your right hand will hold me fast.' Sally said this was my psalm."

"Psalm 139."

"God is so real," Maria said in wonder. "It's kind of terrifying."

"Fear of the Lord is the beginning of wisdom."

"I think God delivered me from darkness today."

"Into his glorious light," Dominic agreed.

"Into his glorious light," Maria echoed with a radiant smile.

"I selected a dress for you to wear when we wed."

"When will we wed?"

"The sooner, the better." He nudged her off his lap. "Let's get you dressed." He stood up and went to one of the valises he'd left sitting on the floor. Opening it, he pulled out the pale yellow silk gown with leaves of lace embroidered on the skirt and on the fitted bodice. "I don't think we'll find anyone to marry us tonight, with everyone celebrating the elections, but tomorrow we'll rouse the good judge from his stupor and put him to work."

He walked over, his eyes lit with adoration. "My lady, I am at your beck and call."

Maria brushed the hair away from her face. She'd washed her locks and dried them by the fire, but Fang wasn't here to pin up her hair or help her into her gown. "You look nothing like a lady's maid," she told Dominic with a nervous laugh.

"I'm doing my best." He fluffed out the gown, holding it up at arm's length for her inspection.

"Sally chose that gown for me." The smile slipped off of Maria's face, and tears filled her eyes. "She said I would make a beautiful bride someday in that dress." Maria arose from the bed and came to him, sliding her fingers down the silky gown.

Dominic grew teary-eyed too. "We have Nicky because of Sally."

"And Sally has Maria Elizabeth with her."

Maria put her uninjured arm around Dominic's neck. The dress was slippery between them. "Neither of us deserved Sally's goodness, you know."

"Does anyone deserve God's goodness?" Dominic held on to the dress with one hand and wrapped his other arm around Maria's waist, drawing her close. The dress still pressed between them.

"I don't deserve God's goodness," Maria whispered.

"Nobody does. Even Sally was a sinner in need of the Savior."

"Sally loved me for no reason at all. I never understood her love until now. Sally's love came from God."

"You know she'd be happy for us." Dominic kissed the tip of her nose.

The smile returned to Maria's face. She pushed him away. "She would never stand here in her unmentionables with you."

"No, she wouldn't." Dominic turned her around and unbuttoned the dress. It took him awhile with all the little satin-covered buttons running down the back. Thankfully, the dress was short-sleeved. Maria hadn't been able to wear a long-sleeved dress with her arm splinted. He lifted it over her head and carefully helped her get her injured arm into it. Buttoning it back up took him far too long. He pulled her in close, pushed her hair aside, and dropped kisses on the back of her neck as he did the buttons, causing shivers to race down her spine.

When she was finally in the gown, he turned her around to face him. Moving her hair aside, he leaned down and kissed the side of her neck, nibbling up to her ear.

She felt boneless in his arms. Her heart was pounding so hard. She was certain he could hear it.

"If we don't eat dinner, I might eat you. You taste so good."

She laughed, tucking her hair behind her ears, forgetting all about the scar she usually tried to hide with her hair. How happy she was. She grabbed Dominic's hand and led him toward the door.

"I forgot to retrieve your cloak from the hotel clerk." Dominic scooped his own cloak off the hook by the door. He draped it over Maria's shoulders.

"Are we going out for dinner?" She resisted the fear that hit her. Wade had found her the last time. What if he found her again with Dominic?

"The hotel has a respectable restaurant. We'll eat here."

She was relieved. She didn't want to leave the hotel.

They went downstairs, collected Maria's cloak and gown, returned the gown to the room, and then walked back downstairs. In a luxurious dining room lit by whale oil lanterns, they were served a delicious dinner. Beef, of course. California never ran out of beef, but vegetables and exotic delicacies too, which were hard to come by in wintertime. A ship from the Sandwich Islands had just restocked the restaurant. With Dominic's eyes upon her and her soul awakened by God, Maria felt reborn. The exquisite yellow gown made her feel beautiful tonight, and for the first time since acquiring it, the scar did not plague her.

"What are you thinking?" Dominic asked her at the end of their meal.

She'd grown quiet and thoughtful, watching a young family settle down at a nearby table. The children were well dressed and well behaved, the parents smiling. They'd probably arrived by ship in the past few days, ready to build a new life in California. Most of the diners were men, so the family stood out.

"I'm thinking I don't deserve this."

Dominic smiled. "I don't deserve it either. But because of Christ, we don't get what we deserve."

Maria hadn't touched her wine. She'd always drunk alcohol in the past to numb the pain. Or ease the way. Or to become more than herself. Tonight she didn't want to numb anything, or ease anything, or become something else. She wanted to feel every bit of life she could with this man she desperately loved for as long as it lasted. She couldn't believe this morning she'd been Wade's prisoner, and tonight she was here with Dominic.

"Are you ready to return to the room?"

The question sent a whirl of butterflies through her. She couldn't get out of her dress without his help. "Yes, dinner was wonderful. Thank you."

"Thank you," he said, rising from his chair and moving to assist her out of hers. He took her arm and led her out of the dining hall. They were about to mount the stairs when a man called her name.

"Maria! What are you doing here, my dear?" Mr. Guzman rushed over, removing his hat and taking a bow. He gazed at Dominic, then returned his attention to Maria.

Everything inside of her came crashing down. Of course it couldn't last. Now Wade would find them. Now Wade would kill Dominic.

Fear clawed up her spine and left her trembling. "Mr. Guzman," she managed to say.

The clairvoyant reached out, took her hand, and kissed it. "My dear Maria. You look so lovely tonight. Are you celebrating the election with this gentleman?"

His kiss on the back of her hand left her skin crawling. Dominic put his arm around her waist, drawing her close to his side. She could feel the tension radiating thorough him.

"I'm Dominic Mason, Maria's fiancé." He extended his hand to Mr. Guzman.

Mr. Guzman narrowed his eyes. "Fiancé? How perplexing. Captain Reynolds was just telling me only yesterday that once your wrist was healed, he was putting a ring on your finger. The ring has been ordered. A tiger ring to match Captain Reynolds's ring."

Dominic's arm around her tightened. "The only ring Maria will be wearing is my ring. A Christian band of gold. Have a good day, Mr. Guzman." Dominic swept Maria up the winding staircase without another word. Maria looked back.

Dressed all in black, Mr. Guzman nodded at her, then stood there watching them go. The look on his face reminded Maria of the darkness she was so accustomed to, the darkness she could never escape.

By the time they reached their room, she was trembling all over. The wind had picked up, rattling the windows once more. Someone had rekindled the fire while they dined. The room was cozy and warm, lit by glowing whale oil lamps covered with rose lamp shades, but Maria shivered, even with her cloak draped over her shoulders. She recognized that cold feeling, like cold from a grave, an otherworldly chill that pierced her bones.

"That was Wade's clairvoyant?"

"Yes." Maria closed her eyes in a silent prayer. She stepped over to the fire and tried to warm herself.

Dominic came right up behind her. He removed her cloak and then wrapped his cloak around the both of them. The heat from his body seeped into her. "God is stronger than the devil," he said softly in her ear. "If God is for us, who can be against us, Maria?"

Chapter Thirty-Seven

Dominic and Maria slept fully clothed that night. Dominic sat in the chair by the fire for long hours after Maria had fallen asleep on the bed. When Wade would come, Dominic didn't know, but he was certain Wade would come. There would be a reckoning. This battle was bigger than man against man. This was good against evil. Mr. Guzman didn't just happen into the hotel on his own accord. The devil had brought the clairvoyant here. The devil would bring Wade too.

Dominic had finally lain down on the bed beside Maria. He stared at her sleeping face for a long time, wondering what would happen to her if he died. Gavilan would take care of Nicky and Chloe, he was certain of that, but where would Maria go? If she allowed Gavilan to protect her, he would, but Maria was her own worst enemy. Chances were she would run from Gavilan too.

Blessed are those who have not seen and yet have believed.

The Bible verse had whispered through his mind on its own accord. Did he truly believe God was for them? And if he did, what did that mean? God's ways were not man's ways. Saints died all the time, and sinners went on with their wicked work. Wade had always come out on top. The man got what he wanted every single time. Dominic had never seen Wade lose at anything. Ever.

The battle belongs to the Lord.

It was his last thought before sleep finally overcame him.

Now this morning as they walked down the grand staircase for breakfast, he found Wade and Mr. Guzman waiting at the bottom of the stairs. Maria saw them too and stiffened on his arm. "The battle belongs to the Lord," he whispered, urging her to keep descending the stairs. She'd wanted to change out of the yellow silk gown this morning, but he asked her to wear it again. He had a plan for that dress today. He wasn't about to let Wade interfere with that plan.

Others milled around the hotel lobby, mostly respectable men in suits, tall hats, and broad coats, walking in and out of the hotel entrance. The storm had finally abated. Wade, like Mr. Guzman, wore a black broad coat and held his black hat under his arm like a gentleman. He wouldn't dare accost them here amongst so many.

"Hello, Maria, Dom," Wade said politely.

The welcome didn't fool Dominic for a minute. He could see the fury on Wade's face. The possessive way he looked Maria over.

"We'd like to have breakfast with you." Wade half smiled, a twisting of his lips that didn't reach his eyes.

"I've lost my appetite," said Maria. Dominic could feel her pulling away from him. Like the night of the Christmas ball, she was ready to flee. He wasn't about to let that happen again. He held on to her more tightly.

"Say your piece here and now," Dominic demanded of Wade.

"Very well. I challenge you to a duel. Revolvers at twelve paces."

"No!" Maria's raised voice drew the attention of all in the lobby.

"Since you have challenged me, it's my right to select the weapons, distance, and dueling site," Dominic calmly replied. In a way, it was a relief to know how this would end.

Wade smiled wolfishly. "There's the Dom I know and love. Choose your weapons, my boy."

"Revolvers at twelve paces," Dominic agreed. He was a crack shot with a rifle, but so was Wade. And he wasn't about to cower to Wade; revolvers would do.

"No! I won't have it." Maria yanked her arm from his. "I will not let this happen!"

"You don't have a choice, my darling," said Wade. "Mr. Guzman tells me you've become Dom's fiancée too. The winner shall have you. It is the fairest thing to do to win the fairest maiden in San Francisco."

"I am not a maiden to be bartered off like a mule!"

"This, of course, is true. You are not a maiden. I have made sure of that." Wade's wolfish smile grew, his eyes full of glee now.

Maria stepped up and slapped his face. The sound of her palm connecting with his cheek silenced everyone in the lobby.

Dominic locked his arm around her waist and hauled her back behind him. Wade came at them, but Mr. Guzman stepped between them. "You will meet on the field of honor

377

at three o'clock this afternoon. Colt revolvers, twelve paces. Choose your second, Captain Mason," said Mr. Guzman.

By now, they were surrounded by an eager audience. Every man in the room had gathered at the base of the stairs. The hotel owner stood there wringing his hands, looked confused and alarmed.

"Gavilan Hernandez is my second." This duel would please Gavilan, no doubt.

"Captain Reynolds, I'd like to be your second," said Mr. Guzman.

"We will need a surgeon on the field," said Wade. "To declare the wound fatal."

A murmur ran thorough the gathered men. Most duels were fought not to kill, but to restore honor. Shots were purposefully missed or extremities targeted. Dueling had been prohibited back east, and California lawmakers were pushing for that here as well; still, most men weren't about to miss a good duel, whether they believed in dueling or not. Rarely did someone die in a duel.

"Name the dueling ground," a man in the audience called out.

"I will not duel today. Tomorrow at three o'clock in front of the Mission Dolores." Dominic said firmly.

He could see Wade was not happy at putting off the duel for a day, but in the midst of so many gentlemen, Wade having raised the challenge, everyone knew it was up to Dominic to decide the time and place of the event. "Now if you'll excuse us, gentlemen, the lady and I are off for a stroll." He wrapped his arm around Maria and urged her through the crowd.

The morning had dawned without fog. The sun shone brilliantly after days of rain. It was a beautiful day, crisp and clear, with only the slightest breeze off the ocean. As they neared the harbor, seagulls filled the air with their piercing calls. Dominic headed for the shipping office, hoping to find Gavilan there. Maria wasn't speaking to him. He could feel anger and fear in every taut move of her body. He kept his hand on her lower back, pushing her down the street. They swept into the shipping office, surprising Gavilan with their abrupt entry.

"Good morning," Gavilan said and then reoffered his greeting when neither Dominic nor Maria answered him. "All right, I see it's not a good morning, but it's good to see you two."

"Wade has challenged me to a duel. I accepted."

Gavilan's face hardened. "Call it off, and then I will challenge him. You have never dueled in your life. Don't be a fool. Let me fight Wade."

Dominic walked over and patted Gavilan on the back. "I am not a fool, and this is my fight, my friend. You are my second."

Maria stormed up to them. "You are both fools! Wade will kill you!"

The two men looked at her for a moment, and then both of them laughed.

"What's so funny?" Maria's cheeks flamed with color.

"You're funny," Gavilan said.

Dominic did his best to stop laughing. He knew it was her nerves. But this fierceness in Maria was funny considering she was a woman and not very big, yet when she was like this, he wanted to hide every weapon in the room. She didn't look capable of harming a man, but he and Gavilan knew better.

"Give me a gun. I will end this duel myself!"

"I'm happy to see you still have your pluck," Gavilan said.

Maria grabbed Gavilan's shirtfront with her uninjured hand. "You can't let him do this." Tears filled her eyes. "Please, Gavilan, you must do something to stop this duel."

Gavilan put his hand over hers. "I haven't seen you cry in years." The look on his face betrayed him. He still loved her. It was so obvious.

Dominic closed his eyes. Said a silent prayer. Perhaps if he died in the duel, Gavilan would finally win Maria's hand. Of course, it would break Chloe's heart, but Maria would be safe with Gavilan.

"I will not cry over men's stupidity," Maria exclaimed. "Please, you must do something, Gavilan!"

Dominic opened his eyes.

Gavilan was smiling at her. "I will," he promised.

"Will you be my second?" Dominic asked, his chest aching with it all.

"Of course I will be your second." Gavilan's eyes remained on Maria.

She threw herself into his arms. Gavilan held her, burying his face in her hair. The two looked like lovers. Dominic looked away. It was too painful to see Gavilan holding her. In light of the duel, he was desperate to make Maria his before time ran out, but Gavilan had consoled her, not him. It rankled.

"What weapon did you choose?" Gavilan asked, untangling himself from Maria.

"Revolvers at twelve paces."

"You should have chosen rifles."

"Would you have chosen rifles?" Dominic tried to keep the anger from his voice. In truth, he was jealous of Gavilan, and hated that he felt that way.

"No, I would have chosen revolvers, but I am not you."

"Are you saying I can't hold my own with revolvers?"

"I'm saying you had a better chance with a rifle at forty paces." Gavilan ran a hand through his hair. Dominic didn't like the look on his face one bit.

"Change it to rifles," Maria demanded.

Dominic swung around to face her. "I will not change it."

Gavilan walked over to his sea chest, opened it, and pulled out a Colt six-shooter. A smaller naval revolver was strapped to his hip, where it always was. Gavilan went nowhere without a gun. He carried the Colt over to Dominic.

"I have my own revolver." Dominic's dander was up. Both Gavilan and Maria were treating him like he'd never handled a pistol before. He'd handled a pistol, just never used one in a duel, God help him.

"This one's better," said Gavilan. "Let's do some target practice today."

"Tomorrow. Maria and I have plans today," Dominic said.

"We do?" Maria looked surprised.

"Yes, we do." Dominic linked his arm through hers. "Today I'm making you Nicky's mother, if you're willing."

Gavilan quietly laid the revolver on the table.

"Gavilan, would you stand as my best man if Maria will marry me?"

"Now I understand the dress." Gavilan looked at Maria. Her cloak hung open, and the exquisite yellow gown showed.

Dominic looked down at her. "Will you marry me, Maria?" It wasn't the proposal he'd hoped for, but considering the circumstances, he decided to forge ahead with Nicky in mind. He wanted to make sure Nicky would have a mother who loved the boy like her very own.

Her eyes connected with his. Maria's green eyes softened, filled with tears. "Yes, I will be Nicky's mother."

Dominic nodded. He didn't trust himself to speak. It wasn't the kind of "yes" he'd hoped for, but her love for Nicky would have to do.

"Well, let's go rouse the judge. I'm sure he was at the Blue Wing Saloon all night. I suspect we'll find him at home this morning."

Gavilan put on his cloak and took up his tall hat. His sailor clothes were long gone. He dressed like a gentleman now, the same way Dominic dressed.

Dominic reached down and fastened Maria's cloak for her. She stood there without a smile. A heaviness settled in his chest. The three of them walked out into the sunshine, a mighty fine day for a wedding, though this wouldn't be more than the taking of vows. They picked their way along the street, avoiding the worst of the mud. Seagulls squawked overhead. Dominic led them to the jeweler's shop. Maria selected a simple golden band that fit her slender finger. It wasn't a tiger ring, wasn't decorated at all, just a solid, unending band of gold. Solid and unending like his love for her. God's love for them.

Gavilan was very quiet. Nobody had much to say.

After purchasing the band, Dominic pocketed it and then linked his arm through Maria's. He expected her to run away at any moment, though the sane part of his brain knew she wouldn't leave. She was in this for Nicky.

It was nearing noon, the streets alive with every kind of humanity. Miners in red-and-blue flannel shirts wearing long boots, eagerly waiting for the snow to melt in the Sierras. Mexicans in colorful serapes. Well-dressed gentlemen going about their business in tall hats. Chilenos in dark ponchos.

Peruvians in light-colored ponchos. Californios in wide-brimmed sombreros and silk-worked leather jackets. Horses and mules wading through the mud. Men walking in and out of gambling halls. The saloons were already so crowded. Loafers hung about the streets doing nothing. Dominic had never seen a city like San Francisco. The vice was deplorable. So were the rats. The large, vicious rodents swam in the harbor like seals, departing the anchored and abandoned ships like sailors from a ship wreck.

He reminded himself that he was a wealthy man now. With the woman he loved on his arm. On their way to be married, in a city bursting with a golden future. Yet he missed the simplicity of the sea. The days when the three of them were bound for Boston and nobody knew about the gold rush. The nights they'd counted the stars and mapped their route east. All the chest games in the cabin. Maria taking over his captain's quarters. Taking over his heart. All the nights he'd lain awake in the cabin boy's bunk thinking about Maria.

The judge's house was one of the grandest in town, and it loomed in front of them now. Holding firmly to Maria's arm, Dominic mounted the steps and tugged her up beside him.

Gavilan followed them onto the porch.

A knock on the door was answered by a butler. "We've come to see the judge," Dominic said.

"May I inquire of your business, sir?" asked the butler.

"We're here to be married." Dominic didn't look at Maria standing at his side. He just wanted to get this over with fast. Make sure Nicky had a mother if he died in the duel tomorrow.

"The judge doesn't conduct weddings here, sir."

"Please ask him if he'll make an exception. It's a life or death matter."

"Life or death?" The butler was an older man. It looked like nothing could catch him off guard. This apparently did.

"I am facing a duel tomorrow afternoon. I'd like to marry my fiancée before then."

The butler looked at Maria and then said, "One moment, sir. Please wait in the parlor." He stepped back and disappeared down a hallway.

Dominic ushered Maria into the parlor. Gavilan closed the door behind them and followed them into the judge's quarters. A fire burned in the fireplace. The room was toasty warm and finely furnished. Wallpaper covered the walls. Tall windows allowed the winter sun to pour into the parlor. The house resembled those in Boston and New York. Just a year ago, most of San Francisco's houses were adobe, and tents and shanties covered the hillsides. Now the city was beginning to rival her eastern sisters with three- and four-story brick buildings, at least down here near the waterfront.

The judge appeared without the butler. He was a giant man, dressed in a fine dark suit, very imposing, but with the look of needing sleep on his face.

"Congratulations on your victory yesterday," Dominic said.

"Thank you. So my butler tells me you're here to take your vows. Normally, I don't marry folks in my home. I do that down at my office. But in your case, I'll make an exception. I hear you'll be stepping onto the field of honor. Where and when will this duel take place?"

"Outside of the city, sir. Tomorrow afternoon, near the mission."

"And the weapons of choice?" asked the judge.

"Revolvers at twelve paces."

The judge looked at Maria, taking in her bandaged arm and the scar on her face. "Are you the cause of this duel, miss?"

The judge's forthright nature wasn't surprising. A city like San Francisco needed a firm hand. Colonels and generals ran the province. This colonel turned alcalde wasn't a man to be trifled with, that was more than apparent.

"I guess I am," said Maria.

"Very well." The alcalde called for his butler.

When the butler arrived, the alcalde instructed him to take their cloaks.

Dominic helped Maria out of her cloak and then removed his own. Gavilan handed his cloak and hat to the butler too. Dominic hardly had time to smooth down his hair before the alcalde began the hasty ceremony. Dominic slipped the golden band on Maria's trembling hand and looked into her eyes.

"Go ahead and kiss your bride," the alcalde said with a smile.

Dominic leaned down and kissed her lightly on the lips.

Maria didn't smile. Tears dripped down her cheeks.

Dominic wished he knew what she was thinking.

Gavilan congratulated them both with a hug. He wasn't smiling either.

Chapter Thirty-Eight

Dominic and Maria headed for their room in the brick hotel, Dominic's mind weighted down by worry. Gavilan returned to the office after dining with them at a restaurant near the judge's home. The sky was so blue, the bay the sky's vivid twin today. Some winter days in San Francisco were like this, clear and breathtaking. Gavilan had congratulated them again after the ceremony outside the judge's house, kissing Maria's cheek. She smiled for him far more than she'd smiled during their vows. Dominic could hardly eat his meal. Maria had picked at her food, seeming so far away from him, though she was by his side. He'd told her not to listen to lies; now all Dominic heard were lies in his head. He hoped they were lies.

She doesn't love you. Gavilan is who she really loves. She only married you for Nicky. You will die in the duel, and Maria will end up with Gavilan. Or Wade.

God help them, not Wade.

The doubts were torturous and so unlike anything he'd ever experienced before. Is this what Maria dealt with all the time? This dark, hounding voice twisting his thoughts? "Devil, you are a liar," he finally whispered while walking up the sweeping staircase inside the hotel.

"What did you say?" Maria looked at him.

"Nothing." He tucked her arm more firmly in the crook of his elbow.

"Please wait, Captain Mason," the hotel owner called, trailing Dominic and Maria up the stairs with a regretful but determined look on his face. "I don't allow folks who aren't properly wed to room at my hotel. My mother would roll over in her grave if—"

"Yes, you've told us about your good Christian mother," Dominic interrupted him. "I assure you we are properly wed, sir. Now if you'll excuse us."

"I'm sorry, but Captain Reynolds challenged you to a duel this very morning because you are bedding down with his fiancée, sir."

Dominic took Maria's hand and raised it to reveal the golden band on her finger. "Captain Reynolds is a blackguard. This woman is my wife. Now good day, sir." Dominic led Maria up the stairs, not looking back at the hotel owner.

When they made it to the room, he closed the door behind them with a heavy sigh. What a day. He removed his cloak and hung his tall hat on the hook. For some reason, he suddenly missed his captain's uniform and longed for the roll of the sea beneath his boots instead of all this mud. He turned to help Maria out of her cloak, but she'd already shrugged it off and was walking over to the window to stare out at the bay. The pale yellow dress accented the gentle flare of her hips and her slender waist. Her red hair hung down. He'd always found her so desirable. She was his wife now, but he didn't feel like he could touch her. Or kiss her. Or do all the things he'd wanted to do with her for so long.

He walked over to the bed and noticed the little toy soldier on the bedside table. *These soldiers are fighting a war for love,* he'd told Nicky. Picking up the soldier, he turned it over in his palm. It was about four inches tall and an inch or so wide, solid as a stone. He squeezed the solider in his palm, then dropped the toy in his vest pocket. Sitting down on the bed, he removed his boots. It dawned on him that the hotel owner hadn't asked them to remove their muddy boots in the lobby. He'd been far more concerned with their muddy lives. Dominic realized that he often judged people this way too.

After removing his boots, he dropped his head into his hands and sat there on the side of the bed. He'd spent his life thinking he was either good or bad, depending on where he was in his walk with the Lord. Had it ever occurred to him that he was simply loved by the God who'd made him? Not because he was good or bad, but because the Savior deemed it so?

Why this all weighed so heavily upon him now, he didn't know. Perhaps he would die tomorrow. Sailors believed their deaths were often shown to them before they perished. A man would tell his mate, "If I die, I want you to have my sea chest, or deliver this letter to my mother, or drink my share of whiskey after the storm." And it often happened that way too. The sailor who spoke of his death would die a few days later, and everyone would be eager for the Sabbath message. But it didn't last. Pretty soon those same sailors would forget about the death of their friend and forget about the Sabbath and go right back to the way they were before.

He sensed Maria had come and knelt beside him. When he opened his eyes, she was there at his feet, her green eyes filled with something he couldn't measure.

"Do you regret marrying me?" Her voice trembled with uncertainty. This woman at his feet with the scar on her face and the broken wrist. So unlike the bold, beautiful Spanish girl he'd fallen in love with before the war.

"Never," he said with feeling. He cupped her face in his palms. "I've always wanted you."

"Please don't go through with this duel. If you die, I will die." Maria closed her eyes, and a silent sob shook her body.

"What is meant to be will be." The ache inside him was terrible. "We must trust our future to the Lord."

Maria opened her eyes. "I want to rage at God, but I know he is our only hope."

"Rage against the devil, Maria. God is for us. He has always been for us."

"God was for Sally, and she still died."

"Yes, God was for Sally, and she is in glory now with him. Someday you and I will be in glory too. The battle is here on earth. In heaven, we are home with the Lord, and all the streets are made of gold. All is well in heaven."

"I want all to be well here." Tears filled Maria's eyes. "I want to bear you sons like Nicky and daughters like Maria Elizabeth. I want you to live. If you die, it will be because of me. This duel is my fault."

"There's the proud girl I know and love." Dominic smiled in spite of the heartache knifing through him.

"I don't understand how you can say I'm proud. I've never felt so humble in my life." Maria wiped the back of her hand across the tears sliding onto her lips. Those lips he'd spent countless hours dreaming about kissing.

"This isn't all because of you, Maria. You think too highly of yourself. So do I. It's our human nature to make much of ourselves and so little of the Lord. Perhaps this was his plan for us all along."

She sat back on her heels. "God planned for me to be ruined in a church? For me to kill the man who raped me? God planned for me to become Wade's whore?" She looked so wounded and appalled and unbelieving.

"God's plan to win your love, Maria. We all are whores at heart. We give ourselves to anything and everything but God until God breaks us. And God often breaks us with our very own sin."

Maria rose to her feet, cradling her bandaged arm. She would have turned away from him, but Dominic reached out and pulled her down onto his lap, leaning back on the bed with her in his arms.

At first, she resisted him. He rolled her over, careful not to hurt her injured arm. "No matter what you've done, no matter what's been done to you, I love you just the same. I will always love you, Maria."

"How can you love me?" she cried, beating her fist against his chest.

"How can I not love you?" He leaned down and captured her lips with his own. He kissed her with everything he had. Every ounce of passion he'd been saving for so long. It was hard to believe she was really his bride after all they'd gone through.

She pressed away from him with one hand. "Your vest is poking me."

"It is our little soldier of love," he said when he realized what she spoke of. He felt lighter, as if the darkness that had oppressed them all day had suddenly lifted. He was about to take the soldier out of his pocket when he decided to take his vest off instead. While he was at it, he removed his shirt as well. He tried to read her eyes, but they were fathomless. Those green eyes that had always beguiled him so.

"Are you cold? Should I build us a fire?" he asked.

"I guess you should if you're taking off your clothes." She let out a little laugh that surprised him.

"Should I put my clothes back on?"

"I'd like to watch you build a fire instead."

He grinned at her. Beside the fireplace sat a tin full of firewood. Dominic went over and took his time making their fire. He shouldn't have removed his shirt so soon. He didn't want to rush her. She'd already been through so much. Even if they only had this night, he told himself to move at her pace. Maria was his wife now. He whistled as he made the fire.

Pretty soon, she was standing behind him, running her fingers across his naked shoulders.

He stopped whistling. Under his hands, the fire flamed to life, spreading a golden glow over the two of them. She continued to caress his bare skin.

"I'm so afraid of losing you," she whispered.

He stood up and turned around to face her. "For now, can we just pretend there's no tomorrow? That this is the day the Lord has made and we will rejoice and be glad?"

She reached out and ran her fingers down his bare chest. "I am glad."

A shiver raced through him. Goose bumps rose on his arms and chest and back. He slid his hands into her hair, pulling her close. She tilted her face up to meet his kiss. They weren't promised tomorrow. Nobody was promised tomorrow. But they had today. And they had each other. He scooped her up and carried her over to the bed. He'd waited so long for this moment. Now all they had was this moment. It was enough.

Chapter Thirty-Nine

Maria knew Wade would not be home. Like Dominic, he was somewhere else preparing for this afternoon's duel. Perhaps out target practicing, as many duelists did before meeting on the field of honor. Such a joke, the field of honor—there was no honor in this duel. Wade was out to murder Dominic. Maria didn't know how to stop it, but she would do her best to try. Now was her opportunity to fetch her sea chest and her belongings. More than anything, she wanted her golden rosary before heading to the mission for the duel.

She walked up Wade's porch steps and didn't bother to knock on the ornate front door. Letting herself into the mansion like she still lived there, she rushed through the foyer and on up the stairs without being seen. Wade's servants tended to stay out of the way as much as they possibly could. It didn't surprise her that none were around when she let herself into the house.

As she stepped into the bedroom she'd called home for far too long, shock washed over her. The room was destroyed, furniture toppled over, the velvet curtains torn from the tall plate-glass windows and shredded on the floor. It had been such a lovely room. Now it was utterly ruined. Wade's rage had reigned here. In that moment, she fervently thanked God she hadn't been in the room when Wade lost it. The man was more than cruel and abusive, he was half-mad. After just one day as Dominic's wife, she knew this and shuddered. She'd been loved more in one night than in her entire life, and now she might lose Dominic forever.

Her sea chest was smashed to bits and scattered about the room. It must have been her knife that had shredded the curtains and bedding and her clothes, but she couldn't find the blade in the mess. Underneath the ripped-up bedding, she found Nicky's soldier. She stuffed the toy in her skirt pocket and kept searching for her rosary. When she finally found it in the room's fireplace, tears filled her eyes. It was covered in ashes, but unharmed. She left the mansion with nothing more than the toy soldier and her rosary in her skirt pocket, determined to somehow liberate Fang too as soon as she was able.

In Wade's stable, she was more than relieved to find the sleek black stallion in his stall. She'd feared Wade would ride the horse to the mission for the duel, but he hadn't. The Oriental stable boy was more than happy to saddle the horse for her. She rode out at a gallop that afternoon. Dominic had told her not to leave the hotel until either he or Gavilan returned to fetch her. Wrapped in his arms, she'd agreed to the plan, but once he was gone, it was impossible to do nothing but wait.

The sand hills were better than the mud of the city. She wasn't the only one on horseback headed for the mission. News of the duel had carried, and dozens of men were making their way across the shrub-covered hills on horseback. Nearly a hundred spectators were already there when she arrived at the mission. On this cold January day, Maria was certain someone would die. She tried to convince herself of how capable Dominic was with a revolver, but Wade would not fight fair, and he was wicked with all weapons. She wondered if he had her knife on him. She'd hoped to somehow use it before the duel to stop him.

Gavilan and Dominic waited together in a field beyond the mission. Wade and Mr. Guzman stood some forty feet away. In the middle of the two parties, a number of men officiated the duel. A field surgeon was there, along with other prominent men of the city. Beyond the field, carriages lined the vicinity. Maria recognized Wade's black carriage with its matching black horses. Numerous saddle horses were tied in various locations. Indians dressed in ragged clothes, animal skins, and draped in beads and feathers had ventured over from the nearby *rancheria*. Even in the winter chill, most of the Indians were nearly naked.

Maria rode straight to Dominic and Gavilan and jumped off her horse, letting the animal go. It trotted off, dragging its reins.

"I told you to stay at the hotel." Dominic sounded like the ship captain of old.

"How could I? You are my husband." She pulled the golden rosary from her skirt pocket. "Please take this." Sunlight gleamed off the golden cross.

He accepted the rosary and stuck it in his vest pocket. "Please, Maria, get out of the way." He turned to Gavilan. "Whatever happens, do not let Wade near her,"

"I won't." Gavilan held a six-shooter. Two more revolvers were strapped around his waist. He looked so much like the hard-eyed vaquero he used to be, only his clothes were much finer now.

After Dominic tucked the rosary away, Maria threw herself against him. "I love you," she breathed, feeling like she might die without him.

His arms wrapped around her. For a moment, he pressed her close. She raised her face to look into his eyes, and he kissed her soundly. "Now be a good wife and obey your husband. Go stand over there." He pointed to a cypress in the distance, twisted and bent by the wind.

"May Jesúcristo protect you." Maria pressed her hand against his vest pocket. It felt hard and lumpy with the cross and something else there.

He reached into his pocket and pulled out Nicky's little soldier, handing it to her.

She squeezed it in her palm and then dropped it back into his vest pocket along with the rosary.

"If I die, please tell Nicky his father loves him." Dominic stroked the scar on her cheek and then turned to Gavilan. "Don't let my son go fatherless."

Gavilan nodded, his eyes dark and unfathomable. "I won't." His reply was so fierce Maria shivered.

"Now go." Dominic pushed her from him and took the six-shooter from Gavilan's hand.

The two men turned and waited for the duel to begin. An afternoon breeze off the bay rushed over the hills, sighing through the manzanita and chaparral. It was a sunny day. Maria gripped her skirt and trudged over to the lone tree. She stood there squeezing her skirt in her uninjured hand, her knuckles turning white. She began to pray more vehemently than she'd ever prayed in her life.

Dominic and Wade were to stand at ten paces, thirty feet apart, with their backs to each other until the command "fire!" was given.

Gavilan left the field where he'd been standing with Dominic and walked down toward Wade's end, which struck Maria as odd. Gavilan had promised to do something about this duel, but he hadn't. Nobody had stopped it from happening. It was Maria's worst nightmare come true.

Dominic will die because of you! Your death curse is upon him. The dark voice came on a gust of wind. In despair, Maria dropped to her knees, clasping her hands in desperate prayer. "Please, Jesúcristo, do not let him die," she begged.

A man in a black cape and tall black hat on the edge of the dueling grounds cried, "Gentlemen, are you ready?" Then he began to count. "Three, two, one . . ."

Wade whirled before the man yelled, "Fire!"

Gavilan shouted a warning.

Dominic spun around as Wade advanced on him.

Wade's revolver cracked.

Dominic answered with his own shot.

Both bullets narrowly missed their targets.

Wade kept coming.

Dominic's revolver jammed. He bent over, clasping the Colt between his knees, trying to force the trigger back to get the gun working again.

Before Maria realized it, she was running toward the dueling field. Gavilan had pulled a revolver from his holster. He stepped into the fray just as Dominic straightened up. Wade's shot staggered Dominic, and he fell back, holding his chest.

Maria screamed in horror.

Wade kept right on coming. Gavilan dashed into Wade's line of fire. The two converged, emptying their revolvers on each other. Both men went down.

The surgeon reached Dominic before Maria did. The doctor hurriedly unbuttoned Dominic's coat. He found Wade's bullet had struck Dominic's vest pocket, denting Maria's golden crucifix and shattering Nicky's toy soldier, causing only a flesh wound over Dominic's heart.

Maria sobbed out his name when he caught her in his arms when she arrived. He scooped her up and carried her to where Gavilan was sprawled on the ground, men gathering around him. Dominic let Maria down beside Gavilan. Other men circled Wade lying dead on the grass.

Two bullets had felled Gavilan. One through his right shoulder, the other ripping into his ribcage. The surgeon unbuttoned Gavilan's coat as he had Dominic's, but this time he shook his head. "The second wound is fatal," he declared.

"No!" Maria cried, letting go of Dominic to fall to her knees beside Gavilan. She gathered his head into her lap.

Gavilan smiled, but his eyes shone with pain. "I promised you I'd do something," he told Maria with a smile.

Dominic kneeled down and gripped Gavilan's hand.

Gavilan looked up at him. "Perhaps you can name your next son after me."

"Of course we will," Dominic promised.

"Do you think Jesus will come for me?" Gavilan squeezed Dominic's hand.

"Of course he will." Tears filled Dominic's eyes.

"I've got a lot of sin I'm sorry for."

"The Lord accepted the thief at the cross. He'll accept you too, my friend."

Gavilan smiled, and a tear rolled out of the corner of his eye.

Maria was crying and didn't even know it until she saw her tears dripping onto Gavilan's face. Gavilan said, "I love you, Maria." Then he closed his eyes and said no more.

Dominic put his arms around her shoulders.

"No," Maria breathed. "No. He can't die. Please, doctor, you must help him!"

"I'm sorry, there's no help for him." The surgeon put his hand on Gavilan's chest. "His heart has stopped. He's gone."

Maria pressed her face to Gavilan's forehead and sobbed out her anguish.

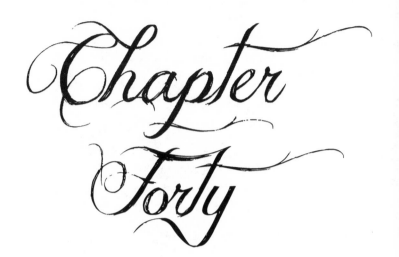

Chapter Forty

They spent that night back at the hotel. Dominic built a fire in their room and then sat there staring into the flames for a long time without saying anything. Gavilan's body had been taken to the shipping office, where it awaited burial. In the city, it wasn't uncommon for bodies to lie in the muddy streets for days if friends or family members didn't claim them. They'd talked of burying Gavilan in the mission cemetery after the duel since he'd grown up Catholic, but Dominic wanted him laid to rest with Sally on Telegraph Hill.

Before the war, there were few non-Catholics in California, and hardly anyone was buried at Telegraph Hill, the sailors' burial ground. Now everywhere Maria looked Yankees abounded. The quest for gold, more than the war, had changed her homeland. The Telegraph Hill Cemetery couldn't hold all the dead Protestants and pagans. She'd longed to travel to a large cosmopolitan city; now the large cosmopolitan city had traveled to her, and it wasn't at all what she'd envisioned. She missed the small, sleepy village of Yerba Buena. The mission bells tolling. The ranchos and fiestas and carefree ways of her people, the Californios. It was all gone.

That night the rain returned. This winter was shaping up to be one of San Francisco's wettest. And most transitional for law and order. The *Alta California* had become a daily newspaper, the first of its kind in California. The paper trumpeted the news of the duel. Both Wade and Gavilan had risen from the origin of simple sailors to become San Francisco's upper-crust elite, said the paper. It wasn't quite accurate, but not that far off either. Both Wade and Gavilan, like so many men in San Francisco, had found their fortunes here.

Now they'd died here before their time. Two men meeting their Maker because of her. Maria held her rosary and prayed, begging God for forgiveness. Wade's death did not bring her any satisfaction, and Gavilan's death broke her heart. Sitting in a chair beside Dominic before the fire, with the rain pounding on the roof, Maria said, "Do you think the Lord can forgive me? Do you think Gavilan is really in heaven with Sally and Maria Elizabeth?"

"Gavilan is face-to-face with his Savior, as we shall be someday." Dominic gave her a bittersweet smile. "You must not carry this guilt. Give it to God. Jesus died for your sin and mine, and Gavilan made his peace. We are all forgiven."

Tears streaked her cheeks. She held up her dented crucifix. "Look at what the bullet did to the cross. Do you think the cross or Nicky's soldier saved your life?"

"God saved my life. God gives and takes away. There is no curse upon you, Maria. All curses end at the cross of Christ." Dominic reached out and captured her uninjured hand, holding on to it. He threaded his fingers through hers, rose from the chair, and pulled her up onto her feet. "We both need some sleep. Let's go to bed."

He led her over and turned her around, unfastening her dress. Last night, their wedding night, she'd experienced such love. She could dry her tears in Dominic's love. Drown in his love. And she did again that night.

The next morning, Maria walked up the porch steps of Dominic's mansion, holding tightly to his arm. Would Nicky even want her for a mother after she'd abandoned him last summer? She could still hear him wailing her name at Christmas as she rode up the hill with Wade. He was just a little boy. How could he understand the forces that had driven her away?

The rain had stopped, but only briefly. Their boots were covered in mud. As soon as they reached the top of the porch stairs, Dominic removed his boots and then hers as well. To her surprise, he whisked her up into his arms and carried her into the house like a bride.

Nicky came careening around the corner and stopped in his tracks, his golden curls bouncing. The shock on his face matched the shock on Maria's face as their gazes collided.

"You let his curls grow back," she said, her arms looped around Dominic's neck.

He gently set her stockinged feet on the rug in the foyer. "I've made Maria your mother," he told Nicky. "She's my wife now. Come and give her a kiss, son."

"Your wife?" Chloe appeared around the corner in Nicky's wake. "When did this happen?" Chloe looked so happy at the news. "Gavilan said you had business in San Jose. He's been taking such good care of us while you were gone, but he didn't come home last night. I've been so worried." The smile wavered on Chloe's face.

Maria absolutely dreaded Dominic telling her Gavilan was gone.

"We wed a few days ago down in the city," said Dominic.

"In that muddy mess?" Chloe wrinkled her nose. "You should have come here. We could have had a wedding party. Let's still have a wedding party! Does Gavilan know you're married? Do you know where he is?"

Nicky had inched over to Maria. When she stretched out her arms, he threw himself into her embrace and then burst into tears.

Maria burst into tears too, holding him tightly against her.

"Gavilan was killed in a duel yesterday," Dominic told Chloe as gently as he could.

"No," Chloe breathed. "No!" she said more vehemently and shook her head in utter disbelief.

"I'm sorry, it's true." Dominic stepped over and wrapped his arms around his little sister.

Chloe fell apart, sobbing against Dominic's chest.

Everyone wept. Rain began to pound the roof, as if the heavens were crying too. Maria held Nicky and stroked his soft curls. He felt so sturdy in her arms. What a big boy he'd become. She pulled his remaining toy soldier out of her skirt pocket and handed it to him. "Do you know one of your soldiers helped save your father's life?"

"How did it do that?" Nicky wiped the back of his hand across his nose.

"The bullet would have entered your father's heart, but your soldier stopped it. God spared your father's life by using your soldier and my rosary."

"But God didn't save Gavilan." Nicky sounded so grown up.

"But God did save Gavilan," Maria said. "Gavilan is with Jesúcristo now. Just like your mama. Just like your baby sister. They are in heaven, where the streets are gold, not mud like they are here. They are all in a better place."

"Jesúcristo?" Nicky looked confused.

"Jesus Christ," Maria translated, a smile flowering on her face. When she really believed that Gavilan was in heaven, a startling joy filled her.

"Do you think Gavilan's playing with my baby sister up there?"

"I'm sure he is." The thought so comforted Maria. "Just like he played with you when you were a baby." She stroked Nicky's cheek.

Nicky clasped his soldier in one hand and held on to Maria's neck with his other arm.

Chloe continued to weep in Dominic's embrace. Poor Chloe. She'd loved Gavilan and hoped to marry him. Maria was still a bit stunned by Gavilan's declaration of love for her after all this time. It tore at her heart. If only he'd loved Chloe and lived to share that love with her the way she and Dominic now shared their love.

They'd all been through so much. It was the way of this golden shore. So many died here, yet the living went right on living. She suddenly longed to see Isabella and Roman and Rachel and their children. "Would you like to visit the rancho where I grew up?" she asked Nicky. "We can ride horses and herd cattle and maybe even capture a wild bull when we go to Rancho de los Robles."

"Can we go now?" Nicky eagerly squeezed her neck, his eyes wide with excitement.

"Soon, I hope." They would need to lay Gavilan to rest first and get Fang and comfort Chloe. Maria wanted out of the city in the worst way, the mud and rats and death were all too much here. She longed to see her family, spend some time at the rancho, and then perhaps return to a life at sea with Dominic and Nicky.

Dominic came and wrapped his arms around both of them. Chloe was no longer in the room. "She wanted to be alone for awhile," Dominic whispered to Maria.

"I just told Nicky we must take him to the rancho to see a wild bull," said Maria, trying to lighten things for Nicky.

"I have seen enough wild bulls in my life," Dominic was able to chuckle, which surprised Maria.

"I haven't seen a wild bull," said Nicky.

"Well, I have. Up close." Dominic pointed to a little white scar on his forehead. "This is from a wild bull that was after Maria. I saved her with a red blanket."

"You did?" Nicky's eyes widened once more.

"By the grace of God, I sure did. That was a mean old bull. He ran me over. But I was tougher than him. I'm here and that old bull is probably shoes in Boston now."

Dominic took Nicky into his arms. "Come on," he said. "Let's go upstairs and show Maria your soldiers. She sent you those soldiers while she was away to let you know she loves you. And God loves you."

Nicky looked at Maria and a smile grew on his face. "The soldiers of love."

"Yes, the soldiers of love," Maria agreed, her heart overflowing with gratitude to God as she followed Dominic and Nicky up the stairs.

Epilogue

Spring, 1850

On the hacienda's front porch, Maria hugged Isabella for a long time. Her sister was heading off to the goldfields with Tio Pedro now that the snow was melting in the Sierras. Tio Pedro insisted on Isabella going against everyone's wishes. It was hard for Maria to believe this beautiful girl with her curtain of long, dark hair was her baby sister, and that she was leaving. The whole family was moving—Roman, Rachel, and the children to Rancho El Rio Lobo, where the land grant Rachel had inherited from her father had withstood the American take-over. Rancho de los Robles's far more ancient land grant hadn't survived the American courts, and Tio Pedro had muddied everything with his gambling losses and mountains of debt.

Many Californios were losing their land under American rule. The Vasquezes were no exception. At least Roman and Rachel could start over at Rancho El Rio Lobo. Many Californio families had lost everything.

All around, the fields shimmered bright green with spring grass. After laying Gavilan to rest, they'd not been able to leave San Francisco to visit the rancho right away. Dominic had to see to his shipping business, and Chloe insisted on returning to Boston. Maria spent the wet, stormy months of winter bonding with Nicky. Within a few days, it was like they'd never been apart. He was her happy little boy again, and she loved him so fiercely, and loved his father fiercely too.

They brought Fang down the hill to live with them before another ship captain took over Wade's mansion. Fang was so happy to have a family who loved her. She doted on Maria and Nicky and shyly smiled whenever Dominic entered the room. Maria couldn't get over the change in the girl. She attended church with them on Sundays now, and was eager to hear Maria read the Bible to Nicky.

By March, Dominic had found a suitable voyage to Boston for Chloe. They put her on a fine clipper ship and hoped for the best. Dominic had wanted his sister to wait until he could sail her home himself when *The White Swallow* returned to port, but Chloe wouldn't have it. San Francisco was a place of broken dreams for her. Maria hoped the goldfields did not prove the same for Isabella.

Wagons filled with mining supplies waited in the rancho's yard, hooked to sturdy oxen. Chickens scratched in the dirt near the wagons. A handful of vaqueros mounted on palominos circled the wagons, their Indian wives and children loaded in the wagons, going along as well. Roman and Tio

Pedro had a terrible fight over Isabella venturing to the goldfields, but in the end, Tio Pedro had his way, and one of Rancho de los Robles's sleek golden palominos was saddled for Isabella.

"I am happy with our new adventure," Isabella assured Maria, the girl's blue eyes sparkling. She was so exotic and lovely with the Russian, Spanish, and Indian blood mingling in her veins. Maria worried for her. Isabella would not be considered a white woman in the Sierras. This could prove very dangerous for her since the Indians in California were treated so terribly. Tio Pedro was blind to all this, his greed for gold overwhelming whatever good sense he hadn't drunk away.

Roman only backed down with Tio Pedro because Isabella assured him she wanted to go to the goldfields and see the elephant for herself. "You have your family, and Maria has hers. I want a life of my own," Isabella said, placing her hands on Maria's thickening midsection. "I wish I could be there when your baby is born. Do you think you'll still be in San Francisco when she comes?" Isabella was convinced Maria was having a girl.

Nicky was set on a baby brother. The boy was mounted in the yard on one of the rancho's ponies. Dominic was also saddled up, waiting for Maria to say her good-byes on the porch. The three of them were headed back to San Francisco, and from there, Maria wasn't quite sure where they would go. *The White Swallow* waited in the harbor, having returned from New England last month.

"I do not know where this baby will be born." Maria smiled. "Perhaps I will give birth on the far side of the sea."

Isabella returned Maria's smile even as tears filled her eyes. "You have had your adventure. I want an adventure too."

"Adventures aren't all that grand. Choose a good man and settle down is my advice."

"This coming from you!" Isabella laughed, and her voice sounded like a bell.

Maria suspected Tio Pedro wanted Isabella with him because she was so pretty and could sing like a songbird. If gold didn't pan out, perhaps Isabella's singing would gather him a fortune with all those lonely men longing for women in the mining camps. Maria reached into her skirt pocket and pulled out her golden rosary. "I want you to take this with you. Keep it close and always pray to Jesúcristo."

Isabella blinked away her tears and tried to laugh. "Where is my sister? What has happened to her?" Isabella didn't take the rosary from Maria's hand.

Maria shoved the golden necklace at Isabella. "Pray you do not lose your way. May Jesúcristo be as merciful to you as he was with me."

Isabella looked at the rosary shining in the morning sun. "I cannot take what belonged to your grandmother. It is worth a fortune and is so meaningful to you."

"The rosary's worth isn't in gold. Its worth is in God. Hide it," Maria said. "Don't ever let your father see it."

"He will gamble it away." Isabella looked worried.

Maria feared Isabella was the treasure Tio Pedro would gamble away. "Take it." Maria snatched the rosary from Isabella's hands and dropped it down into her sister's bodice. "When you get to the wagon, hide it in your humblest shoe. Tio Pedro will never think to look in your old shoes." Pulling

Isabella into her arms one last time, Maria hugged her fiercely. "*Vaya con Dios*, my sister."

If you enjoyed this story, please consider leaving a review on Amazon. Thank you so much!

Historical Notes

In 1849, there were few fine homes in San Francisco. Men lived in tents and shanties, hotels and boardinghouses, but some impressive houses had sprung up here and there throughout the city, and certainly by the 1850s, new millionaires were flaunting their wealth with mansions in San Francisco. I hope you don't mind that I gave Dominic and Wade mansions on the hill perhaps several years too soon historically. On the Internet, I found an original 1850 photograph of some large houses on a hill above Portsmouth Square. Of course, they didn't quite look like mansions, but many times I looked at this old picture as I wrote *Far Side of the Sea*, imagining Dominic, Maria, and Wade living on that hill together.

I read numerous books on 1849 San Francisco, though the best information I gathered was from personal letters written by people in California and sent back home to their families out East. History books said bathtubs were not added to San Francisco hotels until the 1850s, but in an 1849 letter, a young girl who arrived in San Francisco by ship with her family in the summer of 1849 talks about taking a bath with her mother and sister in a hotel room before they went to a Fourth of July party.

The most interesting history I researched was about duels in California. The Golden State experienced the most duels of any state in the Union in the 1800's, most likely because of the gold rush. I'm a fifth-generation Californian and had never heard of all these California duels until recently. I read a book on the history of dueling, and many of the duels were fought in California after gold was discovered. A gold pocket watch did save a senator's life in a duel in San Francisco just as I portrayed Dominic being saved by the toy soldier in his pocket. Sadly, five years later, this same senator would die in another duel in California. Many duels happened between newspaper editors and politicians because the politicians were offended by unflattering newspaper stories written about them. Having written this novel during an election year, I find the duels quite understandable.

The first big San Francisco fire took place on Christmas Eve morning, as I portrayed it in this novel. This was the first of many devastating fires that swept the city. San Francisco really was notorious for its mud and rats, gambling and prostitution. Respectable woman were called "bonnets" by the men, and the appearance of a proper lady in San Francisco stopped everything on the street as she passed by. Seeing a good woman was like seeing a famous celebrity in San Francisco in 1849.

In all my research, I think my favorite story was about the farmer who saw the elephant. Perhaps because we farm, and most summer days we load up our truck and head for market, just like the farmer in the story, except without a wagon and horses. It's so easy to picture a wagon full of our peaches tipped over and scattered across the road because the horses were spooked by an elephant. I'm not sure if this story is actually true about the elephant, but I suspect it may very well be. Years ago, when our oldest children were quite small, a circus came to our little farm town. I paid forty dollars for myself and two of our children to see an elephant, and all the elephant did was poop that day. The poor elephant refused to perform and just stood there and relieved himself, and that was the entire show. My daughters were so impressed because this was the biggest pile of poop we'd ever seen. After that, the girls went around telling everyone Mommy paid forty dollars to see the elephant poop. It was really quite funny, especially since forty dollars was a lot of money for our little family to spend in those days.

I can imagine seeing the gold rush unfold in California was kind of like seeing an elephant poop for many folks. For the Californios, it was the end of their way of life. American settlers poured in and took the Californios land and cattle and horses. It didn't take long for the Californios' unique culture to be stripped from them too. Because of her Indian blood, Isabella Vasquez won't have an easy time coming of age during the gold rush in book three. The Californian Indians faced the worst during this era. Many native Americans were killed simply because they were Indians. Diseases brought in by the miners wiped out most of the California tribes. What we call history, people endured not so long ago. Many of my story ideas come from real events involving real people doing their best to tame California and dying in the process.

The roundup scene where the bull charges Dominic as he carries the red blanket away from Maria came from my dad. I knew I wanted to write about a bull nearly killing Dominic, but wasn't quite sure how to do this, though I've had my own battles with bulls when I was a young girl. Growing up on a ranch, I've been chased by a bull more than once on my pony. I've also encountered an angry bull on my horse, Soda Pop, when my dad, my husband, Scott, and I were trying to return my dad's bull to his cattle herd. I know what it's like to face a raging bull on a horse and I knew I wanted Maria and Dominic to do this together, but I didn't know how the scene would play out. I asked my dad to help me brainstorm this roundup scene and he said I needed to listen to the old country song: *Utah Carol* by Marty Robbins.

Both my dad and I love Marty Robbins. This old ballad inspired the red blanket scene with Dominic and Maria. You can Google *Utah Carol* on the Internet if you want to hear the song. The truth is, my daddy should be the writer in the family. He turns seventy-five this year and says he's retiring from running his engineering firm so maybe he will pick up a pen and craft a tale. Most likely a cowboy tale because he's an old cowboy.

I love my cowboy daddy, and I love California history. Thanks so much for taking the time to read this book. I have so much fun writing historical romances set in California, and I savor how God meets me in the middle of creating a story and speaks his truth to my heart as the tale unfolds. I especially wanted to impart the truth to you that no matter what's been done to you, or what you have done that makes you feel ashamed or ruined or unredeemable, you are precious to God becauses of Jesus. Sin can leave us feeling so ruined, the sins we commit or the sins committed against us, but the blood of Christ makes us brand new every single time. The blood of Christ cleanses sinners and sets us free to be loved by God and by others. I'm praying God touches your heart with his love and grace and endless mercy, I'll leave you with one of my favorite Bible verses: *"The eternal God is your refuge and underneath are his everlasting arms."* Deuteronomy 33:27.

Made in the USA
Columbia, SC
17 September 2017